THE GILDED CAGE

An Evans Novel of Romance

SUSANNAH BAMFORD

M. EVANS & COMPANY, INC., NEW YORK

Library of Congress Cataloging-in-Publication Data

Bamford, Susannah.

The gilded cage / Susannah Bamford.
p. cm.—(An Evans novel of romance)
ISBN 0-87131-643-9 : $17.95
I. Title. II. Series.
PS3552.A4733G5 1991
813'.54—dc20 91-7874
CIP

M. Evans and Company, Inc.
216 East 49 Street
New York, N.Y. 10017

Manufactured in the United States of America

9 8 7 6 5 4 3 2 1

For Rosalind Noonan

December, 1889
Sex and Politics

One

THERE CANNOT BE a great deal of sympathy for the unhappy woman who stands, in her Paris gown, at the most stylish New Year's Eve party of the season, holding a glass of perfectly-iced champagne by its delicate crystal stem while her handsome, rich, and devoted lover smiles adoringly at her across an opulent room.

Columbine Nash told herself this, and continued nevertheless to be unhappy. Clutching her champagne in one hand and her rose-pink gauze fan in the other, she retreated behind an embroidered screen. There, she gave up and decided to brood before someone found her out. She should have about ten seconds of solitude, if she was lucky, for women, in 1889, did not find themselves alone very often in drawing rooms, though what mischief or misery they could come to amidst such a crowd she never was able to understand. Perhaps 1890 would be different, Columbine thought, taking a sip of champagne. She doubted it.

It was ten minutes to midnight, and the wine-colored velvet curtains of Ambrose and Maud Hartley's second floor salon in their Fifth Avenue mansion were drawn back wide despite the cold. Elaborately tasseled gold cord embraced the folds of rich drapery and trailed fecklessly on the Turkish carpet. Across Fifth Avenue, the trees of Central Park loomed, skeletal branches scraping a pale sky with an odd yellow cast. Clouds scudded across a sulphuric moon.

The conversation of the guests, fueled by Pommery, was brisk and animated. It was the most stylish New Year's Eve dinner of New York society's "younger set," and the room seemed almost to spin with its dizzying consequence. The shirt fronts of the men were at their snowiest, the beards at their glossiest. The women glittered in their most formal and extravagant gowns, Nile green and ciel blue, Rose Dubarry pink and the moonlit simplicity of white satin. Clouded moiré collided with broché satin, pearl trimming brushed against spangled chiffon. Diamonds and emeralds flashed, wrapped around necks, sewn in bodices, and cunningly secured in coiffures styled after Paris fashion. They looked resplendent, they knew it, and they had not yet begun to be bored by how familiar it was.

Columbine was wearing her best gown, gold satin with rose-pink crystal trim, but she felt rather cowed at the display tonight. She turned her back on the wide windows with a shudder. Was she the only one to be bothered by that strange yellow sky? She told herself that her uneasy feeling was because she was rather bored, which she was. Columbine had spent the day dreading this party, and already tonight the company had cooperated by behaving even more stupidly than usual.

Tonight, Maud had seated her—and the *placement* had been deliberate, for Maud always seated Columbine Nash next to the guest most likely to annoy her—next to a bore at dinner. Columbine had picked at her mousse de jambon while Gerald Ferrar had jovially but painstakingly explained to her how her feminine mind was unable to grasp the pure, God-given nature of male superiority and the free enterprise system. There was no need for women to have the vote, he said, his mud-colored eyes concentrating on the course to come. For it was women's nature to *influence*, to *guide*. Their sphere was the private one; through their husbands and sons they could exercise their most delicate of talents.

Columbine swallowed her lobster bisque and only politely pointed out that there did exist some women who were not mothers or wives. There were even some women, she said, smiling graciously, who were of the working class. Of course, this was no argument, as she well knew, for what did such women count to a man like Gerald Ferrar? He ignored her comment and charged on while Columbine tried to catch the eye of her lover, Ned Van Cormandt, who was devoting himself to his neighbor as a gentleman should, leaving Columbine to her turbot and her florid partner.

If there was one thing that set Columbine's teeth on edge—and there were many, many things, most assuredly—it was the heavily masculine guest (oh, they were always men) who insisted on converting her to his point of view while she was trying to eat. Invariably, the naivete of their views, their patronizing smiles, and their refusal to listen to even one word of what she had to say, made her drink too much champagne and desperately look for a rescue which never came. It was difficult to be a socialist and a suffragist on Fifth Avenue.

If only she could be rude! But as the daughter of a British baronet, Columbine was incapable of it. It was one reason she admired the anarchists of her acquaintance. They had an impatience for stupidity which they didn't bother to conceal. Of course, they didn't have much time to waste, as the revolution was just around the corner.

A head poked around the screen. So she'd had ten seconds, at least! Ambrose Hartley beamed at her, her host and an excellent target for any anarchist. Guiltily, she summoned up a smile.

"Ah, Mrs. Nash, I find you out. And your glass is woefully empty. Surely you need a touch more champagne." Ambrose inclined his curly head at her. He had the gay but desperate air of a former man-about-town who had married a sour wife. Maud Valentine had roused herself to vivaciousness a year ago during their courtship. But once she had caught Ambrose and returned from their three-month honeymoon in Europe, she'd retreated into her silks, her sulks and her chinoiserie. Already, Ambrose had put on twenty pounds and had begun to sport the ruddy complexion of a man who likes his drink.

"No, thank you, Mr. Hartley," Columbine said with a smile. "I'm content, I assure you. I'm looking forward to your firework display."

"Only five minutes to go," Ambrose said with satisfaction. "And then the nineties will be upon us. The decade will bring more miracles, I'm sure. Just think of all the wonders we've seen in the eighties—the telephone, and the incandescent light. The Brooklyn Bridge, and—"

"—and Haymarket, bloody strikes, Anthony Comstock and his campaign against any device to prevent conception, the continued defeat of suffrage for women . . ." Columbine smiled to assuage the bluntness of her remarks. She was on Fifth Avenue, after all.

Ambrose looked startled for a moment. Then he tilted back his head and burst out laughing. Across the room, Ned looked up from his conversation with Converse Bowles. His aristocratic face collapsed in a grin, his summer-leaf eyes sharing a private joke with her across the room. He no doubt thought she had sent forth a delightful *bon mot*. Columbine was famous for her wit. Unfortunately, people laughed hardest when she wasn't joking in the least.

"Well, leave it to you, Mrs. Nash, to render me speechless," Ambrose said. "Yes, I suppose we had all that as well. But America is still the best of all possible worlds, a shining example of progress and Christian patriotism. We will see even more miracles and ingenuity before the century turns, I'll warrant."

Columbine had seen the same editorial in the World that morning, but she merely smiled and inclined her head. Ambrose was her host, and she was never waspish to hosts. Especially when their wives were so very close to rendering her a large check for her New Women Society. Maud had a tremulous dedication to women's suffrage, although she was nervously waiting until more upper class women found it fashionable.

"And may I say, while we're tête-à-tête here, I'm glad to see that you've settled down, Mrs. Nash," Ambrose continued. "No more of those lectures on free love. I'd much rather enjoy your lovely face across the dinner table than on a podium." Ambrose chuckled. "Thank heavens *that's* over. I'm sure Ned is most relieved."

Stupified, Columbine wasn't sure which comment to take offense at first—the fact that Ambrose felt that she was no longer scandalous, or that he had assumed that Ned was glad she had scaled back her lecture tours. Or was it merely his fatuous tone?

Ten years ago, bishops had thundered against her in pulpits. Five years ago, newpapers had slandered her. Two years ago she had been called a Hester Prynne who gloried in her scarlet letter, a threat to decent society. Today, she was standing in decent society's drawing room. And her leering host was telling her she *belonged.*

This is what I've become, she thought grimly. *A radical pet.* Domesticated, de-clawed, her teeth filed down. She was no longer dangerous at all. She was coasting on her laurels at thirty-five. And it took a fool like Ambrose Hartley to tell her so.

"Actually, Mr. Hartley, I'm planning a new lecture tour," she said demurely. "'The Secret Life of the American Husband.' You know, of course, that my New Women Society has worked with the poor unfortunate girls of this city who sell their bodies, Mr. Hartley, to make a living. I've learned much from their . . . activities. Names, places . . . oh, it's shocking, I assure you, how the men of good society piously deplore the vice of the city in public while partaking of it so enthusiastically in private." She widened her large, luminous eyes at him. "It is *so* necessary to expose hypocrisy wherever we might find it, don't you agree?" She smiled encouragingly at him.

Ambrose swallowed. He opened his mouth and closed it again. "What do you think of Maud's redecorating?" he finally squeaked. "She redid the salon from top to bottom."

"Oh, it's lovely. Remarkable," Columbine said virtuously. It was an appalling room. Maud's famous collection of chinoiserie perched perilously around them, a jumble of ginger jars and vases. The carpet was Turkish, and the furniture was all in the rococo extravagance of Louis XV. Chocolate-colored woodwork and an assortment of gilt-framed mirrors completed the decor. There were a few bad paintings from the worst of the Barbizon school.

Columbine took a very unladylike gulp of champagne, but the room remained hideous. She smiled winningly at Ambrose.

"Mrs. Nash, you must come to the window," Ambrose said, regaining his poise with a grand manner. "I'll find you a good place for the firework display."

He held out his arm, but before she could take it, a butler appeared at Ambrose's elbow. He spoke quietly. "May I have a word, sir? It's about the fireworks."

Annoyance deepened the crease on Ambrose's forehead. He drew the butler away from Columbine, but she could hear them clearly. "Yes, Howell? Not a problem, I hope."

"Devlin needs to speak with you, sir. He's worried about the fireworks. They look damaged, he says. He won't set them off, sir."

"Nonsense," Ambrose said impatiently. "I'll talk to him. I promised my guests fireworks, and fireworks we shall have! Tell Devlin I'll be out in a moment."

The butler nodded and turned away. Ambrose turned back to Columbine. "Just like the Irish to wait till the last minute to complain. Let me bring you to Ned and he'll find a place at the window."

Columbine paused. "But did he say that there was some question of the fireworks being unsafe? If so, I hardly think—"

"Nonsense," Ambrose repeated firmly. "It's only a snag, I assure you. It's almost eighteen-hundred and ninety, and I insist on the proper fanfare."

In a moment, he had delivered her to Ned—like a package, Columbine thought, but then, men did not excuse themselves from ladies in drawing rooms without handing them off to another male—and rushed out.

Ned smiled at her. "What did you do to Ambrose?" he murmured. "He looked like he swallowed a live chicken."

"Not a thing," she said. "I was perfectly charming. He's worried about his fireworks."

"Ah. He hasn't changed much since he was a boy. If it doesn't come off he'll sulk all evening. Come to the window anyway, there's a strange light tonight."

She took his arm and they strolled to the French doors. Cool air emanated from the frosty windows, caressing Columbine's bare shoulders. The salon had been rather hot, and she pressed even closer to the glass. The guests were excited now, and they milled about, laughing about Ambrose and his eagerness. Letitia Garth, the most delicious young ingenue of the season, flirted with graying Converse Bowles behind a fan of white peacock feathers and diamonds. Clara Vandervoon narrowed her small black eyes and whispered to her cousin, Georgina Halstead, about the scandalous behavior. Would confirmed bachelor Converse Bowles fall at last?

"Perhaps we can leave early, as soon as the dancing starts," Ned murmured.

Columbine didn't answer. Something about her conversation with Ambrose pricked at her, and she felt irritated with Ned as well as with herself. She would prefer to end the evening alone in her own room, where she could think.

Shortly after they'd become lovers three years before, Ned had leased a house in Greenwich Village. They met there as often as their schedules permitted, usually taking separate hansom cabs, with Columbine veiled for secrecy. A woman, Mrs. Haggerty, kept the house and her tongue.

But tonight, Columbine's pulse did not race in anticipation. She was a mistress, but she might as well have been a wife, so stately and predictable her relations with Ned had become. What was the use of being a dangerous mistress if you no longer felt thrilled at the thought of your lover? What was the use of secrecy and denial if it didn't add spice to the proceedings? She was so comfortable she might as well be married.

Is that what had bothered her so about Ambrose's words? It wasn't Ned's fault that she had become so predictable, Columbine raged at herself. She was being unfair. She wished Ned would skip the carriage ride to the Village and seduce her on her own parlor sofa, as he once did. Perhaps passion could drive the restlessness from her soul.

"Why don't we leave now?" she asked impulsively. "We can take French leave."

Ned smiled in an indulgent way that told her he didn't take her suggestion seriously for a moment. "Slip away early without saying good night? How wicked of us."

Columbine touched him fleetingly with her fan. "Ah, but it's time you were wicked again, Ned Van Cormandt," she chided. "You are definitely in danger of committing the worst sin of all, in my opinion—"

"And that is?"

"Predictability, of course."

Columbine's tone was light, but there was a hint of asperity that Ned rarely heard. "I shall take that warning under advisement, madam," he said, trying to match her lightness.

Columbine saw the hurt in his eyes and immediately felt guilty. "Don't mind me, tonight, Ned. A devil is on my tongue."

Ned laughed in relief. "As long as you make it up to me later," he murmured.

"Oh, is there any question of that?" she answered dryly. "By two-seventeen in the morning, two-thirty if there is traffic on Broadway on the way downtown, I'd wager you'll be quite satisified, sir."

Ned looked at her sharply, and Columbine instantly felt guilty again. She looked away and fanned her warm cheeks.

"It appears the show is about to begin," Ned said in a cool tone. He flipped open his gold dress watch. Around him, the other men did the same. "It's three minutes to midnight."

Columbine looked out through the glass. A dark figure crossed Fifth Avenue and hurried toward a grassy spot underneath the bare trees.

Moments later, Ambrose rushed into the room. "It's almost time," he said excitedly. He extinguished the gas jets, and the room was filled with moonlight. Some of the guests oohed, and they all pressed closer to the glass doors. Someone opened the latch, and the men and the more adventuresome ladies spilled out onto the terrace. Columbine heard Letitia's soprano laugh as the cold air hit them. Moonlight splashed on her white satin gown trimmed with crystals and pearls.

Columbine shivered, but she welcomed the frosty air. It was intoxicating to feel the fresh night air for a moment. She closed her eyes and breathed in the smell of New York in winter, frost and snow and the faint smell of horses, even here on upper Fifth Avenue, only beginning to attract a fashionable crowd, facing the long rectangle of the Central Park. She returned to London once a year, and sometimes even thought of living there again. But in the past few years she'd begun to realize that New York was her true home. Something about the rough vitality of the city kept her; somehow she could breathe here. There were no bad memories here. She did not have the weight of centuries of family on her back.

"Ten seconds to midnight," Ambrose called. "Nine. Eight. Seven . . ."

He continued the countdown while waiters quickly circulated with thick cashmere shawls for the ladies. Columbine felt the involuntary shiver of excitement that comes with the dawn of a new year. Ned slipped a shawl around her shoulders and she brought her hand up under cover of darkness and placed it over his for a moment. Daringly, Ned leaned forward and kissed her fingers.

A mute apology; a good start to the new year. She looked at him, and he smiled. Her heart squeezed with love and relief. She still loved him, of course, her Ned, with his boyish thick brown hair, his keen eyes, his ironic eyebrow that quirked at her with such quizzical intelligence. Even though the intellectual rebel she'd fallen for had evolved into a surprisingly clever financier on the death of his father, and become a member of the establishment she railed against. Even though she sensed they were growing apart, and it frightened her.

"Three. Two. One! It's Eighteen-Ninety!" Ambrose laughed aloud. Through the clear night air, the faint ringing of church bells could be heard.

Now they all looked expectantly down into the shadows of the park. Ambrose muttered underneath his breath, then said aloud, "Any moment, now!"

Ambrose's exhortation was answered by a series of pops, followed by a tremendous explosion. It had force and weight, ripping through the air like an unnatural, deafening clap of thunder and rolling against their faces. The ladies screamed and shrank back, and the men and Columbine surged forward. A cloud of smoke billowed up from the ground below. A horrible scream pierced the clear night air. Shouts could be heard, along with running footsteps. A slight figure, a woman in the white apron of a kitchen worker, ran across Fifth Avenue toward the trees, disappearing in the smoke.

Ambrose pushed his way to the end of the terrace. He leaned over the terrace railing. "What happened?" he shouted frantically. "What is it?" He strained to hear over the sound of the guests' agitated murmurings and the shouts below.

Those in the front heard it, then: the sound of barely concealed panic in the voice of an unseen man below. "You'd better come down, sir. And send for a doctor. It looks bad, sir."

Ambrose turned, his face white. He pushed back toward the French doors. There, Maud touched his arm, but he shook her off.

Ned spoke in Columbine's ear. "I'll go with him."

Columbine watched Ned head quickly after Ambrose. She could hear a woman shrieking below, and she leaned over the terrace railing while the other guests headed back to the salon. She could see nothing except a tall man heading back across Fifth Avenue, walking quickly, almost running. Then burly Ambrose charged across the street, followed closely by Ned and some other servants. Chaos swirled below, and Columbine shivered.

She made her way over to Maud in the salon. "You'd better send for a doctor," she told her. "Someone is injured."

Maud stood frozen in the middle of her guests. "But the servants have their own doctor," she said idiotically. "Howell knows him. I don't know his name . . ."

"Mrs. Hartley, you must send for your doctor," Columbine repeated fiercely. "Immediately. If he has a telephone, call him." Dropping the shawl and gathering up her full gold skirt, she pushed past Maud and ran down the hall toward the stairs, past the Corot and the suite of Goya drawings, past the medieval armor and the Ming vases.

They were carrying the man in when she reached the bottom of the stairs. The woman in the white apron stood near him; perhaps she was his wife, or his sweetheart. Strands of extravagant red hair were loose from her white cap and waved around her thin white face. Her green eyes were blazing, but they were dry. Columbine wondered at the woman's composure, but then she saw how her work-reddened hand shook as it fleetingly, uselessly, reached out to touch the heavy shoe of the groaning man.

The groans were awful to hear. Columbine felt the lightheadedness that comes with the shock of sudden accident, the smell of blood. Ned was supporting the man's head, black from gunpowder, and Ambrose trailed behind, wringing his hands. The usually imperturbable Howell, the butler, was in his shirtsleeves, frantically directing the bearers to lay the man gently on the carpet in the small salon to the left of the entrance hall.

Ambrose stumbled toward Columbine. He seemed not to see her. His hand flailed out and hit the marble banister.

"Who is it?" she asked him. "Who was hurt?"

"Devlin," he said, his eyes on the salon as the man was lowered onto the rug. "The Aubusson," he whispered. "Maud will be furious. They should have used the cloakroom."

Disgusted with him, Columbine turned away. She sank down on a small tufted bench and clasped her cold hands together. She could see that one of the men, dressed in rough stable clothes, was gently cutting Devlin's sleeve away. What should have been a hand was a mass of blood and tissue. Columbine felt sick, and she looked away for a moment, took a deep breath, then looked back. Someone put a towel underneath the arm, causing Devlin to groan again. Fresh blood spurted out onto the carpet.

Then Ned looked up, caught sight of her, and frowned. He left the salon, closing the door behind him. "You shouldn't be down here," he said. "You look pale as a ghost."

"I'm fine," Columbine said, though she did feel dizzy. She stood up again. "How is he?"

Ned shook his head. "I'm no doctor, but it looks bad. Where *is* the doctor? Has he been sent for?"

"Howell telephoned him," Ambrose said wearily. He seemed to be coming out of his daze. "I'd better see to the guests. Maud will want to start the dancing, I'm sure."

"*Dancing?*" Columbine asked, incredulous. Surely Ambrose wouldn't continue the festivities after a man had been so badly injured. He must be in shock.

"Yes, it was supposed to start immediately after the fireworks." Ambrose grimaced. "You know how particular Maud is about her parties. You two should come to the ballroom. Your absence will be noticed." Suddenly, Ambrose was all business. "There's no need to mention this upstairs, of course. I'll just make a short speech, say everything's all right."

Ned shot Columbine a warning look as she opened her mouth to protest. He said gently, "Ambrose, let me make a suggestion, if I may. Perhaps you should postpone the dancing until we talk to the doctor. The man could be dying."

"Ned, I have responsibilities—"

"Exactly," Ned broke in. "I can go upstairs and explain the situation to Maud. I'm sure when the guests know what transpired they'll understand. You might want to remain here with your servant to demonstrate your concern—"

"Of course I'm concerned, old man. Even though Devlin was not the most reliable of employees. And I regret his carelessness, of course—"

"*His* carelessness?" Columbine broke in. She had to struggle to keep her voice down. "Don't you mean your criminal disregard for his safety? I heard your butler tell you Devlin thought the fireworks unsafe. You knew—"

"Nonsense," Ambrose snapped. "You must have been imagining things, Mrs. Nash."

"I assure you, sir, I do not imagine things," Columbine said tersely. "I heard every word of your conversation."

"Are you calling me a liar, Mrs. Nash? If you were a man—"

"If I were a man, I'd call you a liar in a deeper voice, Mr. Hartley."

Ned looked from one to the other. "Ambrose, Columbine told me after you left the room that you were concerned about the fireworks. Did you know the fireworks were unsafe and order Devlin to set them off?"

Ambrose tried to smile. "I know you're two years older, Neddie, but I hardly think that gives you the right to quiz me. But I will tell you that the accident was Devlin's fault. Perhaps he misjudged the amount of explosives—how am I to know? It was not my responsibility! If he felt it was unsafe, he could have refused."

"He did refuse," Columbine said evenly. "And I am sure if you did not actually threaten him with the loss of his position, nonetheless, that fear drove him to light the fireworks he knew were dangerous."

Ambrose turned back to Columbine with some relief, for she was a less formidable enemy than his oldest friend. "Mrs. Nash," he said with a smile that was all teeth and no amusement, "I wish you would confine your socialist speeches to Union Square. I am not here to baby a servant who had the unfortunate luck to—"

"To what?" Columbine snapped. "Blow off his hand? Yes, it *was* careless of him, wasn't it? How *unfortunate*."

Ambrose stared at her, and she stared back. It was all she could do not to shriek at him. But Columbine knew no amount of shouting would pound the truth into Ambrose. Years of training would allow him to elude his responsibility without the slightest stain on his conscience or reputation.

Ignoring Columbine, Ambrose turned to Ned. He spoke with the gravity of a patriarch dealing with a recalcitrant child. "I'll ignore Mrs. Nash's accusations for your sake, Ned. Obviously, she's distraught. Now, I'm asking you, as my oldest friend, to bring Mrs. Nash and come upstairs now, with me. Maud is waiting."

Ned stood straight as a post, staring at his friend. "Ambrose," he said painfully, "if I do, it would appear that I support your behavior. Your duty is to your servant, Ambrose."

"You need not tell me my duty, sir!" Ambrose hissed. His hands clenched and unclenched. Columbine had never seen jolly Ambrose ever raise his voice except in merriment. And she saw her lover hesitate. The code, she thought bitterly. Ned will not abandon his friend.

"We must begin the dancing," Ambrose repeated. His face was tight. "Maud will agree. I must tell the orchestra to begin. Let's go upstairs."

They heard a movement behind them. Turning, Columbine saw the same red-haired woman who had run across the street and later, touched the injured man's shoe. Now her face was strangely composed, her hair tucked back into her cap. But then Columbine saw her eyes. There was something deep and savage there that chilled her. The contemptuous emerald gaze flicked from Ambrose's face to Ned's to Columbine's and found them all equally despicable.

"Do you have a message for me, Fiona?" Ambrose prodded sharply.

"Oh, but I don't like to interrupt the *dancing.*" The woman's face was impassive. Her strong, reddened hands were still by her side. Yet Columbine felt she had raised a fist. It was the absence of the usual posture—the bowed head, the almost silent murmur, the curtsey—that sent an electric charge through the air.

Ambrose flushed heavily. "Fiona! If you have no message, return to the kitchen."

"The doctor is here," Fiona answered. Again, there was a shock, widening outward like a stone dropped in a pool—the absence of the obligatory *sir.*

Ambrose's voice shook. His face held the rigid lines of panic barely in check. "Howell will see to him. And you may pack your bags tonight, Fiona. There will be no letter of reference. I will not countenance insubordination."

Fiona said nothing. She pivoted and returned to the small

salon, closing the door gently behind her. They heard the man groan again, muffled this time.

Ned took a step toward Ambrose, but was waved off.

"Do what you will, Ned," Ambrose said, turning his back and starting up the stairs. "I must see to my guests." He climbed the stairs heavily and disappeared around the turning.

Ned stared after him. "Columbine, I've known Ambrose all my life. I know his weaknesses. He is afraid, and he's acting abominably, I know, but if I wait until he calms down and talk to him again—"

"Stay then." She spoke the words flatly. "I am not going upstairs to put in an appearance. You may dance the rest of the night away, but I cannot. I cannot remain under this roof. Don't you see that I cannot?" Columbine asked, striving to remain calm. When Ned didn't reply, she bowed her head and closed her eyes for a moment. There, she thought. There it is. The difference between us that will destroy us. He hesitates. And maybe he'll stay.

She turned, her silk skirts rustling, and blundered back down the hall, feeling tears begin behind her eyelids. She tried to remember where the cloakroom was. It must be the carved oak door to the right of the double front doors. Blindly, Columbine reached for the knob.

But Ned's fingers were there before her. He twisted the knob, found her fur-lined cloak. He didn't speak as they waited for their carriage. Their breath clouded in the cold air, mingled and dissipated. Ned's face set in stern lines, and he didn't look at her or take her hand. But whether he was angry at Ambrose or her, she didn't know.

The carriage drew up with a clatter of hooves. Ned ushered her into the leather seat. Columbine sank back with an almost silent groan. She felt twice her years. The decade had just begun, with cries and blood and a yellow sky full of ill portents. She suddenly felt too ill-equipped, old and tired, to cope with any of it.

Two

THIRTY BLOCKS DOWNTOWN and three long blocks west, Marguerite Corbeau heard the bells toll the hour of midnight and the start of the new decade. She wished herself a happy and prosperous new year.

She would turn nineteen in the coming year, and Marguerite was not pleased at the thought. Time brushed against her smooth cheeks like a draft from a rapidly closing door, and she felt the chill. She wasn't beautiful like Columbine or luscious like Bell. She wasn't fashionably round. She was slight and pretty, and she was bored with her brief stint at political commitment. She had given herself two years to marry—and here was one year almost gone. Avid as any debutante, she knew her only way to find herself a position was through a man.

Columbine had rescued her from a life of domestic service, offering her a room in her own home and a job doing clerical work for the New Women Society. It was easy work, and at first Marguerite had been grateful for it. The freedom to do as she pleased on her hours off was enough to convince her she'd made the right decision.

But over the past year, Marguerite had grown more dissatisfied. At the Statton mansion she had watched and listened. She'd improved her speech and her manners. Here, too, at the house on Twenty-third Street, Columbine Nash was a model of grace, and she even knew how to dress. But what was the use of improving herself if she never met any suitable candidates? Here, the only men Marguerite met were poor poets or ragged revolutionaries. Socialists, dreamers, exiles.

She would have to create her own ticket out. If she didn't take charge of her life, before she knew it she would be like Bell, twenty-seven and unmarried, an old maid. Fiercely, Marguerite pulled the mauve cashmere shawl Columbine had given her for Christmas more tightly around her shoulders. She knew more than ever now that it was time to act. Horatio Jones would have to do.

The young newspaperman wasn't exactly what she wanted, but he was a step in the right direction. He came from a good family. He had important contacts, he knew everyone in the city. Through him, she could meet others. If he didn't marry her, he might introduce her to someone who could do just as well. Or better.

Underneath the sapphire blue velvet dressing gown trimmed in white satin—a hand-me-down from the generous Columbine—she was wearing only a summer chemise, half-buttoned. Her bare skin felt cold, and she longed for her warm winter nightgown. But winter flannels didn't fit into her plan. Horatio Jones would soon be seeing Bell home, and if Marguerite was right, he would step inside for a quick cup of hot tea before heading downtown to his rooms.

Marguerite reached for the mirror on her nighttable and looked into it gravely. Her thick black hair was in a state of pretty disarrangement it had taken her twenty minutes to contrive. Her small fingers wandered down to fuss with her unbuttoned chemise. Not too much white skin exposed, just her throat and the tops of her small breasts. When she dropped the book, if he was quick, and she would bet that he would be, Horatio would get a flash of pink nipples. And amid it all, she would be the picture of prettily confused dishevelment.

Marguerite sat up, listening intently, as hooves clopped outside her window. No, they were going past. She settled back against her pillow again. It was too cold to remain outside the covers. Last week she'd been lucky enough to overhear Bell and Horatio after their evening out together. They'd quarrelled over Bell's tiresome insistence on keeping their relations not merely chaste—that, Horatio had insisted, he would understand—but absolutely free of any physical contact whatsoever. It was a wonder, Marguerite thought, that Horatio put up with Bell at all. But the woman was so damnably luscious, full lips and round figure, wasp-waisted, a real beauty. It was a pity Bell's feminine charms ended with her face and figure. She had a straightforward manner that was impressive in its own way. But she had a complete absence of guile, and that was deadly in a woman.

As a result, Marguerite thought, biting her lips to make them redder and studying the effect in the small mirror, the ambitious young muckraker Mr. Jones just might be ripe for the plucking. She might not have Bell's looks, but Marguerite might be willing to give at least a taste to Mr. Jones of what Bell would not. Bell would probably be relieved, for it was painfully obvious to everyone but Horatio that she would never be in the least bit serious about him.

The sound of a carriage on the street below made Marguerite rise on her elbows. The horses' hooves slowed, and she was up at the window, slipping behind the curtain to peer down. Just a glimpse of the top of Horatio's hat and she was moving, gathering her robe in two determined fists and flying across the room and down the hall to the back stairs to the kitchen. Through the kitchen and dining room and scooting into the library. As she carefully closed the door halfway, she heard Horatio and Bell in the front hall. Marguerite took several deep breaths to get her breathing back to normal. Then she plucked a book from the bookshelves and strained to listen.

"If you'll look to the fire, I'll make the tea," Bell said softly to Horatio.

"I'll be happy to," Horatio said. "Hurry back."

Perfect! Thank goodness Bell did not worry about propriety, not that anyone did, in this house. She would not give a second thought to entertaining Mr. Jones so late. They'd probably become involved in some boring political discussion that Bell wanted to continue. Marguerite waited a moment until Bell had rustled back toward the kitchen. She opened the library door, then hesitated, looking down at herself. Quickly, she wet her cold index finger and reached inside her chemise. She pinched both nipples hard until they pushed up against the filmy material. She wasn't blessed with a generous bosom like Bell's. Anything would help.

When she opened the parlor door, Horatio looked up. Disappointment flashed in his eyes for a split second, and Marguerite tamped down her annoyance. Of course he was looking forward to being alone with Bell. She brushed a tumbling lock of raven hair off her forehead and let her lips part in surprise.

"Mr. Jones. I didn't know you were here." Marguerite's hand flew to her open robe, but instead of closing it securely, she merely pulled it together slightly. A full six inches of white throat and bosom were still exposed.

Horatio looked away, then looked back, his light brown eyes embarrassed. "Miss Corbeau. I'm sorry if we disturbed you. B—Miss Huxton is making some tea. She'll return in a moment."

"I was just searching for a book," Marguerite said. She punctuated the remark by dropping it.

In the time it took her to hesitate slightly, then bend over, Horatio was in front of her, stooping for the book. His eyes came level with the curve of one small, perfect breast, and his hand froze on the spine of the book. Quickly, Marguerite stood erect, the picture of modesty, and let him retrieve the book for her. Her fingers slid against his for a second when she took it.

"Thank you." Her eyes didn't leave his face. Confused, Horatio looked away. Marguerite smiled slightly, just a curve of the lips. She felt a surge of delicious power as Horatio peeked back at her. Her mask of modesty clicked back in, and she dropped her eyes.

But Bell should be coming any moment, and this was all she had time for. Marguerite turned and ran from the room without a word. She mounted the stairs, inwardly exulting at her daring. She'd had so little practice, and her performance had been perfect! And it had been enough. Horatio would not forget what he'd seen, and he would wonder if he was being foolish by continuing to scrabble after Bell's skirts. He would wonder. He would imagine. And one day soon, he would come.

In the parlor, Bell closed the door behind her. She noticed at once Horatio's agitation. She put down the tray and came toward him, concerned.

"Horatio, what is it? Has something upset you?"

Suddenly, Horatio gripped her hands and squeezed them. "Bell, we must talk."

"Horatio, you're hurting me." Bell extricated her hands and smoothed her skirt with trembling fingers. She knew what was coming; it was all too familiar to her.

Horatio saw the gesture and turned away angrily. Why did he bother? But how could he not? He turned back. This time, he clasped his hands together tightly. He would not touch her again, he vowed. He would not try.

"Bell, you know I am devoted to you. I love you dearly. I said I wouldn't ask until I felt you were ready—"

"Yes, Horatio," Bell said quietly. "You promised that."

"But how can we go on like this?" Horatio burst out. "It is killing me, Bell. I love you so much. . . . Will you marry me? Will you do me the honor of becoming my wife? I'll treasure you, Bell. I'll be your helpmate, your comrade, your friend—" Horatio paused. "I will even forbare being your lover, if you wish it."

Bell collapsed into an armchair. "Oh, Horatio . . ."

"I mean it, Bell. I'll wait. I'll wait forever, if necessary."

"You say this because you don't believe it will be forever," Bell murmured. "You will always expect . . ."

"There is no answer then, for us?" Horatio asked, his usually humorous face tight. When Bell was silent, he crossed to her side. He crouched by her chair and looked searchingly into her face.

"Perhaps I have no right to ask this, my dear," he said tenderly. "But I know you're not a cold woman. I've felt your warmth. Is there something—someone—in your past who's hurt you, made you this way? I meant what I said, darling. I can wait. Perhaps I can even learn to do without the—the physical. But I have to know if it's an impossibility for you, or if you need time . . ."

"I don't know." Bell startled herself, for she'd whispered the words aloud, the painful answer to the question she asked herself, over and over again.

How she'd hoped to fall in love with Horatio! He was handsome and intelligent and kind. He was committed to reform, as she was. His pieces on the suffragists were weighty and considered, free of the sly tone of so many others. Columbine had approved of him wholeheartedly. "Finally a man who writes of our struggle without a nudge or a wink," she'd said.

And his hands were large and strong, his face alert and humorous, his mouth sensual. At first, she'd thought him dangerously attractive. More than once she had felt close to falling, to blotting out the world in his arms, as she'd heard it was possible to do. But time and again she was able to resist so easily. That had been the worst thing of all. To long for that abandonment, and yet to be relieved when it did not come.

Horatio saw her hesitation, and it gave him hope. He felt anger and heat flood him, and his frustration, fueled by the encounter with Marguerite, boiled over. Grasping her arms, he lifted Bell to her feet.

Her full, beautiful mouth parted in surprise. Her breath fanned his cheek, and he could smell her hair. Horatio was beyond thought now, as raging excitement raced through his blood. He placed his hand on her breast. It fitted against his palm, lush, full, exciting. Horatio made a low noise in his throat as fresh desire flooded him.

Bell tried to twist away, but he held her fast. "Stop it, Horatio. Stop—"

"No. His fingers played across where her nipple would be, underneath the bottle-green silk. "I want to feel your heart beating," he murmured. His eyes glinted. "I want to feel if you have a heart to beat, Bell . . ." His mouth descended on hers, and she felt his rough mustache.

But this time, there was no gentle brush of soft lips. Horatio's mouth was open! His tongue insinuated itself between her lips, tried to go deeper. Bell clamped her teeth down as a shudder ripped through her. Now she used all her strength to twist away.

"No!" She almost screamed it, loud enough so that Marguerite, listening intently at the top of the stairs, smiled. Bell put her hand against her mouth. Her body shook. "No," she whispered. "No, Horatio."

He sank down on the sofa. His head dropped into his hands. For long moments, they both said nothing.

"I don't know what to do," he said raggedly at last. "I want you to confide in me, Bell. Tell me. Is it the act that you fear? Don't be ashamed. We've talked of free love in the abstract many times. Surely you know you can say anything to me."

Bell walked away. She pressed her forehead against the cold glass of the window fronting the street. Words were on her tongue, and again she clamped her jaw, this time to prevent them escaping.

She could never tell Horatio of her shame. Of the uncle who had visited her nightly when she was twelve, sliding into her bed and pressing himself inside her. Of the mother who had looked the other way, up to the heavens to God to protect them all. Bell's father had died when she was ten, a factory worker worn out at forty. His brother had moved in with them, seeming their salvation. Her mother had wept, she was so grateful. And then Uncle Jack sent Bell's brother Sam up to Massachusetts for factory work and had taken to Bell's bed. And then when she was fourteen he had sold her to a "friend" he owed a gambling debt. Archie Taft had been no gentleman.

Bell would never forget the day she had sneaked into a lecture hall to see the famous Columbine Nash speak. Columbine was only a few years older than Bell, and she was on her first lecture tour in America. She'd been brutalized in a marriage and her father had thrown her briefly into an asylum when she'd run away with her lover. The charge was insanity due to "over-education." Columbine had escaped with the aid of her lover and then promptly left him when he'd forbidden her to discuss her experience publicly, saying that it would be unladylike to do so. She lectured and wrote and became instantly notorious in London, a scandalous woman who laughed at her critics and exhorted women to cross class lines and organize for their rights.

Bell had been shocked. Columbine was of the upper classes, her father was titled. And she had been brutalized too! Bell had listened hungrily. For the first time in her life she'd seen that ideas could be a form of comfort. Of strength. Columbine was right; women's problems were unique, and they crossed class lines. Bell drew the ideas she heard around her like a cloak; it held protection as well as warmth. Even while Archie did vile things to her she could think of all women, all the downtrodden of the world and feel comforted. She was trapped in a machine not of her making. But according to Columbine Nash she did not have to be a victim. The only one who could make her a victim was herself. And that was when she began to change. That was when she began to hope. That was when she began to act.

Secretly, she'd written to Columbine, and Columbine had answered. She'd found work for Bell in an office of women working in Columbine's New Women Society. Bell had quit her job at the collar factory that very day. The office was a place of hard work and laughter. Columbine was there every day, fundraising, writing, planning lectures. And when Archie Taft had found out and beaten Bell so badly she could not walk, Columbine had taken her in to her own home. "You will never have to lie with a man again if you don't choose to," Columbine had said to her fiercely, standing over her bed.

But what if I never choose to again? Bell cried out silently now, her lips against the glass. Over ten years had passed, and she was still chaste. She knew she was missing something essential. She could see it between Columbine and Ned, satisfaction and laughter and a closeness not measurable to outsiders. Ease and contentment. Passion.

Bell couldn't bear the touch of a man. Her reputation for chastity was ill-deserved, for she had never once been tempted to lose it. When a man touched her, she didn't feel revulsion; she just felt nothing, even from gentle, strong Horatio, whom she liked so well.

Bell's cheeks flooded with heat at the thought of what this lack had driven her to do lately. Sin. Sin of the blackest and most depraved kind.

"Bell?" Horatio saw her rigid back, the way one hand gripped the faded curtains. He sighed. "I'm sorry I upset you. I'll go."

Bell spun, her honey-colored eyes worried. "You'll come back?"

The question hung in the air while they heard the carriage outside. Hooves clattered to a halt, and Bell turned to look out the window. "It's Ned and Columbine," she said. "I didn't expect her until the early hours of the morning."

They were both silent as they waited for Ned and Columbine. Bell wanted to beg Horatio's pardon, to ask for his patience. Horatio toyed with giving Bell an ultimatum, of threatening never to return to the house again. And then, fleetingly, Marguerite's vivid blue eyes, young but so suggestive, flickered in his mind. He pushed away the image of the white breast, the small fingers with childishly bitten nails brushing against his. He felt himself stir again.

"Damn," he said fiercely, and Bell looked at him, startled, just as Columbine swept into the room.

Her black velvet cloak whirled as she tossed it into a chair. "A fine start to the new year," she said. "How do you do, Mr. Jones. Bell, how lovely you look. I hope your evening was pleasant, at least."

"Very fine, Mrs. Nash," Horatio said politely. His eyes were on Ned, who greeted them stiffly and crossed to the fireplace, his hands in his pockets. Usually, Ned Van Cormandt was the soul of graciousness.

"It's beastly cold in here," Ned observed tightly. "Bell, you'll catch your death."

Columbine looked at him sharply. She didn't care for the omission of her own comfort. But then, they'd barely exchanged a word since they left the Hartleys and Columbine had refused to go downtown with him.

Horatio quickly crossed to the scuttle. "My fault, I'm afraid," he said. "I was just about to rekindle the fire."

"Thank you, Mr. Jones, but Ned is perfectly capable of doing so." Columbine gave her lover an eloquent look. "Mr. Jones, Bell, would you care for a brandy?"

"Thank you, Mrs. Nash, but I've stayed too long." Horatio bowed stiffly to the company. "I'll call tomorrow, if I may."

"Of course," Columbine said. "We always receive on New Year's Day."

"I'll say good night as well," Bell said gravely.

Ned said good night and shook hands with Horatio and returned to poke the fire. Bell walked Horatio to the door. Silently, they looked their goodbyes, for there was nothing to say.

In the parlor, Ned looked into the fire. Not turning, he said, "I would appreciate it if we could keep tonight out of the papers, Columbine."

Angrily, she sat erect in the armchair. "Are you suggesting that I'll tell Mr. Jones to make that tragedy a headline for all New York?"

"I don't think it will do Devlin any good at all. Tomorrow I'll ask

Ambrose what he plans to do. If he refuses, I'll see that Devlin gets a settlement."

"That's good of you, Ned." Columbine sighed. "It's been a very long night."

"I'll go now." Still without looking at her, he picked up his hat.

Columbine stood. She wanted to say something, but she didn't know what. Once, she would have felt the need to say something, anything so that Ned's arms would go around her. But not anymore.

"We're changing, Ned," she said suddenly. "I don't believe I like the way we're changing."

"I don't believe I do, either, my dear Columbine," Ned said, after a pause. "But there it is."

Bell heard the front door close and Columbine mount the stairs. Her step sounded weary. Tomorrow she would have no chance to ask Columbine what was wrong, but she certainly would do so at the office on Monday.

Bell thought about confiding in Columbine herself. She'd never told her of how she could not respond to Horatio, and she wondered if Columbine guessed. For a household of women who believed in free love in principle, they were awfully private with each other.

Sighing, Bell began to undress. She'd wondered many times how long it would be before patient, mild Horatio was no longer able to hold onto his manners in the face of her refusals. Tonight she had seen it, the angry glare of a man too long held off. Bell was twenty-eight and beautiful. She'd seen the look before, with every man she'd allowed to walk out with her.

Sighing, Bell stepped out of her one good gown. It pooled at her feet, and she began on the small buttons on her chemise. Thank goodness Columbine had talked her into giving up corsets.

Her hands paused at her breasts. Why hadn't her pulse quickened when Horatio had touched her tonight? Why did it quicken now?

She fell to her knees on the floor, naked. She loosened her heavy butterscotch hair, and it flowed down her back, caressing her bare skin with its softness. And her skin, too, was soft. Her arms, her breasts, her belly. Her fingertips could feel how it must feel for a man to stroke it, caress it, know every inch of its deep enfolding warmth . . .

Bell's hands snapped up and locked together in prayer. She closed her eyes against the horror. Tears began to slip down her burning cheeks. She begged the Lord Jesus Christ to save her from herself. Thy skin was flayed, she prayed, her eyes tightly shut. What right have I to worship my own smooth skin? Thy mind was pure. What right have I to indulge my own baseness?

She felt on fire, pure as a sword forged in a heat too intense for earth. She felt an angel, white and glowing hot, her hair rippling, glorious in her nakedness and her purity. Her hands again stole down her body to touch her breasts, her legs, her arms. She was pure. She was perfect, a fortress. Her thighs were strong and white. They were soft. They were locked, muscles straining, trembling. She would conquer herself. She—

Bell's head jerked up, her neck muscles straining. It took her a moment to recognize the sound. Knocking downstairs, soft but insistent, on the front door. It was after two in the morning. Who would come to their door at this hour? Perhaps Ned or Horatio had returned, to apologize, to be contrite. How tiresome of them, and how unlike them.

Bell rose on unsteady legs and fumbled herself into her dressing gown. Thinking hard, she decided neither one of those proud men would be downstairs. It could be anyone, really—a woman in trouble, perhaps thrown out of her apartment by her landlord. She would find her way to Columbine's door, for help would be there, bracing advice, and a little money, as much as Columbine could spare.

Her long hair flew behind her as she reached the top of the stairs and started down. She could hear noises from Columbine's room as Columbine most likely roused herself from bed to come downstairs as well. They would need strong tea and a good fire.

She could hear hail pattering against the windows as she walked with quick steps through the front hall. She peered through the long narrow window to the left of the door.

It was a man. He was wet through, and it was hard to distinguish his features underneath his hat and dripping mustache. Bell hesitated only a moment before sliding back the bolt and opening the door.

"Can I help you?" she asked, raising her voice in order to be heard over the moaning wind. She saw small pellets of icy rain bounce off the man's broad shoulders. A drop trickled through his rough cheeks and caught in the mustache over his full upper lip.

"Lawrence Birch," the man said shortly. He blinked back the rain in his eyelashes. "I'm sorry to disturb you. Mrs. Nash?"

She shook her head.

"I've been sent by Tavish Finn," the man said.

Columbine's half-brother in San Francisco. Bell opened the door wider. "Come in," she said.

He came inside the door, and she stepped back, closing the door after he moved forward into the hall. As she turned, Lawrence Birch removed his hat. Water had collected on the brim, and a few drops splashed on her face and neck as he snapped it to his side. Bell recoiled from the shock of the cold water. She felt it on her cheeks, her lips.

"I beg your pardon," Lawrence Birch said. "That was clumsy."

He reached out as if to brush away the drops, but Bell backed up and wiped them from her mouth with the back of her hand. "It's all right," she said quickly, without thinking. "I was thirsty."

He looked startled, then he laughed. Now she saw how handsome he was. His teeth were white and even, and his wet hair was probably blond in the sun. His eyes were ice-blue, an otherworldy color, too pale, perhaps, to be engaging. More odd than beautiful. And his coloring wasn't fair, as you'd expect with a light-haired man. His skin was brown, as if he spent time outdoors.

Suddenly, Bell was aware of her naked legs underneath her dressing gown, and of her hair's wild disarray. Mr. Birch seemed very aware of it, too.

"I'm afraid I've disturbed you," he said. His expression was unreadable, but Bell found herself flushing. It was as though he knew of her struggle upstairs, of her fear, of her secrets. It was as though he could smell her passionate struggle upstairs on her body. Her thighs, her hands.

"Come into the parlor," she said. "I'll fetch Mrs. Nash."

He followed her inside, and she busied herself with building up the fire. By the time she had it blazing again, Columbine was downstairs in her most elegant brocade dressing gown and was holding her hand out to Mr. Birch as though it was four o'clock in the afternoon and he had arrived punctually to tea.

"If Tavish Finn sends you, you are welcome, Mr. Birch. Please sit down. Bell, would you mind fetching some tea? Mr. Birch looks chilled. Perhaps a few sandwiches as well. Thank you."

Bell nodded distantly and hurried from the room. Obviously, Mr. Birch must be in trouble of some sort. Probably political trouble, or Tavish Finn wouldn't have sent him to Columbine. But whatever had brought him to their door, it was no concern of Bell's. It was her job to make tea and sandwiches. But first, Bell took the time to climb the stairs to her room and button herself into her most conservative brown wool dress. Then she twisted her hair into a bun so tight it made her head ache. Only then did she return downstairs to make tea for Lawrence Birch.

Lawrence Birch moved like a gentleman. He tucked his gloves into his hat and laid it on a windowsill, as a gentleman should; his pale, ice-blue eyes were polite, almost bland. He hardly looked the sort of man who would arrive at one's doorstep at two o'clock in the morning.

Columbine wondered uneasily what Lawrence Birch had done as she sank into her armchair and motioned him to do the same. He was far too handsome to have done much of anything. He had an elegant figure, tall and lean, with almost perfect features that were given character by a beautifully curved mouth. His hands were well shaped, and his clothes, though not grand, were impeccable.

"I must apologize again for intruding so late," Mr. Birch said. "If Mr. Finn had not led me to hope of your kind reception, I would never have dared. But I only just arrived, and I didn't know where else to go."

"Are you wanted by the law, Mr. Birch?" Columbine asked imperturbably. She dearly hoped her brother would not send an escaped convict or some such to her, but with Tavish, one never knew.

"No, no, nothing of that sort. But I'm afraid my political activities in San Francisco made things uncomfortable for me there. I was publishing an anarchist newspaper."

Another anarchist. Columbine sighed. "Ah."

"I first met Mrs. Finn. She's one of the few reporters in San Francisco who solicit details of the anarchist position and actually publish them without condescension. She speaks very highly of you, by the way."

"She's a dear friend," Columbine murmured. Only a few people knew of her true relationship to Tavish; for years, they were thought to be lovers because of their intimacy. Not many English baronets recognized their illegitmate offspring, of course. She'd only formed a true friendship with her half-brother as an adult, after they'd both left England. "How is Mrs. Finn? I hope you found her well."

"Very well. She's a remarkable lady."

"Yes," Columbine said quietly. "She is." She missed her sister-in-law. Brought up in the New York aristocracy, once married to the most horrific man Columbine had ever met—with perhaps the exception of Columbine's own ex-husband—Darcy had left it all behind in a scandalous flight to San Francisco with Tavish. And now they were married, and running a newspaper in San Francisco. Columbine had never imagined that Tavish was capable of falling in love so deeply and so happily.

"What is it that led you to leave San Francisco, Mr. Birch?" she asked, as Bell entered and set down the tea and sandwiches.

Lawrence Birch paused, reluctant to answer while Bell was in the room. His eyes coolly followed her progress to the door. He waited until it had shut, then turned to Columbine. "There is a wealthy industrialist in San Francisco, a famous man prominent in society. I heard through a source that a small group of workers were planning to bomb his office. Mrs. Finn had also heard the rumor, and came to me to ask about it. There was to be a secret meeting that evening. I went to it. The police did as well. Shots were fired, and one policeman went down. Two of the workers died. There is some question whether the police shot their own man as well."

"I see," Columbine murmured, pouring the tea.

"Those of us that escaped had to disappear. There is no charge against me, but Mr. Finn felt I would be better off in New York for awhile. However, I'm taking no chances. I would not want to endanger you, Mrs. Nash. If I had any other alternative, I would have—"

"No, don't think of it," Columbine said decidedly. "There's a small room off the kitchen. It has a back entrance, and I'm afraid you'll have to be very discreet. The three of us here get enough tongues wagging."

"Three of us?"

"Yes, three women, living alone. You met Miss Huxton at the door. I also have another boarder, Miss Corbeau. Cream?"

"Thank you. I'll be like a shadow, Mrs. Nash. And I assure you, I'll be on my way tomorrow."

"Tomorrow is New Year's Day. It will be difficult for you to find a place tomorrow. We'll have many callers, it's a New York custom, so perhaps we'll hear something about a room. If not, after New Year's I can find somewhere for you to go. Do you have any plans?"

Lawrence nodded. "I hope to meet Johann Most. I admire him a great deal. Perhaps I can get a position on *Die Freiheit*. Do you know where the office is?"

Johann Most was the publisher of the militant anarchist newpaper, and was a compelling speaker. Columbine had met him, and disliked him personally. She also felt uncomfortable with his ideas. But she had to concede he was a powerful speaker. "Yes," she answered, offering the plate of sandwiches to Lawrence. "Downtown, on William Street. I'm afraid I'm not acquainted with Herr Most, not enough to introduce you, at least. But if you like, I can take you to Schwab's saloon on First Street. You'll be welcomed there."

Justus Schwab's saloon was a famous center for radical politics in New York. Columbine was fond of Justus, who had a warmth and humor Johann Most completely lacked.

Lawrence sipped his tea and watched her. "I sense you're not sympathetic to anarchism," he said.

Columbine took a long sip of tea. "I am primarily a worker for women's rights," she answered carefully. "No, I don't agree with anarchist principles, especially the violent means that Bakunin proposes to demolish the state."

"I don't agree with violent means either. But if the masses are to be galvanized, woken up . . ."

"I don't believe," Columbine said with a thin smile, "that the masses are ever galvanized by violence, Mr. Birch. I'm afraid it has just the opposite effect. It makes the government stronger, for it makes people simply afraid."

"It has not been successful in the United States as of yet, Mrs. Nash. Not that I'm proposing it. But if the demolition of the state—by peaceful means—ensures the emancipation of women, surely you couldn't argue against it."

"If I felt that anarchist men were any more interested in the emancipation of women, perhaps," Columbine said pleasantly. "But Mr. Birch, I've learned something from traveling in your circles. Men are men. If there's any hope for emancipation, it lies with women."

Lawrence sipped his tea, obviously too polite to prolong the argument. "It is a pleasure," he said finally, "to find a woman who does at least consider these matters. I feel as though I've been drinking from a mountain spring, Mrs. Nash. San Francisco is rather a desert in that regard."

"I find that difficult to believe." Columbine sat erect. Nothing made her frostier than a man's attempt to flatter her by denigrating her sex.

He seemed to sense her disapproval, but he merely shrugged. "My fault, I'm sure, as well as my misfortune. In my experience, the formidable minds belonged to men."

"Ask Justus to introduce you to young Emma Goldman," Columbine said lightly. "There you will find a formidable mind."

"I was speaking of San Francisco," Lawrence said. "Of course in New York things will be different. They already are." He flashed a smile at her. "Within five minutes I've found someone to argue with. That is always a grand discovery, almost as precious as finding a friend. It's at least as good for the intellect as the soul. And when that someone is the famous Columbine Nash, my good fortune is doubled. I've admired you for years, Mrs. Nash. You are a brave and true soul."

"Thank you, Mr. Birch," Columbine said confusedly.

Lawrence's smile held and his blue eyes warmed, and Columbine saw sensuality, and heat. The power of that smile was capable of stirring up a woman's wild heart. No wonder he was so careful not to deliver it too often. Good Lord, she thought. No wonder Tavish sent him to me. He probably wanted to get him away from his wife.

Three

Lawrence Birch settled into the small, cramped room off the kitchen as though it were a suite at the Fifth Avenue Hotel. The lumpy mattress felt like the softest down, and the worn sheets like fine linen. He had come through danger and found paradise: He had landed into a household of women.

He was a man that had been often called charming, but never by men. It was always women, delicate, delicious, obliging women who characterized him so. Men might disparage him, ignore him, but women never did, never could. And now once again they would smooth the way.

Lawrence had been blessed since childhood with an extraordinary sensitivity. He found people as transparent as glass. He had learned, living in a household where blows were the usual form of scolding, how to interpret the nuances of voice and gesture to discover what people really meant, despite what they said. It allowed him to move before the blow, sometimes to forestall it completely with the right words. That sensitivity was his greatest gift, and it had gotten him far.

In just fifteen minutes with Columbine he'd learned much. He knew she was unhappy. How unhappy, he didn't know yet. That knowledge was important, but it wasn't the key.

The key was what Lawrence privately termed the one fact about a woman he could turn on to ensure a seduction. Often it was flattery, but the key, the thing most men missed, was the *particular* form of flattery each woman needed. Some women tumbled for their beauty, some for their minds. Some women succumbed because they hated their husbands, some because they loved them. Some because they were bored, some because they were angry. Some because they had never understood sex, some because they understood it too well. Columbine might not be easy. But she was seducible. Lawrence loved celebrity, and she was too famous to resist.

He picked up a ham sandwich and chewed thoughtfully. Columbine was the daughter of a duke, or a viscount—he could never keep track of English titles, but he knew she came from money. That was most likely why she knew Darcy Finn, who had thrown away her fortune to marry that blackguard Irishman with the threatening brows who had sent him packing. Thank God for the absurd delicacy of upper crust relations. Columbine would never know, he hoped, about his pursuit of Darcy Finn.

Lawrence put his hands behind his head and looked up at the ceiling, picturing Columbine slipping out of her dressing gown. He smiled. If every bourgeois had his bomb, as the French anarchists sang, every woman had her key.

On New Year's Day, callers began to arrive at the house on Twenty-third Street in the early afternoon. Columbine, Bell, and Marguerite had been preparing since seven for the guests. Journalists, union organizers, poets, socialists, reformers, society folk, and a few extravagantly-clad ladies who were instantly recognizable as prostitutes, who stayed only a few minutes, to pay their respects to Columbine.

There was no stiff formality, but fast talk and quick laughter, an argument or two. Columbine floated through it all, her honey-blond hair gleaming as the fire caught it on this dark January day. She wore a velvet dress the color of cognac that was trimmed with beaded black passementerie. The tiny diamond earrings Ned had given her for Christmas winked and shimmered in her ears. But Ned himself did not show up.

Across the room, Marguerite saw the diamonds in Columbine's ears and banged down the tray of sugar cookies on a small table. Columbine lived like a pauper, but she still shimmered in diamonds and silks, was still considered one of the most beautiful women in New York. She had an enormously rich lover, and she enjoyed the fruits of those relations. Marguerite wondered if it might be more fun to be a mistress than a wife, but instantly banished those wicked thoughts. Columbine had been married already. It was easier to take a lover when you had Mrs. as your title.

As if her restless thoughts had brought him, Horatio Jones entered the parlor, his hat in his hand. His eyes didn't meet Marguerite's as he wished her an overly hearty New Year.

"Thank you, Mr. Jones. I hope the new year is good to you." Marguerite smiled, deepening the dimple in her left cheek. "I hope you get everything you desire."

Her words dripped with a vague but tantalizing private meaning, and Horatio glanced behind him. Bell was engaged in conversation with Lawrence Birch, and he looked back at Marguerite again. "I wish you the same, Miss Corbeau," he said blandly. There was not a hint of fliration in his tone, Marguerite noted with disappointment. "Can you tell me, by any chance, who that gentleman with the light hair is? There, over by the fireplace. I've not seen him here before."

Marguerite didn't need to turn. "Lawrence Birch," she said dismissively. "A visitor from California."

"An acquaintance of Mrs. Nash, then," Horatio said, his casual tone barely concealing the relief in his voice. Could he really believe, Marguerite thought incredulously, that his problems with Bell had to do with a rival?

"That's right, Mr. Jones," she answered, already bored with the subject. She'd met Mr. Birch at breakfast and was not impressed. He was too poor to tempt her, and she didn't trust his eyes.

"He's a well-looking man," Horatio said. Now that he knew the man wasn't a rival, he could afford to be generous.

"I suppose," Marguerite said with a shrug. "But I prefer a different sort altogether."

"Yes, well," Horatio said gruffly. "I see Mrs. Nash is free. I should pay my respects." He bowed, and Marguerite gave him one last pretty smile. She frowned as she watched him cross the room. Perhaps it was time to step up her campaign. A blunt approach? Did she have the courage? Or, more to the point, would it work?

• • •

"So you work at the New Women Society with Mrs. Nash," Lawrence said.

Bell nodded. "I started as a secretary, but now I'm in charge of the Emergency Fund. We reserve part of our budget to help women who are in dire need of funds—to pay rent, or buy food, or fuel . . . ." Her voice trailed off as she became momentarily tangled in Lawrence's pale intent gaze. "I know what an anarchist would say," she continued with sudden asperity. "A waste of time."

"Yes, some would," Lawrence agreed. "It sounds cruel, but the more reformers try to ameliorate the sufferings of the poor, the longer we shall have to wait for them to rise. Johann Most believes the eight hour day, for instance, will only serve to divert the workers, lull them into complacency for more killing years."

"Perhaps you would not say that," Bell said, "if you saw how they suffered."

"Do you think me so removed, Miss Huxton? Do you think I have no heart?"

Confused, Bell looked away. "I don't know. I only speak of my own experience. The eight hour day can alleviate so much hardship for the working class. The drop in industrial accidents alone—"

"Will mean only more profits for the ruling class," Lawrence interrupted easily.

Her eyes snapped to his face. "So what do a few hands, or fingers, or eyes, of the workers matter?"

Although he didn't answer, she saw now how hard his icy eyes could be. But then he smiled, and the eyes warmed, and she wondered what she'd seen. Still, the thought of the ruthlessness seemed to flood her with warmth, and strangely turned her mind to her struggles upstairs, fighting her flesh, succumbing to her flesh, and sinning. To her horror, Bell blushed.

Lawrence knew she would blush before she did. He'd seen something in her large amber eyes, something that momentarily excited her. Even though she despised him—for he could see by her face how repellent his words had been—she, for an instant, had wanted him. Interesting.

"Perhaps you can show me what you're talking about one day," he said. "Show me Manhattan's working class. Take me to a factory. Or take me to your office, perhaps."

"I'm sorry, I couldn't possibly. I'm very busy. If you'll excuse me." Murmuring an apology, Bell turned away.

Lawrence sank into an armchair and, balancing his teacup, crossed his long legs. His first day in this house was going nicely. Bell was an intriguing puzzle, ice wrapped in a lush body and emotion trapped behind a bland facade. And Columbine . . . she was beautiful. He hadn't realized how very desirable she was.

He watched her without seeming to watch. She was deep in a friendly conversation with the photographer Jacob Riis and didn't notice when Ned Van Cormandt arrived with a companion, a bearlike man with coal-black hair threaded with gray. It hadn't taken Lawrence long to find out the financier was her lover. He felt nothing but scorn for Columbine's choice. It was true that women could have no real political commitment.

He had met Miss Corbeau at breakfast, and dismissed her almost immediately. Remarkably pretty but too slender, with a white face and a pointed chin. Her eyes were dark blue, studded with bristly black lashes. This morning, Marguerite Corbeau's stunning eyes had flicked over him, noted his face, his clothes, and his boots, and dismissed him. Lawrence smiled to himself. He recognized a fellow sexual adventurer when he saw one. He would have to steer clear of Marguerite.

He made his way over to Columbine, who was now trying to pour tea but slopping it in her saucer. Across the room, Ned was engaged in conversation with his companion, and Columbine was alternately frowning and looking at him, then trying not to look.

"I've met so many interesting people here, Mrs. Nash," Lawrence said in a low tone. "Thank you."

"Oh, I'm so glad," Columbine said distractedly.

"You mentioned that you would introduce me to Mr. Schwab. Any time it's convenient for you."

Columbine wrenched her eyes away from Ned. "I have a splendid idea, Mr. Birch. I have business downtown tomorrow. Would that suit you?"

Lawrence gave a short bow. "I am at your service, Mrs. Nash." He moved away as Columbine gave up, put down her teacup, and went to greet Ned.

"Columbine, I'd like you to meet Elijah Reed. Mr. Reed, Mrs. Nash."

Columbine looked up into a kind, weary face. The man was big and looked strong. It was as though the room was a window, and he was blocking her view of everything but the sky. She shook his hand, and his easily enveloped hers. "I'm pleased to meet you, Mr. Reed. I'm an admirer of your work."

Elijah Reed was a famous man, a novelist and social commentator who had achieved instant fame at the age of twenty-two with *Look Away*, his account of his Civil War experiences. He was the son of famous Boston abolitionists, and after his mother died he'd run away to join the war at the age of fifteen.

Columbine had met many famous men. But Elijah Reed was known for his intellect and his fire, and she hadn't expected such a tired, and, well, *old* man. He couldn't be more than forty-five, but he could be sixty, the resignation in his voice and posture was so deep.

He bowed slightly. "Then we are well matched, Mrs. Nash, for I admire yours." She could see now the intelligence in the tired eyes. But still, where was the spark?

He surveyed the room with heavy-lidded eyes and grim-lined lips. Nothing seemed to interest him, nothing could possibly impress him. He didn't look bored, though, Columbine decided. Just projecting the kind of world-weariness that only the Germans could name. *Weltschmerz.*

"Elijah is here for an extended visit," Ned said. "The *Century* is doing a serial."

"I'll be sure to look for it," Columbine said. She kept her eyes trained on Elijah Reed, for Ned was maintaining such a polite, formal tone with her that she wanted to hit him.

"If you'll excuse me," Ned said. He bowed and moved away.

Elijah Reed watched him go, thoughtfulness in his dark eyes. Then he turned back to Columbine. "I understand that there was some excitement at the Hartley home last night," he said.

"Yes, a man was horribly injured when some damaged fireworks went off," Columbine answered. She shuddered, remembering. "It was an awful sight."

"You were there, Mrs. Nash?"

"I was a guest, yes. I left after the accident."

"And why was that?"

She gave him a keen look. "I should think the answer to that is obvious, Mr. Reed."

"Not really," he said. "For I hear that the dancing continued while the injured man was taken away—with no galloping horses or clanging bells to disturb the music. He lost a great deal of blood, I hear, and almost died."

"I wasn't there to see," Columbine said. Elijah Reed didn't strike her as a gossip, but the oddest men were. Ned, for example, always knew before she did what wife was unfaithful, what husband was making a fool of himself over an actress, and who had lost a fortune at Richard Canfield's gaming house.

"I called on the Hartley's earlier," Elijah said. "They both seemed quite recovered from the shock. But it must have affected their memory, for they could not seem to remember the servant's name. He hadn't been there long, they said."

"His name is Devlin," Columbine said. "I believe he worked in the stables, poor man. I hope he doesn't lose that arm. I think Mr. Hartley's behavior was abominable, to continue the party that way."

"It was Mr. Hartley who decided to begin the dancing?"

"Oh, yes, Mr. Van Cormandt and I could not dissuade him. His lack of concern," Columbine said, one corner of her mouth lifting, "was obvious." Feeling she had said too much, she smiled her hostess smile at Elijah Reed. "Can I get you some punch, Mr. Reed, or some tea?"

"No, thank you, Mrs. Nash," Elijah Reed answered, and he watched her say goodbye and move away with imperturbable dark gray eyes, sad and wise and absolutely incapable of surprise at any degradations human nature might indulge in.

Ned stayed until the guests had gone and Marguerite and Bell had retreated upstairs for the night. Lawrence bid them good night and headed for his room off the kitchen. Ned played with an unlit cigar and stared into the flames of the fire. Behind him, he heard the rustle of Columbine's skirts as she nestled further into her armchair. "I've never felt so tired in my life," she said. "Oh, I meant to ask you, Ned—did you find out where Devlin lives?"

"Yes, I talked to Ambrose this morning. It turns out that the red-headed woman he fired—Fiona—is Devlin's wife."

Columbine gasped. "He fired her? But Ned, what will they do?"

"He won't rehire her, he was adamant about that. But he did agree to a settlement, and I hope he doesn't drag his heels. I sent them a note informing them of this, with Ambrose's permission. They live on Gansevoort, near the river. 145 Gansevoort."

"That was very good of you, Ned. I'm glad. But Fiona will need another job, I fear."

"Eventually. But her husband will need nursing. I'll keep an eye on them, Columbine. Now, can we discuss another topic?"

"What is that? How cruel you've been to me today?" she asked, giving him an impish smile.

He almost grinned, but he didn't. "Nonsense," he said gruffly. "I try to save your reputation, and you call me cruel. I can't very well fawn over you in public."

"No. But you could be civil."

"I was perfectly polite. Stop teasing me, Columbine," he said when he saw her smile. "I want to discuss this strange young man you have in your back room. Who the devil is he?" He had to concentrate in order for his voice to come out smooth and unruffled. He was severely irked at the presence of Lawrence Birch in this house.

"I told you who he is," Columbine said, yawning. "He'll find a room soon, Ned. Don't make an issue of it."

That was too much for him. "Don't you think I'm within my rights to make an issue of it? You are my lover. You have a man living in your house—"

"He has nowhere else to turn. And he was sent by my brother, Ned."

"What do you know about him? I hardly think Tavish meant for you to take the man to your bosom."

"Really, Ned—"

"I don't like him, Columbine. I don't trust him. What does he live on, anyway?"

"I have no idea," Columbine said frostily. "It wouldn't occur to me to ask."

"Oh, that British chilliness," Ned said, turning his back to the fire and frowning at her. "You're trying to suggest that I'm a blundering American boor, when I'm merely trying to protect you."

"I don't need—"

"My protection, I know. But I think you do. What the devil is wrong with that?"

Columbine didn't say anything for a moment. "Please. We're tired. Let's not discuss this now."

"We have to discuss things of this nature all the time," Ned exploded. "Because you are too stubborn to consider the alternative to this madness."

"What madness?" she demanded, sitting up. "Having my own life?"

"Yes!"

"Ned, do not try me tonight." Columbine relented, and spoke in a softer tone. "Please. I'm afraid when you talk this way. You told me last year that if you ever asked me that question again, it would be for the last time, and I couldn't bear that."

Ned said nothing. He frowned at his cigar. "You ask too much," he said finally. "You know if we married things would be less difficult for me."

"What a romantic proposal," Columbine said lightly, hoping to tease him out of his seriousness. "Perhaps you should get on one knee when you tell me you wish to make me your devoted bride so that things could be 'less difficult' for you."

Ned waited a beat. "I have proposed to you on one knee, as you well know. I have proposed to you on both knees, sitting up, and lying down. And each time you have refused me."

"You know why," Columbine murmured. "You know that I will never marry again. I cannot marry in a state where I become the property of my husband, where my rights are trampled—"

"Please," Ned said, "please, my dear, can we not discuss the politics of marriage this time?"

"But politics *are* part of marriage, and it is men who make it so,"

Columbine said stubbornly. "They made the laws, did they not? And I must say, Ned, I find it interesting that you choose this moment for your annual proposal. A moment when you are frustrated in your attempts to control who I see, and who I make a friend of. Could it be that you believe, despite everything you say, that if we married you would then be able to forbid someone like Lawrence Birch your house? For it would be *your* house, then, not mine, in the eyes of the law."

Ned sighed. "I find it extraordinary how you refuse to see that occasionally I might be right about something. That occasionally you might need protection, or advice."

"Ned, don't exaggerate. Of course I know you are good and strong, and Lord knows I've never said—oh, do we have to discuss this when my feet hurt so much? Oof, that's better." Columbine slipped off her boots and waggled her stockinged toes.

Ned closed his eyes in pain. It was having her like this that caused him such sorrow. He loved her casualness as much as her gaiety. He turned and smiled at the sight of her stocking feet, raised on a tufted stool. "You look comfortable in body, at least."

She smiled. "But not in mind, thanks to you."

Her smile was so pretty he almost relented. But the brief respite, the light words, had not managed to dispel the frustration in him. He never had enough of her, he was always fighting for more. Suddenly all the unanswered questions of the past months weighed on him. He had to know.

He asked softly, "Do you love me, Columbine?"

Her brown eyes widened. "Of course I—"

He lifted a hand, and she stopped. "Wait. Don't answer out of habit, or affection. You know what I'm asking. Do you love me, Columbine?"

She was silent so long the fear took hold of him. Ned felt his stomach drop. He was falling away. He was a dead man without Columbine's love, and he knew it. She had raised him from a life spent in the margins, looking on at other people, hardly engaged at all. She had made him care.

"Please, Columbine." He was surprised that his voice was so steady.

"Yes, I love you, Ned," she said slowly. "But lately I seem to have fallen away from you somehow. I don't know when it happened, or why. . . . Or maybe something was supposed to happen, and didn't."

"You're not making any sense," he said tersely. Then he bit his lip. "No, of course you are. Of course I know what you mean. God help me."

Columbine heard the pain in his voice and rose so swiftly she took him by surprise. She ran to him and threw her arms around him. "Oh, Ned, don't be unhappy. I *do* love you, so much. You're my best friend. I still want to be with you. I still can't imagine being with anyone else."

She raised wet eyes to his, and the slender hope that had kept him going died. Her arms around him tortured him, the smell of her tortured him, but he didn't have the strength to pull away. Why wasn't what she offered *enough* anymore?

Columbine saw the pain in his eyes and her heart twisted. "Oh, Ned, Neddie," she whispered. "What is it? Why is this happening? All of a sudden, we're so serious. This can't happen. Let's just say good night. Ned, you're making me so afraid—"

He had to keep going, had to know everything. "Columbine—"

She put both hands up to stop him. Her eyes were wild. "No, no, don't say it, Ned, don't ask me, please. Not yet, not tonight. Don't ask me . . ."

He ignored the litany and grasped her hands instead. "I must. I have to. Will you marry me?"

Columbine's eyes filled with tears. "You said if you asked me again it would be for the last time—"

He held her gaze steadily. "And it is."

Columbine broke away from him and walked to the window. "Don't do this to us, Ned."

"I have to. Columbine, I've been thinking. I know you can't be only Mrs. Ned Van Cormandt, with all that implies. The house, the family and social obligations are a full-time job, I know that. But what if we lived differently? I've been thinking of making my house into a public museum. The art collection is extensive, and I've received some support for the idea."

"Oh, Ned. You couldn't. Not the Van Cormandt house."

"You mean that ostentatious pile of marble, that horrifying copy of a castle where some virgin queen was beheaded, that bad imitation of a medieval dungeon where hundreds of heathen were tortured, that shuddering approximation of a bloody feasting hall of Viking warriors? Yes, go ahead and smile, I remember your words perfectly, my dear. Lord knows, I agree. I can't imagine you living there. Am I right?"

She nodded.

"All right, then. What if we lived in the Greenwich Village house? You love the house, as do I. It's certainly large enough. I would like to live downtown—after all, I was born on Washington Square. And you could keep your name, you could have your own study."

"Thank you," she said, but he missed her irony.

"We could have a different kind of marriage, darling. And if you didn't want children, we wouldn't have them."

"But you want children."

"I want you more."

"What about my lecture tours? I've given them up lately, but I plan to return to them."

Ned struggled for a moment. "Of course. As long as they aren't too long." He grinned charmingly. "I couldn't bear to be without you."

Columbine looked out into the night. She pictured the life Ned described, and she saw that it could please her. She could feel happiness tug at her, make a soft bed for her to lie down in, to breathe deeply and slowly. She would never wake up at three o'clock in the morning, gasping in panic at her life. She would sleep the sleep of the contented, next to her husband.

Wearily, Columbine stopped the train of her thought. She'd been married. She knew it could not hold off despair, or uncertainty, or fear. She knew it could imprison. She knew it could bind. Perhaps Ned was right, perhaps they could forge a different kind of marriage. But the thing she most feared about marriage to Ned he could not guard against. Marriage would make her weak. Already, her life with Ned had made her soft. Where had all her anxiety come from during the past months, but the knowledge that she was less than she could be?

"Ned, I've tried to explain this before," she said. She couldn't look at him, so she stared outside at the blackness. "You think I'm a strong woman. You don't know how weak I am. Just in the past three years of being with you I've changed. I work less. I think less. There isn't an edge to me anymore, Ned. I've grown soft. And it isn't your fault, God knows. It's me. I have a taste for luxury and sloth, for love and lightness, and I succumb."

"What's wrong with those things?"

"Nothing except that they should be balanced with hard work. And I haven't been working very hard since I met you, Ned."

"It seems to me you've been working all the time," he grumbled, and she had to laugh.

Her smile slowly faded as she stared out the window. "Maybe to you, I was. Maybe that's the problem."

"But I told you I would change my life. Then you, too, would change to meet it. We wouldn't dine out, we would ignore society. I forced you to go to those awful dinners because I felt some kind of ridiculous responsibility to keep up the family name after my father died. I listened to pressure from my family when I shouldn't have. But Columbine, I was wrong. Can't you see that we can change?"

She turned, her back to the sill. "Why can't you change your life first, and then we'll see? Why can't we decide in a year, or six months? If you really mean it, Ned, if you really want your life to be different, then you'll change it, not for me, but for yourself."

He was already shaking his head. "I can't wait another year."

"And I can't marry you now!" she cried. She raised her hands pleadingly. "I'm so sorry, Ned, but I can't. Please understand."

He stared across the room at her, and his eyes filled. She looked so distraught, so beautiful, with her gold hair spilling out of her pins and her dark eyes soft with misery. "I'll never love anyone but you," he said. "But you're killing me. It's not enough for me anymore, Columbine. I want you at the head of my table. I want you in my bed. I want to go to sleep at night next to you. I can't help that."

Tears were running down her face now. "I'm sorry." She couldn't stop saying it.

He walked to where his hat and stick lay on the front window-sill. He picked them up and went back to her. He kissed her forehead while she shook underneath his lips from her sobs.

"I'll always be there for you, Columbine. Come to me if you need me."

"Ned—"

"Goodbye, my love." Ned walked out of the parlor, taking his hat and stick, but leaving his heart behind.

Four

COLUMBINE SPENT A sleepless night trying to convince herself that Ned would change his mind. She could not imagine life without Ned. Every time he had said he could not go on, he'd relented the next morning. But he had never spoken those words the way he had said them the night before, and in her heart she knew he meant it. It was proof of the folly of the heart that she was surprised to see no flowers, no note, when she came down the next morning. Instead, she saw the smiling face of Lawrence Birch.

He did not mention her pale face or the dark smudges underneath her eyes, and Columbine was grateful. He merely reminded her of her promise to take him downtown.

"Of course, Mr. Birch, I'd be happy to," Columbine answered distractedly. "Would you mind making a stop with me first?"

He bowed. "I am at your service, Mrs. Nash."

After breakfast, they left the house together and walked to the Ninth Avenue El. On the jolting train downtown, Lawrence was caught up in the sights around him, and didn't speak except to ask an occasional question. Columbine turned her mind to the meeting ahead. In preparation, she'd dressed carefully. A plain gray merino dress with her three-quarter length coat of black wool trimmed with gray chenille and silver cord. Perhaps the coat was a bit too smart, but aside from her fur-trimmed cloak it was her warmest coat, and it was blustery today.

When they reached their stop in Greenwich Village, Lawrence

looked around him curiously. This far west was primarily an Irish section, with tenements and crowded conditions prevailing. Garbage was piled high on corners, and many of the windows were stuffed with rags or cardboard to keep out the cold. A group of children in tattered coats played a silent and obscure game near a dead horse lying in the street. Between the garbage and the horse, one had to be grateful it was a cold day.

Columbine looked at Lawrence, but he made no comment. She liked the keenness of his gaze, the sense that he was taking everything in, missing nothing.

"When I see this," he said finally, "I wonder why every person doesn't rise up."

"When I see this," Columbine said quietly, "I wonder why every person doesn't lie down and give up."

He looked at her, startled. "I think you just might need an infusion of hope, Mrs. Nash," he said lightly.

"And will you provide it, Mr. Birch?"

"Oh, absolutely."

"Ah," Columbine said with a smile, "there is no one more romantic than an anarchist."

"Romantic?" He looked startled at the word.

"Don't you believe that after the state is demolished, all its citizens will equitably divide its resources, that all will take only what they need? That scarcities will be rationed, and all will obey this rationing with generous spirits?"

"Yes, of course. But that is human nature, Mrs. Nash. Someday it will be reality, not romance. It's the state that accounts for the depravity in human nature. Once man is liberated, his true soul will have a chance to emerge."

Columbine was struck with how fervent his gaze was. She felt a pang; was he right, did she need an infusion of hope?

Lawrence glanced down a side street. "The docks look as dangerous in this city as in any other," he observed.

"I suppose. But during the day, it's quite pleasant to be near the river. At least on a fine day, not today with this wind. We're very near the markets, as well. You might want to return and sample some oysters—they're shipped in from the harbor right here. But today after our stop we'll walk east toward First Street. It's a long walk, but an instructive one. Some fine houses around Washington Square, some tenements, factories, businesses, New York University. You'll see much of downtown."

"I should like that," Lawrence said.

Columbine led the way to 142 Gansevoort Street, finding her way with some difficulty, for she didn't know the area very well. They reached the address, and Columbine looked at the house dubiously. It seemed to sag with the weight of centuries; it was a wonder it didn't fall in on itself with her first step on the creaking porch. Columbine rang the bell.

An older woman answered. Gray whiskers sprouted from her chin in patches. She looked Columbine up and down suspiciously but said nothing.

"Good day. We're here to see Fiona Devlin," Columbine said. "Would you tell her Columbine N—"

"Round back," the woman said, and slammed the door.

"Thank you," Columbine said to the door.

"Not a good beginning," Lawrence said with a smile. It lightened his features, making his pale blue eyes warm.

"Perhaps they owe her some rent," Columbine speculated.

Lawrence took her arm as they picked their way through a woodpile to a dirt alley running alongside the house. The ground was muddy and encrusted with ice, but a narrow walkway of boards had been set down for passage. Columbine balanced, still holding onto Lawrence's arm, for there were patches of ice on the boards as well. She could feel the bunch of steely muscles underneath his coat. The elegant Mr. Birch was burlier than he appeared.

Around back they found the rear of the building in even worse repair than the front. A dirt-packed yard was crisscrossed with clotheslines. There was a door with cracked, rust-colored paint that seemed to lead to a basement apartment. Columbine knocked at it. It opened almost immediately.

The small, red-headed woman stood, one hand on her hip. Her expression was less strained than the night of the accident, but it was not one whit less fierce. Wisps of red hair from an untidy bun waved around pale cheeks. A clean apron was tied over a plain black dress. If the old woman upstairs had a suspicious look, Fiona Devlin was positively murderous.

Columbine had never been slow to recognize hostility. She didn't smile, knowing it would only infuriate Fiona Devlin. "Mrs. Devlin, I was at the Hartley house the other night when your husband was injured. I've come to inquire about his health."

Fiona Devlin said nothing. She continued to stare at Columbine with opaque green eyes. There was a golden patch in one corner with a dark spot in it. Lovely, hostile eyes.

"My name is Columbine Nash," she continued determinedly. "And this is my friend Mr. Birch. Mrs. Devlin, I've come to see if there's anything I can do for you. I know Mr. Hartley will be forthcoming with assistance, but until then—"

A sneer lifted the corner of Fiona's thin upper lip. "Yes, he will be *forthcoming*, though I'll not be waiting," she said, in an attempted imitation of Columbine's upper crust British accent. "Mrs. Nash," she added. The name was like an insult. Columbine had heard her name pronounced in this way before. One could not advocate free love, family limitation, and votes for women and *not* hear it. But this woman was a master at it.

"If we could come in," Columbine tried.

"My husband is sleeping. He has a fever, you see. The doctor is worried about gangrene, though he won't use that word to me."

"Perhaps you need help with nursing—"

"My sister lives with us. And we have neighbors. Goodbye."

Fiona began to shut the door. Columbine put her hand against it. Fiona's eyes flicked for one contemptuous second at her fine kid glove.

"I work with the New Women Society," Columbine said. "We run an employment agency—for clerical work, mostly. If you need assistance, our office is on Fourteenth Street, at Union Square. And we also have a fund for cases such as yours, Mrs. Devlin." With her other hand, she reached into her pocket and took out an envelope.

Fiona ignored it. Again, she merely stared at Columbine.

"Mr. Van Cormandt and I tried to talk Mr. Hartley into staying with your husband the other night," Columbine said desperately. "I do not countenance his behavior. I am ashamed of his behavior. I—" Columbine stopped and collected herself. She was only making Fiona Devlin more contemptuous, she could see. "I want to help you," she finished quietly. "I hope you will let me." Again, she held out the envelope.

Fiona stared at it. Then she raised cool green eyes to Columbine. "And why would I be taking money from a slut?" she asked evenly.

The breath left Columbine's body. Her hand fell. "I beg your pardon."

"Mrs. Devlin—" Lawrence began.

"I know about you," Fiona said, raising a red hand to stop Lawrence and keeping her gaze on Columbine. "I know you're that rich man's mistress, *Mrs.* Nash. I've seen your fine gowns and your diamonds. And you come here expecting me to welcome you in, when it's your kind who done what they did to my Jimmy? Do you want me to give you a cuppa and cry on your shoulder?" Fiona began to shut the door, until only her white face was visible. "You're a slut, a liar, and an Englishwoman, Mrs. Nash, and I spit on you and your class."

Lawrence stepped forward—to do what, he didn't know. Still, Fiona didn't shut the door. Waiting for the satisfaction of a reaction, perhaps. She looked at Lawrence, her green eyes gleaming with triumph.

"Mrs. Devlin—" Columbine started. But the second door of the day was slammed in her face, and she stared at peeling paint, her mouth still open. She closed it.

"I'm so dreadfully sorry," Lawrence said. "She is obviously in great distress, but—"

"Please," Columbine said. "Can we go?"

She was glad of Lawrence's arm as they navigated the wooden boards back to the sidewalk. Columbine felt unsteady. She'd been spoken of with contempt before, she'd been called names. But never so baldly. She'd been arrested, but she'd always had the protection of the police knowing her class. She'd been treated well. Never before had she seen herself so plainly, through the eyes of a working woman who did not want her help. The women who came to her door, who came to her lectures, *wanted* her help. Never before had she had to offer it to someone who flung her notions back in her face, who mocked her. Strange, Columbine thought. Strange that this had not happened to her before, in all her years of speaking and writing. Catcalls in a lecture auditorium and hostile questions are easy to deal with. Blood pumping from the righteousness of her cause, and words flying from her mouth, and the audience claps and screams at her cleverness. But alone, face to face, looking at the eyes of desperation and contempt, well. That was another thing entirely.

When they reached the street, Columbine began, unaccountably, to shake. She realized, horrified, that she was very close to tears. So strange, she thought again. I used to be so brave.

Lawrence felt her tremble underneath his arm. He saw that her face was white. "Mrs. Nash, you're faint. Let me help you." Murmuring close to her ear, he buoyed her up. He led her to the closest and cleanest stoop, took off his coat, and laid it down for her. Columbine sank onto it and burst into tears.

She cried for some time into Lawrence's handkerchief, which he handed over without a word. "Oh, dear, oh," she murmured as her sobs quieted. She wiped her cheeks. "I must apologize, Mr. Birch."

"But it's only natural," Lawrence said kindly. "Mrs. Devlin said some shocking, terribly cruel things. Words a lady should not hear. It was awful for you."

"Yes. To hear truth is never pleasant," Columbine said.

"Mrs. Nash!"

She sighed and looked down at her boots. "Not the names she called me," she said softly. "Not that. But I saw truth in her eyes. I shouldn't have been at that party. I've lost my way, you see. It used to be so clear. I was using society for my own ends. I told myself that I needed the wealthy classes on my side, needed those women, and the way I dressed and the places I went made them feel comfortable, more inclined to listen and not be afraid. But was it just an excuse to indulge vanity and luxury? I told myself that my ideas became less shocking, you see, if I were wearing a silk gown and diamonds while I espoused them. I needed those women—their power, and their money."

"But all of that is true," Lawrence said insistently. "Look at what you've done."

"But I didn't expect to become one of them. I thought I left that all behind in England."

"You think you're one of them?"

"I don't know," Columbine whispered. "Not to them—to them, I'm still an outsider because of my politics, tolerated because of my background and because of Ned. But what about to the people I want to help? My dream was, when I started, to cross class lines. My dream was that all women would see what they had in common. And today I saw contempt in Fiona Devlin's eyes. She is the woman I'm trying to reach. She is the reason I formed the New Women Society. She is the reason I lecture, the reason I write. But she doesn't read my articles, Mr. Birch. Do you know who does? Socialists, women's rights workers. Elizabeth Cady Stanton sends me letters of encouragement, not factory girls. I am preaching to the converted, I have been for two years now. I'm useless. And soon," she said, her brown eyes pained, "I will be a joke."

Lawrence felt shock crash down on him. Columbine Nash was a legend dating from her lectures in the 1880's. So young, so beautiful, so well-born. And speaking such words of rebellion in that clear English voice so that even the most revolutionary notions sounded like perfect common sense.

And she was *confused*. Lawrence had consorted with dogmatics for so long he had forgotten what it was like to be unsure. And this famous revolutionary was a woman, after all. Helpless, lost, needy.

An enormous sense of power swept over him. He realized that he had her now. Her nerves were fluttering like the wings of a sparrow, and her fine mind was blurred. Her senses were overwhelming her, and she was infinitely attractive, infinitely beautiful, at this moment. For the first time, he was truly attracted to her.

He almost smiled. He knew exactly what to say. Lawrence always knew exactly what to say to women.

"I can't let you feel this way," he said gently. "I know the work you've done over the past two years, and I've seen, even in the little time I've spent with you, how many women you've helped. You've done so much. It's natural to lose your way for a time, or to think that you have. Discouragement is part of your life, isn't it?"

"Unfortunately, I can't seem to get away from it," Columbine admitted. Her brown eyes held glints of green, they were full of tears, and she looked heartbreakingly lovely.

"You just need to rest for a bit. You've worked very hard, and very well, and now you're tired. You must not think this a failing, Mrs.

Nash! You must look at what you've done, and see how good you really are. You must congratulate yourself. You must believe in yourself again, love yourself again."

Columbine stared into pale blue eyes, vibrant, passionate with feeling. If only she could take some of that conviction and infuse it into her veins, be strong again. This young, handsome man beside her was everything she once was, everything she wanted to be again. She felt it impossible to go one more step forward into the life she had made for herself. She didn't have Ned any longer. That was frightening enough. What could she do without her conviction?

"I cannot," she said falteringly. "Oh, Mr. Birch, I cannot."

Lawrence took her hand. "You're the most courageous woman I've ever met. You can do anything."

Columbine shivered, and she withdrew her hand from his. "I'm sorry," she said. "I'm so sorry to impose on you, a stranger—"

"Please, don't say that. Say 'friend.' Sometimes friends can be made in an instant. Something happens, some charge comes between two people, and bonds of steel are formed. I feel that way with us, Mrs. Nash."

Confused, Columbine looked into Lawrence's face again. Bonds of steel? She didn't know. There was something, yes. She'd thought it was merely envy of his optimism. And she wanted to believe him. It was easier to find a way out having a guide. Or at least a friend. "Friend, then," she said. "Thank you."

He took off her glove, and pressed his lips to her cold palm. They were warm; his mustache tickled. Did she feel the faint, ghostly presence of his tongue for an instant? Impossible. But Columbine flushed, just from the thought of it.

"You're cold," she noticed suddenly. "Oh, Mr. Birch, I'm sitting on your coat." She stood up quickly and handed it to him. "We should walk."

"Yes," he said. "Let's walk. Take my arm, and show me your city. Show me what you love, and tell me what you believe in. We'll start from there."

Columbine smiled, her full lips curving, her eyes clear. The key, Lawrence thought, slipping back into his coat. He held out his arm, and after hesitating just a moment, she took it. He held it lightly, carefully, as though it were a precious gift. He'd found it. She felt compromised, and she needed to be told which way to go. Then he would have her, the famous Columbine Nash. And it had only taken a day.

Marguerite stood in front of Horatio Jones's lodgings. She knew she could ruin everything, but she could not wait one more day. She had to force her hand. She had never been good at waiting.

She knew Horatio was home, for he'd written to Bell. Marguerite knew where Bell kept her correspondence, and made a habit of checking on Horatio's letters from time to time. Usually they were full of politics and literature, and insufferably dull. But this last letter had no mention of Prince Kropotkin or Edward Bellamy. It was an ultimatum. Come to me, or else.

Marguerite knew that Bell would not come. She had put on her brown dress and gone to the New Women Society, as usual. Marguerite had improvised quickly, feigning a bad headache. Bell had solicitously advised her, while putting on her hat, to stay in bed. As soon as she was gone, Marguerite changed into her best dress, a peacock blue velvet that matched her eyes. She borrowed Columbine's fur lined cloak and wore the gay beribboned hat that Bell had trimmed for her. She looked very young and pretty, and she hoped that Horatio would finally respond. At least he would be in the perfect state to receive her. Angry at Bell, frustrated. Alone.

Straightening her shoulders, she grasped the brass knob of the front door. She pushed it open cautiously, and saw with relief that the short hallway was empty. Prints were hung on beige wallpaper, and there was a small table to one side that was heaped with mail. It looked perfectly respectable—perhaps too respectable for a lone lady caller in the middle of the afternoon.

Marguerite knew Horatio's rooms were on the third floor, and she ran up the stairs quickly, afraid of meeting someone. That would be dreadfully embarrassing. She fervently hoped she would be able to get in and out of the building without being seen.

By the time she reached the third floor, her breath was coming quickly. She knocked tentatively, and she heard a chair scrape almost immediately, swift footsteps crossing the floor. He thought it was Bell. To forestall the look of disappointment she knew would be on his face, she called softly, "Mr. Jones, it's Miss Corbeau."

After a small pause, Horatio opened the door. He was in his shirtsleeves, and his brown hair was rumpled. He looked very cross. "Miss Corbeau."

She brushed past him quickly. The fool, standing there with the door open like that. "I know you expected Bell," she said boldly, standing over to one side so that she was not visible to the hallway. "But I thought of you here, waiting, and the cruelty of it . . ." She bowed her head and fiddled with a button on her glove.

Horatio shut the door at last. "Bell isn't coming," he said woodenly.

She shook her head.

"You know this?"

"I know everything," Marguerite said delicately. "Bell has confided in me. And I find it so very difficult not to be angry at her. To turn you down, to turn you away—well, I don't understand it. To throw away her chance at happiness. She's had many suitors, of course . . ."

Horatio looked at her keenly. "Many suitors," he repeated.

Marguerite made a helpless gesture. "I'm young, Mr. Jones, and unused to the kind of life that Columbine and Bell lead. It is very different. . . . I'm not sure I understand it. What I mean is," she said, floundering, "that the marriage state is not at all repellent to me. And therefore my conduct changes accordingly. Unlike Bell who can . . . see gentlemen without compromising her morals." Marguerite paused delicately. "If you see what I mean."

He saw very well what she meant, despite her elliptical phrasing, her pauses. Bell had taken lovers before. Horatio felt as though he had been struck. He had never asked her, but she had led him to believe that she had not. That she espoused free love on principle, but she herself had not practiced it. It had given him something to wait for. He had felt enormously protective, willing to wait. And now others had been there before him.

Anger filled him. He considered himself a good man, a careful man. But he had been driven to madness by that woman. He had drowned in her lushness, her softness, and overlooked the steel beneath. He'd admired her intelligence without once honestly examining that curious chip of ice that lay embedded in Bell's heart. He'd never thought it would cut him, he'd never thought he would be her victim . . .

"Mr. Jones? Would you mind if I sat, just for a moment?"

Horatio wrenched his attention back to Marguerite. The girl was so pretty. Her eyes were a deep, mysterious blue, and her slenderness was refreshing next to the maternal bosoms that were so popular these days.

"Of course, Miss Corbeau. Please. And I'll make us some tea, if you wish."

"You're very kind. Very kind to me. And I don't deserve such kindness." Her last words faltered, and he saw her eyelashes tremble as she looked down.

Horatio crossed to the sofa where she sat. He pulled over an armchair and sat, leaning forward. "My dear Miss Corbeau, whatever do you mean? Why wouldn't you deserve kindness from anyone?"

"Not anyone," she said in a rush, "only you." She stared at him, horrified. "Oh, sir. Please forgive me, I don't know what I'm saying." She pressed a lacy handkerchief to her mouth. "I shouldn't be here at all, I knew I should not have come. I should never have come to you," she added in a whisper that throbbed with suppressed emotion.

Suddenly, Horatio began to understand. Why *had* she come? Why had she risked her reputation that way? Surely not from disinterest. "Miss Corbeau—Marguerite . . ."

At the sound of her name, her shoulders shook, as if he had stabbed her. "Please," she murmured. "I should go."

He put out a hand to stop her, and it landed on her knee. "Don't," he said. He felt the curve of her leg underneath her skirts, and wondered what she was wearing beneath. A shock passed through his fingers, exciting him. He remembered that glimpse of her breast, and the knowing look in her eyes he'd convinced himself he'd imagined. But what if he hadn't imagined it?

Her chin still lowered, she looked up at him through her eyelashes. "You know my secret," she breathed. "You can see it in my face. You know I am lost to you."

"Miss Corbeau, I—"

Suddenly, she threw herself on her knees in front of him. "Don't turn me away," she cried passionately. "I couldn't bear it." Tears began to slide down her cheeks.

He brushed them away, feeling the wetness on his fingertips. Passion, and tears, and devotion. He was used to beauty that expressed itself in stillness, passivity, a heart that never beat fast. Now, emotion overflowed into his hands. Who could blame him if he claimed it for his own? What manner of man could turn away?

Before he could allow himself to think, he raised her to her feet. She was so sweetly willing. Her arms wound around his neck and he was kissing her before he could stop himself, feeling her mouth open underneath his as he coaxed it, her lips warm and slack, not tightening in disgust. And that drove him on, and his mouth opened wider, and they kissed, standing close together. Marguerite gave a small moan, more an exhalation of breath against his mouth.

He tore away. "This is wrong."

"Is it wrong for me to love you?" she cried. She stepped toward him again, and he felt her breasts against him. With a cry, he raised his hands and touched them, and she didn't draw away.

Marguerite arched her back slightly. It felt good, a man's hands on her breasts. She had come here purely out of self-interest, but of a more material kind. How strange, she thought dreamily as she raised her mouth to Horatio's again, that she would like this.

I like it, she thought, kissing him. She wanted to go farther, she wanted him to want her, to forget everything but having her. She wanted to forget everything but having him. Her mother's warnings rose in her mind, but strangely, they had no force here. They were hazy, and they meant nothing next to this. No wonder she had been warned against this; it was powerful.

She'd never known, Marguerite thought, as she clasped Horatio to her, as she felt his hands move on her with delight. She had turned out to be that most despicable of creatures. A wanton. A voluptuary. And she did not care.

She did not expect it to be so childishly easy, to have it feel so good, to find her pretty dress pooled at her feet, her dark hair loose on her shoulders, and Horatio picking her up and carrying her to his bed.

He unbuttoned her chemise with a frown that told her he was

concentrating on her completely. He had forgotten Bell, he had forgotten everything. She felt the delicious shock of skin against skin for the first time in her life, and she liked it.

Then, he was taking her, and her mouth opened in surprise. At first she was too shocked at the strange feeling of fullness, tightness, to know how to respond. But then she began to see that it could be pleasurable if she relaxed, if she moved. Experimentally, Marguerite moved her hips. Horatio lifted himself from her and compensated for her movement, withdrawing and plunging in again, letting her move against him, waiting for her. Both appalled and excited by this strange rhythm, Marguerite ran her hands along his hips to guide him. She felt not one whit of shame.

He was taking her, yes, but she was taking him. Now Marguerite used everything, knees, legs, toes, fingers, delighting in this new freedom of touch. When Horatio groaned in pleasure she continued more boldly. She felt unbearably, deliciously hot. She wound her legs around him, and her pelvis seemed to rise of its own accord against his hard body. She wanted all of it, she realized. She had never known she'd want it so much.

Lawrence waited that evening until Bell brought the tea things into the kitchen at ten o'clock. He stepped out of his room, and she jumped.

"I'm sorry, Miss Huxton, I didn't mean to startle you."

"Not at all, Mr. Birch."

"I was thinking about our conversation yesterday. It seems to me you possibly might have a distorted view of anarchistic principles."

"I doubt that," Bell said, stiffly washing out the teapot.

"But you admit," Lawrence continued, lounging against the sink, "that the press does not report their doings with a neutral eye."

"Of course," Bell said, reaching for a teacup. "But I do not rely on the press for my information, Mr. Birch. I've read the anarchist journals, the writings of both Bakunin and Kropotkin."

Lawrence moved closer. "So you're interested, then."

"I am interested in politics in general," Bell said smoothly, putting the cup in the drainer and reaching for another. "I am interested in theories of social change."

"Then I would like to invite you to a meeting."

"Thank you for your kind invitation, but—"

"Don't treat me like a suitor, Miss Huxton, and politely demur. I'm not Horatio Jones," he said deliberately, and Bell flinched. "I'm interested in your mind."

"You know nothing of my mind." Bell's fingers trembled as they placed the cup to drain. She reached for a saucer.

"But I've seen your eyes," Lawrence said softly. "And your soul is in them."

She turned and found him closer than she'd thought. His face was near hers, and she stepped back awkwardly. The saucer slipped from her soapy fingers, but in a quick movement, he reached out and caught it. He handed it to her.

"You see what a team we are?" he said.

Bell felt caught up short. Ah, she thought. He flirts at last. She rinsed the plate and placed it to drain. Then she wiped her hands on the dishtowel and hung it to dry. Now, her clumsy fingers were quick and sure. She was almost relieved; Lawrence Birch had flirted with her. She found him less dangerous when he did that. She was used to that.

"Well?" he asked finally. Impatience had crept into his tone. He'd thought he'd disarmed her.

"Good night, Mr. Birch," Bell said. She walked out of the kitchen, leaving him puzzled at her poise. But up in her room, alone, Bell undressed herself with trembling fingers that lingered, and her face burned with her shame.

Five

JANUARY PASSED SWIFTLY, one cold, snowy day after another. The days seemed especially short, as the clouds formed a dim gray expanse of sky that reduced the sun to only a hint of opalescence. Darkness came early on these gray days.

Columbine told herself that soon she would adjust to the loss of Ned and to her own unhappiness. She kept busy during the day, but then she had to face the nights. She became well-acquainted with three o'clock in the morning. She lay awake, half-missing Ned and half-glad he wasn't with her. She was spinning out of control in a fog of introspection. It was not easy, and it hurt.

Columbine lay awake and thought of her life, the things she had accomplished, and suddenly they seemed puny to her. Sometimes she would cry. If she were a religious woman, she would have prayed. But praying to a masculine God had grown more difficult for her over the years. Masculine patriarchs had a tendency to raise her ire, not soothe it. Recently Elizabeth Cady Stanton had told her that she prayed to Mother and Father God. Columbine tried that. But whoever was up there had no answers for her.

Lawrence Birch had plenty of answers, and he made her laugh. He had fire and a romantic vision of the world, and that was an irresistible combination. The weeks passed without him finding a place to go, and he was so unobtrusive when she wanted him to be and so attentive when she needed it that Columbine found herself not minding his presence in the house. She was so lulled by it that she was surprised, one morning, to discover that the other women did not feel the same at all.

"Lord, is the man never going to leave?" Marguerite asked, handing Columbine the mail at the breakfast table.

Columbine laughed as she leafed through the envelopes. "You don't like Mr. Birch, Marguerite?"

"No. Do you like him, Bell?"

Bell put down her coffee cup. "He can be charming," she said. "But he tries too hard. No, I don't like him."

Columbine looked at the two women. "I had no idea," she said. "Does he make you uncomfortable?"

"Not at all," Bell said quickly.

Marguerite shrugged. "It's your house, Columbine."

"It's yours as well," Columbine protested. "I'll ask him today if he's found a place," she said decidedly. "You're right, of course, he's been here too long." She slid toward her a pile of periodicals she'd neglected earlier in the week.

Bell folded her napkin. "Perhaps it would be better, Columbine. The neighbors are starting to notice."

"Yes, he's not very discreet," Marguerite said. "I heard him come in after midnight—my room faces the back. He made an awful racket, I must say."

Columbine was frowning now, but she wasn't listening to Marguerite. "Oh, no," she exclaimed in dismay.

"What is it?" Bell asked.

"It's the newest issue of the *Century*," Columbine said in an offended tone, as though the *Century* had no right to put out a new issue. "That wicked, wicked man." She stood and left the table, trying to manage the heavy skirt of her velvet dressing gown and read the magazine at the same time as she left the room.

"I'm glad to see Columbine getting excited about things again," Marguerite observed, reaching for a piece of toast. "For the past few weeks even Anthony Comstock only provoked a yawn. It's been dull around here since she developed that insomnia."

"I wonder where Mr. Birch goes at night," Bell said, staring down at the tablecloth. She'd spoken without thinking, and she looked up quickly at Marguerite, to see if she'd noticed.

But Marguerite was too self-absorbed to wonder why Bell was concerned about Mr. Birch's activities, or why she blushed. She spread jam on her toast with a small smile. "Who knows where anyone really goes at night?" she asked, crunching into the toast with her small white teeth. She smiled innocently at Bell.

"What does that mean?" Bell asked, frowning.

"Oh, nothing. I've been meaning to ask you, Bell. Do you think coffee is bad for the complexion?"

"You must tell her," Marguerite said.

"Yes," Horatio said.

"When?"

"Soon. Marguerite—"

"When?"

Horatio groaned. Astride him, naked and poised inches above him, Marguerite moved slightly downward. She brushed against the tip of him lightly. Her tiny teeth caught her lower lip. "When?" she said again. Her husky voice was even lower than normal.

"Soon," Horatio repeated, with a sudden lunge upward. He pushed against her, and now Marguerite moaned. She slid herself downward on him, then moved slowly up and down. Up and down. How easily she had caught the rhythm of sex. She flung her head back and closed her eyes.

Horatio, she knew, had been shocked at her willingness, her avidity to try any position, any variation. The first time she had sat astride him, crossing over during dinner to raise her skirts and swing one naked leg over him, he had even blushed. As much as she enjoyed him, she had a feeling that Horatio's belief in his own adventurousness was certainly overblown. However, there were still things he could teach her.

Horatio sprawled beneath her, his body brown and lithe. He was a beautiful man, a delight of textures, all crisp hair and smooth muscles. Long fingers and feet, a smooth beard that tickled her cheeks and upper thighs and brushed against her nipples. She adored him. But Marguerite was aware that she adored him in what some would say an animal fashion. She had heard Columbine speak about the spiritual nature of love. She had not yet discovered that side of sex.

Ah, there. Marguerite changed her rhythm slightly. Then as Horatio's hips moved and he groaned again, she abruptly withdrew and raised herself above him. This is what he liked, to have her tantalize him, to brush her breasts against his chest and run her lips against his neck while she murmured of her pleasure. Only here, in bed, did she have his complete attention.

He still thought about Bell, she knew that. He still held out a hope that he would win her, incredible as it seemed. This made Marguerite feel impatient with Horatio. As long as they had to see each other in secret, she had no chance of meeting the important people that Horatio knew. Horatio knew everyone in New York—writers and painters, politicians, actors, high society and low society. Marguerite didn't know what she wanted yet. But she wanted to run a finger along her choices before she grabbed at one. And she would have no opportunity to do so if she spent all of her time in Horatio's rooms, in Horatio's bed, as nice as that was.

She breathed against him; she moaned. Her lips slid along his chest and moved downward. This seemed to excite him even more, even as it alarmed him. His dark eyes widened as her mouth followed a path made by trailing fingers. "If you don't tell her," she said, her lips following a line of dark hair descending from his navel, "I don't know what I'll do. I just hate going behind her back."

His hand tightened on her hair. "All right. I promise," he gasped. He raised his hips.

"Oh, Horatio." Her lips curved into a smile, and she took him in her mouth. His gasp of pleasure surprised her with its intensity. Here was something new, some new power she didn't know she had. Marguerite felt the power push her on, fuel her own excitement as her clever tongue and hands ensured her lover's cooperation.

Ned stood when Columbine entered his office. His heart squeezed with pain. She hesitated at the doorway, then walked in and held out her hand. He shook it.

"Columbine, it's a pleasure to see you. Please sit down."

He waited until she was seated and had removed her gloves.

Nervously, she smoothed her silver-willow skirt.

"I'm surprised you'd even receive me, Ned. I read the article in the *Century*. I was a few days behind everyone else, I fear."

"Columbine, I'm not sure what you're talking about."

"Didn't you read the article?"

"Yes, but I hardly know why I'd blame you for it."

"Because I gave Elijah Reed the information. He came to my house as a friend, not a journalist. I didn't know he'd use the story of what happened at the Hartley's New Year's Eve. I'm so sorry, Ned." Columbine gazed at him, trying to discover if he was merely being polite or if he truly did not blame her.

Ned steepled his fingers in a lawyerlike way. "Columbine, set your mind at ease. It never occurred to me to blame you. Elijah Reed got his information from several sources, including the Devlins."

"I gave him their name—"

"He could have gotten their name from many places."

"I told him that Ambrose showed a complete lack of concern, that it was his decision to start the dancing—"

"It's all right, Columbine. It is a story that should be told, isn't it? Though I must admit that the results of the article are unfortunate, however. I wish Elijah Reed had showed it to me before printing it."

She leaned forward. "What do you mean, Ned?"

He dropped his hands and grimaced, looking tired. "Ambrose is furious. Even though Mr. Reed did not mention him by name, there is no doubt to any reasonably aware New Yorker who the man is. Ambrose has refused to make the settlement to the Devlins."

"Can't you do anything?"

"I'm afraid not. Ambrose cut me at the Union Club yesterday. He blames me for the article. I'm afraid our friendship is over."

"Ned, I'm so sorry."

He waved a hand. "Oh, it was over on my part anyway. After that night . . . well, we saw a side to Ambrose we didn't want to see, didn't we."

"But will he influence other friends of yours . . ."

"Yes, he's already done so. I find I'm not welcome in certain homes. Columbine, please don't fret about it. It will blow over, undoubtedly. I'll be spending much of my time in Washington anyway."

"Washington?"

"I've been appointed to a federal commission on labor."

"Oh?" Columbine felt a pang, a little loss. It comforted her to know Ned was in New York. She was truly losing him. She shook off the feeling. "Congratulations, Ned."

"Yes, well, perhaps I can do a bit of good." Ned looked at her, trying to keep the yearning out of his eyes, but needing to imprint every feature, every line of her face into his memory. When would he see her again, this woman that he loved so dearly?

Columbine stood and put on her gloves. "I know you'll make a difference, Ned. If anyone can, you can. And I'm sorry if I caused one particle of trouble for you."

"Columbine," Ned said softly, "I always welcomed your brand of trouble."

She smiled faintly at him. "God bless you, Neddie," she whispered, and walked out.

It hadn't been at all difficult to discover Elijah Reed's address. All her friends seemed to know. Everyone seemed to gather there in the evenings until he kicked them out. For a tired-looking man, Columbine thought dryly, he must have a great deal of energy.

She found the house on East Eleventh Street easily. She was surprised when Reed himself opened the door. He was wearing baggy corduroy trousers and a flannel shirt with a soft collar, and he was wearing small silver-rimmed glasses.

He looked over the top of his glasses at her. "Mrs. Nash."

She nodded determinedly. "Mr. Reed."

"I thought you were my neighbor, Mrs. Stein. She's bringing over my lunch. I'm afraid I'm working now. I receive callers from four on."

She was surprised at such bluntness. It was very close to being rude. "I need to see you, Mr. Reed. I'm sorry to report this is not a social call."

He hesitated only a second. "Please come in, Mrs. Nash."

He ushered her into a front parlor that was set up as an office.

Crumpled papers were thrown on the floor around an old desk. Books were piled on a red sofa, and he quickly moved them off and stacked them on the floor. "Please sit down."

She didn't. "I won't be staying long," Columbine said. "I've come to ask what you expected to accomplish by exploiting the troubles of the Devlins for a magazine serial. And I've come to ask you what kind of journalist comes to a house as a friend and prints information that was given in confidence."

His dark eyes were quizzical behind his glasses. "You didn't tell me the story was confidential, Mrs. Nash."

"You did not tell me you were a journalist, Mr. Reed. I thought you were serializing a new novel."

Elijah Reed sighed and took off his glasses. "Let me understand this. Because of your misapprehension, you blame me for printing a story that is common knowledge around New York."

"Mr. Hartley's behavior downstairs was not common knowledge," Columbine snapped. "And now it is."

"I did not use Mr. Hartley's name."

"Mr. Reed, I assure you that there is no one in New York who doubts your character's true identity."

"No one? Sometimes I am convinced that generalizing is the disease of our times," Elijah Reed said softly.

This infuriated Columbine. She felt she was being patronized, and that always caused bells to go off in her brain. "Sir, I did not come to hear how I happen to embody the failings of our age. If you want to philosophize I'm sure your editor will pay you even more money to do so."

He gazed at her gravely. "Mrs. Nash, you are a reformer, are you not? A progressive. Then why, in heaven's name, do you object to my article? At the risk of sounding grandiose—although I'm sure my editor would pay me to do that as well—I was trying to right a wrong. Factory workers are not the only oppressed workers in this city. Often the plight of the domestic worker is ignored."

"I agree completely."

"Then why are we arguing?" he asked mildly.

"If you had asked for my help, I would have given it," Columbine said in a confused way. "But not at the expense of the Devlins, or of . . . someone who was hurt by your article."

He took off his glasses. "You mean Ned Van Cormandt. I heard he was being blacklisted. But I'm sure the eminently intelligent Mr. Van Cormandt sees that those who would blacklist him would just as cheerfully stab him in the back for less enlightened reasons."

"It's easy for you to say," Columbine answered evenly. "But Mr. Van Cormandt is of an old New York family. He takes his social position seriously. He would not want to embarrass an old friend, especially when he has managed to get that friend to do right by his servant. At least he had. As soon as Mr. Hartley read your article, he decided to withhold the settlement."

"I'm sorry to hear that. But I must confess I had my doubts about that elusive settlement. The Devlins have yet to receive one penny from Mr. Hartley. He would not even settle their doctor's bills. Fiona Devlin is a hard-headed woman. I think she never expected to see it, either. She worked for the man. And I'm sure Mr. Hartley is using my article—and Mr. Van Cormandt—as an excuse to bluster his way past his own culpability."

Columbine sank down on the sofa. "You think he never intended to pay?"

Elijah rubbed his eyes wearily. "I sincerely doubt it. Actually, I advised the Devlins to begin a lawsuit. But there's no way to prove Ambrose Hartley knew the fireworks were unsafe. His butler won't talk, of course. Apparently only Devlin and Hartley were together when the order was given. It's Devlin's word against Hartley, and we know who would win."

"But I heard the butler tell Ambrose that Devlin said the fireworks were dangerous," Columbine blurted.

"Did you? Perhaps you should inform the Devlins of this."

"I doubt Fiona Devlin would even open the door to me again," Columbine said tiredly. "But I'll try."

"Good." There was a knock at the door, and he went to answer it. He returned with a tray, a white napkin covering it. "My lunch," he said. He placed it on top of the messy papers on his desk. "Mrs. Stein keeps me alive. She's a good soul."

Columbine stood. "Thank you for your time," she said mechanically.

"You don't have to leave, Mrs. Nash. It's only some sandwiches, it won't get cold. Or you could join me." He almost smiled when he said it, but not quite.

"No, thank you. I really must go." Suddenly, Columbine was exceedingly sorry she came. She couldn't imagine why she'd felt propelled to come here with such vague accusations. She was whirling around like a top, she thought, exasperated.

"Before you depart, Mrs. Nash, I must ask you something. I've been asked to coordinate a lecture series at Cooper Union. I have my choice of who to invite to speak. Would you be interested in participating?"

Columbine was taken aback. It was the last thing she'd expected from Elijah Reed. "I don't think so, Mr. Reed. I am honored that you asked, but no."

He nodded thoughtfully. "Why not?"

She hadn't expected a direct question. "Because," she stammered, "I—I don't wish to give lectures anymore."

"Why not?" he persisted.

"I don't have anything to say," she blurted out suddenly.

To her surprise, he laughed. His face lit up with the smile, and he looked younger for a moment. She could see for the first time the traces of the young, fierce novelist he'd been. But she still didn't like his laugh.

She turned away. "I hardly think it's anything to laugh about, Mr. Reed."

He stopped immediately. He touched her arm. "I'm sorry if I offended you. After your career, you have to admit it's a surprising admission. I mean," he added gently, "no one could accuse you of not having opinions."

She kept her face averted. "Things change."

"In times such as these?"

"I felt I needed to rest for a bit," she said, recalling Lawrence's words gratefully. They had made so much sense at the time.

"When did you last lecture, Mrs. Nash?"

"Three years ago. I addressed a women's club in Boston. Before that, my tour of 1884."

"Then perhaps you've had enough of a rest. It's time you found something to care about again, Mrs. Nash. You were a fine speaker. I'd hate to see you stop that portion of your career. It reaches the people who don't read articles in magazines."

"I know that," she said, turning back to him. "But what am I to do? I have no subject."

"Then I suggest you find one," he said impatiently. "Why you think you can afford to sit back on your heels, I don't know. I'll hold a date open for you, Mrs. Nash. And now—"

And now? Did Elijah Reed have a plan for her, a way to find her way out of this miasma she'd created?

"And now, I must eat my lunch."

Columbine's mouth opened, then closed. She hadn't been dismissed this summarily since she'd been a wife. But somehow she wasn't put off—not much. She had a feeling that Elijah Reed was just as rude to the men of his acquaintance.

"Just don't pat me on the head on the way out the door," she grumbled, and she closed the door on the sound of his soft laughter.

Columbine thought of Elijah Reed more than she cared to over the next few days. She liked the look of him; she liked the intelligence in his eyes. She liked the way his thick eyebrows descended when he frowned and how one corner of his mouth moved sideways in reluctant amusement. He wasn't very old, really. When she went back to check her copy of *Look Away,* she figured him to be forty-three. And, she had to admit, there was something about a man who gave no sensual heat that made one think about sex.

Sitting in her office at the New Women Society, she looked out the window and thought of Elijah telling her to find a subject. It was odd to find such faith in the eyes of a stranger. It was as though he had no doubt that she would find her way. And while she looked, he would be impatient. She wasn't sure she liked the weight of that. It irritated her, come to think of it.

Bell stood at her doorway carrying a box full of envelopes. "Have a minute?"

She spun her chair around briskly. "How nice of you to ask when you caught me woolgathering."

Bell grinned. "You could have been planning your lecture for Elijah Reed."

Columbine grimaced. "No chance of that, I'm afraid. Every day

I compose a note telling him to give away my date, though I can't bear to send it off to him."

"And why don't you?"

"I don't know. Perhaps I will today. You look worried, Bell. Is something the matter?"

Instead of answering, Bell dumped the box of envelopes on Columbine's desk. Columbine ran her hands through them. "What's this? These look like appeals to the emergency fund."

"That's exactly what they are," Bell said grimly. "I found them hidden in Marguerite's desk."

"I don't understand."

"She was supposed to help me with the emergency fund. She gave me a few priority cases, so I thought she was handling the rest—you know sometimes the requests are for things we don't need money for. Doctor referrals, jobs and such." At Columbine's nod, Bell continued, "So I doled out the rest of the money for the month. I was encouraged—we almost had enough. I didn't know that Marguerite hadn't gone through all of these."

Columbine stared down at the pile of letters. "Have you asked her about this?"

"I haven't had a chance. She hasn't been coming very regularly these past weeks. I didn't want to say anything to you until I had to."

The letters ran through Columbine's fingers like water. There were so many. "Why? If she felt overburdened, why didn't she come to you, or me?"

Bell sighed. "It wasn't a case of being overburdened. Columbine, I know you *want* Marguerite to care. But you have to realize she doesn't have the same commitment we do. She's had a different life—difficult, yes, I know she's an orphan, but . . ." Bell gave up; although she'd lived side by side with the girl for two years, she had no idea what comprised Marguerite's character. "Some women—some people just don't have political minds, Columbine, no matter what you might hope, or want. Marguerite is interested in more worldly things, I think. And I believe she may be seeing someone, a sweetheart. Haven't you noticed the way she's been acting?"

"Well, no. But now that you mention it, she has looked rather blooming lately. And she keeps borrowing things from me—my cloak, or my gloves, and slipping them back in my room without telling me. I haven't said anything. I don't begrudge them to her, I know she likes pretty things." Columbine sighed, looking down at the letters. "Yes, you're right. She is . . . worldly. And young."

"And she's in love—good for her," Bell said dryly. "But we have the letters. I've read through some. Some of the cases are emergencies. We have to deal with this. And we have no money. We should be getting that check from Maud Hartley next month—"

"I'm afraid we won't get it," Columbine said. "Maud will hardly donate money to any cause of mine now."

Bell sank down in the chair across from Columbine. "What are we going to do? We've worked so hard to establish credibility on the East Side. There are relief agencies down there, but they are tremendously overburdened. The women already don't trust us."

"I know. We have to find someone who speaks Yiddish who will work with us. . . . Money again. Can't afford to pay, can't find anyone who can afford to volunteer. Oh, I'm sorry, Bell. I haven't been here enough lately, I know. I've put all this on your shoulders."

Bell looked away. "It's all right."

"No, it isn't. I'll get the money. I'll wire London."

"Columbine, not your estate. You're not supposed to touch it. It's your security. It won't help anyone if you're penniless."

"Nonsense," Columbine said briskly. "I won't be penniless as long as I can write or speak. And I think that Mr. Soames is full of doom and gloom about my inheritance. He's conservative, like all Englishmen—that's why I came to the United States in the first place."

"Columbine, I don't like this . . ."

There was a timid knock at Columbine's closed door, and Bell turned around, a bit irritated. "Yes?" she called impatiently.

The door opened a few inches. A small woman in her twenties came forward a tiny step. A mass of unruly sandy hair was topped by what was obviously her best bonnet, brown velveteen with rather worn trimming. Her plain, freckled face was pale, and she gripped her umbrella as though a high wind might snatch it away at any moment. "Miss Huxton?"

"Yes, can I help you?"

"It's Ivy Moffat, ma'am. I sent you a letter, ma'am."

Bell was on her feet instantly, her impatience forgotten. "Please come in, Miss Moffat. It *is* Miss?"

"Yes, ma'am." Ivy Moffat came a few steps forward into the room.

"I'm terribly sorry, I haven't read your letter," Bell said kindly. "We had rather a backlog at the office."

"That's fine, that's all right."

"Please sit down, Miss Moffat," Columbine said, coming around the desk. She pushed out the armchair reserved for nervous guests.

"Oh, Mrs. Nash, thank you. I knew you first thing, when I came in. I wasn't allowed to go to your lectures, my mam said . . . well, I wasn't allowed. But I read about the New Women Society, and I didn't know where else to go, so—"

"Sit down, please, Miss Moffat."

"I'd rather stand, ma'am, my sister's waiting out by the door, so I can't be long."

"Let's bring her in," Bell said, starting toward the door.

"No!" Ivy Moffat's voice suddenly had strength, and it stopped Bell in her tracks. "I'd like to explain first, you see," she went in her normal soft tone. "Sally is embarrassed, and . . . well."

"Perhaps you should start at the beginning, Ivy," Columbine said kindly.

The young woman nodded several times, as if to go over her story again before launching into it. "Sally is a bit older than me, two years. She married John Hoover over a year ago. He had a good job, a foreman in a shirtwaist factory. But he got laid off." Ivy ground to a halt. She gripped her umbrella more tightly and stared at them, as if asking them to complete her story themselves to spare her the embarrassment.

Bell was used to that look. "You need a little to tide the family over," she said gently. "Just tell me exactly what you think you'll—"

"No." The strong voice came back, the indication that little Ivy Moffat had a backbone of steel. She paused again, but this time, Bell and Columbine waited. "At first Sally wouldn't tell me nothing," she said, her voice very low. "She said she fell down the stairs, or tripped and the pot full of soup fell on her, scalding her. But she'd never been clumsy. Our dad used to say she could be a dancer on the stage, she was so graceful . . ." A solitary tear welled up in

Ivy's left eye. She shook her head as though to send it flying.

Columbine exchanged glances with Bell. Sick at heart, they knew now why Ivy Moffat had come.

"He was beating her, you see. I guess I didn't want to know, at first. And she wouldn't admit it, either. But then finally she did."

"Did she try to leave?"

Ivy nodded. "Six months ago. She came home, but our dad sent her back. She went back, and John threw her down the stairs. She was in the hospital then. So I told her that I'd find a way. I tried to save, and I have a little. But our dad won't take her in, so I have to find a place for us. My mam has a stepsister. She's a hard woman, but she'll do. She never liked my dad, so she doesn't care what he says. She says she'll take me and Sal if we pay rent and expenses. But I don't have enough, and Sal is in bad shape, so . . . I come here."

Columbine went and placed her hand on Ivy Moffat's arm. "You've done right," she said. "You tell us what you need, and we'll give it to you. We'll give you something today to tide you over, and you can have the rest next week."

Ivy's face collapsed in relief, and a smile lit up her plain, fierce face. "I'll tell Sal." She ran out and they could hear a whispered colloquy in the hall. Then two pairs of footsteps returned.

Sally Hoover looked very much like her sister, sandy-haired and freckled. Under any other circumstances one could see that she'd probably once had an amiable, friendly face. But now her face was closed, her eyes flat. Along one cheek ran a livid, yellow-green bruise, and one eye was swollen shut.

Columbine gasped and started forward, but Bell held her back with a quick, light touch on her arm. "I'm glad you came to us, Sally," Bell said.

Sally looked at the floor. "I wanted to thank you," she mumbled.

"We're here to help," Columbine said.

"I'll pay you back," Sally added.

"If you wish the money to be a loan," Bell said, "you can pay us back a little at a time when you and your sister are back on your feet. Otherwise, it's a gift. You can think about it, and let us know."

Sally said nothing. Ivy looked at her. "We'll be going now," she said.

Columbine dug into her purse and gave Ivy all the money she

had. "Come back next week and I'll give you more," she said. If only the emergency fund was available, she could give Ivy what she needed today. "This probably isn't enough for rent, but maybe if your step-aunt knows more will be coming, she'll accept a down payment."

"I'm sure she will," Ivy said. "Thank you, Mrs. Nash."

Silently, Columbine and Bell watched the two sisters walk out.

"I wish we could do more," Columbine said.

"What more can we do?" With a sigh, Bell turned away.

Six

EMMA GOLDMAN HAD a small, compact body that was dynamic even when at rest. Her eyes were soft behind her wire glasses, but her tongue was as sharp as a razor. Only twenty-one, impudent, passionate, and unafraid, she had found her feet in the radical circles of New York within months of her arrival in the city. Lawrence was rather afraid of her, though he didn't like to admit this embarrassing fact to himself.

He had hoped, when he'd invited Bell to this night's informal anarchist meeting and found, to his surprise, that she accepted, that Emma Goldman would not be there. After sitting nursing a cup of tea or a glass of beer for hours at Schwab's saloon, saying nothing, only watching, Lawrence was finally ready to speak. The person he feared most was Goldman. For a moment, Lawrence considered telling Bell the meeting was off.

But when he had time to reflect, he decided it was good that Bell would be there. He always did better with a female audience. He remembered the respect he'd always received in Oakland and San Francisco when he spoke at meetings. New York was no more intellectual, no more fierce, than the West Coast had been.

Bell was dressed in her usual somber brown and black, but she fit right in at this gathering. The men stirred as she entered, for even her drab clothes couldn't hide her beauty. They looked at Lawrence with new respect, and he smiled to himself. He'd never overlooked that ridiculous quality in men that made them respect the ability to capture a beautiful woman. More than money, more than power, more than wisdom, such a prize commanded envy, even here.

A man he knew only slightly, a German, came over and stood in front of them. He looked at Bell but spoke to Lawrence, and Bell stared him down until he dropped his eyes.

"I know you're looking for a room," the man said gruffly to Lawrence while he tried not to look at Bell again. "There's one free in my building on Fifth Street. You can come round tomorrow and look at it if you like."

"All right," Lawrence said to get rid of him. What an unfortunate piece of luck, to have an offer of a place to stay in front of Bell. She would surely tell Columbine, and he might have to leave the house on Twenty-Third Street where he was so comfortable. Columbine had asked him politely several times if he'd heard of anything, but he'd managed to put her off.

He took down the address of the man in such a rude fashion that he hoped the man would miss the appointment tomorrow. After standing a minute, the man walked away.

"Why were you rude to your friend?" Bell whispered.

"I didn't like the way he looked at you," Lawrence answered, and, still annoyed, rose. "I'll get us some coffee."

He brought back the coffee and waited for someone to start. This was not an official meeting, but a general discussion about what position to take in the struggle for the newly formed cloakmaker's union. Lawrence knew the discussion would also inevitably touch on the issue which now threatened to divide them: should anarchists support the struggle for an eight hour day?

The few women who were there did not speak. They deferred to the men, who spoke one after the other, politely at first, then interrupting each other with apologies, then shouting, then standing, then pounding on the table.

"We must never forget the Propoganda of the Deed," one young man with a large drooping mustache said quietly. The others seemed to swivel toward him as one. "We must go back and read Bakunin, we must listen to our esteemed comrade Johann Most. What can the individual act of revolt accomplish if the masses are lulled by promises and concessions? They will never respond to social evils if one by one, that sick tree that is society is pruned occasionally." The man mimed a scissor in the air. "Snip, snip, a leaf here, a branch there. Snip, snip. The eight hour day. Snip. A ten minute break in the morning. Snip. And the masses relax, they are content, the tree still stands. But the root, the root is never nicked!" He raised his voice now. "We must chop out the root—we must not distract ourselves with pruning! The tree will never fall that way!"

Some of the men pounded on the table to show their agreement. Above the din came the clear sound of Emma Goldman's laugh. "Herr Schimmelman, I am exhausted," she said. "All this gardening!"

He gave her a look of pure dislike. "Perhaps that's because women are not strong enough for such a task."

Bell sat up. Her amber eyes were fixed on little Emma Goldman, who casually took a sip of coffee in the silence. How calm she was after such an insult!

"Perhaps they are too busy marching after working twelve or fourteen hours to think of such poetic reasons to justify doing nothing at all," Emma Goldman said. She looked at Herr Schimmelman, and her brown eyes were no longer soft. "I know I am. Perhaps they know, as you do not, Herr Schimmelman, that for us to ignore the struggle of the workers to better their lives means only this: that we will lose them. All the things they accuse us of being will be true—scholars and thinkers, dreamers. Not part of them, but apart from them."

Bell's eyes shone, and she smiled. "Bravo," she called into the silence. Emma Goldman looked over the tops of the male heads and caught Bell's eye. She winked.

Annoyed at Bell, Lawrence nevertheless saw his chance. "But Miss Goldman," he said, "if we distract ourselves from the true struggle, as Herr Most said, we will be corrupted. And while we sit here arguing about cloakmakers we have something right under our noses which if we exploit could set the fuse burning on the ticking bomb that is the discontent of the masses!"

Emma Goldman made a shocked gesture. "Oh, my, another metaphor!" she said, but with a smile.

Lawrence's face flushed, and saw that all faces were turned toward him, including Bell's.

One of Emma Goldman's eyebrows lifted. "And can you tell us what this something is, Mr.—"

"Birch. It was a story in the *Century* magazine."

She shrugged, and looked around at the others, as if to say, and why would I pay attention to that capitalist rag?

"All the city is talking about it," Lawrence went on. "A stable worker for one of the richest and oldest families in the city was forced to set off fireworks that were known to be unsafe. For the amusement of the guests at a party," he said contemptuously. "A big party, with fancy gowns and a big orchestra. And while the man lay bleeding the host resumed the dancing. The rich literally danced over the body of the dying man!"

"And did the man die?"

"No. But he is in danger of losing his arm. The host of the party, the rich man, also fired the man's wife, who was working in the kitchens. They have nothing."

Herr Schimmelman shrugged and said something in Yiddish which Lawrence didn't understand.

"For once we agree, Herr Schimmelman," Emma Goldman said. "Such is life, Mr. Birch. It is a sad story; I'm sorry for the people you mention. In the better world we are working for, such things will not happen. But I do not see how this one event will serve to wake up the masses to the true struggle. You should go back and read your literature, read about the *attentat*," she said, using the word that for the anarchists meant the one blow that, once struck, would illuminate oppression so dramatically that all would rise and demolish the oppressive state. "This is not what Bakunin was talking about. There are thousands of stories like this one, some even sadder. And still nothing is done. No," she said, with a slight, patronizing smile, "I'm afraid such an event will not serve your purpose."

"But all New York has read this!"

"And," she said, "they have gone on to other things." She turned her back on him and addressed a slender man with a high forehead at another table. "What do you think, Sasha?"

The man made a tired gesture with one hand. "Not worth discussing. I'd even prefer to have Schimmelman discuss trees again."

The crowd laughed, and Lawrence's ears burned. He felt acutely uncomfortable with Bell here beside him. Dismissed, ridiculed—and why? Because his idea cut to the heart of things. He was right, damnit. If he had been a Jew, a foreigner, they would have listened.

He waited until the topic had swung back to anarchist support for unions, and when the argument grew heated, he touched Bell's arm and led her out of the saloon.

They walked through the dark streets in silence. Lawrence jammed his hat on his head and then caught a glimpse of himself in a shop window. There was no excuse for an awkwardly tilted hat, no matter how angry he was. He adjusted it.

Bell saw Lawrence's discomfort, and for the first time, her heart went out to him. She had come out of curiosity only, and a desire to prove to herself that she could control this strange tug for this man. But his vulnerability touched her. She wanted to say something, but she knew it would not be welcome. They had been too hard on him, too impatient, she felt. No wonder Columbine had laughingly said that anarchists had no time for manners.

Lawrence was both grateful for and irritated by Bell's silence. He didn't want the woman to know him so well. He would have felt better if she had rushed to fill the silence, rushed to assure him that his point was well taken, that they had been sitting in the midst of fools. He could be angry at her then for her clumsiness.

"That was lucky, to hear about a room," she said finally.

He wanted to strike her. The feeling felt good, and he nursed it.

"Would you like to get a meal, or more coffee?" she asked with unusual timidity. "There's a good place on Second Avenue."

"No. Let's catch the horsecar up ahead." Through the red haze of his irritation, Lawrence noticed how his anger had affected Bell. She was almost eager to please. She was scurrying beside him, her face taut with misery, with yearning. Even though she had no part in making him angry, she was apologetic. He filed the information away for later. Later, he could use this, and it could turn the key. Now, he just enjoyed the sensation of being rude to her.

A few days later, Columbine was frowning over a letter when Elijah Reed tapped on her office door. She had been thinking about him, and when she looked up, there he was.

"Forgive me if I'm intruding," he said. "I found myself in the neighborhood, and I wanted to ask if you'd thought about your lecture."

"I've thought of little else," Columbine said. She felt a mixture of feelings, absurd pleasure to see him, and irritation that he was pressuring her. "Please, come in."

"Thank you." He sat down in the armchair and looked around her office with, Columbine felt, eyes that saw everything, but did not judge and would not even extend the energy to speculate. Her books, her clippings, her papers, were examined with the eye of an impartial God.

Elijah cocked his head, listening to the noise from the street below. It was a cold day, and the cacophony of bells, whistles, and shouts could be heard as wagons, carriages, and horsecars swirled around Union Square. The El passed by, and the building shuddered.

"How do you work in such noise?" he asked mildly.

She looked vaguely out the window. "Oh, I don't mind it. It's always there, like a heartbeat. Except it's wild and erratic, not steady. Fitting for a pulse of a city, isn't it?"

"Yes," he said, frowning. "So, are you going to speak, Mrs. Nash?"

Columbine made a restless gesture. "I think not, Mr. Reed. I appreciate the offer very much, but—"

She was interrupted by Bell, who walked into the office like a sleepwalker. She stood in the middle of the room, oblivious of Elijah, staring at Columbine.

"Bell?"

"Sally Hoover is dead." She said the words flatly, but her forehead suddenly creased, as if she was about to cry but didn't want to.

Columbine half-rose, then sank down again. "Dead? How?"

"Ivy told me," Bell said. "He came to find her. There was nothing Ivy could do. Sally was admitted to the hospital last night. Ivy thought she'd recover. She had some broken bones, bruises. Nothing, Ivy said, that she hadn't seen before. But something was broken inside, Ivy said." Bell began to weep. "Something was broken inside," she repeated.

Columbine stood up quickly and went to her. They held each

other and rocked slowly as Bell sobbed and tears slipped down Columbine's cheeks.

When they pulled apart quietly, Elijah rose. "You've had some tragic news, and I'm sorry," he said. "I'll leave you alone now." He started for the door.

"Mr. Reed." Columbine's voice was thick, and it stopped Elijah in his tracks. "Mr. Reed, you may put me down for that lecture." Gazing at him over Bell's butterscotch hair, she added softly, "I have something to say now."

"I'm glad, Mrs. Nash," he answered. He started to turn away again, but she stopped him.

"Don't go yet," she said softly. Then, embarrassed, she added, "That is, if you can stay. Stay for tea."

"I can stay," he said. And then he smiled at her, the first full smile he'd given her. He looked handsome; ten years fell away from his face.

Then Lawrence was standing in the doorway, impossibly handsome, and young and demanding, "What's happened?"

He strode quickly to Columbine. "You're crying," he said. He looked from Bell to her. "What's happened, for God's sake?"

"It's all right, Mr. Birch," Columbine said. "We've had some bad news, that's all. A young woman who we tried to help is dead." She looked over at Bell, who was now standing at the window, her back to the room. "We just found out."

From his vantage point, with Columbine turned away, Elijah could clearly see Lawrence's face. Not a flicker of emotion showed. He watched thoughtfully as Lawrence composed his face into worry and heartache as Columbine turned back.

"Columbine—Mrs. Nash—I'm so sorry. You must be dreadfully upset. Here," he said, pushing the armchair toward her, "please sit down. You must tell me everything."

Elijah watched what he was now sure was a performance on the man's part, as he held onto Columbine's hand and looked into her face. He waited curiously for Columbine's reaction, and saw that she was a bit flustered by the attention, a bit confused.

Bell wheeled away from the window, and, keeping her face averted said, "I'll be going." Lawrence barely gave her a glance.

"Mr. Birch, have you met Mr. Reed?" Columbine asked, remembering her manners. The two men nodded coolly at each other, for each had taken the other's measure. "Mr. Reed is staying for tea," she added.

"Are you sure you're up for company?" Lawrence murmured solicitously to Columbine. Of course, he was excusing himself from that description.

Elijah noted Lawrence Birch's adhesion to the carpet. He'd be damned if he'd stand here and compete with this gigilo for the privilege of being alone with Columbine. "Yes, Mrs. Nash," he said aloud, "I think we should postpone our meeting."

Disappointment clouded her face, but she was looking down, and Elijah did not see it. "Of course, Mr. Reed."

As soon as the door closed behind Elijah, Lawrence looked down at Columbine tenderly. "You look done in," he said.

"I was too late to save someone," she said. "That is never easy." She looked at him keenly. "That reminds me. Lawrence, will you do me a favor?"

"Do you need to ask? Anything you wish."

"I wonder if you'd be go-between with the Devlins and myself."

He started. "For what purpose?"

Columbine rose and went to the windowsill and leaned against it. "Because of that article, Ambrose Hartley has decided to withhold the settlement to the Devlins, to punish them for talking to Mr. Reed. He thinks—Mr. Reed does—that the Devlins could have a case against Mr. Hartley, if they chose to bring it to court. And I am privy to information that Mr. Hartley absolutely knew the fireworks were unsafe. I want you to tell them that, and tell them that I would be willing to testify in a court of law as to those facts. That's all. I'm afraid Fiona Devlin would slam the door in my face before I had a chance to tell her. But she would listen to you. You're not a tainted woman."

"I'd be glad to help you, Columbine. Of course. I'll go tomorrow."

"Thank you, Lawrence." Columbine discovered that they'd slipped into using Christian names. She hadn't been aware of when it happened. "It's very kind of you. And I hope it will help the Devlins. I have a feeling that even the threat of a lawsuit will open up Ambrose Hartley's pockets." Her face changed suddenly, and she looked down. "Perhaps I can do some good for the Devlins, at least. I failed so badly with poor Sally Hoover."

Lawrence crossed to the window, and suddenly his hand was on the back of her neck. "I'm sure you did not," he murmured.

With her head bowed, Columbine felt drugged by the lazy rhythm of Lawrence's strong fingers against her neck. The touch against the fine hairs of her nape was so soothing. Columbine stopped thinking about the Devlins and Sally Hoover. She looked up into Lawrence's clear blue eyes. She followed the flare of his full upper lip, and she took a breath as subtly as she could. She was suddenly face to face with her attraction, and she didn't like it. It was damnably inconvenient to feel such a pull, she thought. A younger man. And such a radical, such a mystery. There was something there that repelled her even as it attracted her.

He seemed to read encouragement in her eyes. His lips quirked, and he bent his head. The shock of the contact sent her head tilting back against the dusty glass. She kissed him back, felt his lips and tongue move, warm and sweet, against her own lips, inside her own mouth. His hand cupped the back of her head, and she felt suddenly small and girlish next to him. And Columbine never felt small and girlish. She rather liked it, just at that moment.

She was so intent on Lawrence's kiss and these perplexing new feelings that she quite forgot where she was. Unfortunate, since Elijah Reed had paused to light a cigar on the sidewalk outside and think about what he had witnessed, and if he cared. He happened to look up. And what he saw made him stand still and stare, and his cigar went out without him noticing. A blond mass of hair pressed against a window while a tall man bent over a white face. And then, slender arms reached up to encircle the tall man's neck. Elijah felt a strange pain pierce him. Frowning, he headed down Fourteenth Street back toward the solace of his tiny house.

Columbine's unfortunate luck doubled when Bell, at the same moment Elijah turned away, was passing in the hall. She heard the silence and looked in, thinking Columbine alone. She saw the kiss, the complete concentration of the two people in the room, and her heart, too, was pierced. She, too, hurried away.

And, invariably, since the world falls away under such circumstances, Columbine and Lawrence just went on kissing.

• • •

It hadn't been easy to get Horatio to the Twenty-third Street house. But Marguerite insisted. She had plans. All her work—and her pleasure—would be for nothing if she couldn't manage to get Bell out of his heart. He had stalled and stalled, he had promised and promised. It was time for a push.

She was waiting behind the parlor curtain, watching the street, when she saw him walk up. She opened the door before he could knock. "Don't look so nervous," she told him, taking his hand and drawing him inside. "Bell never comes home before five at the earliest. Usually even later. It's only three. We have two hours."

"I don't understand, Marguerite," Horatio said. "Two hours for what? I'm—"

She stopped him by placing her mouth on his. He didn't resist, but his kiss was abstracted, dry. Marguerite persisted, and finally Horatio began to get interested. Just as he deepened the kiss, she withdrew. "I have a surprise for you," she murmured. Taking his hand, she led him to the stairs.

Horatio stopped as abruptly as a horse refusing to take a jump. "Upstairs?"

Taking his hand, this time she placed it on her breast. She kissed him again. "Yes."

Horatio took the first step, then the next. Marguerite's red lips and mocking glance drew him upward. He could feel himself beginning to get excited. She was wearing a loose duster over her underclothes, and he caught a glimpse of black stockings and slender ankles as she lifted her skirts and ran faster, then disappeared around the landing. Horatio followed her, smiling indulgently at her childishness. Now she was hiding, and he would have to find her.

He'd never been upstairs, and he stopped, confused at the closed doors. He tried the first on the left, a corner room. It opened to a large bedroom, a deep gold satin bedspread, a ruby dressing gown thrown across it, a shawl in ivory cashmere with gold fringe. Pins were scattered on a small dressing table, and piles of books sat on a small desk near the corner. He didn't need to see Columbine's spectacles to realize who the room belonged to. Femininity, luxury, intelligence, purpose: Columbine. He closed the door.

"This way, Horatio." The voice was light, mocking.

Now he noticed that one of the doors down the hall was slightly ajar. Horatio approached it slowly; for some strange reason, he had a sudden uneasy feeling about this game. He pushed open the door with a wary finger.

At first, he could only see Marguerite. She was standing in the middle of the room. She'd thrown off the duster and was wearing a plain wool wrapper in a particularly dull shade of maroon. The robe was open, and underneath she was wearing a winter chemise, white with a slight edging of lace. Flannel drawers. Black cotton stockings with a hole in the left one, around the calf.

He blinked as the information slowly sank in that something was wrong. Marguerite's usual underthings were not practical. They were trimmed with flounces of lace, pale delicate ribbons. Sometimes he suspected she pinched things from Columbine. These were serviceable, warm, practical. He could not imagine Marguerite buying a wool wrapper in that dull color. He had never seen Marguerite stand before him in drawers made of such serviceable flannel.

Slowly, he looked around him. The room was spare. There was nothing extraneous, and there was nothing out of place. A painted iron bed was neatly made with a white coverlet. A gray blanket was folded on a chair. A rag rug sat on a swept, polished wood floor. A desk sat in the sunniest corner, books carefully arranged on a small shelf above. Political pamphlets were stacked on the desk, their edges neatly aligned. The windowseat held no cushions, no invitation to dream.

"Yes, it's Bell's room, Horatio," Marguerite said in her husky voice, so adult, so seductively surprising, coming from that small body, that young, fresh face. "I'm wearing Bell's clothes. Her underthings. The robe she wears before she goes to bed. That's her bed, Horatio."

He took a step backward. "This is ridiculous, Marguerite. Come on. Put your own clothes back on. I refuse to—"

"I want her out of your heart, Horatio," Marguerite continued, as if he hadn't spoken. "Look at her bed. It's the bed of a nun. I want you to feel me underneath you on that bed, Horatio. I want you to feel the difference between us."

Marguerite came toward him. As she stood before him, unbearably close but not touching him, he caught it, unbelievable as it was: Bell's scent. It seemed to rise from the dressing gown, from the underclothes, and it sent a flare of excitement through him that made him shudder.

She saw it; she saw his shuddering intake of breath. He took an involuntary step closer and breathed the scent in again. It wasn't perfume, it wasn't flowery, it was clean and fresh, direct. It was Bell.

He seemed to watch his own hand as if it belonged to a stranger. It reached out and fingered the tiny ribbon on the chemise.

"I used her soap," Marguerite said.

He crashed up against a wall of longing. For Bell, for Marguerite? It didn't matter. He pulled her to him and buried his face in her fragrant hair, slid his hands down her slender, boyish body. She was Marguerite, but with his eyes closed, she was also Bell. And did it bother Marguerite? It didn't seem so. She was taunting him, but it wasn't with anger, or pique. He didn't know what it was that would provoke her to take another woman's things, to wash in her soap. He didn't care.

Marguerite wrenched away from him and crossed to the bed. She lay on it, her legs slightly open and waving back and forth. She slipped out of the robe and then, slowly, out of the drawers. Her dark blue eyes burned in her white face.

"Her bed," she said. She threw the drawers at him. They hit his face and fell to the floor.

He drew closer. He was passive as she undressed him, kneeling on the bed and clucking approvingly at his erection.

"Good boy," she said, laying back again. She kept on the chemise, but she unbuttoned it as far as she could and pushed it off her shoulders.

Naked, he eased himself beside her. He lay opposite her, almost afraid to touch her. What manner of a creature was she, to do this? Horatio felt confused and very excited. Prolonging the agony, he breathed in that scent again, that essence that eluded him—Bell, or Marguerite? One tiny breast peeked at him, and he reached out, finally, to fondle it.

"Did you want to do that to Bell, Horatio?" Marguerite asked.

She arched her back, pushing her tiny breasts toward him. "Would she do this? Would she want you like this, Horatio? Would she," and Marguerite reached out to stroke him, felt him leap in her small fingers, "touch you like this? Would she give you such pleasure?" She rubbed him, watching him steadily all the while with that strange blue gaze.

Horatio didn't answer. He was past thinking now, and not capable of a response. He fumbled with the tiny buttons on the chemise. Marguerite reached down and ripped it open, the buttons flying out to nestle in the bedclothes. "Would she want you that much, Horatio?" she whispered, as his lips burned a trail down her fragrant skin.

"She lies here every night," she went on. Horatio reached between her legs and parted them. "And she does not think of you, Horatio."

He rolled on top of her, pinning her slender arms. His face was strained, and sweat dampened the ends of his hair.

"Close your eyes," she ordered, and he did. He felt her skin, hot against his fingers, and he thought of Bell, that exquisite lushness sheathing such dead passivity. She had remained unmoved, all throughout their courtship. There were nights, he remembered, that he'd wanted to lash out, wanted to hurt her. Anything to crack that bland facade. He squeezed Marguerite's breast, remembering. She cried a soft cry, then caught his ear with her sharp teeth.

"You want to hurt her," she whispered. He felt her teeth graze his ear again, not softly. "Take me the way you want to take her."

Horatio had a flash of pleasure in his lover. Marguerite, strong, wiry Marguerite, the little savage, with her red lips and white teeth, her absence of shame.

Her thighs moved underneath him, and he groaned. His eyes flew open, and she was watching him avidly. "Don't think," she said impatiently, greedily. "Just take me. Close your eyes," she ordered angrily.

Horatio closed his eyes again. His head moved to her breast. He took her nipple between his teeth, and Marguerite moaned. Her sound of pleasure masked the creak of the bedroom door, so Horatio didn't raise his head. Then he heard the gasp.

Bell stood in the doorway. She saw everything at once, it seemed. Her amber eyes were very wide as they flew from Horatio to Marguerite. For an instant, she checked the room, as though she thought she had blundered. When she realized she was actually in her own room, she stiffened. And then she was gone like a shadow, flitting away, while Horatio was already slipping out of Marguerite, while Marguerite was just beginning to realize what happened.

"Bell!" she called. She struggled to put on the wrapper, but Horatio, damn him, was lying on part of it, and he was transfixed, unable to move. "Bell!"

She heard the front door slam. Marguerite lay back on the pillows and regarded the ceiling. She devoutly hoped she would continue to have a roof over her head tomorrow.

She was going mad. She would go mad. She was *already* mad. Bell ran down the block, laughing. Tears streamed down her face, and she continued to laugh.

Sex! It was everywhere around her, it filled the house with musk, and she was choking on the thick scent. To hear the news of Sally's death—and somehow Bell connected that death to sex, for what was Sally but a slave to her lover, her husband? And then to see Lawrence bending over Columbine that way—she thought she would die. And she'd run home for solace, wanting only to slip under cold sheets in her own bed, and found Horatio and Marguerite . . . like that.

She couldn't think of it. Lawrence had cupped Columbine's head so tenderly. His hands looked brown and large against her white throat. And Marguerite's nakedness, her black hair spilling over white shoulders, and Horatio, naked against the sheets. She had seen his most private parts, red and angry as an animal's. She had seen everything.

Bell hurried on. She was going west, away from respectability and toward the tenements that crouched under the Ninth Avenue El. Heedless and mindless, she walked quickly to drive out the pictures in her brain, her unbuttoned coat chasing behind her. All she saw was flesh. All she smelled was sex. She felt sick. She felt sweat bead up on her forehead, and she gulped in the frosty air.

She could smell the brewery now, and the sweet air made her

feel sicker. She leaned against a wrought-iron gate. Across the street a squalid red brick building stood, its front crisscrossed with fire escapes and landings. Despite the cold, a few women leaned on their elbows and looked down at the street in a desultory fashion. One sat leaning against the fire escape, a blanket around her shoulders and a cigarette in her hand. The woman waved in a bored but beckoning way at a man who ignored her but started up the stairs.

Bell saw that they were prostitutes. She gripped the gate behind her, and she felt the iron bite into her cold bare hand. A sharp, protruding piece of metal tore the skin on her wrist. She felt a trickle of blood, warm and wet, snake down her forearm and stain her dress. She brought the injured wrist to her mouth. She imagined the smell of sex on her fingers. She swallowed, tasting salt, and, flecks of blood on her lips, she started to walk again.

Seven

COLUMBINE HEARD THE first gasp just one minute into her speech. Good.

She had started simply. She walked out, waited for the applause to stop, then merely set her spectacles on her nose and read, in a quiet voice, from a hospital report. It was a long list of injuries. The details in medical language were no less chilling for being so clinical. The injuries described were a broken arm, a smashed cheekbone, black eye, burns on upper thighs, internal injuries and various bruises from a fall down a steep flight of stairs. At the end of the recitation, Columbine announced the patient's name, Sarah Hoover, her age, twenty-two, and the date of her death, two weeks previous. Her assailant? John Hoover. Her husband.

She heard the gasp, then felt the audience stir, rustle, cough. It was as though one whispering murmur passed through the crowd like a breaking wave. And then attention returned to her. Columbine knew this, even as she went on speaking. She knew she had them in her hand. Her first object now was not to lose them.

She went on with Sally's story, detailing the heartbreaking list of Sally's attempts to find help. The neighbor, the doctor, the police, the family. Those who questioned her loyalty, her sanity, her conduct. At the end, Sally had no one left to go to. When her husband dragged her from her aunt's house, there was no one to prevent her going home to him. He was her husband. He had that right.

By the end of her speech, Columbine imagined that each person in the crowd was leaning toward her. Their pale faces were upturned and rapt. No one coughed, and no one stirred.

"Silence," she said. "They tell us silence keeps us safe. With silence, we remain honorable wives, mothers, daughters. But what honor is this, and who defines it? Our husbands, our fathers. The same husbands and fathers who have raped us, have beaten us. The same uncles who have slipped their hands inside our bodices. The same brothers who have invaded our beds." Another gasp went up, and Columbine charged on. "What happened to Sally Hoover is a crime. And that crime is added to a multitude of similiar crimes too horrific to conceive of. But when we add our silence to those crimes—that becomes our deepest shame. I hear the multitudes crying. I hear Sally Hoover's voice crying. And she is crying 'Shame.'"

Columbine paused. She looked out into the crowd, and she caught Bell's eye. Bell nodded at her encouragingly, and Columbine felt her palms grow damp. She'd discussed the ending of the speech over and over with Bell, and finally, she'd decided to go ahead with her plan. It could backfire, she knew. But now, Columbine let no trace of fear enter her voice. That was the point, wasn't it?

"What would happen," she asked, leaning forward and looking from face to face of the women in the audience, "if we women told the truth about our lives? I say if we told the truth here, tonight, it would surge out of the doorways and run down the stairs in a coursing stream until it was a river of righteousness raging through the streets of our city and our nation." Columbine held the eyes of the women in the first rows of the hall. "Stand up," she said, and a thin-faced woman in the first row jumped. "If you yourself have been beaten, if you yourself have suffered abuse at the hands of your father, your uncle, your brother, your husband. Stand up. If you have a friend, a sister, a mother, an aunt who has suffered that abuse, stand up. Show us. Show this hall, show this city, show this nation how widespread this cancer is. For God's sake—for *women's* sake, stand up. You'll notice," Columbine added, her voice softer but still carrying to the farthest reaches of the hall, "that I am standing, too."

There was a pause. Then, as agreed, Bell stood. It took ten agonizing seconds before Ivy Moffat stood, a few rows away, as she'd promised to Columbine. She saw another woman stand, a stranger, near the back of the hall. Then another. And another. No one spoke, no one moved except the countless women, some dressed in fine hats and cloaks, some in the plain black of the working girl, who rose and stood, erect and silent, by their chairs. Tears burned behind Columbine's eyes but still she waited, then waited longer, for more women kept standing until it seemed the great hall at Cooper Union was filled with women standing, giving silent testimony. When Columbine was sure that every woman who had the courage to stand had done so, she nodded. Then she turned away and walked off the stage. She had prepared a few more words, but this was the most eloquent conclusion she could reach.

She stood trembling in the wings as the hall exploded with applause. Someone pushed her back toward the stage, and she stood for a moment, hearing their cheers, then quickly walked off again. She didn't feel triumphant and exhiliarated, as she usually felt after a speech. It hadn't turned out to be her speech at all. It was the speech of the hundred silent women who had stood in the end.

Columbine reached out shakily to grab the edge of a dusty curtain to steady herself for a moment. Then people were rushing at her, women she worked with, people she didn't know, people she knew. At first she could hardly distinguish the faces. She looked for Elijah Reed, but she didn't see him, and she felt disappointed. Why she felt she needed that man's approval she didn't know. Again, Columbine felt irritated, and then was irritated at her irritation.

She was led to small reception area, where she barely had time to drink a glass of water and catch her breath before they were on her again. Congratulations bubbled from every mouth. Everyone looked energized, excited. But the question was, would anything change? Would they risk embarrassment or anger to question the rights of a husband? Would they still even care a month from now?

She looked over the bobbing heads for Lawrence, but she didn't see him. He had told her he would be first backstage to greet her. Instead, Elijah Reed came forward. He was dressed in a dark suit, and for once, his shirt was pressed and starched.

"It was an excellent speech," he said quietly. "You said what needed to be said."

"Thank you," Columbine murmured softly, to hide her pleasure at his words. "And thank you for giving me the chance. It was good of you to wait."

"I knew you would say yes," he said imperturbably.

She bristled. "Do you know me so well, Mr. Reed?"

He looked at her appraisingly. "No," he said seriously. "But I'm a good guesser."

She couldn't help smiling at that. "Are you coming back to the house afterward? Bell is giving a little reception."

He bowed. "Of course. Miss Huxton has already asked me. I'll see you there."

He moved away. Behind him, Columbine saw Ned moving toward her.

"Oh, Ned, I'm so glad you came," she said when he came up.

"It was a wonderful success," he said. He did not take her hand or kiss her cheek. "I was very moved."

"Thank you," Columbine said. "How is your work in Washington? I see your name in the papers every other day, it seems."

"It keeps me busy. It's a city of charlatans, Columbine. I've met some characters, let me tell you," he said, laughing.

How like old times it was, Columbine thought. Yet how not. Ned's stories had kept her so amused. She'd forgotten that, how his bemusement at fools could make her laugh.

But someone else came up to congratulate her, and Ned slipped away with a bow. She shook hands and chatted and when she looked around again, he was gone.

Columbine began to wonder why Lawrence did not appear. She frowned. He had spoken so eagerly of seeing her speak tonight. Where was he?

Though he hadn't kissed her again, and she was quite sure she wouldn't have allowed it if he had tried, she still found herself drawn to him strangely. They hadn't discussed the kiss, but it lay between them, constricting her behavior now, making her a little shy with him. Lawrence had taken a room near Tompkins Square, but he seemed to be at the house almost as often. And he always seemed to arrive when she was frustrated or bored or needed a break, bringing kuchen from the local bakery near his house, or flowers, or whatever small thing struck his fancy on the way.

A slender arm slid around her waist, and she turned to confront the quiet amber eyes of Bell. "It was a great success," Bell said, kissing her cheek.

"You were as much a part of that speech as I was," Columbine told her. "Thank you for everything. Have you seen Lawrence, by the way?"

Bell's arm slipped off Columbine's waist and fell to her side. "No, I haven't."

Columbine hesitated, but she could see how Bell's spine had stiffened. She knew that Bell wasn't very fond of Lawrence. "I suppose we'll see him back at the house."

"Yes," Bell said quickly. "And perhaps we should think of leaving."

"Bell, are you all right?"

"Of course. I'd better not monopolize your time. I'll see about a carriage."

"All right." Columbine watched Bell move through the crowd thoughtfully. Her head had been buried in her lecture for the past few weeks, that was clear. Bell seemed troubled by something. Ever since Sally Hoover's death, she hadn't been herself. Even little Marguerite had been scarce lately.

Shaking her head, Columbine surveyed the crowd a bit impatiently. Fiery Leonora O'Reilly, who was working on founding a consumer's society, had captured an intent Elijah Reed's attention. Bell had disappeared. Marguerite hadn't come at all. And where was Lawrence?

Lawrence heard the first ten minutes of Columbine's speech, but he felt no impetus to remain. The speech would be another success in one long trail of successes for the notable Columbine Nash. Another speech that explored another issue that was completely beside the point. The world was crushing the spirit of honest men while Columbine and her girls fretted about a few women who had the misfortune to marry bad men. If the system were changed, those men would not need to resort to violence in their homes, they would be free. Columbine was, as usual, focusing on too narrow a vision.

Lawrence was the man for expansive visions; it should have

been him up there declaiming to a rapt audience. He hurried through Astor Place, crossing the dark streets, picturing the adulation, the notices in all the papers about his brilliance. It was time to demonstrate his commitment. It was past time.

It was a long walk to the western edge of Greenwich Village, but Lawrence welcomed the cold air and the darkness. He had a rendezvous which demanded a cool head. He had perhaps an hour or so, no more, before Columbine would miss him. He would have to tell her how wonderful she had been. For a strong woman, Columbine was terribly in need of reassurance.

He was tantalizing her. After that first kiss, he hadn't touched her. He'd merely looked. And she was teetering oh-so delicately on the edge of her resistance. In another week, she would fall. Until then . . .

Balancing carefully on the wooden board so as not to dirty his boots, Lawrence picked his way across the back yard toward the peeling maroon door. He knocked once, lightly. The door opened, and Fiona Devlin slipped out through a crack, adjusting a shawl over her head. Without a word, they started across the yard toward the street. But as soon as they reached the side of the house, Fiona pulled Lawrence to her passionately. Her rough, pale hands drew his face down toward hers. The callouses on her fingers excited him, as they always did.

"I was waiting," she whispered. "Too long."

Marguerite was bored. Now that she had Horatio, she didn't know if she wanted him so terribly much. Since that moment when Bell had seen them together, Horatio's sexual interest in her had waned. Marguerite could no longer tantalize him; she barely seemed to interest him. From the moment Bell had walked in that room, her fate had been sealed. Horatio would forever associate that escapade with Marguerite's irresponsibility, and, being an essentially serious man—she had not realized how very serious was Horatio's nature—he would recoil from her. Oh, he would continue to act in a gentlemanly fashion. He would squire her about, he would be solicitious for her comfort. But he would not slide any farther into love. And he would never marry her.

Marguerite sighed and dangled her empty champagne glass from a negligent hand. She had begged prettily for Horatio to bring her to Rector's champagne palace on Broadway, and finally, the lout had agreed. Horatio had wanted to attend Columbine's address at Cooper Union. But Marguerite had had enough of politics. Her work at the New Women Society would succeed in sending her to a madhouse. If Horatio didn't send her there first. Besides, it was better to avoid Bell these days, even if they were off the hook.

She had waited for days for the ax to fall, for Bell to denounce her, for Columbine to disown her. But Bell merely avoided her. When Marguerite's nerves threatened to crack, she'd had no choice but to seek out Bell herself. She had gone to Bell in her office—for she knew Bell's room would have rather unpleasant connotations—and confessed that she was beside herself with remorse. That she'd fallen quite helplessly in love with Horatio, and she was sorry. Bell had patted her shoulder and said in a expressionless voice, "I'm glad."

So now that Marguerite could see Horatio without fear, the man fell apart on her. Lately, Horatio was a lump on a log. In the middle of glittering Rector's, full of actors, actresses, society folk, society climbers, gamblers, journalists, senators, charlatans, and fools, he was bored! He stared down into his wonderful food as though it were fit only for his dog.

At first, Marguerite had been thrilled just to be there. The head-waiter had bowed to them, and with an imperceptible glance at Marguerite's blue velvet gown and glowing skin, seated them at a prominent table. But she waited in vain to converse brilliantly with the scores of famous people Horatio knew. Horatio was so morose that after a few jovial remarks, people drifted away from their table. Marguerite had never been so frustrated, including when she had been in bed with Horatio earlier.

"Could I have a tiny bit more champagne?" she asked him, trying to hold on to a charming lilt while she wanted to screech at him.

Before Horatio could answer, someone else intruded. "Certainly, you must," came a voice from behind her chair. A deep baritone voice, an interesting voice. "Allow me."

She twisted in her seat to locate the source of that deep voice, and was immediately disappointed. The man had twinkling hazel eyes, true, and he was young, but he was too short. Not a very commanding presence. But at least he was a man. Marguerite flashed her dimples at him, hoping Horatio would be jealous.

"Allow me to present Miss Marguerite Corbeau," Horatio said. "Miss Corbeau, this is Mr. Toby Wells."

"Charmed." He bent over her hand and kissed the air above it. Then he slid the champagne out of its silver bucket and refilled her glass with a flourish. "Not a drop spilled. Perhaps I missed my calling," he said in an odd, mocking way. His eyes traveled over Marguerite with a rakishness that drove the boredom from her mind with a delicious, bracing shock.

"I'd love to join you for a drink," Toby Wells went on, pulling a chair over and sitting next to Marguerite. "How kind of you to ask me, Horatio."

Horatio looked annoyed. "Really, Wells."

"Yes, really, I would love to," Toby continued, still staring at Marguerite. Then he returned his attention to Horatio. "I must tell you, old man, Felix Bartholemew Dillon is over in the corner hiding behind a very large palm. He's wondering aloud why you haven't come over to greet him. And he's already consumed several bottles of champagne, and he's in a, shall we say, expansive mood."

A spark of interest lit Horatio's eyes. Felix Dillon was highly placed in state politics, and was currently involved in a minor scandal involving an Italian opera singer. He'd been avoiding journalists for weeks. "I suppose I should speak to him," Horatio said, rising. "Will you—"

"I'll watch over Miss Corbeau, never fear," Toby answered with a gay smile. As soon as Horatio was out of earshot, he turned back to Marguerite. "He's an awfully dull fellow, your Horatio."

"My Horatio?"

"Mmmm. So serious-minded. I'm surprised to see him here. And," Toby added, after a sip of champagne, "I am especially surprised that he ordered such fine champagne. It must be a tribute to the lady at the table."

"You're an awfully insolent gentleman," Marguerite observed calmly.

"Ah, you're under the mistaken impression I'm a gentleman, then. We'll have to remedy that. But we'd need more champagne, and I doubt Horatio will spring for another bottle." Toby looked sad.

Marguerite laughed. "What *is* it that you do, Mr. Wells?"

"I'm an actor, of course. Couldn't you tell?"

"I've never met an actor before. What are his general characteristics?"

"Well, let's see. John Booth aside, we're very placid creatures. Fond of comfort, very good company. And we love to invent ruses to get beautiful young ladies alone."

"Was that a ruse then?" Marguerite asked. "Poor Mr. Jones. He'll be terribly embarrassed when Mr. Dillon refuses to acknowledge him."

Toby poured them both more champagne. "Oh, I have more faith in Horatio than that, don't you? I'm hoping for ten minutes more with you, at least."

"And what will you do with your ten minutes, sir?" Exhilaration pulsed through Marguerite. She felt flushed, lovely, and witty. So this was what *banter* was, she thought. Horatio never bantered. His jokes were usually over her head, for she never read the newpapers or anything much at all. But everything Toby Wells said seemed designed to let her know that he found her attractive. The words weren't important, it was the eyes that spoke. Marguerite found his manner delightful. And could there be more men like this, she wondered, who could make her feel so beautiful, so alive? Better looking than Toby, and certainly richer?

"Let me see. For the next ten minutes I will try to charm you completely, Miss Corbeau. I will try to intrigue you. And perhaps I will succeed in securing a promise from you that I may call on you again."

He looked at her with dancing eyes, and she couldn't help smiling back. "Well?" she asked. "I'm waiting. Charm me."

He threw back his head and laughed. "So I am not going to be indulged. I shall have to work for my pleasure."

"Most of us do," Marguerite said.

He stopped then, and moved closer to her. "That's where you are wrong, Miss Corbeau," he said in a confiding tone. "Most of us do not. At least in my world. If one has to work for pleasure, how fully can pleasure be enjoyed?"

Suddenly, Marguerite grew vastly more interested in the dandy

Toby Wells. "What is your world, Mr. Wells?" she asked, affecting unconcern as she smoothed the feathers on her fan.

"But how can I tell you with words? I'm an actor, Miss Corbeau, and I know words can confuse, can exaggerate, can lie. Let me show you," Toby cried, as if with sudden inspiration. "A friend of mine is giving a party Wednesday night. I'd like you to come."

"A dinner party?" She'd never been to a dinner party. She'd merely served at them.

"Yes, a dinner party. A very special dinner party."

Marguerite thought it prudent to give a show of reluctance. "I hardly know you well enough, Mr. Wells," she said primly.

"Would you like to introduce me to your mother?" he asked gaily. "I would be honored, of course."

Marguerite's face changed. "She's no longer living."

"Ah, I'm sorry," he said, but he didn't seem sorry at all. "Perhaps I should explain about the party. Can you sing?"

"Can I—"

"Oh, bother, Horatio is coming back." Toby quickly scribbled something on a small white card. "Here is the address. I'll send a carriage, and a note with the details. You must come, Miss Corbeau. And I'll show you a world," he said earnestly, "where pleasure is not preceded by work. Only by more pleasure. Don't fail me, Miss Corbeau." He slipped the card underneath her napkin.

He rose just as Horatio came up. He bent over her hand again. This time, he kissed it. His mustache tickled her knuckle. "*Adieu*, Miss Corbeau."

Horatio frowned as he watched Toby walk away with his lithe, bouncing step. "I hope Mr. Wells didn't annoy you, Marguerite. He can be very impertinent."

"He was impertinent," she said slowly. "But I liked it."

He looked at her sharply. "Did he say anything?"

"Nothing of importance," Marguerite said. She slid the card from under her napkin and, underneath the tablecloth, slipped it into the tiny purse on her wrist. "Nothing at all."

Lawrence made love to Fiona Devlin on an empty Hudson pier. There was no moon. Her back was against a piling, and her red hair was loose. Her face was taut and fierce; her thighs gripped his waist as he drove into her. She made no sound at all, but when she reached her climax her eyes flew open and looked into his. Pale green flecked with brown, a tiny triangle of yellow hovered in one corner. Her eyes had a customary wary look, but at that moment they looked preternatural, frightening. She was a woman who could do violence as easily as a man, he thought, and he came in a blinding flood.

He buttoned his trousers and she straightened her dark skirt. "I have to get back," he said.

"Don't I know that," she answered. She twisted her hair into a bun. "Don't worry, Larry, I won't be wanting any kisses from you."

"Don't call me that," he said, gripping her arm fiercely. Unfortunately, it was through her coat. It didn't hurt.

She shook him off like a child. "All right. Let's be going, then. At least I won't have to listen to your political lectures."

A dark shadow passed in front of them; a rat. Lawrence flinched. Without breaking stride, Fiona picked up a heavy piece of wood and threw it, and the rat skittered away. Fiona noticed Lawrence's revulsion, and she laughed at him over her shoulder. "They're always with me, the rats." Her green eyes glinted at him. "One of them even lifts my skirt occasionally."

She laughed softly again. She loved nothing more than to torment Lawrence Birch. For a blackguard, he could be very stiff—and she didn't mean underneath his trousers. Fiona smiled with pleasure. It was more the dark moonless night that intoxicated her than the satisfying burn in her lower regions; more the freedom than the sex. Jimmy Devlin wasn't a bad man, but the accident had left him mean. And who wouldn't be, with only one arm? It was a sorry day, she thought, shivering, her pleasure suddenly gone, when a wife couldn't bear her husband's eyes.

"So where are you rushing off to tonight?" she asked, brushing the back of her coat.

"Mrs. Nash gave a speech at Cooper Union. I'm going to a reception afterward," he said shortly.

"You'll drink a toast to the bitch who won't testify for me and Jimmy?" Fiona asked in a conversational tone. "She knows that Ambrose Hartley is a liar, and Lady Nash won't say it. Honor among the upper classes."

"So instead of you listening to my lectures, I listen to yours," Lawrence said dryly. "Mrs. Nash has her uses, which you'll soon see." He slid a hand inside her open coat and squeezed her breast. "When will I see you again?"

"Not for a week, mind. I don't want Jimmy to be wondering." Fiona batted away his hand and buttoned her coat with fingers red with cold. The sex had driven out the chill, but it was seeping in again.

"I thought you said since the arm came off he drinks himself into a stupor every day."

"Jimmy in a stupor is sharper than most men," Fiona said flatly. "So next week. Besides, I don't have need of it more than once a week."

"How romantic you are, Fiona."

She gave him a twisted smile. "And you are overcome with my charms, are you, boyo? We both know what this is. Now, I'll be going. Jimmy will be waking soon."

"Fiona," he said, stopping her. "Wouldn't you like to get back at him? Hartley?"

"Of course." Fiona's teeth gleamed. "My dreams about murdering him put a smile on my face every morning."

She drew her shawl over her head and walked quickly away from him, not looking back for a final farewell, a final glimpse of her lover. Lawrence would be surprised if she had. He didn't mind. He watched her straight back until she was swallowed up by the night.

Lawrence pulled on his gloves. Fiona had what he needed: desperation and hate. She would be the perfect instrument. All she lacked was direction, and he was just the man to provide it.

Eight

Bell opened the door to Lawrence and did not smile. Her lovely eyes instantly slid away from his and concentrated on his coat, which he slipped out of and gave to her. He made sure his fingers brushed hers just to see her involuntary jerk away. Lawrence almost chuckled, but he didn't. This was as close as he got to feeling omnipotent, having the trace of one woman on his thighs, about to meet the one he would seduce, but first stopping to fluster the one he would keep in reserve.

"A great night for all of us, Miss Huxton," he said, as Bell folded his coat over her arm.

"Yes, Mr. Birch. I'll have to put this in the back room. There's no room in the hall. Everyone is in the parlor, sir," she added pointedly.

He smiled and lingered. "Yes, I can hear the crowd. Pity you have to run to the door so often."

"I don't mind."

"No, you wouldn't," he said. "You do so much for her."

Her eyes flashed a curious look at him. "And why shouldn't I?"

Lawrence hesitated, a calculated hesitation. "Yes, why shouldn't you," he said slowly. She turned to go, but he put a hand on her arm. "I've been hoping you'd accept another invitation from me, Miss Huxton. Was our last experience so disagreeable?"

She shook her head. "No, but—"

"But?" He was fascinated by the struggle visible on her face.

"Don't ask me again," she said. "Just stop asking me. Please."

"But why—"

She put her hand over his briefly. "If you're a gentleman, sir, don't ask me again. I can't—"

Elijah Reed walked into the hall, and she backed away quickly.

"I'm sorry," Elijah said. "I didn't mean to intrude."

"Nonsense, Mr. Reed," Bell said briskly. "I was just greeting Mr. Birch."

Lawrence nodded at Elijah. "Good evening, Mr. Reed."

Bell took the opportunity to turn without a word and head for the back of the house with his coat. Elijah looked after her. "She's a brave woman," he mused, more to himself than Lawrence. "It took great courage to do what she did tonight." He looked at Lawrence. "Don't you agree?"

Lawrence was confused. Obviously, he'd missed an event of some consequence. Why would Bell have been brave? Had she pushed Columbine out of the path of a streetcar after the lecture? Surely it couldn't be something so dramatic. Mr. Reed, being a novelist, was most likely exaggerating something. Well, he'd give the old coot a thrill and feign interest in the story. "Oh?" he asked. "What happened?"

Elijah looked at him curiously. "At Columbine's speech, I mean."

"Oh," Lawrence said quickly. "Of course. Yes. Great courage indeed."

Elijah looked at the younger man, and Lawrence was suddenly uncomfortable under the acuity of those dark, impenetrable eyes.

"Shall we go in?" he asked smoothly.

Elijah followed him into the parlor. He had a writer's nose for hypocrisy, and he suspected Lawrence Birch. He recognized a smooth recovery, an adept way with a lie. Lawrence had no idea what Elijah had referred to. He didn't go to Columbine's speech at all, Elijah thought.

Lawrence melted away as soon as they entered the parlor. He saw Columbine off in a corner, but he wasn't ready to greet her as yet. Instead, he spoke to a woman Columbine had introduced him to before, a Miss Rosa Giannini from the New Women Society. Ms. Giannini was smart, plump, and prominent of mustache. "Did you enjoy the lecture, Mr. Birch?" she asked, sipping at her punch.

"Very much. Mrs. Nash is a powerful speaker. And Miss Huxton! She showed extraordinary courage."

Miss Giannini nodded gravely. "I agree. To be the first to stand to such a challenge—my heart beat terribly fast for her. But Mrs. Nash made it easier for the women in the hall by adding that they merely had to *know* someone dear to them who had been attacked by a family member. So there was less shame, or should I say risk, involved."

Marvelous. Now he knew everything. "Yes, that was very wise, I'm sure. Will you excuse me, Miss Giannini? I should pay Mrs. Nash my respects."

"Of course."

Lawrence hurried across the room. There was reproach in Columbine's soft brown eyes when he reached her. "Mr. Birch," she said with exaggerated charm. "How *very* kind of you to come."

He felt the slap, and he smiled. "You were extraordinary," he said.

"I looked for you afterward. Why didn't you come back to see me?"

Of course, Columbine would be direct. Other women would merely hold a grudge; Columbine would ask. Lawrence moved a bit closer. He held her gaze, not wavering. "I'm rather ashamed to tell you," he confessed.

"I wish you would, however."

"I couldn't bear to share you at such a moment," Lawrence admitted with a smile. "I am embarrassed to report that I was a child. I wanted you to myself. Don't be angry with me."

Columbine's eyes stayed on him gravely. "I hardly know how to feel."

"I knew I shouldn't have told you."

"Perhaps you shouldn't have, Lawrence."

"I haven't thought of anything but that kiss."

"Don't." Columbine spoke tersely; how could Lawrence speak of the kiss here, in this company? Elijah Reed was heading for them, and she didn't want him to overhear.

As Elijah came up, Lawrence turned to him immediately. "I was just telling Mrs. Nash how moved I was by her speech."

"I thought the end was particularly moving," Elijah said. "What did you think of that technique, Mr. Birch?"

Lawrence could have laughed. So Mr. Reed had suspected him after all. But what a clumsy trap!

"I thought it was an excellent idea," he said, turning immediately to Columbine. "You began so simply with the hospital report on that unfortunate girl. And to ensure that every member of the audience knew how widespread the horror is, you invite everyone who has been touched by that horror to stand. I was especially impressed with Miss Huxton. She showed extraordinary courage, to stand up first like that."

Elijah raised a black eyebrow. "Excellent point, Mr. Birch." He turned to Columbine. "I'm sorry to tell you that I've heard some bad news. Mr. Hartley had a heart attack earlier this evening."

Columbine gasped, but it was Lawrence who looked the most shocked, Elijah noted. It was almost as if he were *angry*. A curious reaction for an anarchist.

"How unfortunate!" he said tightly.

Columbine's eyes were anxious. "Is he expected to recover?"

"Yes, but he'll be abed for quite some time," Elijah said vaguely, still thinking of Lawrence's odd reaction.

Lawrence had regained his composure, and he said, "I suppose there are two people in this city who will not be crushed by the news."

"The Devlins, of course. Have you heard from them about my offer, Lawrence?" Columbine asked him.

Elijah started when he heard Columbine call the man by his Christian name. Exactly how intimate were they? he wondered. He'd told himself that Columbine could not possibly be Lawrence Birch's mistress. He'd also told himself that it was none of his business.

"Yes, I'm afraid they will not pursue the matter through the courts," Lawrence said. "They are very private people, like most of the Irish. And they do not think their chances of success are very great."

"They're probably correct. Still, I'm sorry to hear it," Elijah said.

"How will they ever get along?" Columbine asked in distress.

"I understand they have a benefactor," Lawrence said smoothly, "an anonymous one. The party has settled the medical bills and given them a loan." It was a lie, but he couldn't have Columbine interfering in the Devlins' lives any more.

Ned, Columbine thought. "Thank goodness," she said quietly.

"So that story is over, at least," Lawrence said. "They will not need you to testify, Columbine."

He smiled, and Elijah felt a pang of superstitious fear. Those odd, pale eyes were so frightening. Something nudged at Elijah, a nudge, as a writer, he had come to respect. Something is wrong here, he thought. On the spot, he decided to find out a few facts about the mysterious Mr. Birch.

At three in the morning, Columbine woke with a start.

"Not again," she groaned into the blackness. She flipped over and drew the comforter up to her chin. She'd thought that tonight, of all nights, she'd sleep. By the time the last guests, Lawrence Birch and Elijah Reed, had left at midnight, she'd been exhausted. The two men had sat in her parlor like stones, as though waiting the other out. She wondered why Elijah Reed had stayed so long. Perhaps he was lonely, she mused. He was a widower, had been one for ten years. You'd think he'd have gotten used to his solitary state before now. He certainly seemed to be comfortable with it.

Sighing, Columbine flipped over again. She thought of Elijah's watchful coal-black eyes. She liked the way his name moved on her tongue. *E-li-jah.*

Groaning, Columbine sat up. She hadn't indulged in this sort of ridiculous behavior since she was a teenager, waiting for love and mooning over the local curate.

Well, she might as well give up. She pulled on a robe and padded downstairs softly. The parlor was cold, so she kindled the fire and poured herself a brandy. Gathering up a quilt, she deposited herself on the sofa and leaned against the padded side. She pulled the quilt over her, shivering in the cold, still room. She'd outmanuever her sleeplessness, she decided. She'd let sleep sneak up on her while she pretended not to care.

"Columbine, what are you doing awake?" Bell came in the parlor, her thick, lustrous hair loose on her shoulders.

"I could ask the same of you," Columbine pointed out genially. "It seems my insomnia has returned."

Bell hesitated. "Would you mind some company?"

"Not at all. Pour yourself a brandy and grab hold of some of this quilt."

Bell poured herself a small brandy and returned to recline on the sofa, leaning against the opposite end. She drew the quilt up to her chin. "It was a wonderful night," she said. "You were wonderful. Did you see Ivy?"

"Yes."

"She was very grateful."

Columbine gave a deep sigh and looked into her brandy. "I expected her to resent me. When I first came to her and asked if I could tell Sally's story, she was so grieved she could barely even comprehend what I was saying. I was afraid she would begin shrieking at me, throw me out of the house."

"Why did you think that?" Bell asked softly.

"I felt guilty, Bell. Didn't you?"

Bell shook her head. "No. We did everything in our power, Columbine. We gave her what she needed. Money."

"But she needed safety," Columbine said slowly. "And that we could not give. That's what I keep thinking about, Bell. All those women, all those women who stood up in Cooper Union today, what have I done for them? Where can they go? It all keeps going around and around in my mind. You know I've been so dissatisfied lately with what I've been able to do. This is just further proof of it. I feel so terribly inadequate in the face of this."

"You kept me safe once, Columbine." Bell smiled. "Remember? You have to concentrate on individuals, or you want to lay down and give up. You helped me."

Columbine reached out and touched her hand. "And you've helped me, many times over. What would I do without you?"

"But it's not the same," Bell said urgently. She leaned toward Columbine. "I was trapped. I had no resources. I was abused, I was violated, I was beaten. I took it all as my due. Without you, I wouldn't have known there was another way. Without you, I am quite certain I'd be dead."

"Oh, Bell. No."

Bell cupped her brandy thoughtfully. "I'm not trying to console you, or flatter you, Columbine. It's a fact. I needed more than money, and you gave me what I needed. Ideas, for example. And the first one was that I was not at fault. That was a revolution, Columbine, perhaps a quieter one than is commonly discussed in history books, but it reverberated through my life, and it can reverberate through other women's lives, and *that* is what will change things."

"But until then, Bell. Until then, what are those women who stood tonight to do? What did you do?"

"I had you," Bell said. "Maybe if they're lucky they'll find someone. That's what I'm trying to tell you. You took care of practicalities. I needed a place to sleep. You gave me that. Sometimes the whole world can change if you just have a place to sleep. A place where you are protected. A place where your body can be safe, can begin to heal." Bell swirled the brandy she had yet to taste. "The mind is another matter," she whispered.

Columbine didn't hear the last whispered sentence. She was too busy thinking of what had come before. Bell had never talked about her earlier years, spoke of pain, or anguish, or frustration. She did her work, she was calm and friendly and resourceful. Sometimes Columbine wondered if Bell had any passions at all. She hadn't thought in years of what it must have been like for sixteen-year-old Bell to have a place to go. Columbine had been almost a child herself then, twenty-one and already famous in England. But she hadn't yet known how desperate the poor were, how they lived. She'd known misery, but she'd never known want. She hadn't realized exactly how much her offer of safety and warmth had meant to Bell.

Suddenly Columbine shook her head, as if to clear a fog in her brain. "That's what we need to do, Bell. That's exactly what we need to give."

Bell looked up. "What, Columbine?"

"Safety. We need to give safety." In her excitement, Columbine slowly rose to a sitting position. "We find a house," she continued slowly, vibrantly. "A big one. And any woman who is afraid for her physical safety can have a bed there. Young and old. Women whose homes are not safe. Victims of violence from family members."

"It's a big undertaking," Bell said dubiously.

"Yes, it is." Ideas tumbled through Columbine's brain, clicking like the tumblers of a lock. "The women run the house themselves. We offer protection, perhaps we can hire some kind of protection for them. We'll live there too, of course. We'll need a nursery where they can take turns watching the children. And we'll use the New Women Society for our employment agency. Oh, Bell, it could work. A waystation. A place to rest, to gather forces. And a new direction. We can do that, at least."

Bell frowned. "But where will we get the money, Columbine?"

Columbine laughed. "I've no idea. But I'll get it. We can build on what happened tonight. We can use it. I'll get the money."

Bell gave her a slow, quiet smile. "Yes, I do believe you shall."

Columbine was kneeling now, her face alight. "We can do so much good, Bell. We can take what happened to us and we can use it. Will you help me?"

A man might have shaken her hand. But Columbine was moved when Bell, instead, quietly embraced her. "Of course," she said.

While the house suddenly buzzed with energy for Columbine's new project, Marguerite moved about in a dream. Toby sent her a more formal invitation to the dinner, and she had accepted with pleasure. She had planned for days what to wear as Columbine and Bell discussed their project, which they'd decided to call Safe Passage House. They made lists, argued, and made more lists yet. And Marguerite dreamed of lace and worried about her gloves. She irritably wished she had a jewel for her hair.

She thought the night of the dinner would never come, but then it arrived, and she hardly felt ready. Over breakfast, she received a briefing from Columbine about what to expect, down to silverware and the timing of when dishes would be passed. She went to her room after tea and took a nap to refresh herself. Then she rose and bathed in a scented tub. She dressed with great solemnity. She wore her very best gown, an old one of Columbine's that she'd altered for Marguerite's slimmer figure, ruby-colored broché satin with a low-cut velvet bodice. The gown had less trimming than Marguerite would like, only some delicate white velvet roses with pale pink ribbon, but the material was fine and the color perfect for her white skin and red lips.

Even in the midst of work, Columbine could never resist sartorial preparation, and she knocked on Marguerite's door and offered to help. She was all breathless laughter as she buttoned Marguerite into her old gown. Marguerite watched herself in the mirror while she ran nervous fingertips along the rich velvet. It would be the first time she'd worn it. She'd never had anyplace grand enough to wear it before.

"Now for your hair," Columbine said. "A crystal ornament, I think. Let's pile it high, shall we?" She ran to the dresser to get pins and a hairbrush. Marguerite watched in the mirror as Columbine expertly twisted and pinned. "I do wish you'd tell me who your escort is, or where you're going, Marguerite," Columbine said around a mouthful of pins. "I never knew you were so mysterious."

"It's a trait I'd like to cultivate," Marguerite said, her eyes serious as a child's as she met Columbine's gaze in the mirror. "I want to be a mysterious woman."

"That's all very well, if it's directed at a suitor," Columbine said. She jabbed a pin in to anchor a curl, and Marguerite winced. "Oh, sorry, dear. As I said, I agree that a woman should have mystery. But with your friends, dear, it's quite another thing."

"I'll tell you tomorrow," Marguerite said. "But tonight, I want it all to myself. I don't want to spoil anything."

Columbine stopped, her hands in the air. Her eyes softened. "I remember," she said. "Of course you should have your secrets." She picked up the last lock of raven hair and twisted it into place. "There. You're done." She stepped back and looked at Marguerite in the mirror. "Oh, my," she said finally. "I don't think I realized how beautiful you are, Marguerite. You truly are."

Marguerite gave herself a critical look. She still looked too young, she thought. Too flat-chested. Not very mysterious at all. She needed more bosom for that. But she did look very pretty. "I'll do," she said.

"Aren't you critical. I know, I'll lend you my fur stole, and you'll dazzle all the guests. Just watch what your hostess does, and follow her, and you'll be fine. And don't be afraid to speak up! Remember, no matter how stuffy they appear, guests at a dinner party are secretly dying for fresh conversation from an intelligent and charming young woman."

As the cab jounced downtown, Marguerite tried to compose her nerves. She wished that she was arriving in a private carriage and not a hack. At least Toby had already paid for it.

Not for the first time, she wondered at the way she'd been invited to the dinner. She supposed that actors did things differently, a little more freely. These guests would not think it amiss that she was unescorted, she hoped. Toby had said he'd already be there, waiting for her. And he'd promised her that there would be important people there, society people.

The cab pulled up in front of a large, square building on a street in Greenwich Village. Marguerite's heart was fluttering as she descended to the pavement. She clutched her skirt in both hands—even though Columbine had instructed her once that a lady only used one hand, but immediately added with a laugh not to let it inhibit her—and ran up the stairs. At the top, she composed herself, taking a deep breath, and knocked.

The door opened immediately. The tall, spindly butler nodded, but did not take her wrap. "One flight up, door at the end of the hall, miss," he said.

Marguerite nodded, confused, but followed his pointing finger to the marble staircase. She climbed up in a stately fashion, her skirt held one-handed this time, but there was no one around to approve. At the top of the stairs she paused. Behind the double doors in front of her she heard heavy masculine laughter and shouts. But the butler had said the door at the *end* of the hall. Frowning now, Marguerite turned away and walked the length of the long hall. This didn't seem like a private house, but neither did it seem to have apartments. Marguerite reached the door at the end of the hall and pushed it open nervously.

It was a grand, opulent room, all plush purple velvet and gilded wainscoting, and it stretched the entire length of the building. The drapes that covered one entire windowed wall were heavy velvet, drawn against the dark night. The other walls were covered in lilac damask, and the gas was turned low. Enormous marble fireplaces were at either end of the room, and a huge fire was built in both. Marguerite took a few steps forward, and noticed that she was not alone. A girl sat on a gold satin couch, her blond head bent over some work in her lap. She looked up, and Marguerite saw a pretty, round face with perfect skin and china blue eyes. "Can you sew?" the girl asked. She was wearing a pretty pink gown in velours frappé, velvet stamped with a flowery design.

"Not very well," Marguerite lied, coming closer. She wasn't about to do this girl's mending for her.

"It's my costume. I tore it when I pulled it out of the pile. Look." The girl pointed to a gauzy, flesh-covered confection in her lap. Marguerite could see a tear along a seam, and a couple of crooked stitches that only called attention to the tear.

"I'm sorry," Marguerite said. "Are you in the theatre?"

The girl eyed her indignantly. "I should say I am. You wouldn't have seen Mollie Todd, would you?"

Marguerite sat down and slipped out of her furs. There was no one to take them, but it was dreadfully warm in the room. "No, I wouldn't have. I'm Marguerite Corbeau."

"Oh, Gladtomeetyou. I'm Gem Jackson. Toby sent you?"

Marguerite frowned as she watched Gem pick out the crooked stitches. "He invited me to the dinner, yes. Where is everyone? Am I terribly early? I must have got the time wrong."

"No, dearie, you're on time. They're just getting started in there. Oh, damn and blast this thing, I'll just leave the tear. Let me show you the shawls we have. They're so pretty."

"Shawl?"

"It's a seraglio theme, didn't Toby tell you? That's a harem." Gem giggled. "We're all wearing these Turkish things, and Mollie's going to be carried in wrapped in a rug, can you imagine? At least our shawls are pretty, wonderful silk, I hope we get to keep them." Gem jumped up and ran into an adjoining room, separated from the room they were in by double French doors. She kept the doors open, and Marguerite saw the adjoining room was domininated by a large round dining table. A dozen or so young women were sitting around it, eating chicken and lobster and picking with their fingers at various salads from silver serving dishes. There were three buckets of iced champagne. All of the women were in various stages of undress. Underneath one woman's satin dressing gown Marguerite glimpsed the same spangled gauze that Gem had torn.

Gem picked up a slice of ham and ate it. She licked her fingers. "Where are those shawls?" she asked a woman dressed in a rather soiled pink wrapper. Holding her champagne glass to her lips, the woman pointed to a corner with a delicate finger.

Marguerite stood up jerkily, like a marionette. When Gem returned, she hastened toward her, her blond curls bouncing. "Are you feeling poorly? Do you want supper? There's a nice spread in there for us. It's catered from Sherry's. Come on." She linked her rounded arm with Marguerite's. "I'll sit with you."

"What is this?" Marguerite asked shrilly. "Where am I? Where is Mr. Wells?"

Gem laughed. "Toby's always late. He always says he'll be here to greet us, and he never is. Don't get your dander up, sweetie, it's just his way. Come on, the girls are awfully nice."

"The girls . . ."

"And look at your shawl, isn't it pretty? I picked the blue one for you, it will suit you best. And it covers more than you'd think."

"*What?*" Marguerite almost screamed the word. Several of the women in the other room looked up sharply. Turning, she looked frantically for her bag and furs.

"There's no need to get all het up," Gem said, affronted. "I'm just trying to be make you feel like one of us."

"One of you? No thank you." Marguerite grabbed her bag and threw the fur cape around her neck. She felt on the edge of hysteria.

"Hey now." A tall, shapely brunette stood in the doorway of the dining room, a chicken leg in her hand. "What are you suggesting, Miss High and Mighty? We're all *entertainers* here."

Toby Wells chose this moment to sweep grandly in the door. He was in formal dress, and he swept his silk scarf off as he walked in. "Good evening, girls. I've arrived, and I'm—" Toby stopped short as he saw Marguerite's face. "Miss Corbeau, you're here already."

"Yes, I arrived on time," Marguerite said through clenched teeth.

His gaze traveled to Gem, then to the brunette. "What have you been telling her?"

Gem snorted. "What have *you* been telling her, Toby?" She bent down and grabbed her gauze costume.

"I'm leaving," Marguerite said tightly.

"No," Toby said, frantically signalling Gem toward the dining room while she pointedly ignored him, running her fingers through the gauze. "Miss Corbeau, let me explain. You have blundered onto a situation which—"

"I was invited!" Marguerite shouted at him.

"Of course, of course," he said soothingly. "But—"

"To a dinner," Marguerite continued. She felt close to tears, but she'd be damned if she'd let Mr. Toby Wells know it. "But by the looks of things, I am overdressed."

Gem laughed, and Toby threw her a poisonous look before extending his hands pleadingly to Marguerite. "Miss Corbeau. I ask only one thing. That you stay and let me explain. You could leave now, angry and hurt, and never know why I asked you here. Wouldn't you have the kindness to hear me out before you decide what to do?"

"Toby, didn't you tell her? You *are* a caution," Gem said.

"I'm leaving," Marguerite said icily.

"Wouldn't you rather hear about it than wonder?" Gem asked practically.

Marguerite stared at her round, friendly blue eyes. The girl had a point, she supposed. She pictured herself going home, in her fine gown, and trying to explain to Columbine. She sighed.

"All right, Mr. Wells. Explain, if you can."

"Okay. Okay." Toby ran a distracted hand through his hair. "Next door there's a dinner going on. Among the guests are the most distinguished men in arts and letters in New York. Stanford White heads the table, and around it are artists, writers, architects, the leaders of society—"

"Get to the point," Marguerite said tersely.

"Honey, he's telling the truth," Gem put in. "At least right there he is," she muttered.

"These ladies here tonight have been engaged for the purpose of entertainment. They are actresses, singers. Nothing nefarious, I assure you, will go on, nothing that would compromise your reputation—" and here, Gem rolled her eyes—"everything open and above board, I assure you. Why Gem, here, is an accomplished opera singer. Delilah is a dancer at the Plantagenet Theatre."

"And what is my talent, Mr. Wells?" Marguerite asked.

"You're pretty," Toby said bluntly. "And young. Why, in this light, you could pass for sixteen. Mr. White likes, uh, slender women. All you have to do is pour the champagne at the end of dinner, make conversation."

"And what will I be wearing while I 'make conversation'?" Marguerite persisted.

Toby looked uncomfortable. "A costume would be provided for you. Purely voluntary, of course. Tonight's theme is a seraglio. There'll be Turkish slippers, shawls, some harem outfits. You can choose whatever you want. You'll be decently covered."

Gem guffawed; then, at Toby's look, she smiled at him innocently. "She can't really choose, you know," she said. "The harem outfits are taken, and she'll have to wear the shawl. Mollie's in the rug, of course."

Marguerite felt as though her frozen brain was finally beginning to thaw. She had been so stupid, so naive! She thought of Columbine dressing her for an elegant dinner, and she wanted to burst into tears. But that wouldn't help matters. She wouldn't give that snake the satisfaction of knowing how she'd looked forward to this night.

She dropped her fur cape and picked up the shawl. It was light as gossamer, and heavily fringed. She threw it over her shoulders, and the fringe dripped down to a v between her legs. "Wear the shawl? You mean like this?" she asked innocently.

Gem laughed again. "Exactly, dearie. But without the gown." She held up the spangled gauze. "At least you're covered with *something.*"

Slowly, Marguerite let the shawl drop to the floor. "You swine," she said to Toby.

"Now, Miss Corbeau, I—"

"Procurer!" she flung at him.

"Now wait a minute," Gem put in. She turned to Marguerite impatiently. "No one is telling you to bed them. They're harmless enough, and half-drunk. All you have to do is prance around, and smile, maybe sit on a lap or two. Whatever else you do is your own business. And if you're lucky, you'll catch Stanny's eye. He's not a bad sort, he'll fix your teeth and be nice to your mum and lend you money without ever expecting to see it again. He gave Dolores diamond earrings—and she didn't sleep with him either, mind. This time I believe her."

Marguerite's curiosity got the better of her. "Is he married?"

Gem laughed merrily. "Of course he's married, most of them are married. Why else would they be here?"

"Gem, let me." Toby's voice was kind, even though Marguerite knew he must be terribly impatient. "Marguerite, I apologize most sincerely if I have offended you. I meant to explain before you came—"

"Why didn't you?"

His grin was abashed. "Frankly, I forgot."

"You *forgot*?" Marguerite couldn't believe it. Toby Wells had been on her mind every minute since she'd met him. She'd thought she dazzled him. She felt enormously hurt.

"It wasn't that I didn't think of you," he rushed to assure her. "But I was out of town, auditioning for a part in Boston. I just got back tonight. I didn't get the part, by the way."

"Good."

"You see," he said earnestly, "I saw you sitting there with Horatio Jones, bored out of your beautiful mind, and I thought, here's a girl who'll take hold of life and make it hers. You can have it all, Marguerite. You have the looks, and you have something else. You don't even realize that you have it."

"What do I have?" Despite herself, Marguerite was interested. She'd always been fascinated by what people thought of her.

"You have the ability to walk in the room and possess it," Toby said. His eyes were glowing, and she felt herself picked up by his vision. "People notice you. You *bristle*, my dear. Now, I don't want to offend you, but the best way I can put it is despite your lack of obvious, shall we say, physical charms, men long to bed you. You have something better than talent. If you can act or sing or dance at all, you could go on the stage. Let me know if you want to. If you have a little talent, it will go a long way."

Gem had lost interest in the middle of this speech and wandered back to the dining room for more champagne and chicken. "I'm very confused," Marguerite murmured.

Toby drew closer. "You'll make more money tonight than you'll make in six months, whatever you're doing now. If you're very, very good, you'll make more than you make in a year. And tomorrow you'll wake up and your room will be filled with roses. Maybe even a diamond necklace or two."

"Don't be ridiculous," Marguerite said, but she saw herself waking up to a roomful of roses, and she was bewitched. She had been respectable, and she had nothing to show for it. She had no scruples, so why was she pretending she did? She had already lost her virginity, and that experience had showed her that she was not the girl she thought she was. She was bad.

Toby had, in a few short words, unknowingly touched upon a secret desire she had nursed since childhood. *The stage.* What if he could really do it? What if he could get her on the stage?

And besides, she rationalized, going on the stage was no longer such a scandalous profession. Hadn't Jay Gould's son George married an actress? Now Mrs. Gould was entertaining in a Fifth Avenue mansion. Marguerite wouldn't be spoiling her chances by participating tonight. She might be ensuring her success!

She turned to Toby. "Could you really help me if I wanted to go on the stage? I can sing. I mean, my mother always said I could sing."

"Delightful. I knew it. Of course I can help you. I know everyone. You can come to my rooms tomorrow." He held up one hand. "Just business, I promise. I have a piano."

He took her elbow. There was no erotic charge to Toby; it was the touch of a brother, of a colleague. Marguerite knew, instinctively, that she could trust him. "But start tonight," he murmured, close to her ear. "Show me what you can do, tonight."

Nine

MARGUERITE WAS SMALL, the shawl was large, and she raided Gem's little tufted sewing box for pins. She anchored the shawl securely and prayed it wouldn't slip. The gauze left nothing to the imagination. Every time she looked down, she blushed. There were her legs, plain as day underneath her, soon to be stared at by a table full of strange howling gentlemen.

It wasn't too late to back out. Marguerite firmed her resolve with visions of roses and diamond earrings. She had never been shy; why was this unaccustomed modesty cropping up so inconveniently? But it was one thing to expose her breasts for a fleeting instant to Horatio Jones. Flashing them to a roomful of strangers was quite another thing.

The girls waited around the table toying with empty champagne glasses, for Toby had removed the champagne lest they get sleepy. But the silliness had worn off, and now they were bored. Next door at the grand dinner, the toasts went on and on. The longer it took the better, the seasoned girls advised. The drunker the men, the less agile their groping hands, and the sooner the night would end. With any luck, the old goats would be snoring on the tablecloth by two o'clock.

The elusive Mollie Todd wandered in sulkily at ten. She was the most beautiful creature Marguerite had ever seen, with shockingly white skin, pale as milk and translucent as moonlight, and hair the color of the most flaming sunset. She unpinned it before a mirror, and the girls watched, fascinated, as it spilled from a coil at the top of her head to lay, gleaming red-gold in the gaslight, spread across her breasts. Her eyes were catlike, green dusted with gold, and slanted at the corners. Her eyebrows were perfectly arched. She slipped out of her clothes and into a dressing gown and sat smoking cigarettes by a window, her long, luxurious legs crossing and recrossing restlessly.

"Man trouble, I suspect," Gem whispered to Marguerite. "She's in love with Willie P."

"Who?" Marguerite whispered, and Gem shook her head warningly and placed a finger on her lips. She mouthed "later," and Marguerite nodded.

At a quarter to eleven, Toby finally appeared. "You're on, girls," he said jovially, his amiable face flushed with liquor and excitement. "Mollie?"

Mollie Todd rose negligently, untied the braided cord on her gown, and let it slip from her ivory shoulders. She stood, resplendently nude, her red hair covering her bare white breasts. Marguerite watched, fascinated, as she crossed to the rug in the middle of the adjoining room and lay down on it, arranging her hair to cover her.

Toby was all business now, crossing to Mollie on the rug. "Comfortable?" he asked.

"Just hurry, will you?" Mollie said crossly.

Toby turned to one of the women. "Fannie, call the men in the next room—I'm not John L. Sullivan, I'll never manage to roll her up."

Fringe fluttering, a plump black-haired girl ran out the other door, and twelve huge, muscled black men marched back in. Their chests were magnificently bare, and they wore gold turbans and silky purple trousers that gathered at the ankle. One of them grinned and winked at Marguerite, whose mouth was open in astonishment, but none of the others even glanced at the rest of the girls. They simply crossed to the parlor, and, with great economy, took an end of the rug and rolled Mollie up in it like a crepe. They might have been a crew of workmen, so brawny and professional was their manner.

"Hurry, will you?" came the muffled voice from within. "I'm suffocating."

The men hoisted the rug with ease and settled it on their broad shoulders. Then, in single file, they went to the door of the parlor. Toby flung it open, and Marguerite heard their footsteps going down the carpeted hall.

She started after them, but Gem put a hand on her arm. "We still have time. Mollie's first."

"I want to see!" Marguerite whispered.

Gem grinned. "This way, then."

She led Marguerite through the other door of the dining room, into a smaller room where the men had been waiting. There, too, a supper was laid out, not as grand as theirs. Gem hurried through the room, opened another door, which led into a long room that Marguerite saw was an artist's studio of some kind. Quickly, they ran across the wooden floor to a double oak door.

"Not a sound, now," Gem whispered. She opened the door a crack, and pushed Marguerite forward. Then she knelt below her and placed her own eye to the crack.

Like the drawing room she'd entered at first, this room was all damask and voluminous velvet drapery. Huge paintings of pink nudes in ornate gilt frames hung against the crimson walls. Palms scraped the ceiling, and the chandelier was a magnificent creation in crystal hangings and rose-pink globes.

A long table dominated the room, now cluttered with brandy glasses, wine glasses, and champagne. The men lolled about, heavy with their meal, and most seemed either drunk or happy, or both. Toby had not exaggerated; she could see that these men were prosperous. Their evening clothes were impeccable, their white shirtfronts starched and snowy white. They looked portly and magnificent, and ranged in age from their twenties through their fifties, though most seemed in their thirties. But the effect of their magnificence was offset by their headgear. Each man was wearing a fez, and each man looked remarkably silly in it. Most were tilted askew on balding heads, and tassels waved in a feckless manner as the men reached for their wine glasses or laughed, their hands on their round bellies. Marguerite started to giggle, and she could not stop.

Gem poked her to quiet her, but started to giggle, too. Luckily, the double doors at the other end of the room opened, and the men began to cheer, drowning out any noises the two girls might be making. Marguerite stopped giggling and watched in fascination as the twelve black men carried in the Turkish rug.

They headed for a man at the foot of the table. He had a young face underneath a beard probably grown to make him look older. His red fez tilted precariously on his narrow head. He waved a champagne bottle and laughed uproariously. "So this is my present, Stanny," he said. "A Turkish rug. Original, I grant you."

"I went all the way to Turkey for that damn rug, Stiers," bellowed the man at the end of the table. Large and amiable, his hair was sandy red, and his face was flushed with drink and amusement. "It's one of a damn kind, too."

The table roared as the dozen black men brought the rug to the feet of Stiers. With a flourish, they unrolled it and the exquisite Mollie Todd was revealed. Marguerite couldn't believe the change. Could this be the same sulky, bored creature she'd seen in the other room? This woman was alive and sparkling. Her boredom had changed to an elegant langour. Her green eyes glittered as she stretched and smiled a radiant smile at Stiers. "Happy birthday," she said.

The men roared louder: they pounded the table with their fists and the floor with their boots. Fezzes went flying and champagne spilled onto the tablecloth. Marguerite traded excited glances with Gem.

"She's something, isn't she," Gem sighed enviously.

"Magnificent," Marguerite breathed. She couldn't take her eyes off Mollie. Was this what Toby had told her *she* possessed? Marguerite knew, at that moment, that it was what she wanted. For every man in the room was fascinated by Mollie as she sinuously rose and made her way to Stiers. Their mouths were open, their expressions rapt. Mollie appeared to have no shame about her nudity; she was a wood nymph, a creature accustomed to her body and its loveliness, as natural as a faun. She slipped into the young man's lap and twined a slender arm around his neck. Stiers looked merely embarrassed, and Marguerite found herself liking him for it. He gave a glassy smile as Mollie kissed him lightly on the lips.

"We're up next, dearie," Gem said in her ear. "Let's go."

Marguerite tore herself away from the crack in the door. Gem grabbed her hand, and together they ran back to their rooms. The girls were just beginning to stir, prompted by Toby. They grabbed shawls and smoothed hair and checked each other's appearance. Marguerite fussily adjusted her shawl.

"Who's Willie P.?" she whispered to Gem.

Gem shook her blond curls. "You *are* green. William Miles Paradise, the biggest theatrical producer on Broadway. He has a diamond head on his cane and his dog has a diamond collar. Mollie is the latest of his, oh, shall we say 'special projects.' He'll put her through hell, but he'll make her a star. Lucky girl," Gem sighed enviously.

Toby clapped his hands. "Follow me, girls," he called.

He led them quickly down the hall, pausing before the grand oak doors. He turned to examine them one last time in a professional manner. "Beautiful, beautiful. All right, girls. One, two, three: sparkle!" He threw open the doors, stood aside, and they spilled in.

At first, Marguerite was only conscious of noise and light. A roar of approval met their entrance, and several men stood and cheered. Marguerite tried to head for Stanford White at the head of the table, the man of the extravagant gift-giving propensities, but was swept along with Gem, down the far side of the table, as heads turned, one after the other, to follow their progress. Gem giggled and pranced and flicked the ends of her shawl and appeared to be having a marvelous time. She stopped in front of one gentleman, turned her back and wiggled her hips at him while he banged his wine bottle on the table and cried, "That's it, by jingo!"

Marguerite tried to smile as widely as Gem, but she felt rather silly. Some of the men were standing now, chasing down various girls and trying to capture their shawls. It was an easy conquest. Soon half the silky fringed shawls were drifting down to rest on the carpet. Were these the same bored girls who had disparagingly referred to the men as goats in the other room? Now these same young women blushed and cavorted and wiggled their way around the room. The once-melancholy Mollie Todd picked a shawl off the floor and eluded a pursuer with a laugh as she headed for Stanford White, to all eyes seeming a young girl on a festive picnic running toward a favorite uncle.

Legs and spangled-covered breasts swam before Marguerite's eyes, and she backed up steadily until she hit a tapestry-covered wall. But then she looked over to the double doors and saw Toby watching her with a frown. This was her chance. Was she destroying it because of a sudden, surprising shyness? She was being ridiculous; she could be as captivating as any of these girls!

Squaring her shoulders, she approached an older man sitting morosely at the table. She trailed her fringe along his shoulder and he looked up. Marguerite leaned over and kissed him gently on the lips, as she'd seen Mollie do. "It can't be that bad," she whispered, and he smiled. She sashayed on.

Perhaps champagne would help. Marguerite allowed a bushy-eyebrowed gentleman to pour her a glass while he watched her avidly. She drank a glass down in a gulp, and her situation improved immediately. She accepted another glass from another admirer, and sipped it sparingly while she eluded grasping hands, sat on laps, stroked beards, danced with Gem and then with a red-faced man who presented her with his fez.

Suddenly, the sound of banjo music filled the air, as Toby ushered three musicians into the room. A cry went up for a song. Toby banged a spoon against a crystal decanter until the men quieted. "Perhaps Miss Marguerite Corbeau will favor us with one," he said. His laughing eyes turned to her. There's your challenge, his eyes said. Show me.

Marguerite's lips pressed together for only an instant. She lifted her chin and tossed her head. "Perhaps one," she said flirtatiously. "For I'm in a mood to be generous tonight."

Applause and laughter rang through the air as one of the men stood, and with a flourish helped her up on the table.

The room had gone suddenly quiet. Marguerite felt her mind go blank. The banjo players looked at her expectantly. For the life of her, she could not think of a song other than "The Battle Hymn of the Republic," and that was hardly appropriate under these circumstances. The faces of the dinner guests looked like gaping fish to her. Their little red mouths were open, waiting . . .

A lyric of a popular song floated into her mind, and she grabbed it. The melody was easy, and she began by humming it softly. Behind her, Gem took up the melody and sang a pretty counterpoint. God bless Gem! Then the banjos picked it up.

Marguerite launched into "Father You Raised a Virtuous Girl, But the City is Full of Vice." Her low contralto began on a quaver, but she gained confidence quickly as she saw the men begin to smile. She caught each man's eye as she wrung every nuance of suggestiveness out of the lyrics. Standing on the table, Marguerite felt a strange power infuse her. And she'd thought being in bed with a man was exciting! Some of the pins had come loose on her shawl, and she tore the rest free and slid the silk off a shoulder or parted it to reveal a spangled thigh while she sang a song of innocence corrupted. She trailed the fringe along rapt faces; she clutched it to her modestly only to fling it wide again. The men were roaring their approval by the end, and they joined in on the choruses with energetic, though slightly off-key, fervor.

They stood and cheered when she finished, and she gave a low bow. As she lifted her head, she looked into the glittering eyes of Mollie Todd. Sparks of jealousy and spite jumped across the room at her, but Marguerite forgot them in the heady confusion.

She'd never felt so exhilarated. Pushing aside dishes and coffee cups and brandy glasses with a dainty booted foot, she danced her way to the end of the table and fell into the arms of Steirs, the birthday boy, who caught her with surprising strength.

Under the cheers, he gazed at her with moist hazel eyes. "Say, that was fine," he said. He held her securely against him, and Marguerite realized he wasn't as drunk as she'd thought. She slid down the length of his body and her feet hit the floor. In her high-heeled boots, he wasn't much taller than she was.

"Thank you, sir. You're very kind."

"And you're very pretty, Miss—"

"Corbeau." Her eyelashes fluttered downward. Marguerite thought it rather outrageous to pretend shyness under such circumstances, but why not? Modesty and transparent gauze could be an enticing combination.

"Will you have a glass of champagne with me?" Edwin Steirs looked down at the adorable creature who sang like an angel and had flung herself in his arms. Her black lashes cast shadows on her pale cheeks. She was as delicate as a bird. Most women made him feel small, unmanly. But this girl was all light and air. He could protect a girl like this. She looked up at him, and her eyes were the blue of a midnight sky.

"Thank you, sir," she said. Her voice was low and musical; it seemed to tease him even while it purred approval.

"I'm twenty-three today," he blurted.

Smiling demurely, Marguerite gathered the silk shawl around her. She sat in the red velvet seat and arranged the fringe to cover her like a lady. Holding out a hand, she accepted the champagne with a gracious smile. She noticed that Mr. Stiers wore no wedding band. "That is a very good age for a man to be," she said, while naked spangled girls sang and aging florid men joined in the ribald choruses. She'd had a wonderful time, but she wouldn't want to be trapped in this kind of life. There had to be another way, and she was just lucky enough to find it at once.

"Now, tell me more about yourself, Mr. Stiers. Tell me—oh, *everything.*"

Everyone was bribed not to talk, but the news got out anyway, and the Seraglio Dinner burst onto the New York winter gossip circuit, supplanting the already tired stories of Ambrose Hartley and the fireworks on New Year's Day. Stanford White retreated to his wife on Long Island and birthday bachelor dinners were for the time being off until the furor died down. Mollie Todd became an overnight celebrity, and William Paradise immediately spotlighted her in his newly opened revue and sent her six dozen roses every day for a week.

Marguerite awoke to roses the next day as well, from Edwin Steirs. There was no diamond necklace that day, but one arrived two weeks later, when she slept with him. Marguerite hid it in her purse and only put it on when she was in a private hired carriage heading for Delmonico's to meet Edwin. She enjoyed the thrilling secretiveness of her new life, for Edwin needed time before he announced his love to his family. Meanwhile, Marguerite had Toby Wells, her new friend and music teacher (Edwin paid for the lessons, of course) to amuse her. Marguerite took up smoking and began to buy silk stockings.

She put off Horatio Jones for two weeks, arranging to be out when she knew he would call—he was such a methodical creature—and ignoring his messages. Finally she agreed to see him when she grew afraid he would, in an excess of passion, follow her right to Edwin Steirs' private dining room at Delmonico's, where so far most of their encounters took place.

She met Horatio in Central Park. He looked miserable, his hat jammed down too far on his head. He must have walked all the way there, for his face was red with cold. She felt quite sorry for him. She greeted him with a cool nod, and they turned without a word and headed down a gravel walk.

"Why have you been avoiding me, Horatio?" she asked petulantly as soon as they were past a group of young girls with their nannies.

Shocked, Horatio looked into her still white face. "Me? Marguerite, my dear, how can you say such a thing to me? I've sent you a note every day, I've called—"

"Duty, merely," she flung out. "You've bedded me, and so you'll be a gentleman about it." There was a flash of something across Horatio's face, for she'd hit her mark, and she pressed on. "I knew I could never drive Bell out of your heart!" she cried.

"Marguerite, please, listen to me—"

"No," she said, walking more rapidly, "Every word cuts me to the heart, Horatio. You will never love me, I know that now."

"But, Marguerite—" Horatio tried. He wanted to tell her that he *could* love her, that though Bell would always be part of him, it was time to go on. He felt foolish and callow continuing to yearn for a woman who didn't want him. He wanted to lose himself in Marguerite.

But Marguerite interrupted him again. "Please don't continue," she said. She stopped abruptly and turned to face him. "It's my fault as well as yours, Horatio. I pursued you shamelessly. I let my heart run away with me."

"It is to your credit that you did so, dear," he said gently. "I never blamed you for that."

She bit her lip. "I know, you were very kind." Suddenly, Marguerite felt exasperated. Horatio *had* been very kind. She was grateful to him. But he was in her way! She was terrified that he had begun to love her, now that she was sure that she would never possibly want him. "Horatio," she began again, softly and reasonably, "I release you from your obligation to me. If I cannot be first in your heart, I don't want to be there at all."

He looked around him at the bare trees, confused. Didn't she love him, after all? She had whispered so often of her love, her devotion. And she was giving him up? "But I cannot be with Bell," he said. "She has made that clear. And with time, her image can be supplanted by another. Marguerite, I am being most sincere. I cannot lie to you. I will never lie to you. I was in love with Bell, and such feelings do not die away overnight. But I will be true to you."

Marguerite gave an ironic smile, and suddenly she did not look as young as she usually did. "I have enough vanity to say that I could not wait for the day when you consider me first, Horatio." She touched his arm, and he noticed how fine her glove was. He wondered, fleetingly, how she could have afforded such a fine kid glove, trimmed in sable. "I release you," she said softly. "I will not be an obligation to you any longer."

"But, Marguerite—"

She went up on her tiptoes to kiss him on the cheek. Her lips were cold. "Goodbye, dear Horatio. I'll never forget you."

And then she was gone, walking rapidly down the path the way they'd come. Horatio stared after her for a few minutes, then sank onto a bench and stared at his shoes. He felt dizzy, as though he'd been furiously waltzing in a bright ballroom for hours without a rest, whirling around and around and around, his vision growing blurred and his mind fevered, while a slight young body twisted and turned beneath him. Now his hands were empty, and he had nothing. He felt stunned, and he realized that it was very cold, and he was alone.

"Thank you for seeing me, Mr. Van Cormandt," Elijah Reed said.

Ned nodded. "Of course, Mr. Reed. How are you enjoying New York City?"

"Very much," Elijah answered.

"I read your story in the *Century*," Ned remarked pleasantly.

"Yes," Elijah said, "and I understand it caused you some difficulty. I'm sorry for that."

Ned waved a hand. "Nothing worth mentioning. I thought it was an excellent article, and I was happy to see the story printed, though little good it did," he said with a grimace. "All New York, it seems, is enjoying clucking over the details of the Seraglio Dinner and exactly what shade of peacock blue the shawls were made of. Now, what can I do for you?"

Elijah shifted in his seat a bit. "This is rather awkward . . ." he began. Damn, he hated feeling uncomfortable. He never should have come. But he was here.

"Please don't hesitate," Ned said. His light green eyes were genial, warm. He was a good man, Elijah saw. "If I can help you with something, please be assured that I am at your disposal, Mr. Reed."

"It's about Mrs. Nash," Elijah said, and he saw the other man start. Ned covered it by reaching for his cigar box. He offered it to Elijah, and he took one. While they went through the masculine ritual of lighting them, Ned regained his composure. His eyes were placid when they returned to Elijah's face.

"Yes, Mr. Reed?"

"I've become acquainted with Mrs. Nash through the lecture series I'm arranging for Cooper Union."

"Yes, yes, excellent series, I got a subscription ticket. Unfortunately, I'll be making frequent trips to Washington, so I'll miss a few of the talks."

"I've noticed that she had made the acquaintance of a young man, about twenty-eight or so, a Mr. Lawrence Birch."

Ned's face darkened immediately. "I have met Mr. Birch."

Elijah felt encouraged by Ned's reaction. "I must be frank, Mr. Van Cormandt. I do not know Mrs. Nash very well, so I feel uneasy in interfering in her life, in suggesting that the lady might be taken advantage of by a man of whom she knows nothing. Nevertheless, I felt I had to act. I took the liberty of digging into the man's past a bit." Elijah cleared his throat, a sure sign that he was nervous. "I've done a little investigating, and I believe that Mr. Birch is unscrupulous, and possibly dangerous."

"He's an anarchist," Ned said. He said it to stall; it was a technique of his to state a fact instead of offering an opinion.

"He claims to be, yes. But I know many anarchists in New York, Mr. Van Cormandt. And they themselves are leery of Mr. Birch. There was some trouble in San Francisco, you see. And the group out West sent back reports of Mr. Birch that suggested that he possibly might have been acting as an informer. He was playing a double game, and a profitable one it was. There was a bomb plot on a prominent financier. Lawrence came up with the plot, but the anarchists believe that he warned the man himself and was paid for it."

Ned puffed on his cigar. "But they are not certain."

"No, they are not. But the New York group is wary. It is apparent from what one called his vague and fatuous opinions that he is not grounded in anarchist literature and has but a generalized sense of their ideas. The group is wary, you see, for their cause unfortunately has a tendency to attract the unstable. They doubt his commitment. He seems to espouse the cause for the drama it gives him. These are opinions merely that I'm repeating, of course. I don't wish to slander the man."

"Of course not."

"And I would have said nothing if other things did not come to light, other connections. . . . No one seems to know how he lives, Mr. Van Cormandt."

"Yes, I've wondered about that myself."

"Which gives credence to the point that he was an informer out West, and well paid for it. I cannot discover one fact about his background. But in the course of my story about the Hartleys I discovered something that I dismissed at the time. There was a stranger hanging about that night, this servant said. Everyone was busy with the great party, so security was lax. And this stranger was described as tall, and dressed well. The only specific thing the man could recall were his strange, pale eyes."

"You're suggesting it was Mr. Birch? That sounds like quite a leap, Mr. Reed. There could be many men who—"

"Yes," Elijah interrupted, "I realize that. I didn't make the leap at first. I could find no other account of this stranger, so I forgot about it. I certainly didn't think of it when I first met Mr. Birch. But I've discovered that Mr. Birch has a connection with Fiona Devlin. The wife of the injured man. Mr. Birch has been a go-between for Mrs. Nash with the Devlins. And I believe, Mr. Van Cormandt, that he has passed false information between them."

Ned tapped the ashes on his cigar. "Pray continue, Mr. Reed."

"He told Mrs. Nash that they have a benefactor, though I happen to know they are still living in the direst poverty. Mrs. Nash offered to testify on their behalf, but the Devlins believe that she has refused to do so."

"But what would his object be in such a scheme?"

"I don't know yet. I was told that the Devlins hate Mrs. Nash for this. I haven't talked to them directly to correct their misapprehension. I wanted to speak with you first."

"Is there more?"

"I'm afraid so. Mr. Birch told Mrs. Nash that he only arrived in New York the night of December thirty-first. I have information that he had actually arrived one week before and stayed in a hotel on the West Side."

Ned gave a thin smile. "You have been busy, Mr. Reed."

"It's the writer's disease, Mr. Van Cormandt. Obsession with unraveling a thread. And I'm also a journalist; you'd be surprised how full a city is of eyes and ears."

Ned studied the end of his cigar. "May I ask why you have gone to such lengths for a lady you are, as you say, only briefly acquainted with?"

Elijah said nothing for a moment; he didn't know what to say. He wasn't sure of his reasons, and he didn't think he'd care to admit them even if he were. "May I claim chivalry as my motive, Mr. Van Cormandt?" he asked finally.

Ned studied the man for a moment. The air of gravity, the power that he exuded just sitting in a chair. Could it be that this wise man had no knowledge of his own heart? It was very obvious to Ned why Elijah Reed had become suddenly obsessed with unraveling a thread.

Things ran through Ned's mind, things he could have said, for he liked and respected Elijah Reed. Things about Columbine's independence, and her pride. That she claimed she would never marry again. That she was capable of breaking a man's heart, for she was a woman who would not be possessed, and what man did not want to feel he possessed the woman that he loved?

But Ned said none of these things. If Elijah Reed was to be Columbine's next lover—and it broke his heart to imagine this, but face it he must—he wouldn't listen to Ned. And didn't Ned owe it to Columbine, finally, to respect her views enough *not* to advise Elijah? He wouldn't pass Columbine along to another man like a prize. For she would see it that way.

"You may claim whatever motive you wish," he said at last. "But what is your motive in coming to me?"

"I can hardly repeat this to Mrs. Nash. I'm sure she would not listen."

"I'm sure she would not," Ned agreed.

Elijah leaned forward slightly. "But she would listen to you, Mr. Van Cormandt."

Ned sighed. "I can hardly repeat gossip to Mrs. Nash, Mr. Reed. She would despise any attempt to slander Mr. Birch without proof. Columbine has been maligned and slandered herself. She gives everyone the benefit of the doubt. No, she would not listen to me either."

"But you have nothing to lose," Elijah pointed out. "She won't ban you from her house if you take the liberty."

Ned nodded slowly. "I see," he said. "You want Mr. Birch banished from Mrs. Nash's house, but you do not want to take the chance of being banished yourself. You leave to me to be scorned, since I have been already."

Elijah's color rose. Ned had neatly placed a finger on the flaw in his good intentions, and he felt ashamed. "I assure you, sir, I did not come here for that reason," he said painfully. "I would not want to tarnish your friendship with Mrs. Nash. If you feel that would be the outcome, I certainly would not wish you to undertake such a mission."

"It's all right, Mr. Reed, I'll not hold a grudge. I understand. But I still am not sure if I can do any good."

Elijah leaned forward, his hands clasped between his knees. He would have to play his last card, and he was reluctant. It was just a hunch, after all. "I think he might be planning something that could hurt her," he said. "I cannot prove it. But neither can I leave her unwarned."

"What makes you think this?"

"A few things," Elijah said. "Let me start with California. I should tell you about the job Lawrence Birch had before he began his anarchist newspaper, which, in fact, he did not begin but took away from a man who was arrested."

Ned puffed on his cigar. "What was Mr. Birch's profession?"

"He worked for the railroads. He dynamited tunnels through rocks. He's an expert in explosives, Mr. Van Cormandt."

Ned slowly rose as the implications snaked through his brain. It could mean nothing at all, he told himself. But he looked into Elijah Reed's sorrowful eyes, and he found himself nodding. "I'll talk to her," he said.

Lawrence saw Fiona that night, and, for the first time, he found the sex dull. She wanted him too much now. He tried to think of Columbine, but Bell kept floating into his thoughts. To his surprise, this excited him, and he seized on her image while he had Fiona against the pilings. He pictured Bell underneath him with that passivity, that inert quality, that sense of deadened sexuality. He pictured her not resisting, not joining, only allowing. And that excited him more.

When it was over, he cleaned himself with a handkerchief while Fiona straightened her clothes. "Soon it'll be getting warmer," she said. "Spring is coming. We'll have to find a new place to go."

"We have another month at least," Lawrence said.

"I'll be going. Next week, then?"

"Stay a minute, Fiona," he said, and she leaned against the piling again, perhaps hoping for another time. She would be disappointed, though. He had done more than any man could tonight, God knew. What with this biting wind off the river, it was a wonder he was able to get hard at all.

"Did you hear the news? Ambrose Hartley had a heart attack."

Her lip curled. "Heaven be praised, my prayers have been answered. I just might believe in the Lord again."

Lawrence leaned against the piling, his head against hers. "So a vain, foolish, cruel man is felled. But the hypocrisy he is part of continues to flourish. The machine that crushed you and Jimmy."

"I'm not crushed yet, Birch."

He reached underneath her skirts and squeezed her bare, icy hand. "That's why I admire you, Fiona. You're cruel and fierce and fast. You can strike a blow that the city will never forget. Ambrose Hartley was not a good enough target for you, anyway."

Slowly, she pushed herself off the pole and turned to face him. The moonlight caught her eyes, highlighting the golden patch in one corner. "What are you talking about?"

Lawrence stepped forward into the moonlight. He looked into her eyes, and he felt excited again. "Revenge," he said.

Ten

COLUMBINE AND BELL collapsed on a bench in Washington Square Park. It had been a cold day, but there was brilliant, strong sun, and after leaving one of the brick houses on the square they'd turned without a word and crossed together to the park. They sank onto the first bench they came to. Morosely, they stared across the park at the Judson Memorial Church.

"I don't know where to go anymore," Columbine said. "Admiral Cole was my last resort. All my sources have dried up. We have no money to lease a house, let alone furnish it. I wish I had bought that house on Twenty-third Street instead of leasing it! Then we'd have some capital. Even considering what I can get from England, we come up way too short."

Bell flexed a weary foot. "There must be someone else we can try."

"I'll think of someone. It's odd, how difficult this fundraising has been. Usually we have more success."

"Especially after all the publicity you received from your speech," Bell said. "It *is* odd."

Columbine sighed. "Maybe we should just concentrate on augmenting the Emergency Fund."

"But we agreed that money isn't enough. These women need a place to live," Bell pointed out. "It's the only way we can make a difference."

"I know, I know. But—" Columbine stopped abruptly. "There's

no sense going over it again. I have a feeling this is somehow connected to the Hartley-Devlin incident. I'm *persona non grata* among the aristocrats these days."

"Perhaps Horatio could help," Bell said. "He could write an article about you, keep your name in the news."

Columbine heard Bell finally speak the name she'd wanted to ask her about for weeks, and she immediately dropped her concerns about the Safe Passage House to focus on her friend. "And what about Horatio, Bell?" she asked. "I can't help but notice that the two of you have had a rupture of some kind. Even though he calls constantly."

"He calls to see Marguerite. She's fallen in love with him."

Columbine gasped. "I didn't know."

"She's very discreet. I suppose she doesn't want to hurt me. But I never loved Horatio. I'm glad he's happy—if in fact he is. Somehow I've never been sure of Marguerite."

"Yes, I'm fond of her, but—well. She's very young."

"Columbine, you always say that about Marguerite, as if it excused everything," Bell said with sudden sharpness.

"I'm fond of Marguerite, I can't help it. Even though I'm sure there are things we don't know about her. She's cultivating mystery these days. But Bell, you don't seem hurt by Horatio's desertion. Or are you? You've seemed so . . . spiritless lately. Every time I ask, you—"

"Put you off, I know." Bell sighed. She would never confide in anyone about her struggles, she knew. Especially not Columbine, for wouldn't Lawrence Birch be Columbine's next lover? For all she knew, they were already. "I don't know what it is, Columbine. I feel restless and unhappy without knowing the cause. It will pass."

"You know that usually I do not propose this remedy," Columbine said, "but you need a man, Bell. You need to open your heart to someone. I thought it would be Horatio, but since it's not, there are plenty of other candidates, and well you know it."

Bell blushed furiously. To hide it, she ducked her head, glad for the felt brim of her hat, which shaded her face. "Really, Columbine."

"Oh, Bell, don't be girlish. You're simpering like Maud Hartley. I'm telling you a truth."

Bell sighed. "I do hate that imperious tone of yours."

"Do I sound imperious? Oh, dear. But I *am* right."

Bell decided it was high time to turn the tables. "And what about you and Lawrence Birch?" she asked. Mentioning the name made her blush even more. Luckily, Columbine had looked away to idly watch a baby toddling after his nurse.

"He is diverting, I own," she admitted. "He's filled up some very empty hours. And he *is* the most attractive man I've ever seen, I think. Those blue eyes! But something pulls me back from Lawrence, I don't know what it is."

"You would consider . . ." Bell stopped. She didn't know quite how to put it, even to frank Columbine.

"Being his lover? Well, I *consider* everything," Columbine said with a laugh. "But no, I don't want Lawrence as a lover. He's too young, too volatile."

Bell felt an enormous sense of relief. If Lawrence was Columbine's lover, he would be about the house even more than he was already. She didn't think she could bear that. Her nerves were already screaming from having him around as much as he was. So why had Columbine kissed him? she wondered. And had it been only one kiss, an isolated incident, a passing temptation? She wished she had the nerve to ask.

She tried a different tack. "Is it his politics that give you pause, then?"

Columbine lifted her shoulders. "No, not really. I met Prince Kropotkin in London, you know, and I was almost converted. He is so charming! But I'm opposed to anarchism. It's the violence I abhor. And it's a very naive ideology, and most naive ideologies are dangerous. I said that to Lawrence, of course, and he disagreed. But so charmingly! He talked of Emerson and Thoreau, of an indigeneous American hostility to government authority. He doesn't speak of Bakunin, he doesn't spout that 'every bourgeois will have his bomb' rhetoric. Thank goodness. No, I think his politics are of the soap box variety. He's harmless in *that* way at least. He's been working on an article for *Die Freiheit* over the past few weeks. So I've been spared that test of my womanly virtue," she said with a laugh. "It's easy enough to resist a charmer when he makes himself scarce."

• • •

Marguerite approached Columbine before teatime. She had to seize the moment, even though Columbine was at work, for there always seemed to be people dropping in for tea. If nobody else, there would be the ever-present Lawrence Birch.

"May I have a word?" she asked tentatively, for Columbine was bent over papers, scribbling furiously.

Columbine removed the spectacles she wore for close work. "Of course. You know what we need, don't you, Marguerite?"

Marguerite masked her impatience under a quiet smile. "What, Columbine?"

"A girl who speaks Yiddish. We need to reach the East Side with this issue."

Marguerite's eyes slid away from Columbine's. She smoothed her skirts.

"But you didn't come to speak about work, did you," Columbine said. "I'm sorry. Sit down, dear." Columbine pushed the papers away and turned her desk chair to face the small sofa. She noticed now how blooming Marguerite looked, how pretty in her new dress of Nile green silk with Irish guipure lace. Not for the first time, Columbine wondered how Marguerite was managing on her small salary. Lately she'd noticed new hats, fine lace, gloves lined with sable, and now she saw a tiny pair of emerald earrings in Marguerite's pretty ears. Horatio did not seem the type to shower his lover with gifts, though one never knew. But how could Horatio Jones afford emerald earrings? He came from a good family, but Columbine knew that he did not have such money to spend.

Marguerite sat in a rustle of fine silk. "Columbine, I'll always be grateful to you for taking me in. But it's time I went out on my own. I'll be moving into my own apartments. You see, I've been taking singing lessons, and my teacher thinks I have promise. He's told me, however, that I must practice all the time. I have to leave the New Women Society and devote myself entirely to my music."

Columbine nodded slowly. Did Marguerite really expect her to believe this? Surely the girl was leaving something out, namely how she would finance such a life. Columbine could not imagine Horatio Jones setting up Marguerite in an apartment any more than she could imagine him buying her jewels. Something was not right. "I wish you well, Marguerite," she said slowly, wondering how much she could ask. "I must tell you that Bell confided in me about Mr. Jones. She told me you're in love with him. Forgive me if I pry—it's only out of concern. Do you two plan to marry?"

Marguerite almost laughed. Horatio Jones seemed such a distant memory to her. Edwin Stiers had filled her days and nights for weeks. "Columbine, I haven't seen Horatio in ages. I thought I was in love with him, but it really was just an infatuation."

"I see." There was another man, then. By Marguerite's manner, Columbine knew that the subject was not open to discussion. But she felt responsible. Marguerite was her charge, in a way. The girl had no family. She couldn't stay silent. "Again, forgive me if I pry, Marguerite. But I don't want to see you become involved in a situation which—"

Marguerite stood abruptly. Her small, heart-shaped face was suddenly closed. "Please, Columbine. Please just wish me well. I no longer," she said carefully, "wish to take direction from you. I want to stand on my own two feet."

"And will you be standing on your own two feet in your new accommodations?" Columbine asked dryly.

Marguerite's mouth shut in a thin line. "So you condemn me." Her eyes blazed. "How dare you condemn me? You're the one who taught me about free love."

Columbine sighed. "I hope that I have also taught you about responsibility, Marguerite. The idea of free love was born because of all the women trapped in loveless marriages. It merely said sex should be tied to love, not property. It should be given freely, not forced or coerced. It does not mean license. The essential cornerstone is responsibility shared by two adults. And if you do choose to marry, I want you to marry for love. Not blind love, not passion, but love and friendship both."

Marguerite made an impatient gesture. "That's fine for your articles and such. But Columbine, we're living *now.* You know that a woman needs a man. That her status is tied to him. Why shouldn't I marry for that, if I want it? Won't that better women's state too?"

Columbine looked weary, as she'd heard this argument many times before. "I believe that it's a sad thing if we limit ourselves in life to what things *are.* Why shouldn't our behavior be guided by what *should be*? It's the only way, as women, we can live fulfilling lives. Look at Dr. Dana."

"But she's not married."

"And yet she is happy, Marguerite, for she has work she believes in. Did you know that she *was* married? Her husband would not allow her to go to medical school. It was a very painful decision for Meredith, but she eventually left him."

Marguerite said nothing. She didn't agree with Columbine at all. Dr. Dana seemed harried and half-killed most of the time. She hadn't bought a new dress in ages. How could Columbine miss the desperation in her friend's lives? Even the most fiercely political of them had trouble balancing their domestic lives. She couldn't think of one who was happy in love, not even Columbine. But she didn't want to argue.

Seeing Marguerite's face shut down, Columbine relented. "I just want you to be careful, Marguerite," she said softly. "I care about you."

"I'm obliged to you for that, Columbine, but I still have my own way of doing things."

Columbine nodded. "And that is only right. Let me say one thing, and I'll have done. See Dr. Dana. She's only a few doors down. She has information on ways to prevent conception, and she can help you. Promise me you'll go, Marguerite," she said softly.

But Edwin took care of all that! He said if a man utilized an Eastern method of control, a woman would not get pregnant. He had it on good authority. Still, it would make Columbine feel better if she thought Marguerite would follow her one last—thank God!—piece of advice. "I promise, Columbine," Marguerite said. She bent down and kissed Columbine, for she was fond of her. She'd been more of a mother to her than her own these past two years. "And I'll come see you, often."

Suddenly, Columbine felt sad at the thought of Marguerite leaving. Bell could be so reserved, and Marguerite had added shrieks and yes, sulks and emotion to the house. "Yes, you'll come often."

Not really believing the sentiment, but wanting to, the two women kissed. Behind Marguerite, Columbine saw the parlor door open. Ned walked in. She hadn't seen him in three weeks.

She stood up abruptly, knocking her papers to the floor. "Ned."

"Bell let me in," he said. He stood in the middle of the room awkwardly. "Good afternoon, Miss Corbeau."

Marguerite gave Ned her hand, then left quickly after a hurried glance at Columbine. She felt the tension between the couple, and she felt sorry for Columbine. Marguerite would never bungle things as Columbine had. Edwin might have half the brains of Ned, but at least as much of the money, and a sweetness she found endearing and irritating by turns. She could manage him. She could even love him.

The door closed quietly behind Marguerite, and Ned and Columbine looked at each other. She looked well, he saw. Those violet tinges underneath her eyes were gone.

"You look very well," he said.

"Thank you. I'm actually sleeping through the night, these days. Won't you sit down?"

Ned seated himself in the armchair across from hers. "Bell told me you've had trouble raising funds for the Safe Passage House," he said.

"Yes, I'm afraid so. I thought perhaps it was because of the article in the *Century*. Your friends seem to have closed ranks."

He frowned, and she saw he was truly angry. "Please don't call them my friends."

"I didn't mean it that way, Ned."

"Well, at any rate, your suspicions are correct. Maud Hartley has put out the word. She's never forgiven you for that night, Columbine, and for other things. Capturing me, for starters," he said with a twisted smile.

"So I should not bother attempting to raise funds on Fifth Avenue any longer," Columbine said.

"Well, I'm sure there are some people who don't listen to Maud. You know who they are as well as I."

"I read in the paper," Columbine said, changing the subject, "that you've been busy."

"Yes, my life is primarily in Washington."

"I hope it's going well."

"It has its frustrations, but yes."

Columbine sat, trying to keep a pleasant expression on her face. She had no idea why Ned had come, but she would be damned if she made any more small talk.

Now, Ned looked uncomfortable. He shifted his position. He reached down and adjusted the angle of his gloves in his hat. "Columbine, I've come today for two reasons. I'll get to the second in a moment, but first, I want to make a proposition to you that I dearly hope you will accept."

Columbine hid her apprehension under a smile. "I hope I can do so, Ned."

Ned paused. He fumbled in his pocket and came up with a ring of keys, which he slid onto her desk. "I wanted to give you these."

She picked up the keys, heavy in her palm. "And they are?"

"They are the keys to the house on West Tenth Street."

Columbine gave him a startled glance, then looked at the keys.

"I bought it when I thought we might be married. Now I want to give it to you for the Safe Passage House."

Stunned, Columbine continued to stare down at the keys in her hand. Her thoughts were moving so sluggishly.

"It's larger than you might think. We didn't use but that one bedroom," Ned said without a blush. "Five bedrooms all together, but three floors, so there's plenty of space. And remember the attic studio, with that slanted ceiling and the skylight? I took you up there once, and you said it would make a beautiful room."

"I remember, Ned," Columbine said, looking down. They'd made love on a blanket on the floor, on a chilly spring day.

"It has four baths, one behind the kitchen. It's an odd house, full of angles and stairs, but there is a spacious feeling to it, I think."

"Ned, I can't. . . . The house you wanted to be *our* house," Columbine stumbled over the words.

"But don't you see that you must take it, just for that reason? Columbine, I can never live in that house. But *you* can. And it would give me great pleasure if you would use it for Safe Passage. It would honor me, and us, if that house was used for that purpose."

"Ned—"

He reached out for the first time and touched her, closing his hand over hers. The keys bit into her palm. "You must allow me to do this. I couldn't bear to sell it. I'll be sending over an attorney to go over the details with you." Ned relaxed his grip. She opened her hand, and he saw the red marks of the key on it.

"There's something else," he said.

She looked at him with cloudy eyes, still not sure if she should refuse the gift. "Something else?"

Ned sat down again. "I need to talk to you about Lawrence Birch," he said.

The blue eyes of Johann Most flicked over the manuscript in his hand. His deformed jaw, the result of a childhood accident, seemed to tighten. He was an ugly man, but a compelling one. It had taken Lawrence over a month to get up the nerve to attempt an article for his weekly, famed over the world.

Lawrence waited patiently. He had submitted the article three days ago, and had finally gotten up his nerve to come in to the offices of *Die Freiheit*. He'd only hoped to badger one of the assistants for information. But the great Most himself had called him back to his desk. "Yes, I've read your article," he'd told Lawrence. Then he proceeded to ignore him and read it again.

Now, his eyes slowly lifted from the page. "I wanted to be sure," he said in his heavy German accent. "I read it first when I was tired. So when it seemed like a worthless piece, I threw it aside."

Lawrence's face had been frozen in an expression of agreeable intelligence, but as the words slowly sank in, his facial muscles went slack. "I beg your pardon."

"Do not beg my pardon," Most said tiredly, handing the papers to him. "I will not pardon you for writing slop. Go away, young man. Come back when you have something important to say. This," he continued with more spirit, jabbing a thick finger at the pages, "is merely a *pastiche*, you know this word?"

Lawrence stiffened. "Of course."

"A pastiche of ideas and words you have read and heard. So go home and think harder. Better yet," he went on as Lawrence turned and walked through the fusty office, through dust motes spinning in a shaft of white sunlight, "do not think at all! Do you know what Kropotkin said, that ninny?"

Lawrence turned, speechless. Prince Kropotkin, the brightest light on the anarchist scene, a ninny? The beloved man was a Russian of noble birth, twice imprisoned, now in exile in London. He had swept aside the violent rhetoric of Bakunin to espouse a more philosophical approach, stressing freedom and cooperation as an anarchist ideal. He was a beloved figure, known for his sweet temper. Lawrence couldn't imagine anyone who would dare call him a ninny but Johann Most.

Most gave him a baleful stare. "Even gentle Kropotkin, my young friend, said that a single deed is better propoganda than a thousand pamphlets. You understand the Propaganda of the Deed? Men such as you should not be *thinking!* You are not good at it, my friend."

Lawrence was in agony. He saw the other workers, how studiously they bent over their tasks, how carefully they must be listening. "Thank you, Herr Most," he said at last. He wondered at the power of a man who could command a thank you after an insult. The tips of his ears burned with humiliation as he turned and walked out of the *Frieheit* offices. Once again, he'd been thwarted. Once again! Perhaps that awful Emma Goldman—one of Most's disciples, and probably in his bed—had prejudiced the great man against him. He wouldn't be surprised.

He stood on the sidewalk, wondering where to go. He'd planned to celebrate the publishing of his article with Columbine. He thought it was the first step on the road to matching her celebrity. Opening his fingers, he allowed the pages he had labored over for so many hours to drop to the pavement. A gust of chill wind danced them down the street.

His thoughts turned to Columbine. Yet another failure. Lawrence grimaced and began to walk. He might as well admit that his campaign to seduce her was not going as well as he expected. There were times Lawrence thought she was close to falling, times when her eyes would soften, her body seem to yearn toward him, but if he tried to embrace her, she would move away. Suddenly, anger swept over him at the thought of her. He was tired of rejection. He had had enough.

It was dusk when he arrived at Twenty-third Street. Teatime. His mouth was watering as he climbed the stairs. Columbine always had such fine teas, a holdover from her aristocratic days in

England. There were usually sandwiches, and scones and cream, and wonderful little cakes she bought from Mrs. Tolliver next door.

Marguerite let him in, an odd expression on her face. Usually she ignored him, but today she waited while he took off his coat. And then he heard it, too—raised voices from Columbine's parlor.

He raised his eyebrows at Marguerite.

"It's Mr. Van Cormandt," she said. "Perhaps you should return some other time."

"Perhaps I should," Lawrence said mechanically, but he stayed rooted to the carpet, listening intently. Then, when Marguerite looked at him quizzically, he said, retreating to the back of the hall, "I'll just wait a moment and see if Mr. Van Cormandt goes."

Marguerite gave him a shrewd glance underneath spiky black lashes. Then she shrugged and retreated back up the stairs. Whatever was not directly connected with her, she didn't bother with. And she had to pack.

As soon as she'd passed the landing, Lawrence went to the parlor door. He didn't have to press his ear to the crack. The voice came through clearly. He'd never heard Columbine angry before.

"You should know me better than this, Ned," she said. "To come to me with accusations! With hearsay, innuendo. Do you expect me to adjust my behavior according to this?"

"Yes!" Lawrence heard quick footsteps cross the room. "Yes. You don't have to bar the house to him, but yes, you should be wary."

A chill passed over Lawrence. They were discussing him, of course. What had Ned found out? Had he gathered information from California?

"And Mr. Reed, too," Columbine stormed on. "I would think a journalist had some objectivity. A few doubts, a few hesitations from a few anarchists downtown, and he makes the charge of informer—how ludicrous!"

Reed! He had spoken to people downtown. No wonder everyone was distant with him! Reed had poisoned their minds. He had probably gotten through to Most, as well! Lawrence felt rage overtake him. He began to shake. Always, people were against him. Again and again he found that basic human fear of a superior mind. Columbine understood that.

"There are other things," Ned said. "I have more—"

"No! I will not listen to any more. I cannot. Ned, Ned, can't you remember what I was called? Mad. Adulteress. Prostitute. Wanton. Spy. You name it, I was called it!"

Yes, she understood him. He should have known she would.

Now, Ned sounded angry as well. "And so, because you were called these things once, for the rest of your life you will turn away from any gossip or hearsay of any kind, even if it indicates that a person is not trustworthy? Columbine, surely you can see that at least you must listen, must not completely turn your back—"

"No, Ned, I do not agree. I must trust myself. And I will not listen to any more slander. I think you should go. Take these with you."

"Don't give me those keys, Columbine. They have nothing to do with this. Here, I'm leaving them on the desk." There was a pause. "I'm sorry if I pained you."

Lawrence scuttled backward, for footsteps were approaching. He found the door to the kitchen and quickly stepped into the small pantry. He heard Ned hesitate in the hall, then take his coat from the rack, open the door, and go.

Lawrence stayed a few seconds to compose himself, for he was still shaking with rage. Columbine mustn't know he'd been here, that he'd heard.

He walked into the parlor. She was standing in the middle of the room, her hands clasped before her. She hadn't lit the gas, so dusky shadows filled the room, and the only light came from the fire. She jumped when she saw him enter.

"Lawrence!" She gave a short laugh, a half-gasp. "I thought you were a ghost."

Closing the door firmly behind him, he hurried toward her. "What is it, my dear? You look upset."

"No, no, not upset. Oh, Lawrence, people can be so horrid!" She looked at him earnestly. Was she now looking for a trace of dishonesty, of moral baseness? Damn Ned Van Cormandt!

"Let's sit down," he said, guiding her toward the sofa. He sat down with her and chafed her cold hands. "I saw Mr. Van Cormandt leaving," he said. "Did he upset you?"

"He didn't mean to," Columbine said in a low tone. She looked down at Lawrence's bent head. The fire picked out strands of gold.

Ned had to be wrong, she thought. Lawrence was so kind.

"*He* didn't seem upset," Lawrence said. "He looked . . . triumphant."

"Did he?"

She kept her hand in his, but it was inert. Lawrence leaned down and kissed it. Then he looked up at her and kissed her mouth softly.

Her lips smiled underneath the kiss, and when he pulled away, she said, "Lawrence, you mustn't do that again."

"Don't say that," he said desperately, knowing that now it was time, it was finally time to force the moment. Now, when she had finished defending him, when she was just starting to realize that she was tied to him. "You must know how it pains my heart to think of him with you, to know that you once thought you loved him."

"Why?" Columbine asked.

Lawrence looked surprised. "Because he is evil."

Columbine laughed slightly, and pulled her hand away again. "Oh, Lawrence, no. Ned is a good man. And I *did* love him."

Lawrence felt something tick inside him. She had patronized him. She must never, never patronize him. "It's all right, Columbine. You didn't know," he said.

She seemed bemused. "Know what?" She leaned over to turn on the gas lamp on the table by the sofa.

He grabbed her by the waist, preventing her. "Please don't," he said. The softness of his voice belied the strong grip on her waist. "It's easier to talk without the light."

Columbine pulled back warily. "All right," she conceded. "For a moment."

"You didn't know," he continued, "what your true calling would be yet. You didn't know that later it could hurt you, the fact that you'd been a rich man's mistress."

Columbine frowned. "Lawrence, I'm not following you."

"That's exactly what I want!" he cried ecstatically. "For you to follow me!"

A distant alarm bell sounded somewhere in Columbine's brain. Lawrence's pale blue eyes had a light in them she'd not seen before, and it was not a comforting light. She tried an easy laugh. "If you want me to follow you to the tea table, I agree. Why don't I go prepare the tray? Mrs. Brodge left everything in the kitchen. I'll just—"

His arm shot out and he captured her wrist. "Not yet," he said. "Not yet. No jokes. I want to finish this."

"Lawrence, let go of my wrist," she said calmly, and was relieved when he did. "Finish what?"

"Finish telling you. Ned knew your body, but I know your mind, Columbine. You need my ideas. You need to experience the beauty of what I know. Your view of human nature is so false, so pessimistic. That is what is holding you back from a true philosophical commitment to anarchism. If you believed in the goodness of human nature, you'd see that only when the state is destroyed will we be able to live freely and well. The storehouses will open, and everyone will take what they need. We will live according to a social contract."

"But Lawrence," Columbine said reasonably, "this is all very noble and good. But I do not believe it will work. And even if I did believe it, I would never countenance violence to achieve it."

"But violence is the most beautiful part of it!" Lawrence said. "Don't you see? How else do we purify but through fire? How else do we build if we don't destroy?"

Columbine tried to rise, but he took her wrist again. She tried not to be alarmed. He was just overcome with his ideas, with his emotion. He needed to calm down. "Let me get some tea, and we'll continue the discussion," she said.

"No. Now, now, it must be now." Spittle formed on the corners of his mouth. "If you will only open your heart and accept it, just think what can be done! With your celebrity, and my ideas, you will be the most famous convert to anarchism in history!"

Now Columbine was beginning to get angry. "Lawrence," she said with asperity, "my mind is not the *tabula rasa* you think it is. I have my own ideas. And they do not correspond with yours."

He waved the hand not holding her wrist. "You think you have ideas. What you really need is to learn."

"Lawrence, let go of me. Let go!" Her voice was higher-pitched now, and he looked at her with interest.

"Do I frighten you?"

"No," she said, trying to keep her voice calm. But she *was* frightened, a little. Ned's warnings flew in her brain, and she sorely wished she had heard him out. He had left so abruptly. Perhaps he would come back! She would be very glad to see him. Lawrence was acting so strangely. "It's just that you won't let go of my arm," she added. "Please let go, Lawrence."

He ignored her. "It's because you feel my power that you're afraid. You sense my superiority. That's good. That will make things good for us." With his other hand, he reached out and stroked her cheek. "The time has come to be close, Columbine."

She looked into Lawrence's eyes, and she no longer saw the eyes of a friend. He looked angry; if he was trying to seduce her, he was doing a bad job of it. "No, Lawrence," she said, as gently as she could.

"Yes, Columbine," he said, and he smoothly took her other wrist in his strong grip. He placed his mouth over hers, and it was wrong. His other kisses had been so gentle, the kisses of a young poet, almost shy but with a hint of the sensuality to come. But now his tongue thrust between her lips and into her mouth too eagerly, making her gag.

"Columbine," he coaxed, "Feel the power of us together. You have to know I'm right."

She tore her mouth away from his. "No!" she cried. Panic washed over her. Lawrence was holding her so tightly, and he wasn't letting go. Marguerite was the only one home, and she was upstairs in her room, as she always was these days, her door closed, most likely napping.

"Don't shout," he said crossly. "Why are you shouting?"

"Lawrence," she said desperately, "you're forcing me. You don't want to force me."

"Of course I don't want to force you," he said. But he did not let go of her wrists, and he raised them above her head and maneuvered himself on top of her.

"Get off," she said. "Get off now, or I'll hurt you, Lawrence."

He laughed, but his breath sucked in when her knee came up sharply. "Don't do that again," he said in a constricted voice. His grip didn't loosen.

"Let me go," she shouted. Her heart was thundering so she could barely hear her voice. It sounded so weak.

Now Lawrence realized that he *did* want to force her. Hadn't she tantalized him? Hadn't she kissed him, just a few minutes earlier? Wasn't she waiting breathlessly for a strong man to push her, physically and mentally, into her potential? "You don't realize what you can be," he said with a smile that chilled Columbine's blood. "I'm just showing you the way."

This time, when she brought her knee up, she caught him enough so that he shifted his weight, and she pushed him with all her strength and jumped up. She ran for the door.

But he was behind her, forcing her against the door. Her chin banged against it, and the pain sent tears to her eyes. "Please, Lawrence," she begged.

"Please," he mimicked, tenderly tucking a loose strand of hair behind her ear.

She relaxed for an instant, then tensed her muscles when his fingers moved against her neck. "You liked this once," he said.

"Yes," she said through a constricted throat. When she felt that he had relaxed his hold a bit, she pushed away slightly and hammered at the door. "Marguerite!" she screamed.

His hand clamped over her mouth, and he dragged her backward, away from the door, while she tried to hit him from behind. There was no talking now, no time for it and no breath, for they were locked in struggle. His grip on her arms was powerful, and it hurt. He twisted them behind her back, then held her wrists together with one hand. He seemed to do it so easily, even though she struggled.

Finally, he took her hair in one hand and tilted back her head. He spoke softly in her ear. "Columbine, you don't understand. I don't want to hurt you at all. Do you understand?" His tongue licked her ear, and she shuddered with revulsion.

"You see how you tremble?" he asked. He licked her ear again, and she sobbed a great sob that wrenched her belly.

He put a hand over her mouth. His knee came up and pushed between her legs. And she saw the door open, and Marguerite standing in the doorway. Lawrence's hand dropped immediately.

"She was hysterical—" he started.

"Liar!" Marguerite screamed, and she was flying across the room, fragile, tiny Marguerite, launching herself at him in a flurry of teeth and nails.

He dropped his arms from around Columbine, who fell back, her knees crumpling underneath her. She pushed herself up and went after Lawrence, who was backing away toward the door underneath the fury of Marguerite's attack. A long, bloody scratch went from his ear to the corner of his mouth, and his eyes were murderous.

"Bitches," he spat.

"Get out!" Marguerite screeched, and Columbine picked up Lawrence's coat and hat and shoved them at him, pushing him out into the hall. Together the women managed to open the front door and push him through it. He stumbled and fell to his knees on the stone stairs, and they banged the door closed and locked it, resting against it and taking deep shuddering breaths before Columbine burst into tears and hurled herself into Marguerite's arms, arms she once thought so childish, so slender, and now felt so strong.

Eleven

When Marguerite moved into the house Edwin found for her, she forgot everything she'd known before. She settled into luxury as though she'd been born for it. Now she rose languidly at ten, rather than seven. She did not leap out of bed to dress hurriedly in the cold. Her bedroom was warm as toast, and she merely stretched and burrowed further underneath her satin coverlet. Her maid carried in a tray that contained a silver coffeepot, rolls, jam, and fresh fruit. She would leave the tray on the bed and bring in a vase full of roses. Edwin sent them every morning.

After picking at her breakfast, Marguerite would bathe. Then she would choose one of her many new dresses—they were beautiful, but Edwin promised that next season they'd be from Paris—and take her carriage to Toby's for her singing lesson. She was making great progress, he said. On days she had no lesson, she went for a walk up Madison Avenue. She thought about getting a dog. When she returned, she changed again, for Edwin usually arrived for lunch. If he did, they would usually eat in the dining room, a long luncheon with soup and lobster salad and turbot, sometimes a roast beef if Edwin instructed the cook the day before. Then they would go upstairs to her bedroom. And then Edwin would leave for his office again and Marguerite would perhaps bathe again, or read *Harper's Bazar* to see the new fashions from Paris, or nap. Then she would begin to think about what to wear for dinner.

It was a perfect life. She reveled in her luxury. She licked jam off her fingers and luxuriated in bath water that was always the perfect temperature. She rubbed silk against her cheeks and opened long jewelers' boxes and squealed at their contents. And she got to make love every day, sometimes twice a day. Even though Edwin was not as good a lover as Horatio, she still enjoyed it, very much.

Weeks passed, and Edwin still came, but he sometimes skipped lunch and only made love. In the evenings now, he often arrived after a dinner to which she had not been invited. Their evenings became the evenings of a domestic married couple; Marguerite did embroidery by the fire while Edwin finished a brandy and then looked at her meaningfully and rose to go upstairs. He claimed that now he knew what it was to be domestically inclined. There was nothing he liked better, he said, than to sit in the quiet parlor with her on his knee. Marguerite called him an old stick-in-the-mud. She had to use tears and pouts to get him to suggest a grand dinner out. He wanted to go to Rector's, but Marguerite insisted on the more refined Delmonico's. And no private room this time!

Marguerite swept into the fashionable restaurant, happily reminding herself how wonderful it was to always feel well-dressed. She thought of her old blue velvet gown with disdain. Tonight she was in rose satin bordered with black fur. The godet pleated skirt had a beaded iris design, and the bodice was elaborately tucked and beaded as well. She wore a jeweled aigrette in her hair and carried a tulle fan appliqued with black lace and trimmed with deep pink roses.

Edwin seemed a little distracted, but Marguerite was so happy to be out she didn't care. She hummed as she perused the menu. Pheasant would be nice. Or perhaps terrapin. Or both—of course, they could order both, she realized, her mouth already watering.

Edwin looked bored, or nervous, and she decided it was time to entertain him. "I think I should like a bicycle," she said brightly, sipping a glass of wine. She smiled flirtatiously at him. "Would you like that, Edwin? We could be like Diamond Jim Brady and Lillian Russell. We'll ride through the Park on gold-plated bicycles studded with jewels." She giggled. "And I would have a darling bicycling costume. I saw one in *Harper's Bazar* just yesterday. It had Turkish trousers, can you imagine? Would you like me in trousers, Edwin?"

"Yes, of course," Edwin said. But it was clear he hadn't been listening to her at all. He was staring across the room.

Marguerite followed his gaze and saw that it was trained on the erect back of a woman in a black satin gown. Last year's, Marguerite thought disdainfully. The silhouette for the nineties was already changing to an hourglass figure. Skirts were wider, and bustles not nearly so prominent. She wasn't jealous, for the woman was older, and Marguerite could see, when she turned her head, that she was double-chinned.

"Who are you looking at, Edwin?" she asked, buttering a roll. "Do you know that lady?" she asked with her mouth full.

Edwin looked at her, and she saw distaste cross his delicate features for a moment. "Marguerite, never butter a whole roll. Break off a piece."

She swallowed. "All right," she snapped. She shouldn't mind when Edwin corrected her; she wanted to learn. But she did mind. It was the way Edwin did it; Toby could tell her anything and she would nod and thank him. "But do you know her, or not?"

"She's my aunt Alicia," Edwin said. "She's with my cousins Kitty and Robert. I must greet her. I'm sure she'll see me in a moment."

"Shall I come with you?" Marguerite frowned. "Or should you bring her over to meet me, is that how it's done?"

Edwin stood. He pushed a hand through his curly hair agitatedly. "No, no. Not tonight. I'll return in a moment."

"Edwin, you can't leave me here alone!"

"Just for a moment. Don't worry, dearest." Edwin straightened his vest and dashed off. He looked like a scared rabbit, Marguerite thought scornfully. She broke her roll into smaller pieces and buttered one of them. It seemed rather inefficient, to butter a bunch of small pieces rather than get it over with at once.

"Miss Corbeau?" The waiter bowed slightly. "Mr. Stiers has requested a private dining room. Our largest is available."

Marguerite scowled. "But I like this table."

The waiter, who had just been given a large tip by Edwin, smiled officiously. "Yes. But this is our most elegant room. Mr. Astor has just left with his party, and we've set it up for Mr. Stiers. It's Mr. Astor's favorite room." Edwin had advised the waiter to please drop that piece of information.

Marguerite hesitated. Tomorrow, she could tell her maid and

Toby that she dined in Mr. Astor's favorite room at Delmonico's. She could describe the elegant appointments in detail. She nodded at the waiter, who bowed and helped her from the chair.

Mollified only slightly, Marguerite followed the waiter toward the stairs to the private room above. She peeked behind her but could not get a good look at Edwin's aunt or his cousins. His back was effectively shielding his aunt, and his cousin Kitty was in profile. She seemed to have a pleasant face. Why couldn't Marguerite meet them now? Why did Edwin keep putting off her introduction to his family? He was such a weakling sometimes. She would have to take charge when they were married.

When they reached the private dining room, Marguerite turned to the waiter. "Please bring some champagne," she said. "I don't like the wine. Bring whatever champagne Mr. Astor drank," she added impulsively, hoping it was ridiculously expensive.

The waiter bowed again and left the room, closing the door softly. Marguerite stood and surveyed the velvet hangings, the carved gilded boiserie, the small green marble fireplace. She supposed the room was pretty, but she felt hemmed in. She sighed. So she would have dinner with Edwin alone again. Nothing to look at but his bland handsome face, no admiration to excite but his, which was already familiar and well-tested.

Marguerite sank into a red brocade chair and for the first time, she went over the past weeks in her mind. She knew that Edwin was still besotted with her, but wasn't he coming to see her less frequently? Why was she never invited to those endless dinners he "had to" attend?

Frowning, Marguerite realized that when they did go out, they dined at places where they would run into male friends but she had yet to meet one female cousin, aunt, or distant relative of Edwin's. She realized that she had no friends, except for Toby. She had gone to visit Columbine and felt out of place in the crowded parlor, with nothing to say of her days or her nights. The intimacy that had sprung up between them, that shared secret of that frightening dusk with Lawrence Birch, had seemed to melt away with time and daylight. She saw that she had begun to look pathetically forward to conversations with her maid, an illiterate Irish girl. And she began to see that she was bored.

• • •

Horatio left his office and took the El to Fourteenth Street. Sometimes he liked to take his work to Union Square and think. He told himself he needed some peace and fresh air to puzzle out the perfect lead for his latest story.

His usual bench was empty, thank goodness. Across the square, through the bare branches of trees, he could look across Fourteenth Street straight into the offices of the New Women Society. It was impossible to distinguish forms behind the windows, impossible to see anything at all except for the window behind which he knew Bell breathed and thought, drank tea, scratched, stretched, yawned, was challenged or bored or happy or sad. Behind that window, Bell existed, and therefore he sat in the park and he looked at it. He was in a sorry state, he knew, an object, should the people passing by know his intention, of scorn or pathos. Still, he did not move.

He made desultory notes, but mostly, he thought about Bell and his own stupidity. His days with Marguerite were like a dream, the violent passion she stirred an uncomfortable memory. He had no idea why he had lost his head over her, had no idea why it started or why it ended, and that knowledge filled him with a sort of panic. He realized he had not yet begun to understand himself. He realized that he was as much a fool as any blustering political figure he had lampooned. He was humbled and he was ashamed, and he was still in love with Bell.

At first, he thought his longing had conjured her, but Horatio slowly realized that Bell herself was heading across the square. She was walking directly toward him, wearing a black hat with a green veil, with the businesslike walk he had grown to love. There was no alluring sway of hips, just a straightforward stride, a busy woman getting from one place to another. There was a slight nervousness in that step that only a lover might notice, the hesitation of a beautiful woman who is afraid, at any moment, that she might be examined by a stranger.

She was almost upon him when she recognized him. Her step faltered for just an instant, and she came forward with a smile. "Horatio, how nice to see you."

"Hello, Bell," he said, standing. For once in his life, Horatio felt absolutely speechless. He fished through his glossary of appropriate remarks. "A fine day," he said.

"Yes, very fine," Bell said, politely ignoring the threatening sky above. "I was just going to get tea for the office."

"May I walk with you?"

Bell hesitated. "Actually, I'd prefer to be alone, Horatio."

Horatio struggled with his emotions, but he lost. He couldn't stop himself from pushing her. "Can't we be friends, Bell?" he said painfully.

She looked away, down the long square, and he couldn't see her eyes. "Please, Horatio."

Horatio felt incapable of withdrawing, of making a polite remark since Bell was obviously reluctant to continue the discussion. "Bell, I still love you," he said, trying to say it gravely, with no hint of his vast desperation. "I don't know what happened with Marguerite. I was in despair, thinking you would never love me. I'm not offering this as an excuse, rather some kind of explanation for behavior which was so horrendous, ungentlemanly . . . Can you ever forgive me?"

"Of course," Bell said serenely. She turned her lustrous amber eyes on him with their steady, frank gaze. "I already have."

"Then can we start slowly? Can we be friends again? I assure you, I would ask for nothing more . . ."

She looked down. Her lower lip caught in her teeth. Her skin had a winter pallor that was delicate and lovely to Horatio's eyes. Even the tip of her nose, which was beginning to redden with the cold, seemed adorable to him. "I'm sorry, Horatio," she said finally. "I'll always remember our friendship with fondness. But I truly do not see how we can go on with it. I mean, it isn't what happened with you and Marguerite, not really. I know she must have pursued you." She looked up, and her gaze was no longer serene. "It's me. I'm damaged."

The word hit him like a fist. "Bell, no."

She shook her head, backing up a small step. "Don't say anything." She tried to smile, and she held out her hand in a friendly way. "Let's just shake hands—I'm glad we can do that, at last."

"But you must tell me what you mean."

She continued to hold out her hand, and her smile was distant now. "Won't you shake hands with me?"

What could he do? Horatio held out his hand and shook Bell's mechanically. He could only feel the softness of the kid glove, but closing his eyes for an instant, he thought of the feel of her skin. He wanted to fall to his knees with grief and love, but he merely nodded and turned away, since that was what she wanted. When he turned after a few paces to watch her, he saw that her step was just as brisk, just as businesslike as it had been before.

Marguerite lifted her skirt and arched her foot to study her new boots. They were of the softest leather, lined with fur, and totally impractical for walking, for she tended to trip occasionally from balancing on the slender heel, higher than she was accustomed to. And she shouldn't have worn them to Toby's studio, for her feet felt hot inside the sable. But she couldn't resist wearing them. Toby always noticed her clothes.

Immediately upon arriving, she had thrown herself on his sofa in a most unladylike fashion and announced that she did not feel like singing that day. Toby had laughed at her and complimented her new boots, then sank into his deepest armchair with a glass of brandy. He was a horrid taskmaster most of the time, but today he did not seem to mind delaying the lesson. He was amused, rather than annoyed, at her sulky mood.

"I've been waiting for this," he said cheerfully. "You're bored. Edwin keeps you on a very short leash, I must say."

"Edwin is afraid that the virtue I surrendered to his protection is in danger around any member of the male sex. Except you, Toby." Marguerite sat up in a flounce of lace and a rustle of petticoats. "Which reminds me. Why don't you want to seduce me, Toby?"

He choked on his brandy. "Are you disappointed?" he asked.

"Rather," she pouted. "Of course, I wouldn't surrender, as I'm not attracted to you in the least, and besides, my heart, as you know, belongs to Edwin. But it would be rather nice if you tried, nonetheless."

This seemed to vastly amuse Toby. "Oh, my dear. You are such an innocent, despite how hard you try to be naughty. Don't lose that quality, petal, for you can use it. Now, let's get back to Edwin. Are you terribly bored with him?" A gleam lit up Toby's dark eyes, for he loved gossip, especially of the malicious variety.

"Not in the least," Marguerite said stoutly. "And when we're married, I'm sure he'll let me—"

She was interrupted by a hoot of laughter from Toby. "Married? Surely you don't think he'll marry you, do you?"

A tiny frown appeared between Marguerite's eyebrows. "Well of course I do. Why do you think I'm with him?"

Toby's smile faded abruptly. He put down the glass of brandy. "You *are* serious. Marguerite, Edwin won't marry you. I don't want to be cruel, but it's best you face reality, darling. He'll marry a Miss Clara Vandervoon, or some other pallid debutante. Someone should undertake to teach you the rules. Oh dear, I suppose it's got to be poor me."

"What are you talking about, Toby? Jay Gould's son married his mistress."

"Darling, don't you know the difference between a Jay Gould and a Winthrop Stiers? That's old money—Edwin's father is so revered he should be bronzed. He'd never let his oldest son marry his mistress."

"But Edwin is his own man. He is always telling me so."

Toby had no answer to this, just a lift of sardonic eyebrow.

"You're being very disagreeable," Marguerite said sharply. "I don't know why I came at all today. I wish I hadn't."

Toby groaned. He sat up and poured himself a drop more brandy. "Don't you realize, my petal, that you're part of the demimondaine now? You should just relax and enjoy it. *We're* the ones having the fun. Those swells don't know how to live. I'm all for money, but if I have to sit at Mrs. Astor's table and eat her horrible food for it, I'd rather bow out, thank you very much, for a better meal at Rector's with better company. The dresses are just as pretty, the women prettier, and the talk is vastly more clever."

Foreboding trickled down her neck like icy rain. She didn't want to joke, or flirt. She didn't want him to tease her. "Toby, you don't understand. I met Edwin in an unorthodox way, yes. But I was a virgin. And I told him how you tricked me into that party, that I didn't know what was expected of me—"

Toby gave his hoot of laughter again, which was beginning to have an obnoxious sound. "Darling, they *all* say that."

Marguerite drew herself up. "I am not *they*," she pronounced icily.

He paused, the brandy glass pressed against his lips. "No, you aren't, Marguerite," he said seriously. "I'm sorry I suggested it."

Somewhat mollified, Marguerite relaxed a bit. "Besides, you don't know how much Edwin loves me. Men marry foolishly all the time. The rules are relaxing all over town. Don't you read the papers? Everyone is decrying the collapse of society, you know."

Toby shrugged. "All right, I'm not going to argue with you. I wish you luck, petal. But just in case Edwin doesn't get down on bended knee, perhaps we should have a go at developing a career for you."

"I don't feel like singing today," Marguerite pouted. "Especially since you've been so cruel to me. I should think that you'd *want* me to marry Edwin. That way you'd be sure to keep your position as my singing teacher. Perhaps he'd even raise your wages. Usually, you're so selfish that you'd understand that immediately." The remark was ungenerous, but Toby really did deserve a slap.

To her surprise, he wasn't offended. He leaned forward, earnest now. "I'll ignore that, because you don't know any better. I'm the best friend you ever had, Marguerite. I happen to be fond of you, you know. Sometimes I forget how very young you are. You should know what you got into the moment you accepted Edwin's protection."

"Well, as for protection, Edwin doesn't give me money, you know. I had a little money saved, and he invested it for me. He's an absolute genius with stocks—I've made some marvelous dividends. The money's mine, really, you know. He just administers it." Marguerite trotted all this out with the same firm and reasonable tone Edwin had told it to her.

But Toby didn't look impressed. "Yes, yes," he said impatiently, "that's the way it's done all over town. For some reason, the swell thinks it saves face for the lady, which is ridiculous. It's just one of society's many hypocrisies. Is that house in your name? I don't think so. And with all this money you're supposed to have, I don't see you sitting at Mrs. Astor's dinner table, do I?"

The observation stung, and Marguerite turned her face away. "Stop it. Don't preach at me, Toby. I've had enough of that to last a lifetime."

"I'm hardly preaching, petal. I just want you to realize how very lucky you are. Come, let's not argue. Stand up and practice your scales. I have a surprise for you, and if you're not a good girl, I won't reveal it."

Marguerite concealed her interest underneath a frown. "What kind of surprise?"

"Come on, do your scales and I'll tell you."

"No. Tell me first."

He sighed impatiently. "No."

"Then I won't get up."

"As you wish. Then I'll put on my hat and go out."

Marguerite stuck her little red tongue out at him, but Toby was not Edwin, and he was unmoved. He calmly put down his glass and went for his hat and coat. He had buttoned the last button and was tying his scarf in a distinctly effete manner when Marguerite finally gave in.

"All right, all right, you beast." She stood up and went to the piano. Toby grinned and took off his coat. Tossing it on the sofa, he crossed to the piano and sat down, still wearing the opulent paisley silk scarf around his neck. He tossed one end behind his shoulder.

"Scales," he said. He struck a chord, and Marguerite began. He listened carefully, and he watched her. Today he felt the same *frisson* of possibility he'd felt the first time he'd heard her at the Seraglio Dinner. He had something here. She was almost ready. If that callow ass Edwin Stiers didn't break her heart or get her pregnant. It was too bad Marguerite didn't see that she could do better than Edwin Stiers. But Toby had coached many singers and actresses, befriended many of them. He knew from experience that he could tell them nothing. He could only help them when they arrived at his door, as they inevitably did, pregnant or scorned or deeply hurt and concealing it behind a too-bright laugh.

Under the spell of music, Marguerite's bad mood vanished, and she sang the songs he'd chosen to show off her husky contralto.

What her voice lacked in purity it made up in character. She was an original. She had looks and sex and youth and nerve and a decent voice, and there was no telling where it all might take her. The last test was how she'd do on a stage.

When the lesson was over, she leaned against the piano. "Tell me," she ordered.

"All right. Petal, I think you're almost ready to audition. Three weeks, maybe a bit more. I'm in the process of setting it up with with William Miles Paradise himself." He rolled out the name slowly. It was time to tell her; she'd work harder.

Marguerite had not expected this. She straightened. "Willie P.? Oh, Toby, do you really know him?" she breathed.

"Of course I know him. I know everyone, don't you realize that yet?"

She giggled. "I thought you were a tremendous fibber, Toby, I must confess."

"Shame. Just for that, I'll cancel the appointment."

She threw her arms around his neck from behind. "No, you won't. Toby, do you really think I'm good enough? Don't you think I should start a bit, uh, lower?"

"Why? You'll just pick up bad habits. Besides, it's always easier to go down than up. If Willie P. doesn't take you on, we'll go to the second best, and he will. And then within six months Willie himself will be knocking at your door with his diamond-handled cane."

Marguerite laughed delightedly. "Tell me more."

"And you'll make so much money you'll be bored with it. Real money, your money, free and clear, that you make yourself. You'll live in a grand hotel in a suite of rooms. Admirers will send you enough roses to fill twelve bathtubs, and jewel after jewel will arrive at your door after each performance. You'll do a world tour, and princes and counts will lay their hearts at your feet. Lillian Russell will envy you. Monsieur Worth will beg to design for you. Chefs will name elegant dishes after you. Women will despise you, and men will adore you. And I'll take care of you, petal. I won't let anyone hurt you."

"Really?" she breathed by his ear. "Oh, Toby, you do love me."

"I do." He patted her slender hand.

"And you *know* me," she went on. "You know how horrid I really am."

"I do."

"You know that I'm terribly selfish. That I can be cruel."

"I know you as well as I know myself, because you're just like me," he said, laughing in a rather constricted manner as she squeezed his neck. "Now don't choke me, petal, I'm very fragile, you know."

Marguerite straightened suddenly. "But what about Edwin, Toby? I forgot all about him."

Toby slumped theatrically against the keys, making a dissonant chord. "Oh, please, don't be tiresome. We were having such fun. Edwin's not the man for you. I'll tell you when you meet the right man."

"But I thought Edwin was perfect," Marguerite said, perplexed. "I was so *sure.*"

Toby twisted around on the piano stool. "I thought you wanted to sing."

"I do. But I want Edwin, too."

"You can't have both. Look, William Paradise owes me one favor. Only one. I don't want to waste it. So you'd better make up your mind, petal. Do you want to be a wife?" Toby pronounced the word in a flat, bored tone. He stood up and took her small, determined chin in his hands. Her dark blue eyes were blazing, and that gave him hope. Just a mention of Willie P. and she had gone into heat. He smiled. "Or do you want to be a star?"

Columbine looked overhead at the multi-paned skylight. The sun was beginning to set, and the sky was shell pink with streaks of violet amid the gray. She'd had trouble, over the past weeks, when dusk fell. It never failed to bring back a wave of panic, when she'd felt trapped in her own parlor by a man she'd thought was a friend.

But today, she felt no frightening flutters, and her palms were dry. This house on West 10th Street held no terrors. Ned had first taken her here three years before. It was a place in which she had loved and laughed; it held not one bad memory. Even the arguments she could recall had spice and affection underneath, and merely fueled the loving.

She had forgiven Ned for warning her about Lawrence Birch, of course, although she could not tell him of what happened that day, could not bring herself to tell anyone. It was a secret between her and Marguerite. The truth was, she felt guilty. She felt she must have encouraged him in some way. Hadn't she kissed him? Hadn't she imagined what it would be like to be in bed with all that sleek energy?

She didn't know if Lawrence would have forced her, in the end. Something in his eyes told her that he would have. But only she knew that. He had sent her a letter the next day, which she had not opened. But he hadn't tried to call, thank goodness.

It had taken her a few weeks to recover. The next day, she'd gone to the office as usual, but she'd sat trembling in her office, expecting Lawrence any moment. How ridiculous, she'd told herself. Stop shaking. But she could not, and there it was. She went home that day and didn't go out for a week. Her insomnia returned. For that alone she should kill him.

Columbine laughed aloud for the first time in what felt like centuries. She felt the stirrings of her old self beginning to shake her up. So she had been wrong. And maybe she was guilty. She had misjudged someone, perhaps through her own vanity. But she had escaped, and she was about to embark on a good project. She had so much, and she had no time to lose. She thought of Elijah Reed's impatience, and she decided she should adopt some of it. It would keep her vigorous.

The pink glow of the sky was deepening to orange. It was time to go. There were no lights as of yet in the skylit studio so she had to arrange for gas. The room, she decided, would be used as a common one. For the children during the day, and for book readings at night or lessons. She'd written to Jane Addams, who was beginning, already, to have such a success with Hull House in Chicago, and received generous advice. A reading club was very popular, Jane had said.

Columbine felt her way down the darkened stairs to the third floor, where the bedrooms were. The second floor held the drawing room, a wonderfully large dining room, the parlor, and a small study. The first floor, which was actually below ground in the front, held a large kitchen, two maids' rooms, and a small room overlooking the garden either Columbine or Bell could use as an office. Ned had been right; the house was perfect.

As she stood at the landing, she heard the front door open and shut. Masculine footsteps clicked along the polished wood of the entry hall. Panic sent Columbine bolting backward. She put a hand to her heart, which began to beat furiously. Trying to be quiet, she slid a hand along the wall to search for the gas jet she was sure was there. She wanted light, she needed light. But in her panic, she couldn't find it. A small sound escaped her. She was trapped in this house, it was growing dark, and she was sure, oh, it must be him, it was Lawrence downstairs. It felt so terrifyingly familiar.

"Mrs. Nash?"

At first she couldn't place the voice over the pounding in her ears. She waited, and the man spoke again.

"Mrs. Nash?"

Elijah Reed. Columbine leaned against the banister in relief. She took several deep breaths to compose herself. "Yes, I'm up here." Her voice sounded shaky to her ears.

She saw the gas go on downstairs at the next landing, and she started down. She paused at the bottom. Elijah Reed was waiting outside the dining room, his shadow looming toward her. "I hope I didn't startle you," he said.

"Not at all."

She moved forward and took his hand while his dark eyes held hers questioningly, for he'd known as soon as he'd seen her that something was wrong. But at his touch, something peculiar moved inside Columbine. Ever since she'd seen him standing there in the dim shadows of the hall, she'd felt strange. It was as though she had suddenly been raised to a bird's eye view of her life, and then dropped to earth again, leaving her a little breathless, a little bewildered. She stopped, her hand still in his, unable to place the feeling.

They'd become friends, she and Elijah, since Lawrence's attack on her. Though he had no knowledge of it, he had appeared at her door the next day at teatime and chased away her panic. There was something about his calmness that drew her. They talked about everything and nothing. They talked of books, and reform, and Teddy Roosevelt, and once, fleetingly, he'd mentioned his wife, who died of cancer at thirty-one. He'd seen so much suffering, she'd come to realize, all his life. And it hadn't hardened him, but softened him, in a way she'd come to understand. She had misjudged his manner from the first. It wasn't weariness; it was watchfulness. It wasn't surrender; it was calm.

The fine edge of his mind stimulated her and made her nervous, for she felt that she would know presently that she would not be able to keep up with him in a discussion. But that time had not come. And instead she had known humor, and slyness, and a man fond of jokes.

She'd known all these things, over the past weeks, but she had not known, until this moment, standing in the hall of her new home, that she'd also known her future, and she had not realized it.

"Oh," she said, and she said the word aloud, without knowing it. Oh, she thought, oh, my. So this is it, at last. At long, long last.

He was watching her. "Mrs. Nash?"

"Don't you think it's time," she said, smiling, for good cheer suddenly filled her chest with such lightness she thought she might rise above the carpet with it, "you called me Columbine?"

"Columbine." He said it gravely, as though the name were a gift.

"Elijah," she said, and she was smiling and laughing, for the sound of his Christian name, finally spoken aloud, was such pleasure.

Lawrence waited in the dark outside the house. He was carrying flowers, and he was reviewing his apology. Columbine had a soft heart. He would twist the incident, make her think she had panicked and he was trying to subdue her, and she would listen, of course, she would have to listen. His plan included her; she was to be his convert.

He saw, in the pools of lamplight across the street, a couple approach. They were walking, their steps perfectly matched, absorbed in each other and their conversation. A carriage rolled by, splashing the hem of the woman's skirt with mud, but she did not notice. A boy dashed past them, jostling the arm of the man, but their conversation did not pause.

Lawrence watched, half-envying the couple, half-despising them. It took him long seconds to realize that the couple was Columbine and Elijah Reed.

He drew back into the shadows and watched them mount the stairs. He heard Columbine's laugh as she fumbled for her keys. He saw Elijah take her arm as they passed inside. His enemy. She had gone over to his enemy, and he had lost.

With a curse, Lawrence turned away. He crossed the street and strode down Twenty-third, going over and over in his mind the night he had Columbine at his mercy. How much gold would he give to live that moment again!

He was about to throw the flowers in the gutter when he saw Bell walking toward him. She recognized him, and her step slowed. He kept his eyes locked with hers as she walked, and she did not drop his gaze. He knew then that Columbine had not told her. Bell was afraid, but it was a different kind of fear. She walked toward him slowly, as if in a dream, and he saw that if there was one woman he had lost, there was another who he had only to lift his hand to capture.

"Good evening, Miss Huxton."

"Good evening, Mr. Birch."

"I was coming to see you," he said. He held out the flowers. "Then I felt foolish, and I went away."

She didn't take the flowers, merely stared at them, saying nothing.

"You told me not to ask you again, Miss Huxton. So I withdrew, as a gentleman should. But I find that when it comes to you, Miss Huxton, I am not such a gentleman."

She still stared at the flowers, saying nothing. Her struggle was visible on her face. She had grown thinner, he saw, and in the unflattering light, she was not beautiful. Her cheekbones looked too sharp, and the shadows on her face hollowed her cheeks in an unpleasant way. Some day, he realized, she could lose her beauty. He was glad.

Her hand reached out and touched the flowers, a petal here, a petal there. And then, slowly, her fingers twined around the small bouquet. Her lips were trembling, and her eyes were full of tears as without a word, he took her arm, swiveled her around, and led her down the sidewalk the way she'd come, away from the house on Twenty-third Street.

Twelve

SWEPT INTO A maelstrom, Bell was barely functioning. She didn't know how she got through the days. She felt doped, lodgy, inept. Luckily, Columbine didn't seem to notice.

"Of course she doesn't notice," Lawrence said. "She doesn't notice you at all. You're a servant to her."

"I'm her partner," Bell said thickly. She sat on a hard chair in Lawrence's cold room. She was wondering if Lawrence would want to have sex tonight. She thought the word now: *Sex.* It was for practice; Lawrence sometimes made her say such words aloud.

He was shaking his head at her sadly. "You have so many illusions. That's what I'm here for, love, to teach you. You're her servant. You should see that."

"I don't see it," Bell said. She leaned back against the chair slightly so that her shirtwaist tightened over her breasts. Perhaps then Lawrence would want her. She never knew how to arouse him; something mysterious guided his urges that she could not track.

Distaste crossed his face. "Don't turn into a slut, Bell," he said, turning away. He poured himself more coffee.

She looked down penitently. He was right. He knew her. He saw into the bottom of her black soul, and he pointed out what was there. That was what she needed, he said, and she agreed. Only by facing her baseness could she conquer it. Jesus hadn't helped her any. Lawrence had a better method; he was her teacher, and she was learning so much.

"We were speaking of Columbine," he continued. "She

exploited you. She is a member of the ruling class, and she can never, ever, overcome that, Bell. No matter what nonsense she talks of Fabian socialism and uniting the classes for the common good. It's rubbish. Do you see?"

"I see," Bell said. She did not agree, but she hadn't the strength tonight to argue. She had only a few hours before she should get back to Twenty-third Street, and they had wasted so much time already. She'd had to wait for Lawrence to finish some work on a new article. Then he had to eat.

He grasped her chin and forced her to look at him. "Don't lie to me," he rapped out. "Never lie to me, Bell. Don't tell me you agree when you don't."

Tears spurted in her eyes. "Please, Lawrence," she whispered. "Not tonight."

His nostils flared, and she was afraid. She smelled coffee and rage on his breath. But as quickly as it was there, his anger was gone, and he smiled. His fingers stroked her now, her cheek, her ear. "I love you, my dearest," he said, and the note in his voice made her want to squirm with the power of her lust. "Don't you know that?"

"Lawrence," she breathed, and her head fell back.

"Come to the bed."

Good, the bed. Sometimes, he liked to take her on the floor of the front room, and the wood was so hard. Her back would be bruised the next day, she would wince if she forgot and leaned against a chair.

Positioning her in front of him, he sat on the bed. "Take off your clothes, Bell," he said in a flat voice. "But leave on your drawers only."

That voice excited her, and she obeyed him. When she was naked above the waist and stood in front of him wearing only her drawers, she waited, barely breathing. He touched her between her legs.

"Tell me what I'm doing," he said.

"You're touching me."

"Where am I touching you?"

She closed her eyes and bit back a groan. Her cheeks were hot with embarrassment and desire.

"Where, Bell?"

She told him, using the word he taught her. He cupped her, grabbing her hard, and said the word.

It started again like the motion of a wave, her revulsion and her attraction, beating her forward, beating her back.

He never let her use her hands. He liked her passive. He liked her to keep her eyes closed, and to stand, or to lie, or to sit very still, while he did things to her. If she used her hands he would calmly or roughly return them to her side. When they did it lying down, he liked her to pretend she was sleeping.

And he knew how she liked it, how he could make her come with a few chosen words, or cruel, cold hands on her nipples, or a bite on her behind. How did he know these things? she wondered during the day, pressing her legs together, remembering. Every day she would tell herself that she would not go back to him. And every evening she scratched pathetically at his door.

She wished he would not say things about Columbine, but suddenly, Lawrence seemed to hate her. He pointed to ways Columbine had oppressed her, and Bell could not agree. Columbine could be impatient, sometimes thoughtless, yes. But Bell could not reconcile the Columbine of her own reality—the Columbine who had saved her, who laughed with her and loved her—with the Columbine of Lawrence's imagination.

Suddenly, he pushed her away. "I don't want you tonight."

Her eyes flew open. "Why? Lawrence, what did I do?"

He began to button his trousers. "You have contempt for me. My words mean nothing. How can I love a creature who treats me so cruelly?"

"Lawrence, please. Of course I listen to you. Of course. I love you."

He whirled around as if he'd caught her. "Then why won't you believe me about Columbine? You are her servant. You open her door, you take the coats of her guests, you fetch the tea. 'Of course, Columbine,'" he mimicked cruelly, moving his hands in a mincing way. "'I'd be happy to, Columbine.'" He glared at her. "Are you in love with that woman, or with me?"

"With you!" she cried. She grabbed his hand and pressed it to her heart. His fingers against the bare skin of her breast made her pulse begin to race again.

His cold fingers moved slowly across her breast. "Then you must trust me," he said. "We must trust each other. We must have ultimate trust in each other." He kneaded her breast, squeezing her nipple, and she moaned. Her hand curled around his neck.

"Put your hands down," he ordered, and she did. He positioned her between his knees again. Bell nearly sobbed in relief as his hands began to explore her.

"Tell me," he said.

She bit her lip as his hand cupped her again. "I am her servant," she said.

Columbine pushed down her spectacles to examine the posies on Bell's desk. "Does your admirer own a flower shop?" she asked.

Bell shook her head.

"Then he is a solicitor—a lawyer."

Bell shook her head.

"An opera singer."

Bell looked at Columbine passively; her eyes said that she did not find this game amusing.

Columbine felt rather foolish. "He is very generous, I must say," she said, fussing with the papers she held. "Flowers every day."

"Columbine," Bell said, not looking up, but staring at the letter on her desk, "you can stop hinting. I'm not going to tell you. Not yet."

Columbine put a hand on her shoulder. "I didn't mean to tease you. I'm just happy to see that you've let someone in at last. Good for you."

She's patronizing me, Bell thought. That's what Lawrence would say. She heard the swish of Columbine's skirts as she went into her own office.

Columbine closed the door behind her. She crossed to her desk but paused at the window. The branches of the trees around Union Square were still bare. Spring had not yet begun, but still, on some mornings she smelled the wet earth and knew the season was hovering, waiting for the moment when it could creep softly in. She was tired of winter. She couldn't wait for spring.

Perhaps that longing for spring was what made her press Bell a little too hard. But why hadn't Bell laughed, or teased? It wasn't like her to be so cold. Bell was a private person, but she had never been cold. Columbine had always thought that love made people happy. But Bell didn't seem happy; her face often looked strained. She didn't moon out the window or appear flushed and happy when she came in the house late at night. Maybe Bell was afraid of being too happy in front of her. Columbine's mouth twisted, and she sighed. Bell was all too aware that Elijah Reed was not exactly sweeping Columbine off her feet.

Columbine was used to being pursued. She was used to wooing. She was used to flowers, and lingering glances, and compliments on her beauty. She was used to the soft sound of approving laughter at her wit. She was used to a certain amount of maneuvering at parties, when men stalked her or hovered by her side or smiled at her across bobbing heads. Granted, she was no longer a young, fresh beauty. But she'd be damned, Columbine thought, her hands tightening into fists, if she gave up those things. She still had her vanity, damnit. She still had her romantic heart.

She had known since the dusky evening in the house on West 10th Street that she was in love with Elijah. She'd thought it would be easy, that night, to set in motion that delicious train of events that led to a love affair. She thought something in her voice, in her eyes, would have told Elijah how she felt. She'd believed that night that he did know, that the knowledge had leaped from her to him at the same instant. But as days passed and he did not do all the things she assumed he would do, she'd doubted her belief.

Was the man blind? Was he a stick? Did he care? He seemed to like her. He called at least three times a week and usually more. He discussed his series in the *Century*, "City of Souls," with her. He joined in all the problems and frustrations of the move to Safe Passage House. But the only time he touched her was when, in a gesture which spoke purely of gentlemanly politeness, no more, he took her arm.

"The man is a stick," Columbine muttered, and to put an exclamation point on her statement, she threw her pencil across the room. She felt ruffled and angry and childish and very much in love.

Lunch without Edwin was unappetizing, and Toby was busy that afternoon, so Marguerite sat and brooded. What was the good of having a wonderful life if she had no one to show it off to?

"Oh, hell," she said out loud. Toby always slapped her hand when she cursed, but she was alone, as usual, and she could do whatever she liked.

Rising, Marguerite looked at herself in the full length mirror of her bedroom. She loved her gown of faille and velvet in deep lavender. It had a trimming of Valenciennes lace and the scalloped skirt was drawn up by deep purple ribbons. Marguerite thought of her mother, who loved clothes, and sighed.

"Why not?" she asked the mirror. Pressing her lips together, she impulsively searched for her plainest black three-quarter length coat. Within ten minutes, she was heading toward Broadway and signaling for a hansom cab.

With her heart thumping against her chest, she called to the driver, "Broadway and Broome." She fell back against the seat and tried not to think as the cab trotted its way inexorably downtown. When it reached Broome Street, Marguerite got out and paid the driver. Without looking around, she headed east.

She was glad she'd chosen her black coat, but she mourned for her new boots when she started down the street. How could she have forgotten the muck? The further east she walked, the more crowded the street became. Children dressed in rags, some carrying bolts of heavy cloth as tall as they were, darted or trudged around her, and the sidewalks were jammed with people, carrying huge baskets full of food or clothing.

Marguerite turned the corner and walked down to Hester Street. Pushcarts were everywhere, each peddler crying his own tune. Some cried their wares in mournful shrieks that still grated on her nerves as they had four years before. The crush and stench were overpowering. Women weaved expertly through the crowd with their market baskets, or called over the din as they haggled about the price of fish or potatoes. Marguerite walked quickly, ignoring the men who stared after her. She wished she'd had the foresight to wear a different dress. Even the six inches hanging below her coat was of such rich purple velvet that it marked her as an outsider. She didn't fit in here any longer.

That was what she wanted, she told herself firmly, that was what she dreamed of. She'd come down here to prove to herself how much she *didn't* fit in, how right she'd been to leave. She lifted her chin defiantly as her expensive boots skirted the running water, the garbage, and the rotting vegetable matter on the sidewalk.

She reached the corner of Hester and Ludlow Street, the site of the Pig's Market. Pushcarts and peddlers crowded even more densely into the space, selling everything but pigs. Potatoes, onions, old coats, pickles, eyeglasses, chickens, cabbages, shoes. Marguerite pushed her way south down Ludlow Street and the pandemoniom lessened a bit.

Everything seemed to turn gray on this street. The smoky sky seemed to droop over the brindled tenements, and she could see only gray, the gray of coal and ash. The very air seemed full of tears as a light mist began to fall. No color here, no gay, bright hats, no glimpse of a green square blocks ahead, no canary-yellow carriages rumbling by. Poverty came in monochrome, she thought wearily. She turned into a dumbell tenement that looked like every other on the street. No filthier, no cleaner, no sunnier, no less dismal than any other dismal building on this dismal block.

She pushed open the front door and reeled back. She could never prepare herself for the smell. She took a deep breath of cold air and went in. She would get used to it; she wouldn't resort to a perfumed handkerchief to her mouth, like a silly countess. There was one sink per floor, one sink that was often backed up from the refuse thrown down it. Waste was either thrown out into the airshaft or dumped in the basement. City services were not exactly up to Fifth Avenue standards down here. She heard the hum of machinery—probably a sweatshop on this floor—and the sound of coughing. Coughing was the constant noise of the poor in the cold months. When she thought of Ludlow Street—and she tried never to think of Ludlow Street—she thought of phlegm.

She mounted the stairs quickly. On the third-floor landing, a head poked out of a doorway. "What do you want?" the woman called out in Yiddish. Her tone was half-nasty, half-authoritative.

"It's me, Mrs. Schneiderman," Marguerite answered in Yiddish.

The woman opened the door wider. She pushed a lock of gray hair off her forehead. "Marguerite Blum! Come to see your mama? That's good."

"Is she well?"

The woman shrugged. "Living in this hellhole, as well as can be expected, eh? But your father has the cough. They lost their boarder, that *makher*, he was no good. But I found them another, Mr. Ablowitz, he's a tailor."

"That was kind of you, Mrs. Schneiderman. How is your family?" Marguerite asked politely. She knew she'd hear it from her mother if she didn't inquire about the health of their neighbor's family.

"What you'd expect. Colds, chilblains, but the weather is getting warmer, at least. Spring gives us hope still, God knows why."

She seemed inclined to say more, but Marguerite said quickly, "I'll go up now, then."

Mrs. Schneiderman seemed to notice Marguerite's clothes for the first time. She looked her up and down, and her eyes widened. There was no subtlety on the East Side. Any moment now she would ask Marguerite where she'd obtained such fine clothes—and how. On the East Side, your business was everybody's business.

"Goodbye, Mrs. Schneiderman," Marguerite said quickly, and turned to go.

"Tell your mother I'll be up later with some cabbage soup," the woman called after her. She held the door open and watched until Marguerite was out of sight, craning her neck to see her.

Marguerite pounded out her irritation on each step. She remembered afresh the reason she left. Poverty, yes, she'd hated everything about it. She hated the smell, the look, the feel of it, scratchy clothes against her skin, cabbage, human waste, cold water. And she hated her father, of course. But how she hated this feeling, the penned-in feeling, the difficulty breathing *because* of the close air, the smells, and the goddamn neighbors who know everything, down to how often Mr. and Mrs. Gelb on the sixth floor make love, or how bad Mr. Goldman's cough is, or how long Marguerite Blum had talked to Avi Cohen on the fire escape the night before.

She knocked on her parents' door, heard slow footsteps heading across the kitchen. Her mother opened it and peered at her in the dim light. "Marguerite?" she asked, as if she didn't recognize her at all.

"Hello, *maman.*" Marguerite stepped forward into the kitchen and hugged her mother. She still got a shock, every time. Her mother who had once smelled so light and flowery, whose skin had been so soft, whose body had been so round. Now her mother was as thin and crackly as paper, so transparent that Marguerite almost expected her to crumble into dust when she moved.

"*Ma petite.*" Tears were in her mother's blue eyes. "You look very pretty. Come in. Your father is here today," she added in a whisper.

Marguerite hesitated. "He's home?" she asked in an undertone.

"His chest is bad. He couldn't carry the pack. He's helping me with the sewing today. Come in, he's too sick to fuss at you." Her mother tugged on Marguerite's hand. "Come in, come in. I want to see you."

She followed her mother uneasily down the short, dark hall, inching around a pile of sewing. Her mother took in whatever she could get. It was a good job, better than a sweatshop, but not steady. Sometimes her mother made paper flowers if she could not get piece work. But the bundles of cloth made the apartment look like the sweatshop she prided herself on avoiding. There was no room to move, and the dust from the cloth, carried through the streets, made everyone sneeze. It was piled everywhere, even on the kitchen table.

The light in the main room was not much better. Pants and coats were bundled up and stacked against the walls. An old sewing machine, a precious item, was pushed up against the one window, a cheap pair of knee pants trailing off one end. Next to the machine, a mattress was pushed up against the wall. The boarder would place it on the floor when he returned home that evening, Marguerite knew. She remembered during one bad time that her father had unhinged the doors and used them for beds for more boarders, laying them across the few chairs they had. Marguerite would have to pick her way through the men, in their dirty underwear lying underneath thin blankets, snoring, their beards wet with saliva from their open mouths. One of them used to grab at her legs, try to get underneath her skirts as she passed. She never told her mother.

Her father sat sewing in one corner, his long beard trailing in his lap. Marguerite could see how bad his stitches were. Her mother would probably rip them out and do all his work over again, at night, when he was asleep. It was the unwritten rule of the Blum family that Jacob Blum never be confronted with his many failures, no matter how large or small. Forget to pay the rent, father, so we're thrown out in the street with our embarrassing bundle of belongings? Let the street boys cheat you out of items from your peddler's pack for two weeks in a row? Forget your daughter's birthday? Strike your wife for no reason? No one will mention a word of reproach.

"Look, Jacob," her mother said.

Her father looked up. Marguerite hadn't seen him in three years. "I see, Sophie." He bent down over his work again. She saw the needle shake in his thick fingers.

Sophie crossed the room with rapid steps. She bent over her husband. "Aren't you going to greet your daughter? Aren't you going to say something?" she hissed.

Marguerite sighed. It had been this way since she could remember. Her father ignored her existence and her mother begged him to acknowledge her. It had never been easy. He had struck her only once, at the age of fifteen. She had been ten minutes late coming home from school. After that, she just ceased to exist for him. He would not talk to her, answer her questions, notice her in any way. She had begged him on her knees to talk to her, but he had merely looked past her shoulder and asked Sophie if there was any tea.

He would not go as far as to sit shiva on her, though. That puzzled her, though perhaps it was because he could point to nothing that she'd actually done wrong. She had been dutiful, as far as it went, and she'd gotten a good job uptown, room and board in respectable houses.

Their antagonism had always been silent. She'd left for good at sixteen, returning only for occasional visits when she knew he would not be home. She never knew what she had done to make her father hate her so. She didn't care any longer.

She loosened her coat and leaned against the doorframe. The room was so terrible in its familiarity. Sophie tried to keep the place looking as nice as possible. She'd refused to sell not only her fine tablecloth, only used on the Sabbath, but also the bright pieces of fabric she'd brought from France. So a yellow fringed cloth was draped over the dilapidated sofa, and a red cushion sat in a lonely fashion on a chair with a broken spindle on its back. Marguerite's eyes roamed around the room and finally returned to her father. To her surprise, he was looking at her.

"Sophie, look at her dress," he said.

Marguerite's hands fluttered to her coat. She pulled it closed.

"Good material, I can see from here," he said. "Silk. Fine lace. Velvet. And her boots. Look at her boots. Fur-lined."

"Jacob—"

Marguerite rearranged her skirts hastily, but she could not disguise her boots completely. She met her father's gaze, held trapped in its fiery blackness, suspended, in a dream. She was sixteen, she was fifteen again, still feeling that bewildering rush of shame.

Suddenly, he leaped to his feet, the boy's trousers falling to the floor. "Whore!" he shouted. He took two steps toward her while Sophie grabbed ineffectually at his sleeve. "Did you come here from Allen Street?"

Marguerite stared at him. She kept her face a mask, for she knew it infuriated him more. Tears gave him great satisfaction.

Sophie had begun to cry. "Please," she sobbed. "Please. I just want to visit with her. We'll go to the kitchen. Sit, Jacob. Please."

"Is that why you left your father's house?" Jacob thundered. "And who is your cadet, that Benny Gold? The bum who peddles flesh instead of fish? He has the girls you can get for cheap, I hear."

"Is that what you *hear*, Papa?" she asked deliberately. "Or is that what you paid? You always were a *shnorer*."

"Marguerite! Please." Sophie's sobs were wrenching.

Marguerite glanced at her mother. "I'm going, Mama." She turned and went back into the kitchen. Her hands were shaking as she buttoned her coat. Why had she returned? To tell her mother, who loved music, that she had a voice, a real voice? Or to show off her pretty dress? What did she expect?

Furious at her own stupidity, Marguerite banged out of the apartment and hurried down the steep, narrow stairs. She could hardly wait to get outside, where she could breathe again. As she passed the third landing, she heard Mrs. Schneiderman open her door. "Don't worry, I'm leaving!" she called furiously as she ran down the stairs.

She burst through the front door and took a deep breath of the chill air. She leaned weakly against the railing for an instant. She had to move, had to get off this street, but she felt paralyzed. Suppose she saw someone she knew? She'd kept to herself for the short time she'd lived here, but still, there were those who might recognize her as the scrawny teenager who'd run away and broken her parents' hearts. Marguerite had thought she'd wanted that, wanted someone from her past to see her fine clothes. But they would all think the same thing, that she was a whore. Because she was pretty and because she had a fine dress, she was a whore. Marguerite walked down the steps.

Behind her, the door opened, and Sophie ran out, pulling on her shabby coat. "Marguerite, wait," she said, hurrying down the steps after her.

Marguerite turned a stony face to her mother. She waited for the explanation, the excuses. Your father, he doesn't mean it. He's been sick with the cough. He's never gotten over the shame of being a peddler, Jacob Blum, the richest Jew in Odessa. Can't you see what that would do to a man?

Instead, Sophie gazed at her with calm, beautiful blue eyes, looking very practical, and very French. She shrugged. "I have to put up with him. You don't. Next time, I'll meet you somewhere."

Sometimes Marguerite was able to catch a glimpse of the woman she'd once known, and this was one of those times. Instantly, she softened. "Oh, *Maman*." She hugged her mother and tears sprang to her eyes.

"My baby." Sophie tucked a dark curl into Marguerite's hat. "Come, let's walk, little raven."

"Don't call me that, please, *Maman*," Marguerite said in a calm voice.

Sophie peered at her worriedly. "Of course."

They walked, arm in arm, toward Canal Street. There was no place to walk to, no park, no square with trees or grass. Sophie probably hadn't seen a blade of grass since she and Marguerite had left France nearly five years ago, Marguerite reflected.

Marguerite had grown up in Odessa, that most beautiful of seaports on the Black Sea, one of the few Russian cities with a European accent. Her father dealt in Ukranian wheat, and he was rich.

He'd come penniless from France as a boy, and he'd worked his way up in the grain business. It took him until he was thirty to open his own office, but he did it, starting small, sleeping in the small office next to his files. The business flourished and grew, and Jacob saved his money. When he felt he had more than enough, he bought a house and looked for a wife to run it. He'd wanted someone mature, someone his own age, thirty-nine. But on the street one day he'd seen nineteen-year-old Sophie Marcel, who had come for a visit with her father from France, blond, blue-eyed, with the face of an angel. Jacob had fallen instantly in love. He courted her, and Sophie had been dazzled by the handsome, wealthy man who looked at her so adoringly, who touched her hand so respectfully, so thrillingly. They were engaged within a month.

Jews flourished in Odessa, along with French businessmen, Italians and Greeks, and Armenians. The opera was renowned, the days long and sunny. "Like God in Odessa," went the Yiddish saying, bringing contentment and prosperity to mind. Sophie and Jacob were prominent citizens, enjoyed the opera and the large house Jacob had built on a hill overlooking the harbor. And then came the Easter riots of 1871. The Easter "amusements" they were often called by the Gentiles who perpetrated them.

It started on a Sunday. There was a rumor that some Jewish students had thrown a dead cat upon the altar of a Greek church. Within hours, twenty or thirty roving bands were searching for Jewish victims. Jewish businesses were looted, Jewish women raped, synogogues burned to the ground. Jacob was in his offices, alone, so he did not hear the news for some time. Sophie was home alone. Jacob ran through the streets, running through broken glass and debris, papers and ledgers, for the marauders had left nothing. He passed the Jewish bank where he did business every day and saw that every window was destroyed, and that on a balcony laughing men were throwing down books, accounts, ripping them into small fragments which fluttered down to the street like snowflakes. Now Jacob could smell fire, and the fear moved his legs as he ran, dodging down the alleys that he knew so well, the side streets, in as straight a line as he dared to take toward his house.

When he reached his house he saw, through the broken windows, men in the upstairs room. A group of them stood on the balcony, tugging at Sophie's beloved piano. A window shattered and the glass fell in the street. And then with a roar, the piano went over, splintering on the cobblestones with an awful cry. With his heart in his mouth, Jacob ran to the back and opened a cellar door. He went down the dark stairs and found Sophie, sitting on the dank floor, half-dressed, her blond hair loose and hanging down her back. She would not speak, and he picked her up like a child and half-carried, half-dragged her a few blocks away to a friendly baker who lent them his cellar at peril of his life. They ate bread and pastries for three days and emerged at last to find the Jewish quarter devastated, every window broken. Dazed, they walked through streets that were full of feathers, for it seemed every bed in the quarter had been ripped open. It looked as though a heavy snow had taken place, the streets were so white. They walked through the feathers past the burned-out shells of houses, not daring to hope. When he saw his house standing, Jacob wept. He did not care, at that moment, that all the precious things Sophie loved and cared for were broken or missing. And when he heard of the mother who had tried to prevent the rape of her daughter and had her ears cut off, then bled to death, he thanked God for his wife, whose empty eyes would surely fill with love and hope once again, please God.

Jacob never felt safe in Odessa again, but it was his home, and he loved it, so he said to all who would listen that the riots had been an aberration. He talked of moving his money to France but never did. Jews were too important to the economy of Odessa to destroy their businesses, he said. The czar would protect them. He rebuilt his business and refurnished his house, and he went on and prospered as before, slowly but surely. Marguerite was born in December of 1871, and though Sophie had been depressed during her pregnancy, she seemed to revive at the first sight of her pretty daughter. Life began anew.

Marguerite loved Odessa. She spoke fluent French, Yiddish, and Russian. She was a privileged child, cosseted by her mother, adored by her father. She still remembered her childhood as whole years of sun and warmth, good food, loving arms and generous kisses. She grew up, a beautiful child, with perfect white skin and her mother's dark blue eyes. Her hair was of the deepest black, unlike Sophie's, which was blond, and her father's, which was a dark red. She took after her paternal grandmother, who had been renowned for her beautiful hair, like sable, her father said, showing her a miniature of his mother. He called Marguerite "little raven," and he indulged her every whim.

On March 1, 1881, czar Alexander II was assasinated by terrorists. The czar had been known for his modest reforms, his liberalism toward Jews. Within days, a riot began in Yelizavetgrad, then spread to the neighboring cities, reaching Kiev on April 26th.

This time, news reached them, and Jacob saw it coming. He could not quite believe that it would spread as far as Odessa, but he made plans. He bribed a captain on one of his ships to take Sophie and Marguerite on the next run to France. He gave Sophie a purse full of gold, but he had no time to transfer money from the bank. He sent them away on the morning of May 3rd, just as trouble began in the streets, but Jacob stayed with his home and his business. Marguerite remembered the smoke and the cries from the city as they sailed away, hiding among bales of wheat. She remembered how her mother trembled as she held Marguerite too tightly.

The captain was supposed to hire someone to deliver them straight to Lille, to Sophie's aunt, but he dropped them off at the pier in Marseille and never returned to Odessa with the ship, saying he had had enough of dealing with Jews.

Jacob never spoke of what happened during the riots, but he lost everything. Nothing was salvagable, nothing remained. Consoling himself with the thought of his wife and daughter safe with her relatives, he booked passage for America. It was the only way, he wrote Sophie. Many Russian Jews were going. In America, Jews were safe. He had no money, but he would make it again. Other Jews would help him.

Sophie showed an unexpected strength on the pier in Marseille. She got them to Lille, chattering about the great adventures they were having. She exclaimed over the new house they would live in in Lille, though it seemed small and dank to Marguerite after the grand house in Odessa. And she laughed and sang while she peeled potatoes and dug in the garden.

Marguerite spent four years in France. Her aunt and uncle were not rich, and they weren't very kind, but Marguerite was happy much of the time. She hardly missed her father after a few months, for Jacob, in the past years, had been rarely home, trying to build up his business to what it had been before. Now without a governess, she became closer to her mother. Sophie seemed to blossom without Jacob, and even grew to be a gifted gardener. It came as something of a shock for both of them when Jacob sent the fare for their passage to America.

Still, it was another adventure, and though Marguerite didn't want to leave France, America loomed as a romantic place, full of possibility. Sophie and Marguerite spent days sewing and packing and making sure their wardrobes were perfect for the trip. They scraped together some money so they could both have new hats.

They were blessed with good weather for the passage, and they felt lucky, with second class accommodations, compared to steerage. But their good spirits faded upon their arrival in New York. Marguerite would never forget the shock of seeing her father at the pier. Looking at her mother, she knew Sophie was shocked, too. Jacob was old.

At first, he had tried for a good job uptown, his hopes moving downward from manager to accountant to clerk. Nobody wanted him. He was a Russian Jew, no matter that he had been born in France, and he found that German Jews looked at him with distaste, thinking him a peasant. They would give him a chance, some said, but times were bad. For some reason, he could not hold onto any job he took. Later, Marguerite realized that Jacob was a good employer but a bad employee. He had lost his spirit and his hope, and he was not willing to do menial work. He grew affronted at slights, he lost his temper, and he was often fired. The job as a clerk in a store had given him a burst of optimism and he had sent their passage. But in the time it took for them to make ready and cross the ocean, he had been fired again. Jacob was at his lowest ebb; he was a peddler.

Marguerite was no longer a privileged child. She was sent to school, but it was a public school filled with peasant children. Her mother sewed, and they took in boarders. And instead of the adoring father she dimly remembered, a thin stranger stood in his clothes, a stranger who, after her fifteenth birthday, told her flatly that she would turn out to no good. Things were never the same for Marguerite. She had another year of hell, and then she moved out. She put on her clean shirtwaist and her black skirt and took the El uptown, all the way to Fifth Avenue. She put on her French accent, for she had picked one up in France, called herself Marguerite Corbeau—raven, in French, a nod to a time when her father still loved her—and got a job as a maid. She'd suffered there for two years until Columbine had rescued her.

But her mother was still trapped. Marguerite looked around at the grayness her mother lived with. She remembered the fresh flowers her mother would insist on having all around her in Odessa, and even in Lille. She remembered Sophie, her blond hair spilling out of her bun, her cheeks flushed with triumph over the success of her tomatoes. Now, Sophie would never think of wasting a nickel and taking the El up to Central Park.

"Mama," Marguerite said impulsively, "if I came down and met you, would you take a cab with me uptown to the Park? You could see trees and grass. It's so lovely, Mama."

"Oh, I don't know. That would take a half a day, wouldn't it? I couldn't take the time."

"But I have money, Mama. I could give you the money you'd make that afternoon. Papa wouldn't have to know. Will you think about it?"

Sophie touched a fleeting hand to her hair. "But I have nothing to wear, *cheri.*" She laughed. "You forget I am French."

"I'll buy you a new hat, a beautiful hat, with feathers and flowers, whatever you want."

Sophie stared at her penetratingly. "And where will you get the money for such a hat?"

Marguerite briefly considered telling her about Edwin, but decided to wait until she was actually married. "I'm taking singing lessons, Mama. Remember how you told me I sang like a bird? My teacher says I have great talent. I'm going to audition for William Miles Paradise in a few weeks."

"Who?"

"William Paradise," Marguerite said impatiently. "The most famous theatrical producer in New York, Mama."

Sophie frowned. "On Second Avenue? What kind of a name is Paradise?"

Marguerite shook her head. "Not Yiddish theatre, Mama. *Real* theatre. He put on *The Girl from Abeline*, and *Maisie's European Tour*, and, oh, so many plays. And he does revues, too. He knows everyone—Lillian Russell, Edwin Booth, John Drew . . ."

"He must be a great man. But Marguerite, how are you paying for these lessons?"

Marguerite looked away impatiently. "I have a job, remember? I'm living with Columbine Nash, and I work in her office."

"You never had fine silk dresses from that job," her mother observed.

"You sound like Papa," Marguerite said grimly.

Sophie hesitated. "No. But I'm your mother. I know how men take advantage . . ."

"And what if I take advantage of them?" she tossed out with a laugh.

Sophie withdrew her arm and turned to her. Her blue eyes were sharp with censure. "You are still a child, Marguerite, not a woman. When you are a woman, you will show respect to your mother. Do you think I am without wisdom, without experience? I'm not a peasant, not an uneducated woman. Do you think I am just the meek little wife, running after my difficult husband? You forget how long I was without him, how I made a life for you, alone. And now you toss away my words like chaff in the wind. Don't be so smart, little one."

Marguerite decided not to point out that they had lived with Aunt Mariette and Uncle Max in Lille. Sophie had not exactly been alone. "No, Mama, I don't forget," she said in a concilatory tone. "Let's not quarrel. I have to leave you, and I can't if you're frowning at me." Marguerite dug into her bag and pressed all the money she had in her mother's hands, leaving some change for a cab. "Buy some meat this week. Some medicine for Papa's chest, though he doesn't deserve it."

Sophie blushed as she took the money. "I didn't tell you, but things could be looking up. There's a rumor—this rich man, Baron de Hirsch, he's asked how many immigrants are on the East Side. He's counting the Jews, and they say he'll give one hundred dollars to each person! Jacob is sure of this. Won't that be wonderful?"

Marguerite looked into her mother's eyes. She could see that her mother did believe it. "No one is going to give you anything, Mama," she said. "Don't you see that it isn't worth it, to do piece work, to live like an animal? You have to take a big step, a big risk, to get anywhere."

Now her mother was annoyed again. "What do you know of risks? It doesn't take much courage to risk when you're young and pretty. That's the danger of it."

Marguerite pulled on her gloves. "All right, whatever you say," she said, not listening. "I'll bring more money next time. And Mama, I'm not what Papa thinks I am. I promise."

Sophie looked down at the money in her hands. "But what are you?" she asked slowly.

Marguerite pretended she hadn't heard. She kissed her mother and walked quickly away. *What, indeed?* she thought. But she smiled while she thought it.

Thirteen

FIONA DEVLIN REFUSED to meet Elijah at her home, so they met halfway at a restaurant on Charles Street. It was mid-afternoon, and they were the only customers. Elijah ordered two coffees from the bored proprietor, who poured out two mugs and then returned to nap in front of the coal stove.

While Fiona blew on the coffee and took her first sip, Elijah studied her face underneath the brim of a black hat. For this age, the feminine ideal was of lush womanhood, bosomy and full-hipped in elaborate gowns. Fiona would not be thought terribly attractive. She was a working woman in a shabby black dress; she looked underfed.

But some future age might call her beautiful, Elijah thought. She had a strong, striking face, and he admired it. The nose was straight and long, the jaw a bit too prominent. One of her front teeth overlapped the other slightly. Her skin was pale, but it did not have the creaminess that some women of fair coloring had; it was thin and translucent, skin that would show any change in temperature or emotion. Her eyes were extraordinary, icy green, and in the left one, there was a tiny triangle of deep gold. Next to the skin and the eyes her hair was tangerine colored, wild, extravagant. It was thick and very long, the kind of hair that it is impossible to tame, wavy, kinky and curly by turns, and always unruly.

"Do you see something you like, Mr. Reed?" she asked him mockingly.

He had been caught, and Elijah regretted his rudeness. It was not a good way to begin. "I didn't mean to stare. I beg your pardon, Mrs. Devlin."

She shrugged and cupped her coffee. Her hands looked red and cold; the cuticles were cracked, and one knuckle was skinned. "It's all right. What do you want? Are you writing another article about the poor and downtrodden?"

"No." Elijah remembered now how blunt she was. She had no time for anyone who bored her. "I learned something recently that I thought you should know."

She looked at him over the thick rim of her coffee mug. There was no curiosity in her eyes. She would wait for the information, then decide if it was worth knowing or not.

"I'm afraid that Mrs. Nash's position might have been misrepresented to you," he said. "She has agreed to testify for you, should you wish to bring a lawsuit against Ambrose Hartley."

Fiona blinked, the only sign that this information had interested her. She put down her mug very slowly. She picked at a cuticle, then put her hands in her lap. "She agreed, you say?"

"Yes. From the first. I wanted you to know that."

She nodded several times while she took in the information. "Well, it doesn't matter. My Jim won't go through the bother and expense. We don't expect justice, why would our case be any different from the way things are? And with Mr. Hartley having that heart attack, no judge would rule for us anyway."

"I agree, the chances are not good. But I would help in any way I could, should you wish to proceed. I'm sure I could find counsel who wouldn't charge a fee, or wait until the settlement to take any money."

She waved a hand, then reached behind her for her coat. He noticed how the stitching near the armholes was coming out. A benefactor, indeed, Mr. Birch. "I have something else to tell you," he went on. "An offer, actually."

She paused, then let her coat drop to her lap. "Yes?"

"Mr. Van Cormandt is looking for a domestic worker. A parlormaid. He asked if you would be interested in taking a job."

With an impatient jerk, she turned her head sideways, then glanced at him. "I never did upstairs work. I always was in the kitchens."

"Mr. Van Cormandt is aware of that." Elijah leaned across the table. "He's more liberal than most, Mrs. Devlin. You and Mr. Devlin could live in, or out, as you choose. Sundays and one other afternoon off, and Mr. Van Cormandt is often out of town these days, and doesn't entertain. He said he could use another stable worker, too. Isn't Mr. Devlin up and about?"

She nodded shortly. Her mouth twisted. She looked over Elijah's left shoulder, into the distance. "A one-armed man in a stable?"

"I've seen Mr. Devlin. He's a good, strong man, stronger than most. What do you say, Mrs. Devlin? Would you like to talk to Mr. Van Cormandt?"

She stood up abruptly, surprising Elijah, who reared back as her chair skidded across the tiled floor. The proprietor woke up and looked at them with new interest.

Clutching her coat in front of her, she leaned over the table and locked eyes with Elijah. "I wouldn't work for that man if he danced barefoot to my doorway over broken glass and knelt on his bloody knees at my feet."

Elijah hesitated, then nodded. "A compelling image, Mrs. Devlin. But I do get your point."

Fiona pulled on her coat, thrusting her arms into the sleeves stiffly. Adjusting her hat, she started toward the door.

"Mrs. Devlin?"

She turned. "There's more, Mr. Reed?"

"When did you first meet Mr. Birch?"

Her nostrils flared. "And what business is it of yours?" she asked tightly.

"Was he there that night, at the New Year's Eve party, to see you?"

Fiona met his gaze squarely. Her green eyes glittered. "No," she said, and walked out.

Bell was packing china from the breakfront when Columbine burst into the dining room.

"Bell, I must talk to you."

Bell put down a handful of straw. "For heaven's sake, Columbine, I almost dropped the good teapot. What is it?"

Weakly, Columbine collapsed on a chair. "You didn't take any cash from the Emergency Fund without entering it into the ledger, did you?"

Bell shook her head. "Of course not. Why?"

Columbine's brown eyes were full of panic. "Because there's money missing. Quite a bit of money. I was hoping that you took it."

Bell slid into the chair across from Columbine's. "Did you ask Rosa? She has a key to the drawer."

Columbine shook her head. "No, I wanted to talk to you first. Bell, it's all gone. And since I received those funds from England it was more than usual. It was over a thousand dollars, Bell! I was going to put it in the bank today. I knew I shouldn't have left it in the drawer."

"But the drawer is locked. We're very careful."

"And only three of us have the key. You, me, and Rosa."

"And Marguerite. I gave her one when she started to work on the fund with me." Bell's eyes widened as speculation entered her mind. "But this is terrible."

Columbine moved the toe of her shoe over the carpet. "I can't imagine Marguerite doing such a thing."

"Nor can I."

"Rosa has had trouble at home. Her mother has a problem in her lungs, and can't work. They're behind on the rent."

"You think Rosa—"

Columbine stood up, agitated. "No, I don't think Rosa, and no, I don't think Marguerite, either. But I would rather think that someone who needed money took it."

"Marguerite had all those pretty clothes before she left," Bell said musingly. "Those gloves, the lavender dress—"

Columbine shook her head fiercely. "I don't believe it. Someone else could have gotten the key somehow."

"You have to talk to them, at least," Bell said. "Do you know where Marguerite is living?"

Columbine nodded. She sat down, then stood up again. She walked to the window and looked out into the back yard, lost in thought.

Bell, too, was thinking. Suddenly, she was remembering last night. She had remained after the others had left, waiting for Lawrence to pick her up. Her keys had been on top of her desk when she went out to the hallway to the water closet to wash her hands. Lawrence had stayed in her office.

No, she told herself. It was Marguerite, it had to be. Those fine dresses, those fur-lined boots. And that casual, conniving heart. Lawrence would never steal from the New Women Society. No matter that he didn't believe in it. And when she had returned, had he had any consciousness, any guilt on his face? Not at all. They had gone out to dinner—and she had paid! Bell had a gust of pleasant relief at the thought. Surely the man could not be so black-hearted to let the woman he stole from pay for his dinner.

Columbine was shaking her head. "No," she said decidedly. "I'll not talk to Rosa or Marguerite or anyone at the office. If someone took the money, they must have had very good reason for it. We'll just have to put our energy into replacing it, God knows how." She sighed. "Let's just hope it went for a good cause."

"It's very simple," Lawrence said again to Fiona. He was beginning to lose his patience. "There is no danger, I assure you. As soon as I get my materials, I can construct the device. But first you have to practice with the fuse. You'll have to do it in the morning, when the cleaning women are in the offices. No one will suspect anything."

"Device?" Fiona laughed. "Why are you always trying to talk like a gentleman, Lawrence? Call it a bomb, like a good anarchist should."

"The bomb, then," Lawrence snapped. "What is the matter with you today?"

Fiona turned her head to look out at the harbor. They were standing on the Battery, and the wind was fierce. The sky wrapped around them, aggressively blue. The water was the color of steel with an edging of lace where whitecaps foamed. "It's a dancing day," she said. "My ma would call it a dancing day."

Lawrence stirred impatiently. "Fiona, are you listening to me?"

For an answer, Fiona sighed and said something in Gaelic.

Lawrence scowled. He had enough of trying to decipher the Yiddish and Russian at meetings without dealing with this. Why couldn't they speak English, these immigrants? "What did you say?"

"I said it's a poor man who stares at the ground when there's such a sky overhead," Fiona answered with a shrug. "And why are we always meeting in the wind, Lawrence? There's a danger your words will be snatched away completely. I can't imagine you wordless, Lawrence. Would there be anything there, without the words?"

Lawrence reached up to anchor his hat on his head, for the wind suddenly gusted and almost knocked it off. "I've had enough of this. I'm trying to tell you. I'm going to meet the man who's getting the materials for me. I had to pay him a pretty penny, and I daren't be late. So let's pick a time to meet again."

She stepped closer to him. She tilted her head back and fixed him with her compelling eyes. "What if I don't want to meet you again?"

Lawrence hesitated, for at last he was able to ignore the bite of the wind and her mockery and see the distrustful anger in her eyes. Fear trickled in; he was in trouble. "What is it?" he asked, curbing his impatience under a concerned frown. He laid a hand on her arm. "Tell me. I'm sorry if I was sharp with you."

She looked at him searchingly, then turned away. "It's nothing. Go, then."

But he had seen the need in her face, and he knew he hadn't lost her completely. "Fiona. Tell me, dearest."

"Oh, am I your dearest now?"

He shook his head slowly. "You always mock me. How do you expect me to be tender when you are so light with me?"

She gripped his upper arms and he felt the strength of her hands through his coat. "I'm in this, Lawrence. I'm in this with you," she rasped, shaking him with every utterance. "You have to be true to me. You're my man, Lawrence. You're not near as good as me, nor as good as I could get, but there it is."

So she loved him, after all. Bell flitted across his mind, her amber beauty, her wounded eyes. He needed them both, Lawrence knew, his eyes tearing from the wind. He needed the fierce, wild woman in front of him who he took like an animal outdoors in the cold, in the wind, in the wild winter. And he needed the passive creature who sprawled across his bed in her lace-edged drawers and let him do what he wanted to her.

"Yes, Fiona, there it is. You're my woman," he told her.

"Then why have you lied to me?" she asked impassively. She dropped her hands from him, flinging them off his coat as though he were diseased.

"Lied to you? I haven't—"

"There, you've lied again," she said calmly.

Lawrence quickly catalogued his lies and desperately searched for the one she could know about. But he knew from experience that in a moment she would tell him which one it was. They always did.

But he had underestimated her. "Are there so many, Lawrence?" she asked with a hollow laugh.

He thought of Ned Van Cormandt and Elijah Reed. It had to be what they would know, he decided. He would have to risk it. "Mrs. Nash said all along she would testify for you," he said. The words came out fast. Fiona looked at him, and he felt relief course through him. Perspiration had broken out on her accusal, and now the wind cooled it, making him shiver slightly. He jammed his hands in his pockets.

"Why did you tell me she wouldn't?"

"Because I knew the effort would be fruitless, first of all," Lawrence answered. "People like us get no justice. I knew you'd want to get back at all of them a better way."

"How did you know that?"

"Because that's the kind of woman you are. Courageous."

She put out the flat of her hand to him, her gesture meaning, don't flatter me Lawrence, get away with you. But he'd almost convinced her, he saw.

"I shouldn't have lied about it," he added.

Fiona met his pale, pale eyes. They were a dagger in her heart, those eyes, and they would hurt her someday, most likely. But they were hers. She was trapped in this, with him, her man. But he was trapped, too. At least she had satisfaction in that.

"Lawrence," she said slowly, "you can do anything else but lie. You can murder a man or steal from your mother or take another woman for your pleasure. But don't lie to me again."

He knew better than to embrace her. Holding her gaze, he nodded.

"All right, then," Fiona said, as if that settled the matter. "Let's get out of this wind."

They struck out across the lonely park, empty in the bitter March cold. "Who told you?" he asked her.

"Mr. Elijah Reed, the famous writer. Bought me a cup of coffee at least. Oh, and he had the nerve to offer me and Jimmy jobs in Mr. Van Cormandt's house. As if I'd wait on Neddie Van Cormandt, that blackguard. I'd as soon spit in his food as serve it."

Lawrence stopped in his tracks. "You have to take it."

"I don't," she answered indignantly.

"Don't you see?" he said, turning and grasping both her hands. "We wouldn't have to go to his office. We could set the bomb in his house. It would be foolproof then."

She frowned fiercely, breathing hard. "Do you know what you're asking, Lawrence? I could go to prison. I'd be the first one they'd suspect."

"We'll find a way around it. I promise you, Fiona. But you have to take the job. Not Jimmy. Just you."

She stared out at the water again. "I don't know about this."

"I'll figure it all out," he said, squeezing her gloved hand. "We don't have to decide anything yet. But you have to take the job." He smiled. "And you can spit in his food if you'd care to. Every morning."

She whipped her head around to look at him, saw the look in his eyes, and started to laugh. Lawrence laughed too, throwing his head back slightly, and the wind took his hat and sailed it down the Battery. Lawrence stopped laughing—the hat was a good one, and it was cold—and sprang after it. The hat leaped comically, precariously close to the railing, but he ran harder and snatched it back. He jammed it on his head and ran back to Fiona.

She was laughing harder than ever now, tears springing to her brilliant eyes. "And to think I've never seen you dance before," she said merrily, and when he scowled fresh laughter overtook her.

She looked lovely, with the wind whipping her red-orange hair and bringing a rosy flush to her cheeks, and amusement smoothing out the lines of care around her mouth. She finally looked her age, twenty-four, young and playful for the first time since he'd known her. And Lawrence was struck with the depths of his hatred and his love, and how much he had, without knowing it until this moment, seeing her laughing at him, become so unwillingly at her mercy.

Columbine sat at her dressing table, staring at herself in the mirror. She wished passionately that Bell were home. She needed her so badly. Never had an issue felt so crucial.

Was this the right hat, or not?

She was going to lunch with Elijah at Sherry's today, and she had bought a new hat yesterday for the occasion. She turned her head this way and that, considering it. Oh, when would she grow too old to be so vain!

She had never felt comfortable in those delicate bonnets that perched on the head and thrust feathers in the face of any who might lean forward in intent conversation. No, Columbine preferred a hat that proclaimed its function as well as its beauty. It must have a brim, to ward off the sun, and it must not be overly adorned with netting, in case of rain, and it must never, ever contain a small stuffed bird. But still, it must be cunningly aimed at the heart of a woman, and she must feel beautiful in it.

This one was black felt, large brimmed, with a crown of dark green velvet. The netting was black, studded with tiny bits of jet, and a few dyed black and green ostrich feathers edged the crown. A thick black ribbon crossed the back and supported a cluster of small red roses, which looked rather nice, she thought, against her blond hair. But what would Elijah Reed think? Would he think the hat frivolous and her silly to wear it? Most likely the women he was interested in were serious creatures who would never think of wearing a hat with jet beads and roses and velvet ribbons. They were too busy reading to shop, and could discuss Zola's latest novel with Elijah, which they'd read in the original French.

The man was making her crazy, and she was late for lunch. Columbine made a face at herself, adjusted a curl, smoothed an eyebrow, and ran for her coat.

He was waiting for her inside the door of Sherry's, standing with his unlit cigar—he was trying to quit, he told her—as though he had all day to wait. They were ushered to a side table near the wall. Columbine sat down, feeling very conscious of her new hat.

"Have you decided whether to partition that second bedroom?" Elijah asked as the waiter handed them their menus with a flourish.

Despite her best efforts, Columbine felt the fizziness of her mood flatten instantly. Couldn't he have at least noticed the hat? She had a sudden longing for Ned, who would have complimented her, told her she was beautiful and that waiting fifteen minutes for her had been extremely disagreeable for him, that he had been afraid she'd forgotten. She wanted to tell Elijah Reed this, that some men had actually found her beautiful. She wanted to tell him he was an oaf and a boor, and didn't deserve her.

Instead, she picked up her napkin. "Yes, we have," she said. "I've talked with a carpenter, a handsome young man by the name of Frederic Hanning who has an attachment to tools that borders on the romantic. He measured and nodded and knocked on walls and looked at pipes and rubbed his hands together. He can make one big bedroom into two snug rooms with no trouble at all, he said."

"Good. Now, what should we eat today? Shall we start with oysters and champagne? This is a celebration, you know."

"I didn't. Oysters and champagne would be delightful, but first, you must tell me what we're celebrating."

"Oh, merely that the circulation of the *Century* has gone up since I started my series, so they've contracted for six more articles of my choosing."

"But that's marvelous! I'm so glad, both as a reader and a friend." Columbine *was* happy for Elijah. But she had also been thinking that he'd invited her to lunch because . . . well, because he wanted to invite her to lunch. Though it *was* a good sign that he chose her to celebrate with. Columbine stared at her menu and fussily begged herself to stop her questions and suppositions and be a gracious presence, not a lovesick adolescent. She thought of Bell's serenity and decided to emulate it. She raised her chin and stared into the middle distance with what she hoped was a Giaconda smile.

Elijah peered at her. "Is something wrong? You look rather ill."

Columbine snapped her menu on the table. "I'm fine. Just fine."

"If you grit your teeth like that you'll never be able to eat."

"Maybe you should order soup, then," Columbine suggested pleasantly. "That way I won't have to chew."

Elijah grinned and ordered champagne and oysters to start. While they sipped their champagne, Columbine cast about for a topic. It felt very strange suddenly to be sitting here like this, in a public restaurant. Most of their conversations had taken place at the tea table, or in her office, or walking from one place to another.

"I'm so happy about the series," she said finally. "But tell me, Elijah, why don't you write novels anymore?"

He looked startled, then almost angry. So much for small talk; obviously she had touched on a sore point.

"Why do you ask?"

"I was only wondering," she said gently. "I loved your novels."

He looked away, his mouth tight, and fiddled with his champagne glass. "Did you know I was at Andersonville?"

Columbine nodded, surprised. It didn't seem an answer to her question. She had known, of course, that Elijah Reed had, at the end of the war, spent time in the most notorious of Confederate prison camps. There had been no mention in *Look Away* of any of it, and Elijah had never written about his experience as far as she knew.

"I started a novel based on it five years ago." Elijah took a long sip of champagne. The vertical lines that ran down either side of his mouth deepened. "I haven't been able to lick it, and I can't seem to write anything else. So I went back to journalism."

"I see. But what was the problem?"

His coal black eyes wandered around the room aimlessly. "I've seen much suffering in my life, Columbine," he said finally. "I thought if I wrote about the beginnings of it, I could come to terms with it. You see, I went to war when I was fifteen. I went with all the ideals boys have at fifteen, maybe more. My house, growing up, was full of political activity. William Lloyd Garrison dropped over for dinner. Frederick Douglass came often for tea. I ran away so that I could live up to those men my mother worshipped. And I found, rather predictably, that war was not about ideals at all, but very much about realities. It was my first time away from home, away from Massachusetts, actually. I couldn't get over the land. Cornfields, cotton fields, dense autumn woods, swamps that were as lush as any South American jungle—or what I'd read a South American jungle looked like. The only trouble was, all those places were battlefields. I suppose you've read about the battles."

"Yes, I know how horrendous they were, of course. I mean," Columbine amended, feeling that she was saying all the wrong things, "I've read about them since. But I was still in England during the war, and quite young."

"Of course. I forget that you're so young."

Columbine didn't know how to take that. She felt rather insulted, but whether it was for her physical vanity or her intellectual vanity, she wasn't sure. Did he forget she was young because she looked older? Or did he feel that she was "so young" because she did not challenge him?

"You look troubled," he said softly. "Forgive me. I invited you here for celebratory purposes, and I talk of war. I didn't think about the war for years, I thought *Look Away* had purged me. But that was the book of a young man. I find I have quite different thoughts now, as the decrepit specimen I am."

"Decrepit specimen? Hardly," Columbine said. "Hardly," she repeated irritably. The man with whom she was sitting in a puddle of longing over dared to call himself such a thing?

"Here, have more champagne." Elijah poured her some, spilling a little on the tablecloth.

"I think you should finish it," Columbine said gravely.

"The champagne? I intend to."

"The novel. You know I meant the novel."

"Yes. But that, my dear Columbine, so full of spirit and optimism, is not the easiest thing in the world to do."

Columbine felt irritated again. "I know that," she said. "I mean, I can imagine it. But if you were impatient with me once, I can be impatient with you. It's time to do it. Maybe it's past time."

"Maybe it is."

He frowned at her, but it was a tender sort of frown. Columbine's irritation faded, and she smiled back hopefully. Then she saw a beautiful hand lay itself on Elijah's broad shoulder.

"Elijah! So you're here at Sherry's. I must say I am surprised to see it."

Elijah rose immediately. He bowed to a beautifully-dressed woman. "Elisabeth."

The woman looked at Columbine pointedly. She was lovely, with wide hazel eyes and chestnut hair. Her cloak and muff were sable, and her hat, which was also trimmed with fur and perched prettily on her elaborate hair, made Columbine instantly, fiercely envious.

She had the look of a woman who is seriously dedicated to her beauty; her artifice was practiced and sure. Columbine imagined how all that calculated effect would capture a man, for he would instantly wonder what it would be like to muss that perfect hair, to undo that row of the tiniest pearl buttons to reveal a pink and powdered bosom. This was a woman, Columbine thought, who Ned would flirt with at parties, would enjoy. Perhaps this was the kind of woman he would end up with. In any case, she was the kind of woman Columbine had ceased to be jealous of, long ago.

But then, something about the way Elijah Reed stood and inclined his head, something about his voice when he introduced them, made jealousy burn its hot green way through Columbine's heart. Suddenly, Mrs. Elisabeth Grey was exactly the kind of woman calculated to strike at her weakest point. She could not imagine Elijah in bed with such a woman, she couldn't bear to imagine it, actually, but the way Elisabeth was looking at him made Columbine quite sure that Elisabeth was imagining it, and having a good time doing it, too. She felt stricken; just because she'd found Elijah such a powerful sexual presence didn't mean that she expected other women would.

But Mrs. Grey was smiling at her now, and Columbine had to say something. "How do you do," she said, smiling back pleasantly at Mrs. Grey, even while she wanted to pitch her glass at Elisabeth's glossy head. Why was Elijah *scowling* so?

Columbine told herself that she could continue sitting here with this ridiculous polite smile on her face, and she would not betray one ounce of her jealousy. Elisabeth Grey smiled at Elijah Reed; that hot green poker seared her heart again. The woman had a lovely smile. Columbine realized that she had never felt jealousy before, only pique, only occasional envy. But this feeling was new to her; sexual jealousy of the most appalling, violent sort. It was horrible.

"Cornelius is arriving on Friday from school," Elisabeth told Elijah. "You can imagine how I'm looking forward to that."

"Oh, yes," Elijah said.

"Shall I give him your best?"

"Please do."

"Well," Elisabeth Grey said, looking at Columbine and back to Elijah. "Enjoy your lunch." She moved away with her tall male companion, to whom Columbine had also been introduced, but now, thirty seconds later, had no idea what his name was.

"Mrs. Grey is an old friend," Elijah said, picking up his napkin.

"She's lovely," Columbine managed to say, and she felt, to her horror, tears sting her eyes. Everything crashed down on her: her impossible, crazy love, Elijah's distance, her own silly need of him. She felt like a fool. She was nothing like Mrs. Grey, and wasn't she better than Mrs. Grey? She wasn't nearly as silly, was she, and probably more interesting? Why didn't Elijah want to pursue her, then? He hadn't wanted an intellectual companion at all. He wanted a coquette!

Two tears slid down her face, and she ducked her head. She gripped her napkin, but she was too ashamed to raise it to her cheeks. Perhaps Elijah would not notice.

"Well, shall we order? I think—" Elijah stopped abruptly. "Columbine, what is it? Please tell me. Can I help you?"

"No, I'm so sorry," she said, quickly dashing away the tears. Embarrassment had given her a measure of control. "I'm afraid I'm one of those people who is absolutely incapable of controlling her tears. I cry at the most inconvenient times and places. . . . You see, I haven't been sleeping well, and then I didn't eat breakfast this morning, and I've been working terribly hard—"

"I know. We should go. I'll see you home, you need to rest, obviously." Elijah looked around for the waiter.

"Please don't," Columbine pleaded quickly. "Oh, please don't. I've been looking forward to this lunch for so long. I couldn't bear to go home alone."

Elijah stopped. He looked at her keenly, for there was something in her voice. . . . But Elijah told himself that he had imagined it. He had told himself, over the past weeks, ever since that night in the house on West Tenth Street, that he had imagined everything he thought he saw in her eyes. But how could he mistake this? For once, he had the courage to keep looking, not to make a casual remark, not to turn away with a old man's throat clearing. He saw her heart in her eyes, and his own heart stopped.

"I didn't know," he said. "Forgive me. I thought it was only me. Sometimes I can be stupid."

Sweet relief rushed through her. Her lips curved. "Yes, Mr. Reed, you can be stupid."

"You see," he said, "I wanted you so much."

She was sure of her power now enough to flirt. She was too breathless at the moment to be serious, anyway. "Oh, dear. You used the past tense, Mr. Reed, and I know how exact writers are."

He acknowledged her comment with a lift of his eyebrows, but he did not smile. "You see," he said deliberately, "I want you so much."

Her breath truly left her then, for the whole of Elijah Reed's sexual presence was unfurled for her, and she had never felt anything so keenly. She was more excited than she dreamed it was possible to be, sitting here so decently in Sherry's in her best dress and her new hat. Now she wanted to match him, plain words for plain words. There must never be any mistake with this man. She would have to be the best woman she could be, to keep up with him.

"Yes," she said, holding his dark gaze. "I want you. I've wanted you for such a very long time."

Elijah smiled. "Perhaps then, Mrs. Nash, we should go. We've wasted far too much time already."

Fourteen

ELIJAH STILL HADN'T touched her; they stood in his bedroom awkwardly, a bit apart, still wearing their coats. The bare, cold room had stopped them in their tracks. The compulsion that had propelled them here so precipitately seemed to leave them as soon as they'd crossed the threshold. Columbine picked at a button. She'd felt so free in the restaurant; now her body felt like lead.

Elijah's voice sounded hoarse. "Columbine, let's sit down."

They perched on the edge of the bed. Still, he did not touch her. They stared in front of them at a blank wall. There were no pictures in Elijah's room, no heavy masculine adornments. Just a chest of drawers, a desk, a bookshelf. A bed with a gray bedspread.

"I'm a widower, as you know," he said.

She swallowed. "Yes."

"I've had mistresses, after. But no love."

"And Elisabeth Grey?"

"Yes," he said softly, "Elisabeth was my mistress."

"When did it end?"

"A few weeks ago."

She swallowed again; her mouth felt terribly dry. "Weeks?"

"Yes. After that night in Safe Passage House. Do you remember?"

"Yes. Elijah, what do you want to say to me?" Suddenly, Columbine felt afraid. Her hands felt very cold. She'd thought him solitary and proud; she'd thought him a man of ideas, not of love. But she should have realized that despite his absence of sexual suggestiveness, other women would find him as sensual as she did. She wouldn't be the first to discover the sexual being in him. Why had she thought, like a dizzy adolescent, that she would be the first?

"I haven't had much success in my personal life, Columbine. I've become reconciled to being alone. I'm better so. And it's good for my work. I find that my feeling for you goes beyond anything I've felt in a long, long while. But I want to be honest with you. With the other women in my life, if I may be frank for a moment—well, we both knew the rules from the beginning. Most of them were married. You see, I'm not looking for a partner."

"Only a lover."

"Yes."

Columbine sat, staring at the white wall. She wanted Elijah so much she could hardly breathe. But could she enter into relations with him, knowing that she loved him without limitations, when from the start he outlined those limitations? She saw heartbreak ahead of her, and she knew she should walk away. She should say no to this temptation, this man. She *did* want a partner. She could do without a man, but she could not do without commitment if she did have one she loved.

"I'll understand if you can't accept it," Elijah said. "I should have said all this before. But I was out of my mind at the restaurant, all I wanted was you in my bed. But Columbine, I'll be your friend, I'll respect you, I'll love you. But I can't guarantee I'll be able to stay. And I most likely won't be able to give you what you want. I have always been able," he added with a wintry smile, "to control my heart's urges, I'm afraid."

Barely hearing him, Columbine still stared ahead. She told herself to get up, to tell him they could be only friends, that what he was offering was not nearly enough for her. But some voice was telling her in a seductive whisper that things could always change. That he could come to love her enough to stay with her. That she could live day by day, and not think of the future. Wasn't that what she had begged Ned to do? Wasn't that what she had always done? Was it just a temporary mad love, tied to her lust, that was telling her that she wanted more from this man? Was she counting too much on that mystical moment in the house on West Tenth Street?

Hadn't she always been in Elijah's position, gently trying to convey to a man that her work came first, that she would always be poised for flight?

How had anyone been able to stand her?

"Columbine, please say something. I won't be able to bear not touching you much longer."

Her breath caught. His voice spoke of such hunger. She turned to face him. The look in his eyes took her breath away.

"Touch me, Elijah," she said.

He reached over and took her cold hand. He breathed on her icy fingers, then kissed her palm. Then he took her pale face in his hands and kissed her. She felt his rough fingertips against her cheeks, and his lips and tongue were warm. There was not an ounce of hesitation in his touch, not a particle of doubt. She bent like a lily on a fragile stalk underneath him, and he lowered her to the bed, hat, coat, and all. Decisions and consequences flew from her head. I don't care, she cried silently, as he unbuttoned her dress with practiced hands. I don't care, sang in her blood as he gently uncoiled her hair and breathed in its scent. She opened herself to him with the same absence of doubt she felt in his touch.

They were naked and entwined on the bed; he cradled her, warming her with his large body. He was brown and sturdy, the hair on his chest a mixture of silver and black. The lines around his eyes were exquisite to her, and she traced them with a fingertip. He was on top of her now, and she felt him, urgent and hot, between her thighs. Still, he hesitated, and looked down at her. Lover to lover, they stared into each other's eyes and found love there. They did not need to know, just then, how far that love would take them, or if it would take them anywhere at all. It was enough to see it. And then desire overtook them again, and, fierce and aching, they knew each other completely at last.

It took Lawrence most of the month of April to assemble the pieces for the bomb. It had to be done carefully, and he had not picked the most reliable of associates. Chaim Lepinsky was not a diligent anarchist; he was also a poet by trade. He had connections to get explosives, and his prices were cheap, but he was often forgetful and made excuses time after time. Lawrence would have found someone else, but he trusted Chaim's discretion and he wouldn't improve his chances by involving someone else at this stage.

Fiona was now working as a downstairs maid in Ned Van Cormandt's house. She knew the routine of the household; she knew where the housekeeper kept her keys, and how heavily she slept at night. They fixed on the library as the perfect place for the blast; when Ned was in town he went there punctually every night at eleven to work for a few hours before retiring.

Lawrence left Chaim's rooms on Ludlow Street on a chilly April evening, adjusting his hat and scarf to cover his face. So far, he had limited his visits and always came at night. He covered his blond hair and kept his hat over his eyes, for his coloring made him stand out in this neighborhood.

He was so intent on keeping his head down that he almost missed it. Two women had paused ahead of him on the corner of Ludlow and Hester. They stayed in the shadow of a building, where the smaller one bent forward and kissed the other woman on the cheek. Something about the small, trim figure was familiar. The woman turned halfway, and Lawrence saw by the profile that it was Marguerite Corbeau.

He walked faster, keeping his head averted, as though he were looking for something in the market on Hester. But he came close enough to hear Marguerite laugh.

"Don't worry. Goodbye, Mama. I'll come again soon."

"Goodbye, little one. Keep well."

Marguerite turned and went down Hester Street. Lawrence crossed Hester, heading north; he did not want to take the chance of being seen. He felt exhilarated, lighter than air. The wind struck his cheeks, reminding him of the long scratch from her nails that had taken weeks to heal. He had had to make up a ridiculous story about a nasty cat for Bell.

He didn't know how what he'd seen would come in handy, but he knew it would. It was always helpful to know a secret about another. Marguerite had lied for a reason she thought important. She wouldn't want anyone to know what he saw. The little orphan had a mother. The little bitch was a Jew.

• • •

Bell had embraced a cause as well as a man. The sense of hopelessness that had dogged her days dropped away, and she found the exhilaration of purpose again. Anarchism brought together all the strands of her life and braided them into a coil of hard, steely joy.

Suddenly, everything made sense: what she'd read, what she'd seen, what she'd experienced. The way she'd been raised, her love of Thoreau, even the abuse she had suffered as a child. It all had a place in her new vision, and it all had a new meaning. She had a paradigm for looking at a cruel world that held out the possibility of beauty. She could even incorporate her religious faith, for what was anarchism grounded in but the belief in man's essential good? Of course, anarchists were atheists—the Jewish members even went so far as to pointedly sponsor a dance on the sacred holy day of Yom Kippur—so Bell kept her faith a secret from everyone, even Lawrence. She did not find Christianity incompatible with her politics, and she would not allow anyone to preach to her that she was inconsistent.

She hugged it to herself, this new faith. Her work with Columbine still seemed important, in terms of individual lives. Despite the slight distance between them which had sprung up, despite Lawrence's disapproval, Bell still felt happy there. One could not face that need every day and not feel necessary. She was still weak enough to need that. Lawrence claimed it was because she was weak in her faith.

Lawrence mightn't understand it, but Bell got an unexpected source of strength for her position from Emma Goldman. They met every now and then for coffee; Bell would not tell Lawrence until afterwards, because of his inexplicable dislike for Emma. She was not the easiest friend to have, but she enjoyed teaching Bell her views on anarchism and class struggle. Bell was aware that Emma saw her as a child, even though she was older. But her new friend's fierceness and wit kept Bell hungry for more. And Emma was strong enough to oppose Johann Most and work for the eight hour day. She also believed in Columbine's work, to a point.

"Safe Passage House is a good idea," Emma had said over a glass of tea. "I've seen what goes on down here, all over. Don't listen to the men. We have to help our sisters, even as we fight for the revolution. Mrs. Nash might be cowardly in her politics, but I cannot say she doesn't have good ideas."

But when Bell told Lawrence this, after supper, when they were reading by the fire, it only irritated him.

"It is reformist gibberish she talks," he snapped. "I should tell her hero, Herr Most, what the Goldman woman is telling you."

"She's not afraid of Johann Most, or of any man, I think," Bell answered quietly. Her eyes returned to her book. She was studying Russian at night, at Lawrence's insistence. There were many papers he needed to read, hot off the presses, to be current, and he missed many important discussions because he could not speak it. She was also learning Yiddish from Emma, but she wanted to surprise Lawrence with this. She planned to compose a birthday card for him in Yiddish in the fall.

Her life was full, her love filled her heart. Despite their differences, she and Lawrence were working together in a common cause: they were comrades. With the coal fire warming her feet and Lawrence studying across the room, she felt that her life was at last complete.

Except for one thing. "Lawrence," she said, looking up, "I really must tell Columbine about us. She should know. And it would make things so much easier for us. You could come to the house and not be afraid you'll betray us."

"She will try and break us up Bell, I know it. She's a jealous woman. She's never forgiven me for spurning her."

"She'll understand. She's with Mr. Reed now." Lawrence said nothing, and Bell returned to her book. She read slowly, translating as she went. When he said her name, she was concentrating so hard it took her a moment to realize it.

Lawrence spoke again. "Bell?"

She put a finger in her book to mark her place and looked up. His head thrown back, his legs sprawled in front of him, he was watching her. His blond hair fell on his forehead, and his blue eyes were piercing. A pulse beat deep inside her, as it always did when his beauty struck her afresh.

"Yes, dear?" she asked affectionately.

"You must talk to Columbine tomorrow."

"You think I should tell her about us, then."

"You must talk to her," he said deliberately, "and tell her that you are leaving. You will not participate in Safe Passage House."

"But my darling, I can't do that. We're moving in a few weeks. Columbine can't run that house alone."

"She'll find someone else. You have better things to do."

"I don't think so. I'm needed there."

She expected him to be angry, but he shook his head sadly. "I understand. When it comes down to a question of loyalties, I see now who wins. Not your cause, not your lover. That woman."

"That's not true. But I have work there. And a paycheck," she added dryly. "Don't forget that."

"I can get you a job with Jacob Schimmer's wife."

"In a factory?" Bell couldn't believe her ears. "I did that work once, Lawrence. I swore I would never return."

"It's more fitting for an anarchist. Do you know how you'll embarrass me if you work at a settlement house?"

"It's not a settlement house," she argued. "It's a place of refuge. No, I cannot work in a factory again. I cannot go back to that life."

His hands tightened, but he crossed his legs indolently. "As you wish," he said.

Bell felt her blood run out of her face. Her hands began to tremble. She knew that look. His face was closed to her, indifferent; he looked back at his papers. He would not speak to her for the rest of the night, or tomorrow, or the next day. It could last a week. She could come to his door, and he would let her in, let her cook for him, but he would not speak to her, no matter how she begged.

"Please don't punish me like this," she said. "Please, Lawrence."

But she got no answer. Her nerves screaming now, she returned her unseeing eyes to her book.

After Bell left that night, Lawrence saw his mistake. If Bell backed out of Safe Passage House, she would have to tell Columbine why. And if Columbine knew Bell had been converted to anarchism, she would naturally make the connection to him. Bell wouldn't be able to lie, damn her.

He should have kept his mouth shut, for a few more weeks at least. Lawrence wanted to kick himself. But as he drifted off to sleep he told himself that Columbine was bound to find out sooner or later. He'd have to face her wrath, and if Bell wasn't tied to him enough by now, she never would be.

He rose early the next morning and scrawled a quick note to Bell, telling her that he would prefer they both tell Columbine about their love. It was more honest that way, he wrote, and Columbine deserved that respect. He would be there at four o'clock, and they would tell her together. Frowning, he dispatched the note by messenger. Better he would be there to deflect any accusations. But it would still be a rocky meeting. Everything would depend on which way Bell jumped.

Columbine was just pouring her first cup of tea when Bell knocked on the parlor door. Bell opened the door and hesitated on the threshold.

"Bell, why did you knock? You're just in time for tea. Elijah was supposed to join me, but he had business to take care of. Well, come in for heaven's sake. Mrs. Brodge made a seed cake."

Columbine nattered on while she poured milk in another cup and added hot tea. When she looked up, Lawrence Birch was there, standing next to Bell.

Columbine counted off a few slow seconds. She told herself to keep her voice level. "What is that man doing here?" she asked Bell, her tone low and vibrant. "He's not welcome in this house."

"I'm in love with him, Columbine," Bell said quietly. "That's what we came to tell you."

She couldn't absorb the information at first; it was too enormous. "That's impossible," she said numbly. "I don't . . . How could you—?"

"Columbine," Lawrence said, "we don't know how ourselves." He shrugged; the tenderness in his blue eyes nearly made Columbine gag. "I'm inclined to think I fell in love with her from the first moment she opened the door to me." He glanced at Bell with a smile. "Who would not?"

Columbine's rage was a small, hard thing in the very center of her. It burned. Her voice shook with fury as she leveled her gaze on Lawrence. "How dare you come to this house. How dare you expect me to accept this? Bell," she said, rising and coming toward her anxiously, "I didn't tell you this before. But—"

"Don't listen to her, Bell—"

"He tried to attack me, Bell. He would have raped me I think. Right here, in this parlor, a month or so ago."

Bell backed away. "I don't believe you."

"Bell," Columbine said desperately, "have I ever lied to you? Why would I lie to you?"

"I don't know myself," Lawrence said sorrowfully. "I cannot believe that you, no matter how bereft or angry you might feel from my rejection, would invent such a story."

"Rejection? My God." Her hand to her mouth, Columbine saw that Lawrence was prepared for this, and that she was not. He was as cool as a cucumber, and the pitying look in his eyes was frightening to see.

Tearing her gaze away from him, she took Bell's icy hands in hers. Bell tore them away. "You must listen, Bell," she said rapidly. "He is lying. He lost control one evening, right at this time it was, at teatime. Something happened to him, some violent streak was unloosed. Surely you must have seen intimations of this in him. Think, Bell."

Bell cried out and dropped her face in her hands. She couldn't think of such a thing. Of any of it. Of Lawrence lying, of Columbine lying. Of Lawrence forcing Columbine . . . It was impossible. She loved him so much.

"No," she sobbed. She looked at Lawrence beseechingly. "Please. Tell me the truth.

"All right," Lawrence said quietly. "I'll tell you the truth. I've already told you that we were friends, Columbine and I. I didn't tell you the whole truth because I didn't want to hurt you. Columbine and I were lovers, for a very short time."

"Bell, he's lying. We were not, you know we were not!"

"I saw you kissing," Bell whispered.

"It was only one time—"

"No," Lawrence said quickly. "It was more than once." He rode over Columbine's denial; she did not seem to be aware that Bell had interpreted her words to mean that they had only been to bed once. Bell gave a low moan, as if she were in pain.

Lawrence went on hurriedly. "It was for a very short time, darling. I realized that it could not go on, and I told her that as gently as I could. But I suppose her nerves were strained, for she exploded with rage. I didn't know what to do, Bell! She tried to hit me—she scratched my cheek, remember that scratch?—and I pinned her arms at her sides. That is all, I swear it!"

"No, Bell!" Columbine cried. But her desperate hope died when she saw the look on Bell's face. She would lose her. She would lose her friend. Lawrence had gotten hold of her somehow. Even the closest woman friend could not compete with the mystery that lies between a woman and a man.

Then Columbine remembered. "Marguerite!" she said aloud, shooting a triumphant glance at Lawrence. "She saw! She helped me kick him out of the house. You can ask Marguerite, Bell."

Bell looked at Lawrence. He nodded slowly, wanting to kick himself for telling her it had been Columbine who scratched him. That could trip him up. But he'd figure that out later. "Marguerite was there. If you feel you need confirmation of my story, you can ask her everything," he said. "As a matter of fact, I insist on it." Lord knew Marguerite would back him up. She was an opportunitistic little bitch, and scruples would not get in her way.

Columbine looked at Lawrence. What did he have up his sleeve? she wondered. Marguerite wouldn't lie to Bell. Or was his power strong enough that he knew Bell wouldn't approach her? Had he bound Bell to him that tightly, so tightly she could not step away and see him clearly?

"Bell, you have to believe me," she repeated. She didn't know what else to say.

And then Bell smiled. The smile, so passive, so accepting, and so sorry for Columbine, struck her at the heart.

"Oh, Bell," Columbine whispered. "No."

Bell wanted to collapse with the joy of relief. The scene was over; it was all over. And she would never have to see Columbine again. The thought of Lawrence touching another woman made her want to scream. But she would never have to see Columbine again.

"I don't need to talk to Marguerite," she said, turning to her lover. She knew she was saved now. For the first time in her life, she was able to trust completely. She felt exalted now, looking into Lawrence's blazing blue eyes. She was his forever.

With that new found strength, she was able to turn to Columbine without emotion. Her calmness was born of the shield that was her love. She felt enormously protected, for the first time in her life, standing next to her love.

"I'm sorry if Lawrence hurt you," she said. "I assure you it was not deliberate on his part. And I also must tell you that I cannot go forward with the plans for Safe Passage House. I have more important work in the movement. I'm sorry; I know it will inconvenience you. I'm sure you can find someone else to take over my duties at the New Women Society. Ivy Moffat is a good worker, you might want to approach her."

Columbine was frantic. She knew if Bell walked out the door she would never see her again. "All right, Bell. Whatever you want. But we have to stay friends. Promise me we'll still be friends."

Bell's beautiful mouth curved in a gentle smile. "But Columbine, my life will be so different now. I don't think it's realistic for us to expect to go on as we were."

Lawrence held out Bell's coat, and she slipped into it. She smiled over her shoulder at him and took her muff from his hands.

"Bell," Columbine said desperately, "Please wait. You can't go with him. He'll destroy you."

Bell put her hand on Lawrence's sleeve. Her smile was placid, benign. "Destroy me? Oh, Columbine. You always had a taste for melodrama. Don't you see?" she said in a such a bland, rational tone Columbine wondered if she was quite sane. "Lawrence has saved me."

Elijah found her sitting with the lights out, the tea cold, at six o'clock. He slid into the armchair across from Columbine's and looked at her. She smiled wanly. The firelight flickered across her still face.

"What is it?" he asked.

"Bell's left," she said, turning away to look at the fire. "We've been together for more than ten years."

Cautiously, afraid of prodding her, he asked, "Why did she leave?"

"She's in love with Lawrence Birch. And she's an anarchist. She's given up reform."

"She's in love with Birch?" he asked incredulously.

Columbine nodded. She wanted to confess everything to him; what Lawrence had said, what she had said, what Bell believed. But something stopped her. She loved Elijah with all her heart, but it was a careful love. If she confided all her hurts and joys to him, it would be harder to go on after he'd left. So she gave herself to him physically and she loved him without regrets, but she kept the everyday cares to herself. She would not grow to depend on him more than she could help.

Sensing that he'd heard half the story, Elijah looked away and stared at the fire. He wanted to press her, but he didn't. He wanted to ask why she seemed angry as well as sad, but he didn't. He sensed the deep, roiling emotion Bell's departure had stirred up, but if Columbine did not wish to tell him, he would not ask. In his experience with women, some had wound him into the fabric of their lives. Some had kept themselves aloof and mysterious, from the fear that if he knew them completely he would grow bored. And some were merely private, like Columbine. He wished, for a moment, staring at her brooding profile, that Columbine was not one of those women, for her life was varied and complex and interesting, and he would like to share it.

He wanted to share her sorrow, he realized. Her slant on her friendships. Her irritation and her amusement at the minutiae of her life. Everything.

He almost sat up with the enormity of the jolt this revelation gave him. Instead, he stretched out his legs. He was a slow thinker, and even slower to act. He wanted to chew on this new feeling for awhile, figure it out. Did he want something different from this, after all?

Columbine looked at Elijah. His leonine head was sunk a bit on his chest, and his sturdy legs were extended toward the fire. He could be asleep. If she had been a different kind of woman, she would have imagined that her troubles bored him. But she knew it was not boredom that led him to withdraw from her. It was that sense of privacy in him; it was the last barrier to complete intimacy between them. And it would never be breached.

She had to keep loving him, though. She had to take the companionship and the hard loving between them, and leave the dissatisfactions behind, for as long as she possibly could.

"Shall we have a sherry?" she asked.

He looked at her, and he saw such sadness. Her deep brown eyes were bright; was she close to tears? Elijah couldn't hold her gaze; he coughed and looked away. "Let's," he said.

Lawrence had no way of finding Marguerite—he could hardly ask Columbine—so he waited a week. He stood on the opposite corner of Hester and Ludlow at the same time he'd seen Marguerite before. She did not appear that week, but the following one he saw her walking to the corner with the older woman in black. He waited until they separated, then trailed down Hester after Marguerite.

She was walking quickly, her spring green skirt swishing behind her below the dark gray of her three-quarter length coat. They were fine clothes, he noticed. And if she wore these to the East Side, she must have even grander ones at home. Lawrence flirted with the idea of extorting money instead of promises, but decided the promise was too important to risk.

"Miss Corbeau?" he called, when he was just a few paces behind her.

She stopped, but she didn't turn, not for a few slow seconds. Then she slowly twisted to look behind her. Her dark blue eyes were wary.

"Or should I say," Lawrence said deliberately, "Miss Blum?"

Shock showed clearly in her face, but a moment later it was gone, replaced by a smooth, polite mask. She nodded shortly. "Mr. Birch."

"May I walk with you?"

"I'm not going far, just a few blocks to the Bowery for a cab."

"Perfect," Lawrence said. "I'll accompany you. Young ladies are not safe on the Bowery these days."

"I assure you, I—"

"Come," Lawrence said, interrupting her and taking her arm. "I won't take no for an answer, Miss Blum."

Marguerite extricated her arm and drew herself up. "I don't know why you continue to refer to me by that name."

She started to walk again, at an even faster pace, and Lawrence swung into step beside her. Ignoring her last comment, he said in a conversational tone, "Such a fascinating neighborhood, don't you agree? Squalid, certainly. But such energy! You feel it hum around you like a giant machine."

"Really, Mr. Birch. How fascinating," Marguerite said icily.

"But the thing that impresses me," Lawrence went on, "is the friendliness of the people. Why, I was in one of the worst tenements on Ludlow Street the other day, and I met a woman who couldn't have been nicer. Mrs. Schneiderman, her name was. She came right out to the stairwell as I came up, and we chatted for quite some time."

Marguerite stopped. Her eyes flicked toward him. Her delicate upper lip curled slightly. "What do you want?" she asked.

"She told me about the Blum family upstairs. Russian Jews. The father is a peddler. He kicked the daughter out when she went bad. Mrs. Schneiderman had seen the daughter just the other day, all dressed to the nines, with fine boots."

"Get to the point, Mr. Birch," she said steadily.

He grasped her elbow and moved her forward, for people were beginning to notice them. "I do so admire the culture of the Jews," he said, speaking in her ear. "It is a shame that they cannot mix in the best society. I think it terribly wrong. Of course, it's whispered that August Belmont is a Jew. Jay Gould. Just think, Miss Corbeau, if those men admitted to their heritage! Perhaps attitudes would be changed. For who could shut their door against August Belmont? He is so charming. Who would refuse to do business with Mr. Gould?"

Now they had reached the bright lights of the Bowery. Marguerite stopped again and resolved not to budge. "Pray go on, Mr. Birch."

"Ah, you become interested, Miss Corbeau."

"I very much doubt I would be able to stop you. Please hurry, for I'm late."

"I'll take my time," he said fiercely. "You'll do well to act polite, Miss *Blum*."

"Just get on with it!" she snapped. "What do you want? Money?"

"Certainly not. Merely a promise that you may never even have to fulfill."

Marguerite watched him warily. "What is this promise?"

"That if Miss Huxton ever comes to you with an explanation of what happened that night in Columbine's parlor, you will tell her the truth. That Columbine was wild with anger, that she lost control and I had to subdue her. She was upset about the fact that I ended our affair."

Marguerite snorted. "That is hardly the truth."

"It doesn't matter what you believe," Lawrence said. His pale eyes gleamed in the lamplight with a menace that chilled Marguerite. "You will tell her that."

She shook her head. She was frightened, but she would not let him know that. "I cannot lie about Columbine. I will not."

"Would you like your lover to know that you're a Jew, Miss Blum? Do you think he will still keep you? Or do you want to marry him? Do you think the Stiers family would let a Jew taint their blood?"

She backed away. "You are an animal."

He shrugged. "I am only a man. Like you, I have something I wish to conceal from my lover. Tell me how we are different."

"Let me count the ways," Marguerite spat out.

He laughed. "Do I have your promise then? It's an easy one to give, for I doubt Miss Huxton will approach you. She trusts me, you see."

"God help her," Marguerite muttered.

"Do I have your word, Miss Blum?"

Marguerite hesitated, though she already knew her answer; she wanted Lawrence Birch to sweat a little. What was this promise anyway? As he said, Bell probably wouldn't ask her. And if Bell actually believed this man, she deserved what she got. Anyone could see what a monster he was. No one would ever know, she told herself. And Edwin could not discover the truth; he could not, no one could. That would be the end of her.

"Yes," she said finally. Her arm reached up to hail a hansom cab; she could not bring herself to look at Lawrence Birch again. "You have my word."

Fifteen

DRESSED ONLY IN her lace-yoked corset cover and her drawers and stockings, Marguerite perched on Edwin's lap. She fiddled with a tiny curl by his ear. She had already finished her lunch, and she was bored. Edwin had insisted on setting up a table in the bedroom, so she couldn't even look out the window at the street to pass the time. Her bedroom overlooked the back.

"Must you go?" she asked.

Edwin took a bite of fish. "I must."

"And can we go out to dinner tonight?"

"Not tonight. Perhaps on Monday."

"Do you know," Marguerite said in a bright tone, "that Toby told me you take me out on Mondays because that's the fashionable night for the opera—we won't run into any members of your family then." She peeked at him, wondering how he'd take it.

"That's ridiculous," he mumbled. He cut another piece of fish and held it out to her on his fork. "Come on. You hardly ate anything today."

Marguerite felt her stomach roll over at the smell. She was too full to take another bite. She rose. "Toby says I'm getting fat. That's because all we ever do, Edwin, is eat and make love."

Edwin sighed and continued to eat. He waited, hoping this afternoon would not turn out like too many afternoons lately.

She went for her dressing gown. Wrapping herself in it moodily, she sat on the small couch upholstered in some old French tapestry. She crossed her legs and jiggled a foot. Marguerite felt irritated; a month ago, she had given Lawrence her promise. Bell had not come to her, but Marguerite was nervous about Lawrence's knowledge. There was no telling when he might return with more threats. She wanted to be married and safe.

Edwin took a sip of wine. "I have a present for you at my house," he said. Presents always improved Marguerite's mood.

"Perhaps I should call there and pick it up," she flung at him.

He sighed. "I have to get back to the office."

Immediately Marguerite rose and ran to climb into his lap again, despite the fish. "I'm sorry I was cross, Edwin. It's just that I love you so. And you said we would be engaged by now."

She smelled of powder and perfume, and she was so beautiful. Her heart-shaped face shone with adoration. Edwin picked up a raven curl and pressed his lips to it. "I know, dearest. But I also explained to you about father. The whole family knows to tread carefully with him. He has to get used to things. He's from the old school, you know."

She pouted. "He sounds a perfect ogre."

"No. He comes round eventually. As with my sister-in-law, Rosamond." Edwin grinned. "He wouldn't hear of Albert's engagement for months. And now Rosamond is his pet. I believe he loves her better than his own family now."

Marguerite laughed. "Do you think he'd like me?" she asked eagerly.

He gazed at her. Lately, Edwin had noticed that though he was still enthralled with her, he was able to see Marguerite more clearly. In the beginning, he had been simply besotted. He'd thought her beauty and freshness would win his father over. Now, he realized it would be harder than he'd anticipated, much harder. Perhaps impossible.

He kissed her soft cheek. "He'll adore you, my dear. Now, I really must go."

Marguerite rose. "All right. Shall I expect you for dinner?"

"Of course. And we'll go out to dinner next week. You can wear your new gold dress. We'll go on Thursday." He gave her a meaningful glance. "There's no opera that night."

Marguerite started to smile, then stopped. Her audition with

William Paradise was on Friday. She wouldn't want to stay out late; she'd be too tired the next day, and Toby would notice. He noticed everything. She'd been terribly tired lately; she never could seem to get enough sleep, and Toby had been sharp with her, saying she yawned her way through her lessons.

"Why not Wednesday?" she asked. "I don't want to wait so long."

"I can't go any other night next week. Thursday it must be." Edwin buttoned up his coat and set his hat on his head.

"All right, Edwin. Thursday." She kissed him goodbye, then hurried to dress. On the way to her dressing table, she had to sink on the bed, she felt so dizzy. It was that fish; it stank so. She rang the bell furiously for Bridget to come and take it away.

The move to the Tenth Street house was harried and chaotic. Columbine had spent five years in the Twenty-Third Street house, and there were piles of papers and magazines and books and clothes to go through and give away, then pack the rest. The days were exhausting, but the fresh start was exhilarating.

She'd come to love the house even more as she supervised the move. It had a certain air of shabby elegance that she liked. A thick vine ran up one side which would bloom with red flowers in the spring. There was a large bow window in front with a curved windowseat, and a wrought-iron balcony at the top. The house was a weathered, dull red that seemed warm and welcoming to Columbine, though Ivy Moffat laughed and said it just needed a fresh coat of paint.

The housekeeper agreed to stay on, and Columbine moved into the back bedroom on the third floor. She decided her first project would be to transform the skylit attic into as cozy a space as she could make it. Ivy Moffat would move in next month, and the New Women Society would begin to refer women in a few weeks. The house had to be done by then.

"Everything is going well," she told Elijah as they walked together on a chilly spring morning. One of the best things about the house was that it was a short two blocks to Elijah's. "Actually, it's lucky that the house is empty at present. Tavish and Darcy Finn arrive next week."

"Old friends of yours?"

"Yes, I knew Tavish in England. He grew up on my father's estate." Here was another example of how she kept herself apart from Elijah. She would not tell him that Tavish was her half-brother; that was a secret that very few knew, at Tavish's request. "I can't wait to see them," she went on. "I've missed Bell very much this past month. Ivy is delightful, I'm glad she's moving in, but it's not the same. Darcy and I will talk for hours and hours." She slipped her arm into Elijah's. "I want you to meet them."

"I'm looking forward to it. I've heard of their newspaper from friends in Oakland. They tackle controversial issues with great courage, I hear."

"Yes, they're doing splendidly." Columbine felt Elijah stiffen underneath her hand. "What is it, Elijah?"

But he didn't answer. He was already raising his hat to a lady who looked to be in her sixties. She had a pleasant face with small bright eyes. Her bonnet was a bit old-fashioned, but her carriage was elegant, as though to say, yes, my clothes are a bit shabby, but who are you to judge me?

"Good day, Mrs. Pollard."

"Mr. Reed! Well, what do you know. I was just thinking of you the other day. I read your article in the *Century*."

"May I present Mrs. Nash."

"How do you do."

Columbine greeted Mrs. Pollard, but her thoughts were on Elijah. Something about this woman disturbed him. When they passed on, would they talk of the weather, or their work, as it was all too possible for them to do? Well, she would not. Not this time. She would ask for a change, she would pry if she must. Elijah was so stiff; it was obvious to her he was making a great effort.

"I'm just visiting a friend," Mrs. Pollard was saying. "I live uptown, on the West Side. It's so nice to see you, Mr. Reed."

He bowed. "It was lucky for me. I'm glad to see you looking so well."

After a few more pleasantries, they said goodbye and moved on. "Who was she, Elijah?" Columbine asked, as soon as they were out of earshot. "You seem disturbed."

"I knew her husband in the war. He died."

"Oh. Were you close to him?"

"Yes, I suppose. In a way. He was older. Shall we turn back? I should be getting back to work."

"Of course." Columbine was silent for a few paces. "Were you in his company?" she asked timidly, for she knew that Elijah had closed the subject, and this was her signal to back off.

"No. We were at Andersonville together, near the end of the war."

"Is this what you can't write about?" she guessed.

His face was stony. "Columbine—"

"Please tell me."

"Yes."

"Tell me about it," she said softly.

"Columbine, no."

She stopped. His face was turned from her, and she touched his sleeve. "Please, Elijah."

"Why must you know?" he asked roughly.

"Because I think you want to tell me," Columbine said frankly. "And I think I would know you better if I knew. And I'm tired of *not* asking when I know these things."

After a pause, Elijah began to walk. "It was near the end of the war, so things were especially bad. The Confederates could barely feed their own troops, it was no wonder there was no food for us. We had corn, the cob and husk ground together. Or sometimes if we were lucky we'd get some molasses. There was no shelter, not enough anyway. Thirty-five thousand men were in an enclosure of less than thirty acres. I know it can't have rained every day, but it seemed so. Some men went mad. All of us were starving. I didn't have a coat."

"You were just a boy," Columbine said. "Surely they should have sent you home."

He shrugged. "There were other boys there. Transfers didn't happen that often. By the time I landed in the prison, they weren't doing it at all."

"And Benjamin Pollard?"

"He was in his mid-thirties. He was from Massachusetts too, from Cambridge. He was an educated man, an officer. He'd heard of my parents—admired them for years—so he watched out for me. He went to get our food, so that no one would steal the food from me. He got me a pair of shoes and a blanket. He arranged a pool, you see, of the men in our section. When someone died, we'd draw lots for his effects, pitiable though they were. But a scrap of blanket could mean the difference between life and death. So Ben won the pool a few times, and always managed to get me something. Food, too. For a few days we could conceal the death and get the man's rations. Maybe Ben knew he was dying; I think he probably had tuberculosis, when I think back. I saw him cough up blood a few times, though he tried to hide it." Elijah paused. "I was closer to him than I'd ever been to any man. I loved him."

"And what happened? How did he die? From consumption?"

"No . . . I found out he was cheating. In the pool. We drew straws—actually they were sticks. We all trusted him completely, you see. But I found out that he was cheating. That he knew which was the shorter stick. He didn't take it himself that often. He bided his time."

"But he gave you the blanket, and the boots."

Elijah smiled thinly. "Precisely. But I was fifteen, and I was enraged. Or at least as angry as I could be, half-starved. What I thought of as 'honor' was important to me then. Of course now I realize what Ben was doing—he devised a system to let the neediest profit. And he would also decide," Elijah said painfully, "when a man was too weak to be able to benefit. Now I can see why such measures were so necessary. We could have murdered each other otherwise for a coat or a scarf. But I was fifteen, and I accused him of dishonor. I said terrible things."

"And what did he do?"

"He was too weak to do much of anything. And he knew I would not listen, I suppose. He just told me that he knew it was important I survive. It was the oddest thing, Columbine. He was emaciated by this time. But on that rainy afternoon—it was so cold, so gray—his spirit seemed, this is difficult to explain, but it seemed that he had a foot in both worlds. His face was almost transparent. He told me that he *saw* something in me. He had to save me. I was worth saving."

"What did you do?"

"I laughed. I told him he was trying to justify cheating, and there was no justification for that. But even I could see at that point how weak he was. And I was ready to fall down myself. So I left. Later he deliberately crossed the 'dead line,' and he was shot down. We didn't have a pool that night. He had willed me his coat, which I would never take from him before. Everyone respected the request. I took it. Winter was coming on; I wouldn't have survived without it. Later one of the other men there told me that Ben, all along, had been halving his rations and giving them to me. I never realized it. I just ate what he put in front of me. He was starving to death in front of my eyes, and I ate what he put in front of me."

Columbine was silent. She didn't know what she could possibly say. Elijah's hands were shaking.

"Whitman said that the sight of the Union prisoners was worse than the bloodiest battlefield. That the real story of the war lay in its hospitals and its prison camps. I didn't understand that twenty years ago. The battles were what haunted me. But now when I wake up at night, I think of Andersonville."

They had reached the front steps of Columbine's house, and they paused.

His eyes were dark and grave. "So now you know why it was painful for me to see Jessie Pollard. She was young once, in her late twenties when Benjamin was captured. He loved her, he spoke of her often. She never married again."

"You were so young, Elijah," Columbine murmured. "Somehow you have to forgive yourself. Somehow."

He didn't respond. "I'll be going." He turned away.

"No," she said, and her voice stopped him in his tracks. "Come inside with me," she whispered. "Please."

"Columbine," he said, shaking his head, "it's no good. Can't you see? I can't bear it."

"No," she said again.

She reached for him, her hand outstretched, and he took it. She grasped his hand, laced her fingers through his. "We can both bear it together," she said, and she drew him up the stairs and into the cool stillness of the hall. They went up the stairs together and she took him into her bedroom. The morning sun was streaming through the freshly-washed curtains, and her dressing gown, ruby silk, was thrown across a gold armchair. The rose and gold satin coverlet was thrown across the large bed, and her pins lay scattered on the nightstand. Some sort of perfume seemed to rise from it all, Columbine's scent.

Elijah looked at the room and felt the possibility of healing there. He had never been one to go to a woman to heal, or to blot out the world in passion. But this was different; there was the strength of a woman here, softness and steel, backbone and a yielding art, and it could help him.

He brought her to him, and he kissed her, his mouth open, wanting to drink her in. She was all softness and fire underneath his hands. He undressed her hastily, needing her nakedness, and he threw off his own clothes, barely conscious of what he did, his eyes never leaving her body, her face, her eyes. He loved the daylight on her skin. Everything about her body was beautiful to him; the curve of her breast, the small mound of her belly, the way her hips flared. He kissed her again, more urgently, while he took the pins from her hair. She moaned into his mouth, and he felt her excitement propel him into a need for possession.

He could not wait, it seemed intolerable to wait one second longer. She lay back on the satin coverlet and pulled him to her with strong, urgent arms, and he entered her instantly in one long thrust. Columbine gasped, her eyes wide. Her fingers clutched his shoulders. He waited, feeling himself swell within her, accommodating every enfolding soft curve. And then she began to kiss him, lightly, along the chin, her lips brushing against his beard. He moved, and she moaned again, and a sob caught in her throat. She pressed her cheek against his as they rocked together, and he felt her tears. She was crying and moving and her legs wound around him and her arms clutched him to her. Her skin felt hot; her lips were slick with tears as she kissed him, over and over, and held him against her tightly.

For an instant, against his closed lids, he saw Ben's face, pale and spectral, and he screwed his eyes shut tighter, seeing red flares. His rhythm grew more rough, but Columbine, with another deep sound of pleasure, matched it. He breathed her in and felt her skull against his fingers against the softness of her bright hair. He cradled her head. Love burst through him; his heart swelled and his senses drowned in her. He was lost in her, and he gave himself up.

And then she was crying out, and coming with him, and he was weeping too.

Lawrence found Bell work in a corset factory. It was strange, she thought, how quickly she adjusted back to that life. It was like a remembered dream. She went to work in the dark and came home in the dark. She had to pay rent for her chair and her sewing machine. The manager of the shop disliked her on sight, seeing in the tilt of her head and her posture a troublemaker, and he never let up on her.

Misery filtered down like ash through her days. The weight of returning to factory work was like an anvil on her chest. She would walk to work from Lawrence's rooms, timing her steps in concert with deep breaths of air. She felt she was about to be buried alive. She began to take a small volume of poetry with her, and she would memorize lines every morning. She was almost through "Dover Beach."

But slowly, as the weeks passed, Bell began to have certain satisfactions. The first, of course, were her nights. Living with Lawrence was intoxicating. She called herself his wife now, though of course they could not marry, since they did not believe in state sanctioned marriage. Bell got a secret thrill out of calling herself "Mrs. Birch," though of course she would never admit this to anyone. But it was nice to belong to someone. To have someone belong to her.

Bell never got used to the work, but she did begin to enjoy the workers. On lunch breaks and after work she would listen to the other women talk, and she saw that for these women their job was not purgatory. They were proud of earning their bread; this job was miles ahead of domestic service in status. They viewed their bosses with a cynical eye, and many were polticial, keeping up with the progress of the cloakmaker's new union. As May Day approached, Bell surreptitously talked a group into going with her to Union Square, where a great rally to support the cloakmaker's union would be held. Even the anarchists were attending, though Johann Most had blasted the effort in the *Freiheit*. Of course, ever Most's disciple, Lawrence refused to go.

But Emma Goldman disobeyed Most, and, using the oratory

skills he'd been teaching her, gave an impasssioned speech on the platform, standing next to Joseph Barondess, who'd emerged as the the fiery hero of the new union. The cloakmakers were among the worst paid of the garment workers; only nine dollars a week, working fourteen or fifteen hour days. Their hard struggle to form the union showed no signs of easing; recently, the bosses had begun lockouts of union workers.

Bell positioned herself as close to the speakers as she could. She was thrilled when the charismatic Barondess urged all workers to support their struggle. She had come to see, from attending meetings with Lawrence, that unlike her lover, many anarchists *did* support reform. She felt more comfortable with that side of the movement. Her commitment to anarchism was as yet a philosophical one; she still shied away, to Lawrence's disgust, from the *attentat*. Bell was more interested in the ideas of Dyer Lum, who thought that worker associations would be the natural core groups within a future anarchistic society. He believed that unionism was on the way to that goal, and the young firebrand Voltairine de Cleyre, who Bell admired, also spoke eloquently of the need for worker organizations.

New ideas, new speakers, constantly filled Bell's head. Despite long hours at the factory, her nights sparked with energy. She had only to cross the threshold of their rooms on Tompkins Square and see Lawrence bent over *Liberty*, Benjamin Tucker's anarchist journal, to feel strength fill her limbs again. A quick meal and coffee and they were off into the night, to a lecture or a meeting or a Second Avenue cafe, where talk swirled around them, dramatic and dangerous. She would put her head on the pillow every night, her brain busy, her trust secure that the strength of these ideas would change the world forever.

With the first hint of spring, when the still-biting breeze held the smell of damp earth and the pale sun had a fleeting warmth, fishing began again on the piers. Lawrence and Fiona's old spot was taken, but since she was living, five nights a week, at the Van Cormandt mansion, she managed to get away on her day off and come to his rooms. It was handy that Bell had agreed to take the factory job, for there was no chance, as there had been when she was only a few blocks away at Union Square, that she would appear during the day.

For the first time, Lawrence had Fiona in a bed, and he did not like it nearly as much. Somehow she sensed this, being a creature of the devil, and one day she took his hand and led him upstairs to the roof, where they lay on his coat amid the laundry lines and took their pleasure. Lawrence was excited by the windows surrounding them, empty eyes, and the soaring blue sky above. The light caught the strands of gold in her orange hair and turned her eyes pale green.

"Do you love me, Mr. Birch?" she asked him afterward, one white arm flung out among the cinders, and her skirt still bunched around her pale thighs.

"Aye, Mrs. Devlin," he said, imitating her lilting brogue.

She gave him a sidelong look. "Would you marry me then?"

Lawrence was taken aback; he'd never dreamed Fiona would be so conventional. "And what would Jimmy say?"

She made a face. "Jimmy and I don't have much of a marriage, as well you know. We're not even living together but two nights a week, now. And I've been thinking if things go wrong with the bomb. If Ned lives. You tell me I can disappear and take a new name. Can we have one together, man and wife? Go away together, out west?"

He grimaced. "I came from the west."

"Europe then."

"I don't have any money for such things, Fiona."

"What about what you lifted from that society of Mrs. Nash?"

"I had to pay for the bomb, you know," he said impatiently. "And I had to live."

Her reddish eyebrows came down in a deep frown, and she looked across the rooftop. "Are you telling me no, then?"

There would be no danger in agreeing; his plan was perfect, and he would have to trust to her wits to keep her head afterward. And she was Catholic; she would never divorce her husband. Jimmy Devlin was hale and hearty, though only one-armed, so there was no danger in agreeing. "Yes, I would marry you," he said, taking her hand. "And I would go with you, should you have to run. Would you do the same?"

She pulled down her skirt. "I suppose I would, yes."

"Of course," Lawrence continued, glad to see that she'd relaxed, "it's against my principles. I don't believe one needs the state to sanction a union."

She waved her hand. "I'm not interested in your theories, Lawrence. I wouldn't feel right otherwise. You'd have to overcome your scruples for me." She lay back and met his eyes mockingly. "Even though you have so few, I'm sure you can sacrifice one."

He kissed her. "I'd kill for you and die for you, so I suppose I'd marry you, too."

Fiona laughed, her teeth catching her bottom lip. "You're a liar," she murmured, running her hands along his chest. Lately, she'd been affectionate with him, her brusqueness tempered with tenderness.

"So how do you like your new master?" Lawrence asked lazily as he buttoned his trousers.

"We don't have conversations, if that's what you're asking," Fiona replied, sitting up again. "As a matter of fact, I rarely see our Ned."

"Let's go over the plan again," Lawrence said, smoothing the crease in his trousers. "You leave the inside lock of the summer parlor open when you clean it sometime during the day. Then you plant the fuse at night, running it underneath the rugs. What time does Mrs. Campbell go to bed?"

"I told you already—"

"Tell me again."

"She's in her room by eleven-thirty," Fiona said in an exasperated tone. With strong fingers, she wound her loosened hair into a tighter bun and stuck the pins back in. "Then Mr. Granger takes Neddie his brandy and soda at midnight and goes to bed himself. His light goes out at twelve-thirty. Everyone's asleep, then. The place is as quiet as a tomb."

"And Mary is a heavy sleeper, you said."

"There's but a foot between our beds, and for three nights now I got up and banged her blessed Bible on the floor, she didn't wake up. She'll sleep on, never fear."

"So you can get the keys earlier—"

"Mrs. Campbell sneaks out and takes a drink from the brandy bottle while Granger is taking our Ned his drink. She leaves the keys on the kitchen table. Since she's been tippling all day the brandy is all she needs to go straight out like a light. Sometimes she leaves the keys all night on the table, or the counter. She won't miss them if I take them, not till morning. And I hear her snoring fit to beat the band by twelve-twenty."

"And our target goes to bed when?"

"One-fifteen, I told you, just like clockwork."

"So I'll have about fifteen minutes between when Granger goes to bed—allowing time for him to be in a deep sleep—and the target goes upstairs." Lawrence put his hands behind his head and looked up at the sky. "That's hardly enough time," he mused. "But it will have to do, I suppose. As long as you can plant the fuse the night before."

"That will be the tricky part, make no mistake," Fiona said gloomily. "Mary is always poking about with her dustrag."

"You'll have to manage it. So when does he leave for Washington?"

"Two weeks, I think."

"Next week then," Lawrence said.

Fiona shivered. "So soon?"

Lawrence didn't notice the shiver; he was thinking hard, staring ahead of him. "He's going to Washington to meet with the president," he said. "I wish I could get that bastard, too, but I'll have to settle for his lackey."

"Next week," Fiona said dully.

Lawrence turned to her briskly. "Let's go over it all again. What time does Mrs. Campbell retire?"

Sixteen

MARGUERITE HAD SAILED through Toby's lessons over the past months without any nerves at all. Whatever he asked her to do, she did. If he wanted her to extend a note, she did. If he wanted her to use her hands on a phrase, she did. If he had asked her to dance around the room in her drawers, she would have. She trusted him, and somehow that trust belied any nerves on her part. Toby told her she was remarkably free of any fear of failure. Secretly, he hoped that would carry her through the grueling pressure of an audition with the great William Miles Paradise himself.

He was already a legend at thirty-two, starting out as a playwright at twenty-five and after two smash hits turning to producing. Whatever he touched seemed to turn to gold. He worked with the greats: Adelaide Ristori, Richard Mansfield, Edwin Booth, Maurice Barrymore, Ada Rehan, Maude Adams. Recently he had turned his eye to the revue, and his current hit was called *Potpourri!* The exclamation point was pure Willie P.

Toby had escorted Marguerite to the theater on the nights when Edwin was not available due to family duties. Even her disgruntlement at Edwin's desertion faded the moment she swept through the doors of the theater and sniffed the air. All theaters smelled the same to her; it was a perfume that went straight to her head and heart, better than anything from Paris, and instead of violet and musk she picked out floorboards and velvet curtains and sawdust and hammers and nails as well as the scent of furs and satins and silks of the audiences who crowded the seats night after night. When the house lights came down and the show began, good, bad, indifferent, tears would spring to her eyes. She would forget Toby next to her and lean backward, not forward, for her emotion was so overwhelming she was embarrassed by it.

As the play progressed she would lose her self-consciousness and begin to lean forward, rapt. She concentrated fiercely if it was a musical play, memorizing the words to songs and practicing the dances in her mind. The next day, she'd do them for Toby in his room. She had an excellent memory for steps and tunes, impressing even the blasé Toby.

She had approached her training with Toby as a lark; it was something she possessed that had nothing to do with Edwin. She had that, at least, for herself. And secretly she had planned to use the audition with William Paradise as a lever to get Edwin to marry her. He'd had enough time to vacillate. She would tell him it was either him or the stage, that the great William Miles Paradise wanted her. And, as it was with men, that would make Edwin want her more.

So if her confidence was high, if Toby told her her arrogance knew no bounds, why, on the morning of her audition, did she wake absolutely sick with fright? Just the thought of standing and singing for William Miles Paradise made her run to the bathroom directly after breakfast and deposit her rolls and coffee in the basin. She dressed with icy cold hands, feeling light-headed. She tottered her way to the carriage.

The stairs to Toby's rooms seemed endless. Along with her queasiness, she felt a bit guilty as she climbed. Poor Toby; if the audition went as he wanted, he would be losing her to marriage. All his work would be in vain. Marguerite told herself that she would not exclude Toby from her drawing room after she married. Of course, she couldn't invite him to dinners, just large receptions. But she would continue her lessons, he would like that.

Marguerite gathered herself at the threshold of Toby's door. She straightened her hat and her shoulders. She wouldn't want Toby to see how nervous she was. He was an awful scold.

He opened the door, handsome in a new light gray suit. His boots were impeccably polished. "Good morning," he said. "Are you ready to become a star, Miss Corbeau?" Then he stopped abruptly and really looked at her. "Good God, you look awful!" he burst out furiously. "Did you stay up late last night, you wretch?"

"Oh, do let me sit down, Toby." Marguerite pushed past him and sank onto his sofa. "I didn't go out last night at all, for your information, even though Edwin wanted to. I said I had a cold. I think I *do* have a cold. I feel wretched." She turned up her face to him pleadingly. "Don't be angry. Just give me some tea, I beg you."

Toby ignored the request. He put his hands on his hips. "However do you expect to sing today?"

"I don't know. Maybe you could postpone the audition. I was thinking that might be best." She looked at him hopefully.

"Oh, you were thinking that, were you. Well, forget it, petal. Willie P. is too important to cancel on. Who do you think you are, Lillian Russell? You're just going to have to pull yourself together, that's all there is to it. Do you have any rouge? No matter, I have some. We'll give it a try, anyway."

Marguerite sighed. "Do I look so very bad, Toby?"

He relented when he saw how distressed she was. "No, not so very bad," he said in that special voice that meant he was going to fuss over her. Marguerite leaned back against the sofa, glad to have back the Toby who petted and made everything all right.

"I'll have you fixed up in no time. Did you eat this morning? I'm sure not. Well, there you are. No wonder you're so pale, petal. You'll have some toast and tea, and you'll be as right as rain. Why didn't you eat, for God's sake?" he asked her, fussing impatiently with the teapot. "I told you to be sure and have something."

"I did," she insisted. "But then it came up again."

Toby's hand froze over the tea things. He stood stock still for a few seconds, then turned to her. "Oh, my God. You're not pregnant, are you?" He shook a piece of toast at her. "Don't lie to me."

"Don't be silly. And don't use that awful word." Marguerite removed her hat placidly. "I'm feeling better already."

"Do you *know* you're not?" Toby persisted.

"If you mean what I think you mean, yes, I know. I mean, I'm never regular—I can't *believe* I am discussing this with you, Toby! And I'll murder you with my bare hands if you keep standing there with your mouth open not pouring my tea." Toby turned back, and

Marguerite quickly went over dates. It *had* been over a month, but Edwin had promised that she could not get pregnant. "I'm not," she said aloud. "I'm not."

"You'd better damn well not be," Toby said, handing her a teacup.

Fortified with tea and toast, a spot of rouge on her cheekbones, Marguerite climbed back into the carriage with Toby for the ride to William Paradise's theater, where *Potpourri!* was currently packing in audiences.

"Don't be nervous, petal, you'll be wonderful," Toby said as he took off his gloves and put them on again without seeming to be conscious at all of what he was doing.

"Please stop telling me not to be nervous, Toby," she replied through gritted teeth. The carriage was swaying back and forth, and she felt carsick. Marguerite pressed her handkerchief against her forehead, which had drops of perspiration on it. She dearly hoped she could keep her food down.

It seemed ages before they pulled up in front of the theater. Marguerite took several deep breaths of fresh air and immediately felt better. Optimism surged through her again, and she smiled at Toby.

"That's better," he muttered.

She composed her face into its prettiest attitude, her lips slightly parted, her eyes shining with innocent enthusiasm—Your freshness, petal, we must use that!—but William Paradise had not yet arrived, and it was wasted on the worried-looking stage manager. He told them to wait, and they took two seats in the orchestra. Marguerite sank into the red plush, glad to have a few moments to herself. Her nerves were humming now, acute and sensitive. But it was so stuffy in the theater. So delightfully warm, actually . . . It only took a few minutes for Marguerite's head to droop, and she fell deeply asleep.

The next thing she knew, Toby was shaking her. "He's here," he hissed. "Wake up, Marguerite, for God's sake."

Marguerite shook her head slightly and focused on the stage. William Paradise had arrived through the stage door, and he was earnestly in conversation with the morose stage manager. He wasn't much taller than Toby, and though he was beautifully dressed, his figure was not elegant, like Edwin's. As a matter of fact, he was almost stocky. Marguerite preferred tall, slim men.

The stage manager pointed them out to him, and he started down the stairs and across the front aisle to meet them. Toby tugged her to her feet.

As William Paradise came closer, Marguerite was still not impressed. He had dark hair and dark eyes and a dark suit; he was mid-sized and middling handsome. This was the famous producer, the notorious lover, the man who, it was said, had broken more hearts than anyone on Broadway? She passed his like every day on the street.

He greeted Toby like an old friend and asked about his mother, of all things, who apparently had been an actress herself twenty years before. William Paradise seemed to have a genuine interest in this woman; too genuine, for Marguerite was standing there, trying to "look like an angel," as Toby had advised her, and growing a bit sulky. And then, finally, he turned to her.

"Miss Corbeau." He took her hand for an instant and looked at her. Marguerite saw that his eyes weren't brown, but a dark, woodsy green. His gaze was keen and focused and alive; it drank her in without being in the least offensive. He smiled, and suddenly, Marguerite wanted very much to please him.

"Will you sing for me?" he asked, as though she would be bestowing a favor.

And even though they all knew very well how much Toby had schemed and pleaded and scratched for this audition, she followed Willie P.'s lead and nodded her head shyly, as though he had asked her to sing in his parlor, for his most intimate guests.

She mounted the steps to the stage with Toby. He went straight to the piano.

"Toby?" William Paradise's voice was soft, but it carried up to the stage. "I'd like George to play for Miss Corbeau, if you wouldn't mind."

Toby looked startled, but he nodded. "Of course."

"Thank you. Miss Corbeau, I'm going up to the balcony. George will signal you, and then you may begin when you wish. Abram, the lights please."

The footlights flicked on a moment later. Marguerite blinked. It was her first time standing on a stage, and she was overwhelmed. The floorboards seemed to vibrate underneath her feet and send up shock waves all the way out to her fingertips. She liked being high like this and looking over empty seats. She imagined them full of people, all looking at her. Through her nerves, her queasy stomach, she felt a sharp thrill, as though she'd just looked into the eyes of a new lover, and she had the same strong sense of fate. I belong here, she thought.

"Take off your things," Toby hissed. He handed the music to George on his way back down the stairs.

She slipped out of her coat quickly and fumbled with her hatpin. Toby had gone over and over her wardrobe, and finally selected her new gold gown. It was her most flattering dress, accentuating the narrowness of her waist and giving her a bit of bosom, as it was low-necked and cunningly tucked and embroidered on the bodice. Marguerite had stuffed several handkerchiefs down the dress for good measure. A design of pale pink chrysanthemum petals was embroidered on the gold damask, and a double garland of pearls mounted on tulle with crystal pendants was drawn up in a series of loops diagonally down the skirt, held by jeweled clasps in the form of scallop shells.

Marguerite tried to imagine that she was the luscious Lillian Russell. She struck the pose she and Toby had practiced, and when George nodded at her a moment later, she was ready. She took a deep breath and looked out into the empty seats. "Sing to the last row," Toby had advised her. "Picture someone sitting there, someone you want to impress, even someone from your past . . . your father? No, I can see that's a bad idea. Well, how about me, then, petal?"

Marguerite smiled a bit, remembering that. But she pictured her mother, in an extravagant hat Marguerite would buy her, sitting in the last row. She nodded at George, and as the opening bars began, she took a breath and sailed in exactly as she'd practiced, over and over again.

They'd chosen "A Bird in a Gilded Cage" for her to sing. Though the song was written from the point of view of someone looking at a young woman who'd sold herself in marriage to a rich, older man, Toby had coached her performance to suggest that Marguerite was the young woman herself. "You may think she's happy," Marguerite had sung, over and over on those sunny afternoons, "but she's not, though she seems to be . . ." Toby had been thrilled with the result, telling her that she packed a wallop better than John L. Sullivan himself.

But today, she couldn't seem to capture that plaintive fire. Maybe it was the accompanist, who played at a slightly different tempo than Toby. Her voice was fine, but Marguerite knew, even as she sang, that she was not giving her best performance. Her tiredness showed in her voice, and she could not seem to pull herself together. As she sailed on, she frantically tried to inject life into the song, and it came out wrong. It was bad, it was wrong, she was trying too hard, and she was relieved when she could finally stop, on a note that was slightly sharp. Marguerite wanted to stamp her foot in frustration. She was never sharp. Toby had been the first to tell her that she had something known as perfect pitch.

She didn't dare look at Toby. She wouldn't get another chance, not with William Miles Paradise, and would even Toby want to continue with her when she'd let him down so badly?

William Paradise stood up in the balcony. "Thank you, Miss Corbeau," rang out through the darkened theater. The footlights clicked off. Marguerite missed the warmth of the lights on her face. George got up from the piano and wandered off into the wings. It had taken less than five minutes, and it was over.

Slowly, Toby rose from his position in the fifth row. She could sense it rather than see it, for her head was down. Suddenly, she felt ill again. Sweat popped out on her forehead, and she was dreadfully warm. Marguerite pressed a hand to her mouth.

"Well—" Toby began, but he stopped abruptly as Marguerite picked up her gold skirts in both hands and ran to the wings, where she deposited her second breakfast of the morning on her new gold kid boots. With Toby standing over her, exasperated and angry, catching the jeweled hair ornament when it tumbled from her curls, she retched and sobbed bitterly.

When she'd finished, she weakly lifted her head and looked straight into the cool, amused eyes of William Miles Paradise. She hated him more than she'd ever hated anyone.

"I'm sorry," she gulped. She was dreadfully afraid that her nose was running, but she'd be damned if she'd swipe at it with her hand. She'd already been humiliated enough.

"Don't worry, it's happened before," he said. Then before she could realize what his intention was, he reached into her bosom with two respectful fingers and extracted a handkerchief. With a mock bow and a twinkle in his eye, he handed it to her with a flourish. "Your handkerchief, Miss Corbeau," he said.

Darcy and Tavish Finn arrived with smiles and presents and large trunks, for they were planning a two-month stay in Europe. "We need ideas," Tavish said, "new experiences, new people, and I want to learn French."

"And I want to spend time with my mother," Darcy put in. "I haven't seen her in more than twenty years. It's a fine thing to forgive someone by mail, but it's time we faced each other. Though I must say I don't like the timing one bit."

Darcy's mother, Amelia Grace Snow, had been a famous beauty who scandalized New York society by running off with the painter James Fitzchurch. The family had never heard from her again; Darcy had been forbidden to speak her mother's name. She'd written to her mother soon after she was married, however, and they'd struck up a thriving correspondence. Since Darcy's father had died in the great blizzard of '88, Amelia and James had been able to quietly marry at last.

"What's the matter with the timing?" Columbine asked as she poured them all glasses of sherry. "I would think spring is the perfect time to go to Paris."

"She means now that Amelia is married she can't shock everyone by seeing her," Tavish said with an arch glance at his wife. "Darcy would much rather visit her mother while she is living in sin."

Darcy laughed. "You are too awful, Tavish. You know that's not true."

"It is true, and I had the black eye to prove it."

"Oh, dear, have you two come to blows so soon?" Columbine asked with a grin.

"Not that old story, Tavish. I declare, you must tell everyone you meet. I think the entire train thinks I beat you."

Tavish raised one eyebrow at his wife and turned to Columbine. "It was at a very elegant dinner party at the Vesey Montclairs. They tolerate me, but they adore Darcy because she's a Grace and a Snow, you see. Why do all society people in America feel compelled to use two names? Anyway, needless to say they've never read one word of what she's written, or they'd ride her out of town on a rail."

"We should never go there again," Darcy put in.

"So Mrs. Vesey Montclair turned to Darcy and asked her if she would actually receive her mother should she leave a card at our hotel. And Darcy replied sweetly that she was going to call on Amelia first thing *without*, of course, mentioning that Amelia is now Mrs. Fitzchurch. Darcy almost killed poor Matilda. I swear, Columbine, the poor thing choked on her fish—I thought my own filet terribly bony—and Reverend Collier had to pound her on the back. Whereupon Mrs. Vesey Montclair's emerald brooch popped its clasp, flew across the porcelain dishes and landed a mean one on my left eye." He turned back to Darcy. "Case closed."

Darcy swatted him. Her quiet gray eyes were full of merriment. "I can see why you are opposed to marriage, Columbine," she said. "How I wish sometimes that you had converted me. Or perhaps I should become an anarchist."

"That blackguard Mr. Birch certainly tried to convert you," Tavish said, scowling.

Columbine sat up. "If he's such a blackguard, Tavish, whyever did you send him to me?"

"Send him to you? I didn't."

"But he said—"

"Oh, I might have mentioned you—perhaps at one time might have said, if you get to New York, look her up . . . something like that. Before I knew what he was, that is. I know how much you adore radicals," Tavish said, grinning. "But you didn't get a letter of introduction, did you?"

Columbine shook her head. Lawrence had told her the letter had been lost in the haste of his journey. She had meant to write Tavish about it, but she had forgotten, and soon it seemed unimportant.

Darcy looked concerned. "Mr. Birch came here, Columbine?"

"Yes, a couple of months ago," Columbine said neutrally. "He had some trouble in San Francisco, he said."

"I'll say," Tavish growled. "Some say he caused it."

"There was no proof, Tavish," Darcy said quietly.

"I know. But it was a bad business. I hope you didn't get entangled with the man, Columbine. Frankly, I don't trust him a bit."

"Columbine probably saw through him in the first five minutes," Darcy said decidedly. "She's such a good judge of character."

"Mmmmm," said the cowardly Columbine. She picked up the decanter. "More sherry?" she asked brightly.

Marguerite wore her white bengaline gown with Irish lace and no jewelry. She arranged her hair in a simple style. She had the cook make Edwin's favorite lunch. She was tender with him while he ate, solicitously asking him about the brokerage business, and only letting an occasional soft sigh escape her. When he had finished, he poured himself another glass of Bordeaux and pushed back his chair.

He patted his lap. "Come here, little one. Something is troubling you."

Marguerite slipped off her brocade chair and went to sit on his knee. His arm curved around her waist. "Tell me," Edwin said softly. He loved solving Marguerite's little problems. "It can't be so bad, can it?"

She leaned against his shoulder. "Oh, Edwin. I'm so happy, and yet I can't seem to stop weeping. I hardly know how to begin."

"At the beginning, dear," Edwin said. He thought he sounded wonderfully masterful. Like his father, nearly.

Tears sparkled on her thick black lashes. "I'm going to have your child, Edwin," she whispered.

Edwin felt as though ice water had been poured over his head, having the dual effect of shocking him and freezing his brain. "What?" he asked stupidly.

"At first I wasn't certain. But now I am." Marguerite peeked at Edwin. He looked awfully, well, stupid, with his mouth open like that. "Isn't it wonderful, darling?"

He pushed her off his lap so he could stand. That action, the first curt gesture he'd ever made toward her, started Marguerite's heart beating. She leaned against the table. The queasiness was constant with her now, and she desperately told herself she could not be sick, not now.

He fumbled in his pocket for a cigar. She closed her eyes. Not a cigar! She would lose her composure for certain.

"Please, Edwin," she said weakly. "I must ask you not to smoke. I'll be ill."

Automatically, Edwin returned the cigar to its case. "How could you do this!" he burst out, wheeling around to glare at her. "Father will never forgive this."

A slight widening of the nostrils was the only sign that Marguerite was furious. She must not show it. She must salvage this, she must. She must not lose her temper. "He doesn't have to know, Edwin. We can marry."

"We cannot marry in time, I would have to elope. Even if we *could* marry, it is impossible."

"Even if we *could*? What are you saying, Edwin?" Real tears gathered in her eyes now. "I thought you loved me."

"Marguerite," he said desperately, "don't you understand? My family, my position? This is impossible."

"Stop saying it's impossible! I'm afraid it *is* possible, Edwin, for I am standing here carrying your child. Despite your 'Eastern method of control,'" she added bitterly.

He stared at her. "Exactly. I timed myself, I controlled my fluids—"

She made a disgusted noise. "That's ridiculous. In the beginning, perhaps. But there were many times that—"

"There's someone else," he said. "You have another lover. I can see it in your face. My God, I should have listened to my friends. I should never have trusted you."

Her mouth was open. She wanted to fly at him in a rage. Her Edwin, her pale, elegant Edwin, was accusing her like this, like a bully, like a . . . *man*?

"You are despicable," she said.

"You see that Toby Wells almost every day. The driver told me."

"What are you saying? You know I take music lessons from him."

"Sometimes you stay for two hours or more—"

"Because what do I have to return to? An empty house with only an Irish maid to keep me company. You keep me here, I can never go out—"

"I demand an answer!" Edwin shouted. "Who is the father of that child?"

Marguerite stood rigid, her hands clasped into tiny fists at her sides. She wanted to fly at him, she wanted to scratch his eyes out, she wanted to murder him. But instead she turned her back and left the room.

She went to the library and sat on the sofa, her whole body shaking. She could hardly think or move. Where to turn? she wondered dizzily. Where to turn? She heard footsteps down the hall, heard the slam of the front door. Edwin was gone.

"What will I do?" she asked the empty room. Never in her worst nightmares had she imagined this.

Bridget knocked lightly on the door. Her blue eyes rounded in concern when she saw her young mistress. "Can I do something for you, ma'am?" she asked solicitiously.

Marguerite shook her head. "Just leave me alone, please." But as Bridget nodded and turned, Marguerite spoke up. "No, Bridget, I'm going out. Will you put out my gray cloak, the one with the white velvet trim, and my new hat?"

A kind of calmness came over her as she dressed to go out. She knew the answer now. Edwin was terrified of his father. For all his talk of his independence, he still answered to Winthrop Stiers. How Toby had snickered whenever she blithely said that Edwin was his own man! She should have listened to Toby; he had tried to warn her about Edwin. But now even her best friend had turned his back. Toby was furious with her for humiliating him at the theater. She would have to solve her own problem.

Winthrop Stiers was the key, she thought as she hailed a hansom cab on Madison, for Edwin had taken the private carriage. She remembered clearly how Edwin had said that his sister-in-law Rosamond had won his father over. Well, she was prettier and more charming than Rosamond, Marguerite felt sure. And Rosamond, in her fifth year of marriage, had yet to produce a child. Winthrop Stiers was heavily disappointed, Edwin had said.

The carriage pulled up in front of the Stiers' quiet brownstone on Fifth and Thirty-Sixth street. This was the neighborhood of the Old Guard, those venerable New York families who refused to follow the steady drive uptown, as millionaires pushed farther and farther up Fifth Avenue with their palaces and their limestone castles. Here the money and the mood was quiet and restrained. Marguerite knew that these brownstones were vastly more confident than those grandiose piles, but she still would prefer to have a Renaissance palace like the one Alva Vanderbilt had commissioned than an ugly old brownstone. When she and Edwin married, perhaps his father would build them a new house farther up Fifth, near the Valentine Hartleys, the epitome of the smart younger set.

But still, even the brownstone cowed her a bit. She hesitated on the walk, looking at the curtained windows. A momentary still voice within her told her to stop and reconsider. But Marguerite was on fire from Edwin's reaction. She knew in the very depths of her that Edwin had not meant to be cruel; it was just that he was still a boy, unable to stand up for himself. She would have to arrange everything. She would have to do it, for Edwin would hem and haw and put her off for weeks, even while her belly grew rounder and she was bursting the seams of her dresses. And what else could she do? Where else could she turn?

That thought propelled up the stairs and made her hand strong as she let the knocker fall. She gave the butler her card, folding over the left corner to let him know she wanted to be received. She'd already written "an urgent matter concerning your son" on the back.

She was left to wait in the front parlor. Marguerite nervously noted how elegant the room was. She had read of the Vanderbilt drawing rooms in the Japanese or French mode, of jeweled butterflies sewn in the velvet curtains, of the carved wainscoting, the marble fireplaces, the ebony furniture inlaid with gold. But here the elegance of the furnishings lay in their rich, discreet velvets and fine woods. Family pictures were collected on a small table, and over the mantlepiece was a luminious landscape of a Hudson River school painter. There was a minimum of the jumble and display of most parlors, however, and something in the room seemed chilly to Marguerite, despite the cheer of a small fire. Perhaps it was the absence of books, or periodicals, or even a pair of glasses forgotten on a table. Nothing personal was in this room. Used to Columbine's clutter, and her own messes, Marguerite found it strange.

A throat cleared behind her, and she whirled around to find the butler had returned. She was afraid that he'd been sent to escort her out again, but he told her that Mr. Stiers would receive her in the library, and to please follow him.

She walked down a long red carpeted hall to a room at the back of the house. Her first impression on entering the room was of strong masculinity; she could smell cigars and leather and fine old brandy. Mr. Winthrop Stiers stood in the middle of the green Persian rug looking at her with a bland expression. He was almost seventy, she knew, but he still had the same elegance of form that Edwin had inherited. He waited until the butler had withdrawn and closed the door behind him. "Miss Corbeau," he said neutrally.

"Mr. Stiers, you must forgive me for intruding like this. If it weren't a matter of the greatest urgency, I would not have disturbed you."

He nodded slightly. "Please sit down."

Marguerite sat in the straight-backed chair he indicated while he went back behind the desk. She wished they could have sat in the armchairs in front of the fire, but this would have to do. She knew she created a pretty impression in her white velvet hat trimmed with lilac grosgrain ribbons and violets. Even though her cheeks were pale, she told herself that it gave her an aristocratic look.

"You know my son?" he asked.

She nodded. "I became acquainted with your son several months ago, sir. We became . . . attached. He asked me to marry him some months ago."

He nodded again, only slightly, but at least he gave no sign that this information distressed him.

"Edwin wants to tell you," she said. "But he can't. It's that he wants to please you so much. He reveres you, Mr. Stiers. And I," she said softly, her lashes trembling as she looked down at her prettily clasped hands, "revere him."

"Shouldn't it be my son's place to tell me this, Miss Corbeau?"

"Of course. But I thought if I came to you, bold a step as it may be, and presented myself to you as your future daughter-in-law, we could be frank with one another. Edwin is proud, Mr. Stiers. He would think it an insult to explain his choice, to have to answer questions about my background. But I know there are things you must ask, and I wanted to give you the opportunity to do so. I am an orphan, but I come from a good family in France. My father was a very prosperous grain merchant. He was a gentleman, and I was educated to be a lady. My family emigrated five years ago, and unfortunately my parents died soon after arriving in America. I was raised by my aunt, who had fallen on hard circumstances. But still, she had a respectable house upstate. She died a year ago, and I moved to New York." Marguerite prayed that none of these details would be checked. She would just have to risk it.

"I see," he said. "Are you aware, Miss Corbeau, that Edwin is already an engaged man?"

Marguerite swallowed. "No," she said confusedly, "no, I was not. Edwin never said—"

"It is not official as of yet. Certain arrangements still have to be made with the father of the lady. But it is a matter of time." He reached for a silver box and extracted a cigar. Marguerite's stomach rolled over at the thought of the smell. He did not ask if she minded, and she could hardly ask him to abstain. She'd already spent all her courage to come to him at all. She leaned back.

"I think Edwin would have told me if he was serious about this," she said slowly. "Perhaps it is you who want the engagement, Mr. Stiers, not your son."

"Are you so sure of that, Miss Corbeau?" He clipped the end of the cigar and lit it, puffing slowly. "I must confess I am still puzzled as to why you have chosen to come to me. But you have, and you've said your piece, I assume, so can we consider the interview closed?"

Perspiration gathered under Marguerite's armpits, and she was glad she had not removed her cloak, even though she felt hot. "No," she said. "I have not finished." A cloud of cigar smoke rolled over the desk toward her.

"Ah. Now comes what you would call the payoff, eh?"

What you would call. So despite her pretty dress, her hat, her careful words, her cultivated manner, he had seen through it all. He knew she was not of his class. Marguerite tamped down her anger; she reminded herself that she must charm this man. "No," she said, "not a 'payoff,' whatever that may be. I'm carrying your son's child, Mr. Stiers."

He lowered the cigar slowly. His face went white, tense. His nostrils were tinged pink. Something about the look in his watery gray eyes frightened her, and she understood now what Edwin told her the family called his father's "dead eye." And suddenly, she was reminded of her own father. It was the same look, frightening in its opacity.

"What do you want?" he asked.

"Only acceptance," she said, swallowing. "I was wrong. But I was in love. Edwin and I lost our heads, as well as our hearts. But I think we would do a greater wrong to you if we were forced to elope. Only you can make the marriage happen with any speed. Sir, I'm here before you to show you who I am, to show you that I'm a respectable person. Accept me into your family. I am carrying your grandchild. I love Edwin with all my heart. I'll make him a good wife, Mr. Stiers."

He continued to stare at her, his face a mask. Marguerite held his gaze as long as she could, then looked down at her lap again.

"You are a pretty child," he said in rapid French.

"Thank you, sir," she responded in French. "But I do not consider myself still a child. I am a woman in love with a man."

It was a test, and she'd passed it. She knew her accent was perfect. Her mother had the accent of an aristocrat; she'd made sure that Marguerite did not pick up the peasant French in Lille.

Winthrop Stiers pressed his lips together. He seemed to be struggling with a decision. The smoke from the cigar assaulted her nostrils. Marguerite couldn't help it; she turned her head away.

Immediately, he put it out, standing up as he did so. "You look very pale, Miss Corbeau. I think you could do with a rest. Jameson will escort you to a guest room, where you can lie down. I'm going to summon Edwin home and discuss this with him." He came around the desk and helped her rise. He seemed almost kind now. "Don't you see, this has come as a shock."

"Of course," she murmured.

He raised her chin with a finger. "You're very beautiful, Miss Corbeau, and very forthright. I quite see why Edwin fell in love with you."

Her eyes dropped. "Thank you, sir."

"Now, you've had a very upsetting time, and you need your rest. Then we'll see what we'll do, all right?"

She nodded gratefully, glad now to put her fate in his hands. She was so tired.

She fell asleep almost immediately in the guest room, her cheek against cool linen. It was a light, pleasant sleep, and she dreamed of being on stage again. But this time her voice came out silvery and pure. She could not sing a wrong note, and roses were heaped at her feet. William Paradise smiled at her, his forest eyes approving.

When there was a tap at the door, she woke immediately. "Come in," she said, raising herself on her elbows, thinking it would be Edwin.

But it was the butler. "I'm to escort you to the front door, miss."

"But where is Mr. Stiers—I mean, Mr. Edwin?"

"If you'll follow me, miss. You're to go home now, Mr. Stiers said."

Puzzled, Marguerite put on her hat and coat. Perhaps Edwin was meeting her at her house. She followed the butler down the hall. "How long have I been asleep?" she asked him.

"Over two hours, miss."

Marguerite found herself on the front stairs without quite knowing how or why she was there. She looked back, but the door was already shutting in her face.

It was past five o'clock. Edwin was most likely waiting for her in her house; it was thoughtful of Mr. Stiers to realize they should discuss their future in privacy. Marguerite hailed a cab and sank back against the upholstery with a sigh. She supposed Edwin might be angry that she had gone over his head. But he could not stay angry, for her idea had worked. That solicitiousness of Mr. Stiers had not been faked. She was carrying his first grandchild. He would not compromise that.

She got back to her house with a great sense of relief. It had started to rain, and she was still groggy from her nap. It would feel like heaven to be in front of a roaring fire with a cup of tea. Marguerite climbed the stairs wearily. She pushed at the door, but it was locked, and she hadn't taken her key. She rang the bell for Bridget.

It seemed a full minute before the door opened a crack. A frightened Bridget peered out at her. "Oh, Miss," she said stupidly.

"Let me in, Bridget," Marguerite snapped. "Can't you see I'm getting wet?"

"I can't miss." The maid said the words in a hurry. "Mr. Stiers forbids me to, miss. I'm so sorry, miss," she said in a low moan.

"This is impossible," Marguerite said. "This is my home. What about my clothes?"

"You're to have nothing, miss. Goodbye, miss. I'm sorry." Bridget slammed the door. The lock slid home.

Marguerite stared at the closed door in shock. The rain began to fall faster. She ran down the stairs, yelling at the driver to wait, for he'd hesitated at the curb.

"The Union Club," she called to him, and stayed erect, her face set, for the short ride to Edwin's club.

She guessed that he would go there for dinner, or at least a drink, to get away from his father. Mr. Stiers must have laid down the law; that evil man had done this to her. He had tricked her. Edwin didn't know that his father had done this. But she would fix Winthrop Stiers. She would get his precious son to elope with her. She'd never let him see the baby, never . . .

She dismissed the cab without thinking, for her money was low. But now she had to wait on the sidewalk in the rain. She positioned herself across the street, under a tree. She was wet through now, and she wrapped her arms around herself to stay the shivers that racked her body. She was on fire with her purpose, and hardly noticed the cold.

She seemed to wait for hours, but it was about fifteen minutes, when she saw Edwin alight from a hack. "Edwin!" she called, running across the street.

He turned, shocked, when he saw her. "What are you doing?" he hissed. He looked behind him nervously at the windows. Then, taking her arm, he led her across the street.

She began to laugh. His hurry was so comical, and the rain was falling, and they were so wet. "Edwin," she said breathlessly, "your father locked me out of my house. Can you imagine such a thing? Bridget was terrified—" She stopped abruptly when the look on Edwin's face registered. It was a look of shame, and defiance, and now, suddenly, she felt the cold in the marrow of her bones.

"You did it," she said.

"Father made me," Edwin said, not meeting her eyes.

"Edwin, how could you do this to me? I'm carrying your child. And you love me," she said with a sob.

"Marguerite, Father thinks it best if I have no contact with you," Edwin said uncomfortably. "I wanted to give you money, but he said it could be construed as blackmail. He said there should be no ties between us."

"But the baby . . ."

"I can't be sure it's mine, you see," he said. "I can't even be sure there's a baby at all. I met you at that dinner, for God's sake, with all those naked women. I had to tell Father how I met you."

He sounded like a boy. A foolish, wavering boy. And he looked like a boy, with his wet head, his calf eyes. Betrayal wasn't always cruel. Sometimes it came in the guise of weakness.

Rain and tears fell down her face, and she drank in the taste of salt. She could hardly see now; a film of rain and rage clogged her vision.

Edwin pressed something in her hand, and her fingers closed over it. Marguerite wanted to fling the money in his face, but what would that get her but satisfaction?

Edwin felt rain seep down his collar, and he thought of the roaring fire in the Union Club with longing. "I'm sorry, Marguerite," he said. But along with the remorse he felt relief; the worst was over. And Marguerite did not look as pretty now, with her red nose and her lank hair. And the men at the club, his friends, the men he'd gone to Harvard with, wouldn't laugh at him, the way his father said they would should he be foolish enough to marry his first mistress, one of Stanford White's chippies that a dozen men had had, most likely. Or at least that was what would be whispered.

And he wouldn't ask Georgina Halstead to marry him, no matter what his father said. No, he would stand up and be a man. He would choose his own bride. But he would not choose Marguerite.

Edwin turned away because he could not stand her eyes. "I'll get a cab for you," he mumbled.

"And where will I go, Edwin?" she asked him dryly.

He had no answer. He looked callow and stupid. She didn't want him, anyway. Marguerite turned and walked away, down the long sidewalk, and left him standing there. And as she trudged away she left behind any tiny bit of harbored, giddy innocence that had remained in her heart.

Seventeen

ELIJAH AND TAVISH had gone off to a meeting of Elijah's reading group, which tackled everything from Henry George to George Eliot, and Columbine and Darcy had the long evening to spend together. They settled into armchairs pulled close to the fire, with a small table with tea and sandwiches between them.

"I like this room," Darcy said approvingly. "I loved your old parlor, of course, but this is so elegant and light somehow. I like the proportions, and the big bay window."

"Yes, I think I'll be happy here," Columbine said with a yawn. Now that she had Darcy all to herself, she was chagrined to find that she was sleepy. She straightened up and moved a bit back from the fire.

"And are you happy with Elijah Reed?" Darcy asked, picking up a chicken sandwich with a show at unconcern.

Columbine laughed. "I remember when you used to have to circle round a tender topic, Darcy. Is it your journalistic training that's taught you to strike right at the heart?"

"No, just my curiosity," Darcy answered with a grin. "I just want to know if you are happy, Columbine. It's not clear to me, or to Tavish, I'm afraid. It's obvious that Elijah loves you, but—"

Columbine looked into the fire. "But?"

"Well, there is something . . . Something that he holds back. You talk of your life, and he of his, as though they are totally separate."

"But they are. After all, we're not married."

"This from a free lover? You are committed to each other."

Columbine's voice was muffled. "I don't know if we're committed to each other or not. Or rather, I don't think that Elijah is capable of it. He told me that from the beginning. The nature of his work, his life, is so different. He doesn't like to be settled. Do you know that he's lived in six cities in the past five years?"

"Yes, he seems a man who avoids entanglements."

"It's because he's lost so many people, from a very early age. And he saw horrors in the war. Then he married, and his wife died a long and particularly awful death from cancer." Columbine gave a deep sigh. "But it's not just those circumstances, though they shaped him. I'm inclined to believe that we're formed from the cradle, able to love well or not to love well, and whatever life brings us we fit into that scheme of things."

"But Columbine, what about redemption?" Darcy asked, startled to hear such pessimism from the normally sunny Columbine. "What about the human capacity for change, or surprise?"

"Oh, we have the illusion that we can change our natures," Columbine answered. "That's the romance of life. What is life for, but striving to be good, to be better? But can Elijah Reed break out of an emotional prison formed since childhood—or can I help him do so? I don't think so."

She sounded so sad that Darcy reached over and took her hand. "I changed, Columbine. How can you forget that? You're the one who helped me. My emotions were crippled. I had been locked all my life in that same prison. And yet, I learned how to love. Through Tavish, and you."

Columbine gave her sister-in-law's hand a squeeze, but she was not comforted. "I think the two circumstances are so different. You were longing for change, Darcy. Your true nature *was* for frank love, commitment. From the moment you realized you loved Tavish, despite everything, you were for him to the death. You opened yourself to Tavish with all the innocence of a flower."

"Nonsense," Darcy said in an acerbic tone. "Now who's being romantic? A flower, indeed." She gave an unladylike snort. "More like a hoyden, most likely."

Darcy's words broke the ice, and they laughed together like

young girls. They quieted, leaning back in the chairs again. Darcy bit into a sandwich.

Columbine's eyes were dreamy as she gazed into the orange flames. "The thing is, if Elijah did love me," she said quietly, "I'd be the last to know."

Darcy didn't get a chance to reply, for there was a knock at the door, and Mrs. Haggerty stood at the threshold, wiping her hands on her apron. The stout, gray-haired lady was constantly working, no matter how vociferously Columbine begged her to rest.

"There's a visitor for you, Mrs. Nash. A Miss Corbeau, she calls herself." She gave a pronounced sniff.

"Indeed, that is her name, Mrs. Haggerty," Columbine said dryly. "Will you show her in, please?" As Mrs. Haggerty retreated, she said to Darcy, "Marguerite Corbeau, do you remember her?"

"Of course," Darcy said. Marguerite had been a parlormaid in Darcy's grand Fifth Avenue mansion when Darcy had been married to Claude Statton.

Darcy greeted Marguerite cordially when she entered, but she could see immediately that the young girl was upset. Her dress and cloak were soaked and splattered with mud, and her hair was loose and hanging down her back in wet clumps.

"How do you do, Mrs. Statton—I'm terribly sorry, Mrs. Finn. Please forgive me," Marguerite said, summoning up dignity from somewhere, "it's just that I've walked far."

"Please don't give it a thought, Miss Corbeau," Darcy said. "And come closer to the fire, you're wet through."

"Why don't you come upstairs, Marguerite, so you can take off your things and put on one of my dressing gowns?" Columbine suggested. "I must insist. You'll catch your death."

"No, please," Marguerite begged, sinking into an armchair. "I'll dry off soon, I promise. Let me just sit here for a moment."

Columbine and Darcy exchanged looks over Marguerite's wet, dark head. Then Darcy gave an imperceptible shrug, as if to say that it would upset Marguerite more to insist. So she slipped her own cashmere shawl around Marguerite's thin shoulders.

"I have some packing to do upstairs," Darcy said, for she sensed that Marguerite would only speak of her trouble if she was alone with Columbine. "If you'll excuse me, Miss Corbeau."

Marguerite's earlier shaky poise had deserted her. She didn't seem to hear Darcy. She was staring into the fire, shivering violently now. With another worried glance at Columbine, Darcy left the room.

Columbine knelt by Marguerite's chair. She picked up one small, frozen hand, then the other, and chafed them. Then she stood and removed Marguerite's bedraggled hat. She coaxed her out of her three-quarter length coat and drew the shawl around her shoulders more firmly. Then she began to spread out Marguerite's thick hair so that it would dry. Through all of this, Marguerite stared into the fire, shaking. Finally, Columbine picked up Marguerite's hands again and rubbed them gently.

"Can you talk now, dear?" she asked tenderly.

Marguerite turned and looked at her. "I don't deserve your kindness," she said. "But you said I could come to you. And I didn't," she said, a sob breaking loose, "have anyplace to go."

Columbine moved to embrace her, but Marguerite stiffened immediately. "Please don't," she whispered. "I want to stop crying, and if you hold me I won't be able to."

Columbine was unaccountably moved more by those words than anything else Marguerite might say. She looked so pathetic with her wet hair and still face, so lost. She had never seen Marguerite look lost.

"I hate my tears," Marguerite said bitterly. "Everything was my fault, everything. I had two eyes to see with and two ears to hear and a brain, a working brain, and still I persisted in my folly. And I hate that my falling is so predictable!" she said, her two hands curling into fists. Her dark blue eyes were bright with tears, but they did not fall. "I can't forgive myself for that, either."

"Has your lover left you?" Columbine asked timidly.

Marguerite nodded. "Of course. And I'm pregnant, how about that?"

Columbine nodded; she'd suspected something of the kind. First things first. "Are you certain?"

"Dizziness, fatigue, and this constant sickness. And I'm over three weeks late, I believe."

"It sounds like it, then. But a doctor will be sure. And is there any chance the man might marry you?"

"No," Marguerite answered flatly. "None."

Columbine was used to counseling other young girls with the same problem. Briskness and practicality was usually a good approach, for they usually thought their situation hopeless. "I can help you," she said to Marguerite. "We can take care of this, and no one will have to know. The New Women Society has a fund, as you know." Columbine briefly thought of the fact that she had suspected Marguerite of stealing from the fund, but she pushed the thought away. "We can send you away, to a place in the country, and you can have your baby. Should you wish to keep it, we'll help you move to another city. I assure you, it's done all the time. Just invent a husband, nothing could be easier."

Marguerite shook her head. "No. I want to get rid of it."

Columbine sank back into the other armchair. This was another thing indeed. "I see," she said.

"I'm not cut out for motherhood, Columbine. You might imagine that. And how could I bring a child into the world with that stain? I could not live with that. I could not live with the knowledge that I left my child in an orphanage with no hope, no money. I couldn't. I want to get rid of it. I want you to help me. Does Dr. Dana do abortions?" When Columbine hesitated, she said impatiently, "It doesn't matter if you don't tell me. There are other places to go."

Columbine closed her eyes, thinking of the girls, bleeding, dying, she had seen before. Dr. Dana was not one of those butchers; she was a good doctor. She'd help Marguerite. "Yes," she said reluctantly. "But only occasionally, if the mother is desperate, or the pregnancy will kill her. No one knows this, Marguerite."

"I will keep the confidence," Marguerite said.

"But Marguerite, I must urge you to think again. You have other options—"

"No, I do not. This child will kill me." Marguerite's eyes were screaming a kind of hell Columbine did not understand. "And if I have to bear it, I will destroy myself. Don't you see?" she asked flatly. "Don't you see I have nothing? I have a bit of money he pressed into my hand. I have the clothes on my back. I have no home, no job, no friends."

"You could live here—"

"No, I could not take the place of someone who needs to be

here, Columbine. As soon as you open the house, people will be coming, and you know it."

"Marguerite, no. There is room here for you for however long you need it."

Tears filled her eyes. "Thank you. But I cannot." How could she throw herself on Columbine's mercy, when she had promised Lawrence to betray her? And she had to keep that promise, for Lawrence could destroy any chance she had of a singing career. And she had to hold on to that, she had to believe that she would have a life, a chance, after this pregnancy was over.

"Let's sleep on it," Columbine said. "You'll stay here tonight." She rose, and for a moment she was struck with dizziness. She leaned on the back of the armchair, and it passed. "I'll prepare a room for you."

She made one of the beds in the small upstairs room on the third floor. It was at the end of the hall, next to the bathroom, and Marguerite would have privacy there. She laid out a dressing gown and nightgown and some toilet articles, then brought Marguerite upstairs.

Marguerite undressed quickly, visited the bathroom, then slid immediately between the covers. Her dark hair fanned out against the pillow, and she looked wan and very young. Columbine kissed her forehead. Marguerite's eyes were already closing when she shut the door.

She went to Darcy's room, needing her friend's calmness. Darcy was reading in bed, and she put down her book and listened gravely to Columbine's account.

Columbine stretched out on the bed while she talked. "I must be having sympathy pangs, or something," she said. "I feel absolutely exhausted, and I had a dizzy spell earlier." She smiled. "Do you think pregnancy can be catching?"

Darcy smiled, but she gave a worried frown. "You have been tired lately, and it's not like you. Perhaps you should see Dr. Dana."

"Oh, I'm fine," Columbine said. "I *have* just moved, you know. I think fatigue is natural. And the queasiness in the mornings is just nerves, I'm sure."

"You've been queasy in the mornings, as well?" Darcy asked, sitting up. "Columbine, could you be . . ."

Columbine shook her head, then stopped. "No. Oh, Darcy. This is impossible, ridiculous. It's only because of Marguerite . . . Oh, Darcy." Her hand flew to her mouth.

"No, pregnancy is not contagious," Darcy said dryly. "But you could have caught it in the same old way."

Marguerite left early the next morning, before any of them were awake, and Columbine had no idea where she'd gone. She hoped that Marguerite would be back in touch after she had thought more about her predicament. But Columbine was drawn up in her own problem. She marched back to her room and climbed back underneath the covers to ponder. The thought of pregnancy filled her with her panic. She kept telling herself that it could not be true. She had used a pessary provided by Dr. Dana, and she'd been careful. Of course, Meredith had warned her that the womb barrier was not foolproof. And when Columbine thought of the deep, fierce loving she'd had with Elijah, she wondered how careful she could have been. They had made love so often, and if passion alone could assure pregnancy, she should give birth to triplets.

Darcy knocked firmly on her bedroom door at noon. "I've called Meredith," she said, tossing a dressing gown at Columbine. "She'll see you tomorrow after her other patients, at five o'clock. Now get dressed. Tavish and I are going to take you to lunch. Pulling the covers over your head won't help matters. What you need is distraction."

Columbine gave herself up to Darcy and Tavish, the two people she loved most in the world, with the exception of Elijah, who she didn't want to think about right now. She allowed herself to be taken to lunch, to tea, for a walk around Madison Square. They went to the theater that night and walked through Central Park the next day until Columbine was too tired to be nervous. Columbine pushed away the thoughts of what she would do if she *did* happen to be pregnant. She concentrated on praying that she was not.

So when Dr. Meredith Dana looked at her gravely and told her she was with child, she was not prepared. She didn't burst into tears, and she didn't smile. Her hands did not curve protectively over her belly, and she did not feel a secret satisfaction, knowing that she and the man she loved had conceived a child.

"How *do* you feel, Columbine?" Meredith asked, her blue eyes scanning her keenly. "Besides queasy, I mean."

"Numb," Columbine replied frankly. She stared down at her ringless left hand. "And terrified."

Meredith switched on a light, for the room was growing dim in the gathering dusk. "There are many ways to go," she said neutrally.

"I know," Columbine said. "I never wanted children, you know. My life is not fashioned that way. And Elijah—I don't know what he thinks about it. What do you think, Meredith? Would the stigma be too awful for a child of mine, if I do not marry?"

Meredith shrugged. "You are already notorious, my friend. Already considered a radical in most circles. Other women in your position have had children. But no, it won't be easy. And your child will bear the scars. I can't paint a very rosy picture for you." She patted Columbine's shoulder. "But you always seem to manage, Columbine. You have a remarkable ability not to care what people say."

"For myself, yes," Columbine said. She raised troubled brown eyes to Meredith. "But what of my child?"

"Would you marry Mr. Reed if he asked you?"

Columbine was struck dumb by the question, for she had never considered it. She could never imagine Elijah wanting to marry. "Yes, I would," she confessed slowly. She was surprised to find that she would. "I was never opposed to a good marriage, a marriage made out of love and respect. I have Tavish before me as an example." Tavish was also before her as another example; he was illegitimate. She knew how difficult life had been for him because of that. And he was a man. What horrors would a daughter be subjected to?

"But I don't think Elijah would feel the same," Columbine went on. "And I would never want to marry simply because of a child. I suppose I could give it up," she said reluctantly.

"Well, then. You have some thinking to do," Meredith said briskly. "And I'll be here if you need me, you know that. Columbine, you're not young, so promise me you'll come and see me within a few days so we can discuss the pregnancy."

"I promise. Thank you, Meredith." Columbine slipped into her coat. She still didn't know what to do, or how to feel. She didn't feel pregnant; she felt empty. When she reached the street, she began to hail a cab for the ride downtown, but changed her mind and walked toward Fifth Avenue.

It was almost night. The sun had set, and the sky was a deep, dark blue. The air caressed her cheek as she headed down Fifth. People were rushing by her, hurrying home from work on a soft night in early spring, with the promise of summer in the air and an end to winter at last. Their faces seemed excited to Columbine, and happy to be alive. Tonight, there seemed to be no weariness in the world. And suddenly Columbine was happy to be alive, marveling at the cleverness of her body as it moved her through the streets, as her muscles flexed and her joints moved just so, as her heart beat and her cheeks flushed and her fingers tingled with new awareness. She was a miracle, they were all miracles, imperfect and striving, but miracles nonetheless, all walking under a benevolent sky.

She tilted her head back and she saw the first stars of evening. They twinkled in the midst of that vast mysterious blue, but she could think of no wish to whisper, for she felt complete at that moment, as complete as she had ever felt. The soft spring air and the enveloping night and the faces rushing past her vision, the sound of their heels clicking, it all sent a message to her, straight to her heart. She was part of miraculous life, and she knew, as that ecstatic moment flowed into another and another and another, that she had been given a gift. Before it was too late, before she was too old, before Elijah had left her. She would have part of the man she loved forever. Their blood, the links of their family lines would be joined, forged tightly into a new golden link, and they would create a new generation. A new miracle. A child.

Marguerite was waiting for her, a forlorn figure on the stairs. She stood when Columbine walked up.

"Good evening." Marguerite noted Columbine's flushed face, her shining eyes. Something good must have happened to her, she thought distantly.

Columbine hugged her. "I'm so glad to see you. We have to talk, because . . . well, because something's changed. You might say we're in the same boat, Marguerite."

Marguerite didn't understand at first. Then she raised her eyebrows inquisitively at Columbine, and the older woman nodded.

"Yes," Columbine said. "I am, too."

Marguerite smiled thinly. "We're not in the same boat anymore, Columbine."

She looked into Marguerite's face searchingly. "Already?" she breathed.

Marguerite nodded. "It was very simple, really. Dr. Dana didn't do it, but she told me about someone else. I've just come from—from there. I only have a little cramping. Otherwise, I'm fine."

"You should lie down. Come upstairs." Columbine linked her arm with Marguerite's.

"I've come to ask if you saved any of my old dresses," Marguerite said as they climbed the stairs together. "I left quite a few."

"Yes, I saved them for anyone who might need clothes. You can have them back, of course."

"That blue velvet gown, too?" Marguerite asked, pausing as Columbine opened the front door.

"Yes, I think so. Come in, Marguerite."

"I'll just get the clothes and go," Marguerite said. Her face looked very pale, and her mouth was tight.

"Just stay one more night," Columbine urged. "You don't look well."

From the light in the hall, Marguerite could see Columbine's features more clearly. "You're happy, aren't you," she said slowly. "You're happy about the baby."

"Yes, I am," Columbine admitted. "Not at first. But yes."

"You must think I'm horrid, then."

"Oh, dear, not at all," Columbine said quickly. She touched Marguerite's arm, but the girl shrank back. "Not all women want to be mothers," she said gently. "And I'm older than you; I have a little money. It's not the same for me. I think you are very brave, Marguerite. It was your decision, and you knew best. Now, come inside. We'll have a good dinner together, just you and I. Darcy and Tavish are going to a concert tonight."

"I'll just get the gown," Marguerite insisted stubbornly. She could not sit across a table with a pregnant Columbine, and she had already made her plans. "I have somewhere to go now," she added.

Columbine saw the resistance, and the return of fierceness in Marguerite's expression. She would always set her chin and face the world alone. She would not let anyone in. A chill passed over Columbine's heart then, for she thought of Elijah.

"I'll be fine, Columbine," Marguerite said.

Columbine nodded slowly. The exhilaration had faded from her face, and she looked weary. "Yes, I'm sure you shall," she said.

Toby took her in; he had to. He had been frantic for two days, wondering where she was. He'd even tracked down Edwin at the Union Club, and was shocked to hear that Edwin had abandoned her. If he hadn't been such a coward, Toby would have horsewhipped him. But how could he handle a whip? He'd grown up on Fourteenth Street. Toby settled for calling him a callow ass, and left.

He put Marguerite to bed and fed her soup and sandwiches for two days and let her sleep. He took her to the abortionist and waited in the other room, perspiring madly. He gave her all his best handkerchiefs, for she'd caught a cold from walking in the rain. She was exhausted, and she didn't say much, and after the first day, she didn't cry. Toby fussed over her and worried about her and railed against Edwin.

"I should have horsewhipped him," he said for the tenth time while he fixed her toast.

"Toby," Marguerite said weakly, "I don't think you realize how much pain you give me by mentioning his name. I never want to hear it again, all right? It's all over with now. I have to think about the future, not the past."

Toby was instantly contrite. "Of course, petal, I'm terribly sorry. It's just the thought of all those beautiful clothes . . . and the jewelry! It's just so déclassé, to say the least. A woman should always keep the jewelry and the clothes. And you'd think he would have offered to pay for the—"

"Toby! Please! Shut up!" Marguerite turned her face to the wall.

Toby wasn't hurt in the least by her sharpness. He set the toast aside and went to sit by her on the bed, stroking her hair until she fell asleep.

Toby was playing a Confederate soldier in a bad play that was in the final weeks of its run, so he was away every evening. Marguerite came to enjoy her solitary evenings, even as she looked forward to when Toby would arrive at one or two that morning, fresh from a dinner at Rectors or drinks at the Hoffman House, and full of jokes and stories. She would wait up for him, and then they would sleep into the late hours of the morning, Toby on the couch in the parlor. They knew the situation could not last, but Toby didn't dare ask Marguerite her plans, for fear she would think he wanted her to leave.

One evening, Marguerite sat, in Toby's silk paisley dressing gown, by the window, the latest issue of the *Century* open on her lap. Her gaze was unfocused as she flipped the pages. She was planning. Could one have a comeback if one had never been a success? she wondered with a thin smile.

A knock at the door surprised her, and the magazine slid from her lap. Marguerite debated whether to answer the door. It was a tiresome friend of Toby's, most likely. There was a sharper rapping on the door now, and, sighing, Marguerite got up to answer it. She padded across the floor in her bare feet, and opened the door to find Bell there.

Marguerite didn't say anything for a moment. She had been dreading this moment, and it was here. Bell had come for information, of course; it had only been a matter of time.

"Hello, Bell."

"Good evening. I hope I'm not disturbing you."

"Not at all. Do come in."

Bell looked strained and pale, Marguerite noted. Her usually rosy complexion had changed to a pallor with a sallow tinge. Her hair was swept up any old way into a bun at the back of her head. But she was still beautiful, Marguerite thought with the same old envy, as Bell turned and looked at her. There would always be that surprising impact of her beauty that struck one at the heart.

"Please sit down," Marguerite said. "I'm sorry I'm not dressed, I wasn't expecting anyone. If you'll excuse me, I can change."

Bell gave a thin smile. "Please don't on my account. I've certainly seen you in a dressing gown before. No, I won't be staying long."

"How did you know where I was?" Marguerite asked curiously.

"I asked Horatio. He said the only friend he knew you had was a man named Toby Wells. I came here expecting to ask him how I could find you."

"Yes," Marguerite said, embarrassed under the compassionate gaze of those amber eyes, "Mr. Wells has graciously allowed me to trespass on his kindness. I lost my home, you see." She added briskly, before Bell could feel any sorrier for her, "What brings you here, Bell? Can I help you?"

Bell hesitated, and for the first time Marguerite realized what really was different about her. It wasn't the paleness, or the slightly shabbier clothes. The calmness was missing, the serenity in those wide, long-lashed eyes. What would being with a wolf like Lawrence Birch mean to a doe like Bell?

"I need to ask you something," Bell said awkwardly. "It's about a night about six weeks ago or more, I'm not sure. You interrupted Mr. Birch and Columbine in the parlor."

"Yes," Marguerite said neutrally.

"And I was wondering," Bell said, stammering slightly, "if you could tell me about that." She twisted her hands together in her lap and wished passionately that she had not come. Aside from humiliating herself in front of Marguerite, she was committing the worse sin in Lawrence's view—she was questioning him. She wasn't believing in him. But she couldn't help it! She was tortured. Her bed was like a rack, as she lay next to Lawrence and imagined him attacking Columbine. To make things worse, she'd begun to suspect that he was seeing another woman. If he *hadn't* attacked Columbine, could he still be her lover? Bell knew the thought was insane, but stranger things had happened. Remembering her last meeting with Columbine, she could conjure up the disturbing sense that there was something running between Columbine and Lawrence, something obscure and dark. It wasn't attempted rape; it was passion.

Watching her, Marguerite pitied her. She could see the struggle and the desperate need to know. But that desperation was not for the truth, Marguerite saw, but only for confirmation. Despite her intelligence, her good judgment, Bell would stay with Lawrence. Even if Marguerite told her the truth, Bell wouldn't believe it. She would find some excuse not to. That made it so much easier to lie.

"Columbine told me that you and Mr. Birch are together now," Marguerite said with the proper amount of hesitation. "I would hate to tell you anything that would cause you pain."

"It's all right," Bell said eagerly. "Pray, go on."

"Columbine and Lawrence Birch were lovers for a short time. I gather that on that night he broke things off. You remember that Columbine was troubled during that period, often unhappy. I suppose she reacted badly, and when I walked in Mr. Birch was trying to restrain her. Columbine was hysterical," Marguerite said calmly, watching the greedy relief in Bell's eyes. Yes, she was telling her what she wanted to hear. "He left. That is all I know."

Her hands clasped at her breast, Bell closed her eyes. She wasn't even angry at Columbine for lying. If another woman had stolen Lawrence from her, Bell would have lied or cheated, too.

She stood. "Thank you," she said quietly. Then she remembered her manners. "Are you well, Marguerite?"

Marguerite almost snorted. As if Bell cared. "I'm very well, thank you."

Bell nodded and started toward the door. Halfway there she paused and turned back again. "And how is Columbine?" she asked shyly.

Anger filled Marguerite's heart. She hated Bell for her weakness, for her illusions, believing a bad story full of holes in order to clear a man who was obviously no good. "She's blooming," she answered. "Extremely happy in Safe Passage House. And she's going to have a baby," she added. Let Bell wonder.

Bell's face changed abruptly. "A baby? I didn't know."

"She only just found out herself," Marguerite said. "It's not very far along," she added cruelly.

"I see." Bell's steps faltered as she went to the door. Without another word, she opened it and went out.

A baby. Columbine was pregnant. Columbine was going to have Lawrence's child. With every step, the baby grew in Bell's mind into a monster. A living, growing thing, a fungus. Even as she walked home, the baby was getting bigger. It was growing inside Columbine.

And Columbine would tell Lawrence, and he would want her again. Or at least he would want the child. Lawrence wanted children. He said it was the highest role for women. Bell had secretly hoped to get pregnant herself, but nothing had happened yet. Columbine had beaten her to it.

She couldn't let it happen, couldn't let it happen. They were probably already seeing each other again, perhaps having relations again. Planning how to tell Bell. How to break it to her.

But she would forestall them. She would fight for Lawrence. Bell's steps slowed. And she had an ally she was just desperate enough to use. She had Elijah Reed.

Eighteen

THE NEXT DAY was Sunday, and Bell left Lawrence sleeping and eased her way out of their rooms at eight o'clock. It was a short few blocks west from Tompkins Square to Elijah Reed's house on East Eleventh Street.

He was in his shirtsleeves and wearing his reading glasses when he opened the door, and he blinked at her in surprise for a split second before welcoming her inside. She saw that she had interrupted his breakfast. A small table was set up in the parlor, and newspapers were strewn about on the floor. She thought of what a perfect match Columbine and Elijah would be; the parlor looked very much like Columbine's on a Sunday morning. Lawrence would have a fit at the mess.

"Forgive the appearance of the room," Elijah said comfortably, making no attempt to clear up any of the papers. "I'm slow to get started on Sundays."

"You should be the one to forgive me for intruding like this," Bell said, pushing aside a book of poetry to sit down on the couch.

"Not at all. Would you care for some coffee?"

"No, thank you."

Elijah pulled up an armchair. He looked slightly quizzical, but amiable. A strong, intelligent man, Bell thought. He was older, settled, and famous. Good for Columbine, better than Lawrence would be. So it wasn't really bad, what she was doing.

"What can I do for you, Miss Huxton?" he asked politely.

"I've come to you today because I believe we have an interest in common," Bell began. "And I believe that you and I are the best people to work out a distressing situation. But it doesn't have to be distressing. We can make it . . . comfortable for all of us."

"Miss Huxton, I must confess that you have me at a disadvantage. I have no idea what you're talking about."

"I'm talking about Columbine and Lawrence," Bell said, aggrieved. "You know that she is pregnant with his child, don't you?"

Elijah's knees jerked, and he rose and turned his back on Bell. He needed a moment of privacy to absorb this. Loss spilled in him, washed through him, loss and love, and unreasonable anger. He'd suspected the affair, knew it had been over for some time before he approached her. But a legacy from that affair—a child! It was monstrous.

"I'm not certain what they want to do," Bell said to his back. "But I am certain that Lawrence will do right by the child. That's why I'm here. Why should we all be miserable because of this? I know Columbine never wanted children. Did you, Mr. Reed?"

Startled at the effrontery of the question, Elijah didn't answer, and after waiting a moment, Bell went on calmly. "But I do want children. So if I offer to take the child and raise it with Lawrence and myself, would you support me in this? You could persuade Columbine that it's the best thing, you see. Because it is. And this way you'd still have her."

Bell's voice went on, steaming onward with the stately logic of an oceangoing vessel. Elijah stopped listening and tried to think. Bell talked on, embroidering her arguments calmly. In the middle of a sentence, he turned.

"How do you know the baby is his?"

She shrugged. "Because I do. The timing, you see." Of course the baby was Lawrence's, the product of his virility. Elijah still looked doubtful, so she added, "Columbine told Marguerite that it was." It was an exaggeration, but it didn't matter.

Elijah looked down. He nodded several times. He spoke without looking at her. "And why do you want to raise it?"

"Because it is Lawrence's," she said serenely. "I could not bear that a child of his be raised by another woman. He is my husband, if not by law, then in fact."

Elijah wondered for a moment if she was a little off, a little deranged. Surely no normal woman would have such composure under the circumstances. But there she sat, as beautiful as ever, not a trace of misery in those serene eyes.

"Well, Mr. Reed? Will you help me?"

Elijah went back to the chair and sat across from her. He leaned on his knees and stared at his clasped hands. "Let me explain, Miss Huxton. I cannot interfere in this. It is up to Columbine what to do about her child."

"But you love her. So it's your decision, too."

Annoyed, Elijah blew out an exasperated puff of air. "Miss Huxton, I don't want to discuss my relations with Mrs. Nash with you. And I must say that I feel this entire conversation is an invasion of her privacy." He spread his hands. "I can't help you."

Feeling herself dismissed, Bell rose. She was furious. "It will serve you right to lose her, with such an attitude," she said. And then she swept out the door.

Elijah stood. He poured himself another cup of coffee but did not drink it. It sat cooling on the mantel while he stared at a letter on his desk, a letter he was going to answer today. Would this—should this—information change his decision? He didn't even know if Bell was correct. He didn't know anything.

Love was beside the point. Of course he loved Columbine. But she stood apart from him, from his life, and he from hers. Despite his yearnings to share more of her life, he fought the inclination and won. Columbine seemed to want it that way.

They had both led uncommon lives. He knew that she'd lived through hell. She'd been locked in an insane asylum for wanting to leave her husband. She'd been spat at in the streets. And he—well, he'd seen misery, too. For both of them, work was what had saved them. Work was what they clung to, work was what drove them, words on a page, ideas. Being wedded to ideas made them free and fluid in their personal lives. They could not, would not center their lives on the intransigence of flesh.

But he was entangled in her life, for he loved her. If he stayed, he would be entangled even further. He could be a part of the upbringing of another man's child. If the child was half Lawrence's, a man he distrusted, it was also half Columbine's.

He could open his heart and engage with life, taking his courage and his love in each fist and striding forth to meet it. He could cleave to flesh, to blood, to human love. Or he could pack up his books and have none of it.

Columbine had instructed Mrs. Haggerty to lay the good lace tablecloth down and set the table with the best china. She lit candles and put out the cut glass amethyst water glasses. She arranged violets in a crystal vase. Then she stepped back and surveyed the table. The table breathed of spring, she thought approvingly. What feeling could be more appropriate for this evening?

She felt like a young girl as she ran, humming softly, to dress. As she pulled out a pale yellow gown of mousseline de soie, she reflected that she'd never really had that first romance in her life, never that budding, dizzy sense of possibility. Her father had arranged her marriage to a man she detested and locked her in her room when she refused to obey. She had married Charles Edward Nash with none of the illusions of youth. And after having gone through hell to leave him, she had never been young again.

It was a miraculous rebirth, then, to feel this way, she thought, turning in front of the mirror. She fussed with the pale green velvet ribbons on the dress and adjusted the lace yoke. It was a pretty dress; Darcy had gone with her to the dressmaker for the fittings. And soon, Columbine thought with a grin, it would not fit.

Elijah arrived promptly at seven. He seemed discomfitted by her appearance as he came into the parlor. "You look very beautiful," he said gruffly.

Columbine dimpled. "You seem to begrudge me my beauty this evening, Elijah."

He smiled slightly and bent over to kiss her cheek. "On the contrary."

When he was settled in his chair with a whiskey and Columbine had her glass of sherry, she realized nervously that for all her preparations, she had not prepared how to broach the subject of her pregnancy. It was hardly something she could tell him flat out, just like that. But how did one ease into such a topic?

"So tell me," Elijah said. "Did Mr. and Mrs. Finn get off with a minimum of trouble?"

Relieved for the reprieve, Columbine smiled. "Oh, yes. They left yesterday. Perfect sailing weather, and they believe they'll have a good crossing. Of course the boat is very crowded, since it's the beginning of the season in Paris. All the crème de la crème were there. It was highly amusing to all of us, since we could not decide which of us they were trying to snub—me, or Darcy."

Elijah smiled and took a large sip of whiskey. It wasn't a very good opening, but it was an opening. And he had to tell her now, before he sat down and ate her dinner. "Perhaps I shall see them in Paris," he said lightly.

Columbine's face changed, but so imperceptibly one who didn't love her would not have noticed. "Oh, are you going abroad?"

"I received a letter a couple of days ago. A friend of mine, a writer, is making an extended trip to the United States. He's offered me his apartment in Paris for a year, possibly more if he decides to stay here. So I could book passage for next week, if I wanted to go. He'll be traveling here."

"How amusing," Columbine said brightly. "You could wave to each other across the Atlantic from your separate ships."

"I thought I would go, Columbine," he said gently.

"I can see that," she said. A sob formed in her throat and she swallowed hard. It was plain that he was to go alone.

So here it was. She was caught. She had no ties to this man other than those of love. He had warned her, she told herself desperately. He had told her, right at the beginning. She had listened. But she had not understood.

"What about your articles for the *Century*?" she asked. She would ask about details, because she could not ask about reasons.

"They would be glad to take my last article for City of Souls, and then I could start a new series in Paris, if I wished," Elijah answered. "But I think I will not. That's what I wanted to tell you, that's why I'm going. I have a place to stay for a year. I want to start the Andersonville novel, Columbine. You were right. I need to write it. I don't know what form it will take. It won't be strictly autobiographical. But I do know that somehow I'll be writing about what happened to all of us. To Benjamin Pollard. It's because of you."

The irony almost destroyed her. That day, the day he'd talked of

Andersonville, she'd made love to him without protection. She'd always assumed that that encounter had been the one. And she'd been glad, thinking of that; the love had been searing, she'd never felt closer to him. For the first time, she'd felt part of him, and he of her. She'd felt his tears on her skin, and she'd known that she'd held love in her hands that day, that she'd had everything from him. And that was the day she'd sealed her fate.

You've got to tell him, Darcy had said. *Marriage isn't so bad, Columbine. It's quite wonderful, actually.*

"Elijah." His name came out cracked and uncertain, and Columbine swallowed and began again. "I don't want you to go."

"I know, Columbine. But we can write. And you can visit. I'm keeping my house here, so I'll be back. Do you see, I need this solititude. And I need to be away from this country so I can write about it. I need a clear eye, I can't explain it better than that."

"You don't understand," she said. "I need you." She was afraid to look at him. The admission hurt her. She'd never made it before, to anyone. That word, *need.* How she'd always hated it. But now such words made sense to her. Need. Belong. You belong to me. I belong to you. And you shall cleave unto me, and I unto you. We are one flesh. With my body I thee worship . . .

It all made sense to her. So late. Too late . . .

"I'm sorry," Elijah said. He put down his whiskey glass. He couldn't look at her. In a dress of silk and lace, pale as the first buttercup, her gold hair shining, her skin glowing and exquisite, she was all that was fresh and exciting to him. But he knew he would fail her, should she ask for his help. And if he let her ask for his help and he refused, she would never forgive him.

She would be all right, he told himself. She was strong, she never let her head be turned by anyone. She had many friends, many strong women to help her. And she moved in a society that would not condemn her should she keep the child. Perhaps she would give it to Bell. She would find a way.

"Elijah," she began again. "You don't understand."

He rose swiftly, without thought, and knelt by her chair. His eyes were dark, darker than midnight, and full of pain. "I do," he said. "I understand everything. But I'm doing the best thing for both of us."

"What do you mean?" she whispered. "Can it be good for us to be apart?" Her mouth twisted, and she looked away. "The best thing for you, I think."

"Best for both of us," he said firmly. "I would not be good company, Columbine. This book is burning me. I must do it. Perhaps in a year's time, things will be different. We can come together again."

She began to cry softly, with her head still turned away. "Please go, Elijah."

Suddenly, Elijah felt unsure of his decision. He was being unkind. Perhaps she needed him, needed a man to help her. Perhaps she'd counted on that. "Do you want to talk to me?" he asked. "Tell me what I don't understand?"

It took several long moments before she turned back to him. The tears had stopped, but they still marked her cheeks. Her face was full of grief. But the emotion had drained out of her eyes, and they were cold. "No, you were right. You understand everything. So do I. So go."

Ned Van Cormandt had extended his trip to Washington, but he returned on a Thursday. Fiona sent a message to Lawrence, and they met by the stables that night. She had thrown a coat over her nightdress, and she was shivering, for the nights were still cool. Her fiery hair was loose and he ran his fingers along its waves.

"Tomorrow night," Lawrence said. "You remember everything?"

"Everything."

He grabbed her to him, and they kissed to seal their pact. Perhaps it would be the last time, Lawrence reflected. Fiona's connection to the injured man at Ambrose Hartley's house could come out, though Lawrence was counting on the police overlooking it. Never had he felt more excited by Fiona's cool lips against his own than tonight, thinking of the morrow. In twenty-four hours, Ned Van Cormandt would be dead. Lawrence would leak his part in the *attentat* to only one man: Johann Most. He would keep his secret, but a bond would be forged with the great man to last a lifetime.

He pushed her up against the stable wall, grinding against her. He tried to lift the skirt of her nightdress.

"Lawrence, love, no. We can't. We cannot risk it."

He didn't answer. It was a risk, Fiona was correct, it was a great risk. But blood pounded in his ears, and he was harder than he'd ever been. It wouldn't take long. He tore at her drawers, and now she was helping him, excited by his roughness. He pushed inside her, and her head went back, her throat white and straining in the moonlight. He grunted as he thrust, one, two, three, and then he had his release, felt warmth spill out of him, warm seed, and he wondered if he had begat a child. He wouldn't mind. Fiona would take care of things, Jimmy would think it was his, but Lawrence would have that secret satisfaction of knowing his son was in the world.

She quickly pulled down her skirts. "I must go."

He grabbed her arm before she could move away. "Don't fail me."

Her mouth was slightly swollen from his rough kisses, and her eyes were full of a fire that sent a spark across the space between them, making it nothing. They were together in this; she would not fail.

Lawrence did the final assembly of the bomb in his bedroom the next day, while Bell was at the corset factory. He planned to go uptown and meet Fiona for only a moment. He would pass the package through an open window in the summer parlor. Sweat beaded on his forehead as he worked, and he had to pause to wipe it away. He knew the danger of working with explosives, and he was careful, but the thing was tricky. You never knew. He was nervous at the thought of transporting it uptown.

He was startled when he heard the sound of footsteps heading for the door, and he paused, listening. A key was thrust into the lock, and he quickly slid the apparatus underneath the bed. He walked into the other room just as Bell closed the door behind her.

Fear turned immediately to anger. "What are you doing here?" he demanded. He thrust his hands in his pockets so she wouldn't see them shaking.

Bell's hands paused as she reached up to remove her hat. "I was fired," she said, removing the long hatpin.

"Can't you do anything right?" he exploded. "Was your sewing that bad?"

"No," she said. Her movements were awkward as she removed her hat, for Bell knew she would have to tell Lawrence why. He would find out eventually; he always found out everything. "For organizing," she said.

He wanted to strike her. He was so angry that he had to turn away to compose himself for a moment. Why did this always happen to him? His plans, the plans he'd brooded over, worried over, honed, perfected, would be ruined. "I told you," he said evenly, "to let that reformist garbage alone. I told you how you'd compromise the movement."

"I wasn't trying to organize a union, Lawrence," Bell said quickly. "I just asked some girls to go to Union Square on May Day to hear the speeches, that's all. And maybe I said a few things about anarchism. The foreman found out. He would have let me stay if I'd have slept with him," she added. She wasn't going to tell Lawrence that, but perhaps it would focus his anger on other things.

"Why didn't you?" he asked, turning away. "How do you expect me to support you, as well as myself?"

"You don't mean that," Bell said.

"You know how important my writing is," he said. "You constantly work to sabotage me."

"No, Lawrence," she said quickly. She touched his sleeve. "I'm proud of you," she said softly. "I want to see you recognized, I do. I'll get another job."

"Do you mean it?" he asked. "Do you really respect my work?"

She smiled tenderly; this was when she loved him so, when he was like a boy. "Of course," she said, stroking his shining hair gently.

"Then will you do something for me?"

"Anything."

"Ned Van Cormandt has asked for some copies of the articles I've written. He's on that presidential committee—"

"But you said it was rubbish."

Lawrence shrugged. "And it may well be. But it's encouraging that he's asked me for the anarchist position."

"I think it's wonderful!" Bell exclaimed, her eyes shining. "But how can I help you?"

"I have so much work to do, and a headache besides. Would you deliver the package for me?"

"Of course, darling," Bell said. "Of course."

Fiona was at the window at the appointed time, but Lawrence did not appear. She was hard put to keep returning there, since the housekeeper had suddenly become officious. Fiona had had to pretend to make a mistake that morning, for the summer parlor wasn't due to be aired until the following week. Mrs. Campbell had sniffed and said she might as well continue with the cleaning, though she didn't like to mess up the rotation, not one bit, and Mr. Granger would hear about it, sure as Fiona was standing there. The old bitch, Fiona thought savagely, stealing toward the window again.

She had already placed the fuse as they'd planned. They were lucky, for Ned's desk was close to the summer parlor door, for both rooms led into each other. His library had originally been built as a summer dining room, but Ned, on the death of his father, had changed its function. His father's library remained, untouched, and Ned moved his books and his desk into the smaller room at the back of the house. He liked the sun during the afternoons, Mary had told her. And didn't it drive Mrs. Campbell crazy, she said with a giggle; she seemed to consider it sinful to switch rooms around, making trouble for everyone.

But it made things perfect for Fiona and Lawrence. The fuse could be run from the small parlor into Ned's library with no trouble. Since the desk was close to the door, which was rarely used, the fuse was only exposed for a short distance, where it lay flat against the wall and was barely noticeable. Then it ran underneath the Turkey rug. Fiona would flip the rug a bit later tonight, counting on the fact that it was behind Ned's back and he would not notice it. The bomb would be placed behind the heavy velvet curtains. Lawrence, next door in the parlor, would then light the fuse. He would have enough time to slip out the window and would be to the shadows of the stable by the time the bomb went off. With any luck. Fiona would be in her room, deliberately waking Mary so she would have an alibi.

Fiona looked at the grandfather clock in the hall again and wondered if Lawrence had changed his mind. She would hardly believe it. She had finally found a man with the same bloodthirsty passion she possessed; he must not fail her now.

The doorbell chimed, and she jumped. Mrs. Campbell hurried out from the kitchen a second later. "What are you waiting for, child?" she scolded. "You know Mr. Granger is down cellar, seeing to the wines. Answer the door. And straighten your cap, mind!" she hissed after her.

Sighing, Fiona straightened her apron and cap. She hurried down the long hall and opened the door. A woman stood on the step. She was dressed like a working woman, but her figure was lush and elegant, and her beauty was astonishing. Long-lashed eyes of the purest amber held an expression that was as serene as that of the finest lady in New York.

Fiona remembered to curtsey. "Can I help you, ma'am?"

The woman held out a brown package. "For Mr. Van Cormandt. From Mr. Birch."

Fiona had reached out her hands, but jerked them backward involuntarily. She knew what the package was. The woman stared at her, puzzled. Fiona took an imperceptible breath and reached for the package. Her hands closed on it. "I'll give it to him," she said. Her breath was short, and her heart had begun to pound.

"Thank you." The woman turned, and Fiona saw her hair, the color of whiskey, lustrous and shining in the sun. She suddenly realized what she should have known immediately; this was the other woman in Lawrence's life.

"Would you like to leave a card?" she blurted, not thinking clearly, only wanting to see the woman's face again, to find a flaw in that beauty.

Bell turned. For the first time, she saw the features of the maid; the face had hardly registered before. She saw fierce green eyes, a determined jaw, improbable, fiery hair. Something about the woman sent a chill to her heart. Something about the way those eyes were watching her. "Oh, of course," she said. She fished inside the reticule hanging from her wrist and extracted her card. She handed it to Fiona. "Good day."

Fiona watched the woman for a moment, but she was afraid that Mrs. Campbell might be spying on her, so she shut the door. She stared down at the small white card in her hand. *Bell Huxton*. So that was the woman Lawrence was keeping! She'd known for some time, but what could she say, when she was living with her husband? She had expected anything in the woman Lawrence had, things that Lawrence wanted that she did not possess—money, gaiety, lightness, tenderness. Any of those things. But she had not expected such serene, perfect beauty as that.

Mrs. Campbell scuttled around the corner. "And do you have time to waste, standing there like that?"

"A package," Fiona said blindly. "Mr. Van Cormandt got a package."

"Put it in the library then, with the mail. And put the card with the others on the tray, don't you know any better? Hurry along now. And finish that summer parlor. You've been in there half the day."

Mrs. Campbell hurried off. Fiona pushed aside her jealousy, her burning heart. She would think about it later. Lawrence had warned her to handle the bomb gently, to put all her concentration on that. But he'd also assured her it could not explode until he armed it. So why should she have to handle it so gently? Fiona wondered for the first time.

She unwrapped it carefully and placed it behind the curtains. When Ned went for his air on the terrace with his cigar, Lawrence would make the final adjustments. It was all in place. And she was the one, only she, who would be with him in this. The woman had no idea what she was carrying; nobody could have that kind of serenity carrying this thing. Only she knew. She had him. Even with her startling beauty, the other woman was nothing. Fiona's lips curved. And after tonight, Lawrence would be bound to her with more than ties of love. She would have her revenge on those that maimed Jimmy. And she would have her man.

Ned was thinking, as he too often thought, even still, of Columbine, as he walked to the library after his solitary dinner. He reached for a cigar from the silver box on his desk and lit it meditatively. He hadn't seen her in weeks, but he had received a note from her, telling him that she'd reconsidered what he'd said about Lawrence Birch and was dropping the acquaintance. He'd been gratified by that, but it only made the urge to see her burn more in his heart. He missed her too much.

Opening the French doors, Ned moved out to the interior terrace. He smoked and looked at the moon and thought of Columbine. Once he'd had a dinner party, and they'd stolen away from the guests and come outside for a kiss. Memory was strange. He could remember how her smell made him feel, he could remember her features, but he could not seem to put them together to recreate anything close to the living reality of her presence. He could ache for her, but he could not completely conjure up that lift in his heart when he saw her.

Ned would be thirty-nine soon. He was a young man—or, at any rate, he had years ahead of him. It was not possible, he thought, that he would live those years alone, solitary, childless. There must be another woman in the world who he could love as dearly as the one he'd lost. Just because he could not imagine such a woman, could not form an image or a character in his mind, didn't mean she couldn't exist. How could he have ever imagined Columbine, before that first time he'd seen her?

It had been at a large party at Delmonico's. He'd been there with his wife, desperately unhappy, desperately bored. There was a frisson of titillation running through the crowd, for the gathering was large enough that it included those who didn't "belong," a few notable writers, even an artist. And there was Columbine Nash. Ned had thought her beautiful, from across the room, in her ruby dress. Cora had refused to be introduced to her, of course, but Ned had made his way across the room to shake her hand, for his interest was piqued by her political work. And he had ended up angering his wife and shocking the company by lingering at her side, engrossed in conversation as he'd never been before, with man or woman. Forthright, intelligent, arch, sardonic, she was all of those things. He had been bewitched, and he had ceased, from that moment on, to be bored.

Ned ground his cigar underneath his heel. He had started out trying to cheer himself, and he had wound up entangled in his memories again. He should get to work. He had a pile of reading to do.

Ned pushed open the doors. Fiona was fussing with a curtain.

He was surprised to see her; usually, by this time, the maids were in bed. "Fiona, it's late," he said. "You should be upstairs."

"Yes, Mr. Van Cormandt," she said, her eyes downcast.

He turned and went toward his desk. "Good night, then, Fiona."

"Good night, sir." She moved out silently; he approved of a parlormaid who could move like a cat.

Ned sat at his desk and reached for a report he'd been meaning to get to. He pushed aside regrets, memory, desire, and started to read.

The work was done. There was nothing more to do. Shaking badly now, Fiona ran upstairs and wriggled out of her clothes, slipping into her nightgown, ripping the seam in her haste. She slid between the cool sheets. Immediately, she began to moan and thrash about. No response from the sleeping Mary. Nearly hysterical now, Fiona moaned louder. She heard Mary stir, and the young maid slipped out of her bed and padded over.

"Fiona, love, wake up," she called sleepily. She shook her arm. "Wake up."

Fiona shot up in bed. She didn't have to manufacture the fright in her eyes, or her pounding pulse. "What is it?"

"A dream, love," Mary said. With a yawn, she perched on the edge of the bed. "It must have been something, eh?"

"Awful," Fiona whispered. Her ears strained, as though the blast would be a murmur on the air, instead of an explosion. She thought of the night the fireworks had exploded, of the terror that had struck her when she realized that Jimmy was out there setting them off. Her trembling grew more violent.

"Fiona, you poor thing." Mary's eyes were soft with compassion. She was a dim soul, but she was kind. "Do you want me to get in bed with you? I used to with my sister Kate."

"Would you?" Fiona asked. She scooted over to make room, and Mary climbed in.

"Why, you're still wearing your stockings," she said.

"I was cold, getting to bed."

"Funny, I thought I remembered seeing you take them off. And you're so cold! Here, I'll warm you." Mary began to rub her warm palms against Fiona's arms. "Do you want to tell me your dream?" She yawned sleepily. "I could interpret it, me mam taught me."

Would she have to manufacture a dream now? Fiona wanted to scream. Thinking hard, she lay back against the pillows. "Oh, it was terrible," she said. "I was walking along a field in Ireland, and—"

And then the blast came. It was louder than she'd expected, and Fiona jumped as Mary shrieked and grasped her arm, hurting her. Her light brown eyes widened in fear. "Holy Mother of Jesus!" she cried.

Fiona crossed herself. "God help us all," she said.

Panting, Lawrence crashed against the stable wall. He felt the explosion move against his skin. One light came on in the house, then another. He heard a cry.

He wanted to see Ned Van Cormandt's broken body, wanted to make sure he was dead. But he knew it would be madness. He would have to wait for his ultimate satisfaction. Exhilaration pushed him forward, and, keeping to the shadows, he ran.

Nineteen

COLUMBINE DRAGGED HER eyes open at seven that morning. She'd barely slept; misery had kept her awake and tossing. Pain lodged in her throat, felt heavy in her chest. Elijah was gone. She woke to a world without joy; she wondered dispassionately if and when she would get it back.

Ivy Moffat would be arriving tomorrow, and there were things to do to make ready. Columbine splashed water on her face and did her hair without looking in the mirror. She pulled on a plain gown of light gray pongee. The weather was getting warmer. Soon it would be summer. She would no doubt be uncomfortable, as she would begin to put on weight. Perhaps she should try to escape to the shore for more than two weeks this summer.

Columbine thought of these things, but she hardly connected them to herself. She could barely imagine the child inside her now. Her whole being was crouched over her anguish. She was afraid to examine it; it was like something that was glowing too brightly to look at directly. She had to sneak peripheral peeks at her pain; if she faced it dead on, she didn't know if she could stand it. She took shallow breaths, closing her eyes, thinking of Elijah's face.

She moved downstairs to the parlor, deciding to make a list of tasks to be performed. The newspapers were ready at her desk; in another moment, Mrs. Haggerty would come in with her tea. She would have to tell Mrs. Haggerty about the baby soon. She hoped the good woman would not leave, but it was possible. Why should another woman live with shame? She should look for another place for Mrs. Haggerty, should she need it. That should go on the list.

Columbine reached for the newspaper on the top. She spread it out on the desk, so as not to get ink on her skirt. She wasn't really looking at it, so it took several slow seconds for the headline to penetrate her brain.

She thought her heart would stop. She could not take this, too, she told herself. Ned. Not Ned.

And then her hand was ringing the bell furiously, she was showing Mrs. Haggerty, who crossed herself as she listened to Columbine read the details in a shaking voice. Then Mrs. Haggerty ran to get Columbine's things. Within ten minutes Columbine was in a hansom cab heading uptown to St. Luke's Hospital on Fifty-Fourth Street. The streets, the people, the buildings were a blur. "Mr. Van Cormandt is not expected to live," the paper had said.

Mr. Van Cormandt is not expected to live.

She ran into the hospital, looking around wildly as she sped through the doors. There was a stone-faced, white robed nurse at the desk. "Mr. Van Cormandt," Columbine said breathlessly.

The nurse looked at her. "No visitors."

"May I talk to his doctor, please?"

The nurse gave her another bland look. "Are you a family member, Miss—?"

"Nash. Mrs. Nash. I'm a friend. A family friend." Tears sprang to Columbine's eyes. "A very dear friend," she added softly.

The nurse who had seemed so inhuman softened a bit. "His sister is here. Should I send a note to her?"

"Would you?" Columbine extracted a card from her silver case. She scrawled, Olive, may I see him? on the back.

The nurse took the card and disappeared down a long hall. Within a few minutes she was back and beckoning to Columbine.

Columbine followed her up what seemed to be endless stairs and down corridors and through passageways, past closed doors. The breakfast carts were going around, and trays and silver clinked softly as nurses distributed the food. The smell of the hospital was in her nostrils, only increasing Columbine's anxiety. Carbolic would always remind her of the ten days she'd spent in the asylum in England.

Olive Van Cormandt was waiting alone in a small, comfortably furnished room. She had obviously dressed hurriedly, as had Columbine; it was the first time Columbine had seen Olive without the cameo her mother had left her pinned to the front of her dress. There was a stain on the lace of her cuff, as though she had spilled tea from a shaking cup.

Olive Van Cormandt had never married, but she had plenty of money, and she liked her own way. She had her own house on Madison Avenue, refusing to stay with Ned and Maud after the death of the elder Van Cormandts, as was the custom for mature unmarried ladies. In her matter-of-fact, unsentimental way, she kept track of the entire large Van Cormandt extended family. She always knew which of the many young Van Cormandt cousins were being courted and by whom, and which uncle was a drunkard and which niece was having trouble with her pregnancy. She was a spare, intelligent woman with a private life of which Ned or Columbine knew nothing. Sometimes they had speculated if she had a lover. After an initial period of hostility, she'd accepted Columbine, once she'd seen that Columbine loved Ned. She and Columbine had become friends, and Olive had donated large sums to set up Safe Passage House.

Now, she stood erect, saying nothing. She moved slightly, and Columbine sensed what she wanted, and went to embrace her. Olive held her tightly for a moment, and her body gave one convulsive shudder.

"The papers say there's no hope," Columbine whispered, drawing back to search Olive's long, handsome face.

Olive nodded. Her eyes were like Ned's, light green, as green as a summer leaf. "That is what the doctors tell me."

"Can I see him?"

"He's not conscious. The doctors are with him now. I'll ask them." Olive pressed her hand. "Of course you can see him, Columbine."

"Thank you."

The two women sat down in the creaking brown leather chairs. "Why would anyone do this to Ned?" Columbine asked as she unbuttoned her jacket.

"The police came this morning," Olive said. "I couldn't tell them anything. They suspect anarchists, but then they always do. Of course, Ned is on that presidential commission. There's talk of him running for Congress. He's become a public figure. So they could be right."

"Oh, God." Foolishly, Columbine hadn't thought of anarchists. She hadn't thought at all. She thought fleetingly of Lawrence Birch, and of Bell. Perhaps they would know something, hear through the grapevine of who could have done this awful thing.

The door opened quietly, and a doctor came in. He was older, with silver hair at his temples. His authoritative air and his kind eyes sent a tiny spurt of reassurance through Columbine.

Olive stood. "Doctor Temple?"

"He's still unconscious, I'm afraid," Dr. Temple said. "It's a blessing, for if he comes to, he'll be in great pain. He's been badly injured. The bomb was packed with bullets."

Olive gave a soft cry and turned away to face the wall. Her shoulders shook, but she did not make another sound.

"He was lucky that he wasn't closer to the bomb. The window shattered. Apparently, his back was to it, and he was starting out of the room. But the bullets did their work. They penetrated his back. We were able to remove all of them, thank God, but he's lost a great deal of blood. I'm sorry, Miss Van Cormandt."

Olive turned. Her face was wet, and she nodded at the doctor. Her voice was thick as she said, "This is Mrs. Nash, Doctor. She is a dear friend of the family. May she see Mr. Van Cormandt?"

The doctor hesitated, then nodded. "Yes. But if he wakes, please let us know immediately. You may follow me, Mrs. Nash."

Columbine followed the doctor down the hall. She felt such a sense of unreality she thought she was almost capable of forgetting why she was there. A bomb, Ned, hospital. She could not seem to put the elements together and make something coherent that her mind could grasp.

He paused at a corner room. "The injuries you can see are the superficial ones," he said. "Some of the glass did cut his face, for the explosion twisted his body a bit."

Columbine bit her lip, her hand on the door. It was the first time she'd been able to picture the actual blast, Ned's body propelled through the air. She gulped in air. The doctor hesitated, then slowly walked back the way he came.

She pushed open the door. A man was lying in the bed. His face was bandaged, and he had only wisps of hair. His scalp, the parts that she could see, were a furious red. It seemed impossible that the man could be Ned, but as she inched closer to the bed, she saw that it was. One hand was outside of the sheet, and it seemed the only part of his body that was intact. But then she noticed there was no hair on his wrist or his fingers.

It was the hand that undid her. Columbine began to cry helplessly. She could not control herself, and she pressed her hand to her mouth to stifle the noise. She turned from the body in the bed and went to the window, where she stared outside at the spring morning and told herself to shut up and get her courage back.

In a few moments, she was able to turn and approach the bed. "Ned," she murmured. "It's Columbine, Neddie." She was afraid to touch him, afraid anything would hurt him. She knew he was unconscious, but she had to tell him things; perhaps somewhere he would know, somehow. "I love you, Ned. I'm here. Olive's here. We're waiting for you, Ned." She leaned over and touched his hand with her lips as lightly as she could. "Don't die, Ned," she whispered.

When she went out into the hall again, the doctor was telling Olive that Ned would not last a week.

New York erupted with the news. Anarchist papers were raided; Johann Most's presses were smashed. Several cafes where anarchists were known to congregate were found with broken windows when their owners went to open up that morning. The President of the United States, Benjamin Harrison, sent a telegram to Ned Van Cormandt and made a statement deploring the action to the press.

In fever pitch of anxiety, Lawrence debated what to do. He could visit Jersey City, or Boston. But that might serve to bring suspicion on him. He reminded himself that nothing linked him to the bombing, except Fiona. And Fiona would not talk. If he kept his head, he would be all right.

Bell had given him a look when she opened the paper that first morning, but he hadn't avoided her eyes, and he'd manifested the same amount of shock she did. He must have been convincing, for Bell didn't question him. Luckily, she'd been sleeping soundly the night before, thanks to a sedative he'd provided in her tea, and had no idea he'd been gone.

The first day seemed a year, with Lawrence jumping every time he heard heavy footsteps on the floorboards outside his door. He wanted desperately to see Fiona, but they'd agreed to wait two weeks before attempting a meeting. On the second day, as each edition of the newpapers screamed that Ned Van Cormandt was failing fast, he began to feel more confident. And on the morning of the third day, they came for him.

They were eating breakfast, coffee and rolls. The knocks were loud, purposeful. Bell looked at him apprehensively. "Who could it be, calling at this hour?"

Fear dropped in a clean plumb line down through him until it hit his bowels. Lawrence forced himself to sit, to nod at Bell to answer the door. When she turned her back, he closed his eyes and took shallow, quick breaths. So be it. If he was arrested, he would be notorious, famous. It wouldn't be so bad. Herr Most had been arrested more than once, Bakunin, Kropotkin. A chill passed over him at the thought that if Ned Van Cormandt died, he would get the death penalty. That he could not accept. Lawrence glanced quickly at the window. Only four stories, perhaps not high enough. Why hadn't he figured a plan to kill himself in the event of being arrested?

All this passed through his mind as the two men came in. A uniformed man stayed outside in the hall. Lawrence could see that the two men were taken aback, for a moment, at Bell's looks. It was clear they hadn't expected to see a beautiful woman.

The taller one spoke first. "Miss Huxton?"

"I am Mrs. Birch," Bell replied calmly. "May I help you?"

"Miss Huxton," the man said deliberately, and Bell flinched, "You are known to be an anarchist, miss, isn't that true?"

"May I ask your name, sir?"

"All in good time, miss. Did you deliver a package to Mr. Ned Van Cormandt's house on Friday last?"

Behind Bell, Lawrence saw her spine snap to. Her hands clenched behind her back. Why were they questioning her, he wondered? Were they spinning out the suspense, wanting him to crack?

"Yes," Bell said, "I did."

"May I ask what was in that package, miss?" The detective's voice was affable now.

Bell didn't hesitate. "Papers."

"Papers, miss?"

Lawrence felt sweat break out everywhere on him; he was drowning in sweat. He wanted to tug at his collar, but he kept his hands at his sides. The other detective's eyes flicked toward him and back to Bell.

"Mr. Van Cormandt is on a presidential commission. I am the former secretary of Mrs. Columbine Nash. He asked me for copies of her speeches and articles. I delivered them. If that's all, sir, may I return to my breakfast?"

The detective's eyes flicked over Lawrence. He looked from Bell to Lawrence and back again. "We'll give you some tea at the station house, miss. If you'd get your things."

Ned lingered on, but the doctors still gave no hope. He did not regain consciousness, and Olive, for some perverse reason, saw that as a good sign.

"It's as though he's gathering up his strength," she whispered to Columbine as they sat by his bed. "He's waiting until he knows he'll be able to bear the pain."

Columbine felt herself at a loss. She admired Olive's faith, but she did not want Olive to be destroyed when Ned finally slipped away. He was now fighting an infection, and his fever was shockingly high. Olive had remarked approvingly on the color in his face. "Olive," she said gently, "Doctor Temple says—"

"I don't care what he says!" Olive cried vehemently. "I don't like him. He wants us to give up on Ned. He wants the whole city to think him almost dead, so that when Ned lives, Dr. Temple will be the genius who snatched him from the jaws of death. Pah!" Olive snapped her fingers. "I give that for the famous Dr. Temple."

Columbine sighed and turned back to Ned. She was done with crying now. She only sat and looked at him, and waited. The long hours had given her time for reflection. She had thought of Ned, of course, but Elijah was never far from her thoughts. It struck a dagger in her heart to think that Elijah was willingly giving up love, when Ned was lying here, having wanted love so badly in his life. Never had Columbine wanted so much to live as when she sat here at Ned's bedside and watched him die. She once again felt connected to the child in her belly, and her hands curved around it for comfort during the long days.

Life was meant to be lived, it was as simple as that, and Ned had always known it. Elijah's way was only a half-life, Columbine thought. Ned had wanted everything. Olive was right, in a way, for it was Ned's strength that was in this room, and it was awesome. He clung to a thread while the doctors shook their heads. He wanted to live.

Columbine dreamily began to count the things that Ned loved, the things that anchored him to life. When she was alone in the room, she would whisper them to him. Kensett landscapes. Newport. Parsnips. Women's gowns. Guy de Maupassant. Mozart. Vermeer. Peach cobbler. Veuve Cliquot. Lenox, Massachusetts. Paris. Her gold gown.

Olive's whisper broke into her silent chant. "Don't you see, Columbine," she said, "that he can't possibly die?"

"Yes," Columbine answered. "He can't possibly die." Cognac. Cigars. Bicycles. Central Park. The new Turkey rug in your bedroom . . . .

Hours later, Olive went for a walk, and the doctor called Columbine into the waiting room. "I'm worried about Miss Van Cormandt," he said gravely. "I think it would be better if she faced things, Mrs. Nash. Perhaps there is some way you could help her prepare for her brother's death."

"Are you so certain, Dr. Temple?" Columbine asked.

"I'm afraid so. He won't last the night."

Her knees gave way, and she sank into a chair. "I see."

His hand came down on her shoulder, and he patted it gently. "I'm sorry. I see that you and Miss Van Cormandt are devoted to him. But these things must be faced. He's nearing the end." He left, gently closing the door behind him.

Columbine sat staring at the walls, wondering how she would

tell Olive. And would Olive brush this away, along with everything else Dr. Temple had said?

It was only a few minutes later that Olive came in the room quietly. Columbine looked up; she could see immediately that something was wrong.

She rose shakily. "Is it Ned?"

Olive shook her head quickly. Her hands were cold as she grasped Columbine's. "No, no. There's no change. It's something else. Columbine, sit down."

Columbine sat like a child. "Please tell me."

"The police have made an arrest."

"Yes?"

"They've arrested Bell Huxton."

Columbine stared into Olive's eyes, absorbing the knowledge. "Bell? That's impossible! She liked Ned, they were friends—I don't believe it."

"She took a package to his house on Friday afternoon. The maid confirms it. She put it in the library. Ned must have opened it."

Columbine's hands flew to her mouth. "No."

"She's converted to anarchism, you know. It's possible."

"Is she admitting she did the deed?"

"She will only say that she acted alone. The police have solid evidence, it's said." Olive saw Columbine's expression, and she took her by the shoulders. "You have no responsibility for this, Columbine. Do you hear me?"

Columbine nodded, but hell was in her eyes. "I hear you," she said numbly. "Let's get back to Ned."

Ned regained consciousness that evening. He was in terrible pain, and did not recognize them. He was given morphia and relapsed into a fitful sleep.

At two in the morning, while Columbine was nodding in her chair, Olive touched her shoulder briefly. "Would you like some tea?" she whispered. At Columbine's grateful nod, she said, "I'll see if I can get that dragon of a nurse to let me make some. That bilge she serves is hardly fit for consumption. I brought some Earl Grey from home this afternoon."

Olive rustled out, and Columbine, fully awake now, rose for a turn around the room. The moon was full; pale, silvery light flooded the room. The moon seemed tangled in the high branches of the crabapple tree outside the window. Columbine could make out the delicate blossoms, faintly pink in the light. She and Ned had first met in the spring.

"Columbine."

His voice made her jump. She turned, and saw the one eye that wasn't bandaged was open. "Ned," she breathed, hurrying toward him. "Oh, Ned."

"For a moment," he said with difficulty, "I thought I was in our house."

"Yes," she said. There was an apple tree outside the bedroom window at the Tenth Street house. "The apple tree," she said, smiling softly. "It's in bloom now."

"I rather think I'm dying, Columbine," he said groggily.

"No. Don't say that." Tears began to slip down her cheeks. "Don't, Ned."

"I wanted to tell you that I loved you."

"And I love you. I should get the doctor—"

"No, don't go. Take my hand."

She slipped her hand into his. He grasped her fingers feebly.

Columbine swallowed. "You have to live, Ned. We've been sitting here, Olive and I, waiting for you to come back to us."

"It's funny," Ned said. "I remember everything so clearly. I was working, I couldn't concentrate. I was thinking of you. I was thinking . . ." A small grunt escaped him.

"Ned, let me get the doctor."

"No, not yet. I want to talk to you, just for a minute. I was thinking what it would be like, to live my whole life without you. How I would ever come to find joy in things again. Do you know?"

Columbine nodded, thinking of Elijah. "I know."

"And I got up from the desk, thinking it useless to work. I would pour another cognac and go upstairs and think of you, I decided. Give myself up to it. To memory. That's when it happened. So you see, you almost saved my life. I was moving away toward the door. I should have been . . . quicker."

"Oh, Ned."

"But that isn't what I wanted to say at all. Damn. I was thinking,

I was thinking—what if it isn't over? What if a year from now she'll come to you? What if she could make a life with you after all? And now I'm wondering, were those foolish thoughts, Columbine? Is there really no hope for me?"

Columbine's breath went out of her. Ned was dying, she could see it in his eyes. And it was through her that it had happened. She had brought him heartbreak and she had introduced his killer to him. But she could do one last thing for him now.

"There's hope for you, Ned," she said. Tears ran down her cheeks. "I'm here, aren't I? I've been here every day."

"If I asked again—"

"I would marry you. Ned, perhaps we're meant to be together after all." And at that moment, Columbine believed it.

He closed his eyes. "My love," he said.

"Ned?" Columbine pressed his hand. "Ned?"

The door opened, and Olive came in, following by the nurse carrying a tray of tea things. She took the situation in with a glance and put down the tray immediately.

"What is it?" Olive asked frantically.

Columbine stepped back from the bed. The nurse bent over Ned, checking his pulse, his pupils.

"I'll get the doctor," she said, turning away.

"Nurse!" Olive's voice was panicked. "Is he worse? Is he dead?"

The nurse smiled under the white veil. "No, my dear. I think he may be quite a bit better."

Elijah had been packing his books when he heard the news about the bombing. He stopped packing. He went to Columbine's and discovered from Mrs. Haggerty that she was spending all her time at the hospital. He left his card and went back to his own parlor.

He sat in his parlor for a week while his trunks went unpacked and his letters unsent. He must have taken meals, slept, tried to read. But to Elijah, whenever he thought of those seven days, he thought of himself, sitting heavily in his chair, not moving. Thinking, in a way he knew was slow and ponderous, almost confused, about who he was and the decisions he had made.

It wasn't merely that death could strike some surprising evening over cognac and a cigar in one's own study. It wasn't only that Ned was a good man and an inexplicable target for any anarchist. It wasn't just the awfulness of the crime, or his own friendly feeling for Ned. It was all of those things, and it was more. It was Columbine.

It was how fiercely he wanted to go to her. It was how desperately he wanted to see her face. It was how piercingly he wanted to share her pain. It was how deeply and irrevocably he loved her. Great tragedy had done its work. It had brought so freshly home to him how important life was. Elijah would have despised himself for succumbing to such a cliché, but he was too puzzled.

His body trembled as he sat, thinking these things. There had been a worm in the center of his love, and he hadn't examined it before. The worm was Lawrence Birch. It was how secretly, in his heart, Elijah had despised Columbine for loving, however briefly, that man. How could someone like Columbine not see through such a man? He had pushed the question away, not wanting to answer it. Now, he looked at the question, and he also looked at the arrogance of the man who had asked it. What right did he have to judge?

But now, what must she be thinking? Elijah felt sure that Lawrence Birch must have been involved in the bombing plot. As he remembered Bell's visit, went over it in his mind, he saw that her mind was possibly unbalanced; at the very least, it showed an alarming susceptibility to Lawrence's direction. Had Lawrence used that to suggest such a course? It was possible. And if Elijah was thinking these things, surely Columbine was as well. Could she bear it, knowing that Lawrence had possibly been instrumental in the attack on Ned?

He saw culpability there, but he did not care. The question was, could he offer himself to her and wipe the slate clean?

Should she choose to keep the child, could he raise it? Should she want to marry him, would he do it? Should she tell him that she loved him irrevocably, could he answer truthfully that he felt the same?

It took him seven days to realize that the answer was yes.

Elijah arrived at it in no blinding moment of clarity, no spinning, dizzying revelation. It was just there, quietly in front of him, as he stirred his coffee on the last morning. He loved this woman, and suddenly, that love was enough for anything.

He read in the paper that Ned Van Cormandt had turned a corner, that he was sitting up, receiving a few visitors, though he was still in great pain. Dr. Temple was hailed as a savior. The Van Cormandt family was donating a wing in his name to the new St. Luke's hospital which would be built on Morningside Heights.

Elijah put on his hat and went out. Columbine was at the hospital, Mrs. Haggerty told him when he rang the bell. He caught a horsecar going up Fifth and got off at Fifty-Fourth.

He left his card at the desk and in a few minutes the nurse came back to tell him Ned Van Cormandt would be happy to see him. He followed her upstairs and through passageways and down a long corridor. Elijah was not at his best in hospitals; he'd spent long months recuperating in one, after the war. He came to a corner room with relief, and the nurse pushed the door open.

The window was open, and sun was streaming in through lace curtains. A group of chairs was clustered around a small table with a silver tea service. Apparently the Van Cormandt money could buy amenities, even in a hospital, Elijah thought. And then he looked at the bed and wished Ned Van Cormandt all the silver tea services in the world.

He was thin, and bandages covered much of his body. He'd lost most of his hair. In silk pajamas and a paisley dressing gown, he appeared the height of sartorial elegance, but Elijah could see immediately in what great ways Ned had changed. It wasn't only his injuries, and his bandages. Great pain had marked his face. Even though the smile was still as generous, the eyes had changed.

"How good of you to come, Mr. Reed," Ned said.

"I heard you were receiving visitors, so I took the liberty," Elijah said. "It's good to see you back among us, Mr. Van Cormandt."

"It's good to be back."

"I see that Miss Huxton hasn't been formally charged as of yet."

Ned frowned. "Yes, there is some uncertainty still. They thought I had unwrapped a package, but I did not. The bomb suddenly went off, so they think now that a fuse was set and the bomb was detonated outside. There was a window open in the summer parlor. And the remnant of the papers which Miss Huxton brought were found with the evening mail, though of course they were unreadable. The only discrepancy was that I had not asked for any of Columbine's papers. Miss Huxton volunteered that she'd often brought me articles of Columbine's she'd thought would be of interest, which is true, though she hasn't done so since . . . well, for some time."

"Puzzling," Elijah said. "And how are you feeling?"

"Well, I'd rather be bicycling in the park," Ned said, flashing an unsteady grin. "I have my bad periods, I must admit, but I'll be back on my feet in no time. And, may I add, I have the best nurse in the world. Columbine has been here every day. She'll be sorry to miss you, she just went for a walk on the grounds."

At that, the door opened, and Columbine walked in. When she saw Elijah, she blushed deeply. She was wearing a summer dress in a light blue and white pattern with lace at the throat and wrists, and her hair was drawn back simply in a bun. Elijah drank in the sight of her.

He bowed. "Mrs. Nash."

"Mr. Reed." She closed the door behind her. "It's kind of you to come and see Ned."

"Come, Columbine." Ned held out his good hand, and she took it slowly. "I was just about to tell Mr. Reed the good news."

Foreboding snaked through Elijah. Something about the way Ned reached for her hand. Something proprietary in that. It was not merely the clasp of friendship. "Yes?"

"We're going to be married. At the hospital chapel next week. We hope you can be there."

It was probably three seconds, but it felt like three hours, before he was able to reply. Columbine had looked away, out the window, and he couldn't see her eyes. She was staring fixedly at a crabapple tree. "I'm sorry," Elijah found himself saying pleasantly, "but I won't be able to. I leave for Paris at the end of the week. But do let me offer my very best wishes to both of you."

When the door closed behind Elijah, Columbine heard the click, and her shoulders shook with a convulsive jerk.

"You were lovers, weren't you," Ned said.

"Yes, Ned."

"It's funny, I thought it in the cards at one time, and then I ceased to think about it. I wouldn't have told him that way if I'd known."

"It's all right. It was over already."

"For him, or for you?"

"For him," Columbine admitted. "And Ned, there's something else. Something I haven't told you. The doctors tell us not to upset you, so I haven't, but I must before next week. Before we marry."

"Don't listen to the doctors," Ned said. "Tell me."

They hadn't looked at each other. Columbine still stood by the head of the bed, holding his hand. "I'm pregnant," she said. "It's Elijah's child."

His hand tightened on hers, but Ned said nothing.

"I want the baby, Ned. And obviously, I'll understand if you want to call off the wedding. I've felt dishonorable, agreeing to marry you without telling you about it. But I was worried about your health. I thought, well, I thought you'd be a good father, if you could find it in your heart to take it on. It's a big decision, and I very much regret having to place it before you."

Ned didn't speak for several minutes. She waited, still holding his hand. All of her future would be directed by this one moment, she knew. She didn't know what was right anymore, what she needed, what she should do. All she knew was that she wanted her child, she wanted Ned to get better, she wanted to get back to her life and her work. She wanted to give up her life to someone else to manage. She wanted someone to tell her what to do.

When he continued to be silent, Columbine tried to extricate her hand from his, but he grasped it more firmly. "I've been quiet," he said, "not because I was reconsidering, but because I was considering you. Columbine, I would be happy to marry you and become a father to your child. But I also know what I'm honorbound to say. It's just that I find it so difficult, now that I have you at last . . ." Ned paused. "I release you from your promise, should you wish it."

She looked at him searchingly. She saw that he was in pain; the drugs must be wearing off. How could she abandon him when it was because of her that he was here? Wasn't it time she brought Ned happiness instead of grief?

That idyllic, brief period when she had tasted true love was over. She would never feel that way again. But she had always loved Ned, could still love him. And there was a child to consider. Columbine honestly did not know how she could bring an illegitimate child into the world. That would be a sin to her, in these times. She reminded herself that she loved Ned, she loved his sister. She would create, at last, a family, not just a marriage. She would not live to please only herself any longer. That was a wrong way to live, and too narrow for her now. Ned would give her a direction. She felt as though she was poised between two high places, with a yawning chasm beneath. She put out her foot, and it slid along the outcropping rock, found a foothold, and she crossed over.

"No, Ned," she said. "I don't want to be released."

Twenty

TOBY HAD PLANNED to go out for lunch with some friends to celebrate the closing of the show, saying it was his last chance for festivity for awhile. He did not say that after this, there were no prospects, though Marguerite knew, of course, that this was the case. Money would soon be even more of a problem for them. Already they were skimping on meals and coal. Toby had not mentioned an audition for her again. He was tender with her, waiting until he thought she'd regained her strength.

Toby was a puzzle to her, there was no doubt about it. He never implied, by word or touch, that he wanted to sleep with her. Still, why was he so kind? Marguerite turned this over in her mind as the days went by. She had never met with such kindness, and she waited every day for him to come to his senses and call her a slut or a tease, and throw her out of his house. She thought it quite remarkable that time went on with them remaining merely comrades, giggling like brother and sister together.

As soon as the door closed behind Toby that day, Marguerite sped to the closet. She reached for her blue velvet gown and shook it, smoothing out the creases. Once she had thought the gown sumptuous and elegant; the months with Edwin had shown her how plain it was. But still, Marguerite knew there was a simplicity to it that made it fresh and pretty. She hesitated, a pair of sharp scissors in her hand. She'd planned this, but she hated to ruin her only good dress. Sighing, she began to cut away at the simple lace on the yoke.

Within ten minutes, she had carefully cut away all the lace, leaving an even simpler, deeper neckline. While she worked, she ran a bath. Marguerite bathed quickly but carefully, washing her hair with the last of Toby's fine shampoo. She dried her hair by the coal stove and left it loose, tying it behind her with a blue velvet ribbon. Then she slipped into the dress and went to examine herself in the mirror.

She had lost weight over the past weeks, and she looked even more childlike than usual. But the low, dramatic neckline of the dress showed a slight swell of bosom, even without handkerchiefs stuffed in her chemise. Marguerite rubbed a tiny bit of Toby's rouge on her cheeks and put a touch of salve on her lips. She rubbed cream into the tops of her breasts and her shoulders. Then she put on her gray spring coat and hat and went out.

She didn't have enough money for a cab, so she took the horsecar to the theater. She knew that Willie P. always arrived at four, so she'd have a little while to wait. The side door to the theater was open, thank goodness, but there was no one in sight as she crossed the back of the theater toward the center aisle. As she started down the aisle, she heard voices raised in anger. A couple was arguing in the front of the theater, and before she had gone a few steps Marguerite saw that it was William Paradise and the gorgeous Mollie Todd.

Mollie's bright hair shone even in the dark theater, gleaming against her white face. She dropped her summer furs off the shoulders of her silk ensemble. "Don't tell me any more lies, Willie," she spat out. Her voice, that cooing, seductive instrument, was hoarse with rage. "By God, you'd think I would have learned the first time."

Willie leaned negligently against a theater seat. "Really, Mollie? But you know how long it takes for things to penetrate that beautiful head of yours. Think, for example, of how long it takes for you to learn your lines."

Marguerite could hear the sharp, indrawn breath. She inched slowly backward until she was underneath the shadow of the balcony.

"So you're not going to deny it?" Mollie demanded.

"Why should I, when you have obviously appointed yourself

judge and jury? Why don't you just tell me my punishment? A diamond necklace this time? Another fur piece?"

Mollie seemed to wilt. Her voice was barely audible now, low with sorrow. "You really are a bastard, Willie. You think that's what I wanted all along."

"Well, you seem too well-outfitted to deny it, dear," Willie answered in the same murmuring, bland tone.

In one stride she was on him, and she cracked her hand across his face. Then, Mollie burst into tears. "Damn you, Willie! I hate you so!"

"Mollie, this is tedious—"

"Damn you! It's the humiliation that's so unfair. Everyone knows. You took her to Rector's, to Tony Pastor's. You took her to my own dressmaker, for God's sake!" Mollie broke out into fresh sobs. Her furs fell off her shoulders and landed on the carpet. She buried her face in her hands.

"So it's that, then. You're embarrassed by Miss LeClerc. It's not the loss of my love, I fear."

Mollie didn't answer. She was trying to regain control of herself now. Willie held out a handkerchief, but she ignored it and took out her own. Marguerite could see at least two inches of embroidered lace on the border.

"Well," Willie continued, his voice lower now, but still perfectly audible to Marguerite, "perhaps now we should discuss the show. I don't want this to interfere with your performance, Mollie. You are still my star, you know. You're on the threshold of becoming great. Why should we spoil that part of our partnership?"

Mollie Todd raised her head. Her wide cat eyes glinted. "What partnership?"

Willie waited a beat. "You have a contract," he said evenly.

"And you have a new mistress," Mollie said with a toss of her head, fully in control now. She picked up her furs from where they lay and smoothed them over her shoulders. "I think she'll be perfect in the role. She sings like a banshee, I hear." She flung one end of the fur around her throat and headed down the front toward the side door of the theater. She pushed the curtains aside in a grand gesture, and the door shut with a muffled thud.

Willie P.'s sigh was audible. He sank down in a front row seat with a groan and lit a cigar. Marguerite hesitated, wondering if he would hear her if she went out and came in again. Or perhaps she should come back tomorrow. This was not Willie P.'s day.

"Miss Corbeau?" The voice drifted back to her with cigar smoke. A hand lifted, beckoned her forward. A diamond ring caught the faint light and winked at her. She had never seen a diamond ring on a man before and she was fascinated.

Marguerite headed for Willie P.'s back in the front row seat. Her knees were trembling with fear. Now that she was here, she forgot all her rehearsed words, her sallies, her smiles. She stood in front of him and he squinted at her through the smoke.

"Well?" he said.

Her chance. Her last chance. He was sitting there, still simmering with barely-concealed anger, now doubly annoyed by her presence. Looking at her with cool hazel eyes. Almost laughing at her.

And suddenly, Marguerite lost her nervousness. It was simply gone, without any effort on her part. She unbuttoned her coat with sure fingers and lifted off her hat. She tossed them both on a chair. She didn't flinch or smile prettily as his gaze moved over her professionally.

"You want to audition again," Willie said with another deep sigh. "God help me. Tell me, Miss Corbeau, why should I listen?"

"Last time I was Toby's creation," Marguerite said. "Today I am only myself." She gestured to her gown, her hair. "You see how simple I am. You can create me, Mr. Paradise."

There was a pause that stretched out into an agonizing full minute. His eyes took her in, but gave no hint of what he thought. "Go ahead, Miss Corbeau," he said finally. "But I'm afraid there is no accompanist for you today. I think I can manage the footlights."

She nodded, knowing better than to show her fear when she heard she'd have to sing without a piano. She gathered her skirts and walked on stage. William Paradise disappeared and the lights flicked on.

Marguerite felt them again, those warming lights, like something physical, something sexual, moving inside her stomach, going lower, exciting her. Those lights. Taking his time, Willie P. walked down the side steps of the stage and headed down the side aisle. She lost sight of him in the dimness, with the lights in her eyes. She could not tell at first where in the theater he sat. She waited, standing there, until she felt the whole theater of empty seats looking at her. And then she sensed him. She knew somehow that he was in the middle of the theater, to her left.

Marguerite began, slowly, to hum the melody. Her voice came out sweet and low and perfectly on pitch. Encouraged, she began to vocalize, singing la, la, la, along the melody line instead of words. And then she began to sing.

She sang "A Bird in a Gilded Cage" again, and she sang it easily, letting her voice speak, leaving off the gestures Toby had planned for her. She had practiced night after night while Toby was at the theater, singing it her way. Toby had given her professionalism and strength, a knowledge of tricks other performers used, and breath control. Marguerite kept some of what he taught and threw away the rest. She gambled everything on being herself.

In the dark theater, William Paradise watched the girl sing. He'd been prepared for the same artificiality that had so bored him the time before. But this time the hairs on his arms rose, and he saw his future on the stage. The girl was an original, and she had something new. She was singing under the most difficult of circumstances, a cappella on a bare stage, and she was charming him.

As he usually did, he tried to get beyond his emotional response and analyze it. Somehow this girl managed to project a sense of youth and corruption at the same time. She sang of knowledge learned too early, of innocence forever gone, and yet one sensed she had relished every second of her slide into sin. She was half willing accomplice to her downfall, half innocent child. When she sang, he thought of desire and regret and innocence and sex all at once. Something about the combination of child and woman mixed in her to combust into fire. The sexuality was combined with just enough of the perverse, just a hint, so that the audience would not recognize it but know it was there. And there would be no threat in such sexuality, Willie saw, because she looked so sweetly childlike that it seemed indecent to look at her bosom and legs. But they would look.

The audience wouldn't be able to put their finger on Marguerite's attraction, and there would lie her power. They would take this slight girl to their hearts and make her a star, and countless words would be written trying to explain why. Women would seize on her sweetness, her boyishness; men on her suggestion of wantonness. The men would make her a star, Willie thought. Especially the men.

Marguerite lifted her childish arms and he nodded at the perfection of the gesture. Her quality murmured in his ear and sang in his blood and he knew he could take it and build a star around it.

He eased out of his seat and started down the aisle as she swung into the chorus. She was pretty, no doubt about that. And there was boldness in her as well as freshness. No virgin would wear a dress with that neckline. She had no bosom, but what she had was well shaped, the breast a Frenchman would call perfect, one that would fit in a champagne glass. He would like to see her legs.

Quietly, Marguerite ended her song, the last note held until it was scarcely a whisper. She stood there, waiting. She did not peer out into the audience or duck her head shyly or take even one step backward. She didn't do any of the obvious things. She would never be obvious.

Willie was reluctant to speak. As soon as he spoke, he would begin to lose her. She would begin to believe in her talent, and she would begin to change. She would begin to be corrupted. He would have to be careful. She couldn't know yet. She had to be hungry enough to work.

Marguerite stood, waiting. She was totally at ease in the middle of the stage, underneath the lights. She looked enraptured, not bored, not nervous.

"Miss Corbeau," Willie said brusquely, "raise your skirt, please."

It was obvious that he shocked her, but she hesitated a bare fraction of a second. She lifted her skirt to her calves.

Good ankles, Willie thought. Not too skinny. Good. "Higher," he ordered.

Her lips tightened, but she raised her skirts to her knees. Good calves as well, nicely rounded. Thank God she didn't have skinny legs. Her stocking had a hole in it. He liked that. He could see her on stage as a waif, a naif, with a hole in her stocking. "Thank you," he said, and she dropped her skirts.

"I'm sorry, I've forgotten your first name," he said.

"Marguerite," she answered.

Not Marguerite, he thought. Daisy. She would be Daisy Corbeau. And he would always dress her in blue.

He returned his attention to her face. Pretty and impudent, and mysterious, too. Dark blue eyes, a slightly puffy upper lip, perfect skin, a dark, curling abundance of hair. He thought her perfect. He'd been waiting all his life for her. He wanted to fall on his knees before her, for he knew that at this moment she was an angel to him. It would not last. But the next important thing in his life had begun.

On Columbine's wedding day, she woke and stared her mistake in the face. The amazing thing was that she rose anyway and dressed in her wedding dress, a two-piece suit of French faille in soft ivory with pink velvet bands running down the skirt and Irish guipure lace on the bodice and sleeves. Ivy Moffat helped her into it, cooing softly at how lovely it was, and Columbine saw dispassionately that it was true, and that she didn't care.

The incredible thing was that with this heavy knowledge in her heart she still took up her small bouquet of pink and ivory roses and got in the Van Cormandt carriage with Olive, in her best navy silk, for the ride to the hospital. Olive, in a touching gesture that was quite unlike her, held Columbine's icy hand all the way there.

In a dream, Columbine waited in the small anteroom off the chapel. She heard the noise of the small organ. Ned's uncle Thomas arrived to give her away. She glanced at him as though he were a stranger, then took his arm.

She found herself walking down the aisle, thinking, this is so silly, I really should tell them I've changed my mind. She somehow managed to smile uncertainly at Ned, who looked horribly pale and ready to fall down. She wanted to laugh at her pathetic wedding, but Ned took her hand and she felt his desperate grasp and she didn't. She turned toward the priest, and he began.

And the most unbelievable thing of all was that she found herself repeating vows for the second time in her life, vows that she wasn't sure she could believe in. She felt a ring slipped on her finger. The priest said something, and Ned turned to her, and they kissed. And then they were turning, and Olive was crying, and she was heading down the aisle with Ned. It was as though there were cotton in her ears, for she could not hear what anyone was saying. There was something she was trying desperately to remember and could not. And then there was a noise like a ship's horn, but it was the organ, not a ship, and she remembered, walking out of the chapel with Ned into the sunny side garden of the hospital, resplendent with roses, that Elijah was sailing that day.

Bell waited in her cell in the Tombs for a trial, and for Lawrence. She'd been waiting since she'd been arrested. He had not come, but she continued to wait confidently. He would know when it was safe.

Columbine had spoken up for her at the hearing. She did not believe that Bell could be involved in the bombing plot. Bell hadn't quite been able to look at Columbine, for she could see that Columbine was putting on weight. Or maybe she imagined it. At any rate, the thought of Columbine pregnant while Bell was in jail was so awful she couldn't face it, and she certainly couldn't face Columbine. She had refused to allow Columbine to see her, and then, embarrassed, had sent word that she would receive no visitors at all, except Lawrence.

Jail wasn't bad. Bell had met prostitutes before, since Columbine had helped a few through the New Women Society. But those were a higher class of prostitute, not these tough streetwalkers and pickpockets. They jeered at her, but one day she offered to sew one girl's torn skirt, and another brought her a hem going down, and Bell demanded needle and thread and got it. She sewed and listened placidly to their troubles, and she was accepted.

Columbine had found a lawyer for her, a Mr. Chandler Ross. He was young and earnest and horribly worried about her situation. Her placidity annoyed him, she could tell. He was all on fire to defend an anarchist, and he'd expected more passion from her. Nellie Bly had asked for an interview, and when Bell refused Mr. Ross had been furious. What she needed was publicity, he said. This case, he said, would be tried on the streets of New York, and it was important for the public to like her. It was obvious that he didn't believe her story and thought she was guilty; she knew he suspected Lawrence was her accomplice.

"The only thing you have going for you," Mr. Ross said, "is that there is absolutely no evidence. But that's not much at all. You must tell me everything, Miss Huxton. I'm very much afraid you're going to jail."

But Bell said nothing. She smiled her serene smile, and she waited for Lawrence to come.

When Fiona could stand Lawrence's silence no longer, she sent him a note asking him to meet her. She waited in Central Park, in a wild stretch called The Ramble. Under the shelter of trees, it was quite cool, and Fiona tilted back her hat to feel the breeze against the drops of perspiration on her forehead. It had been a long, hot walk from the Van Cormandt house, but she could not think of a safe place to meet and could not risk asking Lawrence to send back a message with a meeting plan in it. So perhaps he would not be able to come.

She leaned against a tree tiredly. It felt good to be out, smelling God's good earth again. The strain of the past weeks was getting to her. She didn't realize how hard it would be. She was trapped in the Van Cormandt house with that awful old maid sister of Van Cormandt. Olive had moved in and taken over the running of the place. And Mr. Van Cormandt's new wife, that baggage Columbine Nash, would be moving in when Ned got out of the hospital. Fiona was already looking for another place. That is, if she didn't end up in jail.

She heard footsteps along the path coming toward her, and Lawrence strode into view around the bend. He looked extremely cross, and he did not even smile when he saw her.

"That was dangerous, sending me that note," he burst out as soon as he was close enough. "I told you to let me make the arrangements."

"I would have waited forever, then," Fiona shot back tartly. "I have things to tell you, things you should know. And I can't stand that house anymore, Lawrence. I've got to get away. Can you find me a place somewhere? You have to find me a place."

"How can I find you a place?" he asked irritably. "I don't know any swells, for God's sake." He did not like this new view of Fiona, vulnerable and demanding. She reminded him too much of Bell, and he did not like to be reminded of Bell these days.

Fiona saw the digust in his face. Her green eyes hardened. "To hell with you then," she said. "It's every man for himself, is it? Fine with me." She turned in a whirl of black skirts, and Lawrence's fingers were on her arm in a moment.

"Don't go," he said. "I'm sorry. Tell me what you came to tell me."

Still turned away from him, she relaxed against his body. "They're asking questions," she said in a rush, relieved to have someone to talk to at last. "They finally put my name together with what happened at the Hartleys. They're asking how I came to work there and why. And they asked about when I cleaned the summer parlor. I'm scared out of my wits, Lawrence. And they've questioned Jimmy, too. They've been to my house, Lawrence!"

He waited, barely noticing the weight of her body against him. He had to think.

"Lawrence, what are we—"

"Shut your mouth!" he snapped. "I must think."

Fiona stiffened and moved away, but she was quiet. Footsteps were heading toward them, and without another word, Lawrence took her arm and began to walk. "Turn your head as they come up," he whispered. Within another second, a young man appeared. He was carrying binoculars and a notebook, and appeared to be just what he was, an eager bird watcher. But Lawrence had already turned slightly and was saying to Fiona, "Yes, I believe it's a Siberian elm," and she was looking at the trees blindly, nodding, so the friendly bird watcher did not bother saying good day.

As soon as he was past, Fiona tried to draw her arm away, but Lawrence held it against him. "Just let me think," he murmured, and she looked into his set face and nodded.

It was five minutes or more before Lawrence felt ready to speak. He catalogued his thoughts and dealt with them one by one. First, he had to put away his anger at Fiona for disobeying him. Then, he had to subdue his panic at the knowledge that the police had put together the connection. Then, he had to wonder why they hadn't been on him yet. They had questioned him a few times, but he knew it was merely for background information about Bell. They hadn't linked him with Fiona, thank God. They weren't looking at him as a suspect, for some reason. Suddenly, Lawrence's steps slowed. He was not a suspect because they already thought they knew who did it, he realized.

"What did they ask you about the summer parlor?" he demanded.

"They asked me if I opened a window. The window that you climbed in that night, Lawrence. They found it unlocked the next day, you know."

"They were supposed to," he said irritably. "I didn't want suspicion on anyone in the house."

"I know that," Fiona answered, just as irritable now. "The point is, they suspect me of opening it in the first place. And they asked me why I cleaned the parlor that day, out of the cleaning rotation. And why that window was open, because under it is a carriage block hidden in the bushes there. Apparently the stable was moved, it used to be where the parlor is now. That wing was added later."

Lawrence remembered the carriage block; he'd struck it with his foot. It had been an unexpected boon, giving him excellent leverage to hoist himself over the windowsill. It had been child's play. Even a man with only one arm could have climbed in that window . . .

Lawrence stopped completely, jerking Fiona's arm. "Jimmy," he said.

"Yes, they've been at him, too."

"They suspect him," Lawrence said. "They suspect it was him that planted the bomb. And they think you opened the window for him, Fiona."

"No," Fiona said, shaking her head wildly. "Not Jimmy."

"But it's obvious, don't you see that?"

"He only has one arm!"

"You don't need two for this work," Lawrence said.

"And he's a drunkard. He can't even tie his own shoes half the time, everyone knows that. The doctor told him he'll be dead in six months and he keeps on drinking."

"Dutch courage." Lawrence began to feel excited indeed. "Where was Jimmy that night, Fiona?"

"Where he always is, drunk in his bed."

"And your sister? Was she watching him?"

"Colleen is living somewhere else now, you know that. It wouldn't be proper for her to be there with me living at the Van Cormandt house."

"So he was alone," Lawrence said. "You're sure of that?"

Fiona nodded. "He's not one for company these days. And there's no one who'd sit with him anyway. Yes, he was alone."

"They think it's him, Fiona, I know it. Now there's one thing for you to do. You have to confess."

"Confess? Are you daft?"

"No," he said. He reached out and grasped her hands. "This can save us. Say he asked you to open the window. That you thought he was coming to see you that night. They won't blame you, Fiona."

A chill ran through Fiona. She searched Lawrence's face with agitated eyes. "Are you asking me to put my husband in jail for a crime I committed?"

"I'm asking you to save us," Lawrence replied. He gripped her hands more tightly. "That's all."

She broke away. "That's all!"

"It's everything, I know," Lawrence said desperately. She had to do this; it was the only way. Even though no one would ever know that it was Lawrence who struck the daring blow. He couldn't tell Most if Jimmy Devlin went to jail for the crime. That would seem cowardly of him, sending a one-armed laborer to jail in his place. But Lawrence didn't belong in jail; he was too fine for jail. Fiona had to listen.

"But what happens if you don't tell them about Jimmy? They're just words, Fiona. You can find a way to say them. And then we'll be free."

"And Miss Huxton?" she asked fiercely, turning back. She saw Lawrence's face change. "Oh, yes, Lawrence, I know about your woman. You're asking me to do this so you can go back to living with her!"

"No," he said. "No, that's not it. It's you I love, Fiona." He grasped her around the waist and pulled her to him roughly. "Only you. I want you to save *us*, not her."

Fiona hesitated. She didn't know whether to believe Lawrence. He was most likely lying. But still, she'd always known that he lied.

And she also knew that he didn't realize yet how completely they were bound together, man and woman. He still thought he controlled her. He didn't know that they had given up control the first night they'd lain together.

"You said the doctor told him he would die if he didn't stop drinking," Lawrence said softly, insinuatingly in her ear. "You know he won't stop. He'll die out here. He won't get a harsh sentence, Fiona. Just a year or two. How can a jury be ruthless to a one-armed man? They'll understand. Revenge, they can understand. Anarchists, they hang. A man's life destroyed by Van Cormandt's best friend. And Van Cormandt dancing with Jimmy bleeding on the carpet. They'll say these things. The jury will hear them. It won't be bad. And he can't drink in jail. He could come out a better man, Fiona."

"Don't feed me such lines," she said. Her face was ashen. "You don't care a fig about Jimmy."

"It's only us that matters," Lawrence said. "Isn't it?"

He waited. He knew better than to push Fiona. He could taste victory, though, and sweet, blessed relief. He'd known fear these past weeks that had paralyzed him. He hadn't been able to go out of his rooms. For whole mornings, he'd stayed in bed. It would be his secret for the rest of his life, his cowardice. He knew he could not go to jail.

Fiona had run her fingers absently through her hair, and it had come loose from its pins. Tendrils waved around her thin face. Her thin, bloodless lips opened and closed. "He's my husband," she whispered.

Lawrence took her hand again. "It comes down to this," he said. "Him or us. Choose."

The news reached Bell faintly, as if through a haze. She was thinking of Lawrence, and she didn't want to be distracted by Chandler Ross. She had a special way now to fill time. She would think of quiet times with Lawrence. Early mornings, when he lay behind her and combed her long hair with his fingers. He would do it for thirty minutes at a time. Bell was to the point where she could almost completely recapture that feeling of drowsy contentment, Lawrence's fingers in her hair, the pleasant tug on her scalp, the faint gray light.

"Did you hear me, Miss Huxton? They've arrested James Devlin, the man who was injured at the Hartley party."

She blinked at him slowly. "I remember." The news sank in. "Can I go, then?"

Mr. Ross coughed and shuffled his papers. "Unfortunately, there is another charge," he said.

It seemed that the foreman of her old factory had shown up and accused her of rounding up the workers and bringing them to the May Day parade, inflaming them with anarchist rhetoric. He claimed that she had told them to seize the factory for themselves.

In court, Bell objected to this. What she had said was that one day workers would seize such a factory. She wouldn't have advocated such a thing, she told the court quietly, for she wouldn't expect anyone to follow her advice, and anyway she wouldn't want any of the girls to lose their jobs. Though, under questioning, Bell did admit that she believed in the demolition of the state, absolutely. The people would seize factories and banks and redistribute the wealth and privileges—someday. And she supposed there would be some violence involved in this, though she did not advocate it.

Bell was a beautiful, serene presence on the stand. But her serenity served as a burr under New York's collective saddle. Her likeness was on the front page of every city newspaper for two weeks running. They said that she claimed that James Devlin had done them all a good service. That she wished she'd thought of it. That she wished Ned Van Cormandt had lost an arm, like Devlin. The beautiful anarchist who lived with a man outside of marriage was said to have supported her lover by prostitution.

Mr. Ross told her he expected a verdict of innocent, for he found Bell impressive on the stand. But she was convicted of inciting to riot and sentenced to five years in jail. The unusual severity of the sentence was seen as just punishment for her other crimes, immorality and sedition.

Bell was sent to Blackwell's Island. Emma Goldman brought books, and Columbine sent a basket of food weekly, which Bell shared. Several other anarchists sent pamphlets and letters frequently, and Bell looked forward to novels sent by Ivy Moffat. The intellectual Alexander Berkman sent candy, which touched her. After the first hellish months, there was a kind of peace gained from being so close to Manhattan, yet not part of her life there. She was not forced to engage with people, she did not have to endure the thousand deaths she had died daily while living with Lawrence. The pains of love were replaced by a numb reliance on future joy.

Lawrence wrote, saying he would wait for her, but he could not visit her yet. Bell smiled, serene. One of them was a martyr for the cause; it did not signify which. Lawrence would wait for her. With good behavior, she could be out in two years.

The day after *Wait for Sally* opened and Marguerite had been proclaimed a star, Willie moved her into a suite of rooms at the Fifth Avenue Hotel on Madison Square. The rooms were grand, all pale satins and vivid velvets, and Willie added to the splendor by sending dozens and dozens of roses every day.

It had been inevitable that they sleep together; Marguerite had always been adept at spotting a man's lust for her, and she'd seen it in his eyes as she took her bows on opening night. But they did it the right way, waiting until after the glowing notices came and opening a bottle of very expensive Bollinger. Willie was compact and muscular and energetic, and Marguerite enjoyed him tremendously. They were giddy and silly with delight in their good fortune, and they were seriously lustful about each other's bodies. Afterwards, they lay on the living room rug completely naked, unself-conscious, and plotted her career.

Overnight, Marguerite's life took off. She was Daisy Corbeau now, and she was a star. She had a clever, immensely rich man for a lover. She lunched at the hotel in silks and velvets and extravagant hats; she bought Toby wonderful ties and beautiful handkerchiefs. She gave interviews by the dozens, and jewelers opened their shops on Sunday afternoons when they knew Miss Corbeau took her walk with the generous Willie P.

It happened fast, but Marguerite was not breathless. She was aware of every single second of her happiness. She lapped her success up like cream and clamored for more. She watched her money and her publicity and the attempt of her vain co-star, Errol Finley, to upstage her like a hawk. She kept her eye on Willie, too, for she was growing rather possessive of his attention, which was notoriously fluid. She knew all too well how devastated Mollie Todd had found his rejection and subsequent interest in Marguerite. Not to mention poor Lorena LeClerc, who had captured him so fleetingly and had only a ruby bracelet to remember him by. Marguerite felt rather fierce about Willie; if it wasn't love, it certainly was excessive fondness.

On Christmas Eve, they dined alone in her suite. This was a rare occurrence, and Marguerite found herself suddenly afraid she would bore her lover. Christmas was always a time of melancholy for her, a time where she pretended interest in trees and nativity scenes that held no charm or significance for her. She did not feel like chattering gaily or telling Willie some piece of salacious gossip. Willie loved gossip more than women or even Toby.

Willie picked at his pheasant, and his glass of champagne was untouched. Marguerite was halfway through her plate of food, which was delicious, when she noticed that Willie wasn't eating.

She put down her fork immediately. "What is it, darling?" she asked. She put her hand over his. "Is it Christmas? Do you miss your family?"

Willie's parents were dead. He'd grown up in Chicago, an only child, and he never spoke of his early years. Since Marguerite preferred to keep her own past a secret, she never pressed him.

Willie looked startled. "No. To tell you the truth," he said with a laugh, "I was worrying about your Christmas present."

She sat up immediately, her face flushing with pleasure. Marguerite had not become inured to presents in the least. She hoped Willie had gotten her something extravagant, something positively vulgar. "I'm sure I'll love whatever it is," she said. She had bought him a diamond stickpin and matching cufflinks. They had cost a staggering amount, but Marguerite loved to give presents as much as she loved to receive them. And how could she give anything less than extravagant to such an extravagant man?

"I want to give it to you now," Willie said. He knocked against the table as he rose. China clinked and her champagne glass wobbled alarmingly. It was the first graceless move she'd ever seen him make.

Fishing in his pocket, he walked around the table and held out a small velvet box. A ring, Marguerite thought, a bit disappointed. She would have preferred a necklace, or earrings. She thought rings called attention to the childishness of her small fingers.

With a soft smile up at him, she opened the box, prepared to squeal in delight. The biggest sapphire she'd ever seen flashed up at her. It caught the candlelight and flashed again. It was a deep, dark blue, thrown into relief by the diamonds that were clustered around either side. They winked up at her, too. Slowly, Marguerite realized that this was no ordinary gift.

"I thought maybe we'd marry," Willie said in an offhand way.

Marguerite was afraid to look up. She stared down at the ring. "Marry?" she asked.

Willie fumbled for a cigar. He couldn't see her face, she was keeping her damned head down. He needed a cue to proceed, needed someone to feed him a line. He knew Marguerite didn't love him. But he was banking on the guess that she wouldn't *allow* herself to love him, that perhaps with care, and time, she would come to do so. All he knew was that he was possessed by her. A feeling had lifted him, buoyed him up during these past months. It was so new that it swept out any emotion he had ever felt in his life, any woman he had lusted for, any woman he'd wanted. Those feelings were completely inauthentic next to his feeling for Marguerite. This mixture of slyness and affection, of artifice and freshness, this woman who looked like a child. He realized that the mad lust of his time with Mollie Todd had been merely a taste of what would overwhelm him with Marguerite. Or it wasn't even a taste, for the two were as different as rotgut and champagne.

A rage for her was in his blood, but also a wish to protect. He felt the child in her, the hurt and the pain and the secrecy, and he recognized it. For the first time in his life, Willie wanted to hold something. He didn't want to let it go. He wanted to tell her that, but he didn't know how, so he waited.

Marguerite turned the box in her hands, watching the jewels catch the light. Willie's silence confused her. She knew that he didn't love her. Horatio had lusted for her, Edwin had been devoted for that brief time in his feeble way, but Willie's indifference, his casualness, told her that he was not smitten in the least. She was used to men out of their minds with passion, and she could not understand a man who could hide love under banter.

She was never sure of him. And when she *did* have him, he was all lightness and jokes, even in bed much of the time. So the question was, why did he want to marry her? Publicity? Come to think of it, the newspapers would go wild.

"Just think, Willie," she said slowly. "We'd be in all the papers for at least a week. No news happens at Christmastime." The thought had popped into her head just like that, and Marguerite was not used to censoring her conversation with Willie. That was what she loved about him; she could say anything. She looked up, her blue eyes shining, but she'd missed the look of pain in his face, for he was turning away.

"Exactly, my dear," he said, lighting his cigar. "Box office receipts will double. And after our honeymoon—we'll have to wait until the show closes to marry, of course—we'll find a new play for you and you'll return in triumph. A good plan, don't you think?"

"New Yorkers love marriages," Marguerite said. "And I guess this way you'll know I'll always appear in your plays. How clever of you. You'll never lose me."

She dimpled up at him, and Willie felt his heart squeeze with pain. He'd lost her already, he supposed. Her marriage would be a business deal. "So I take it the answer is yes?" he asked lightly.

Marguerite gave what Willie called her pagan grin. "How could I refuse this?" she said, waggling the box at Willie.

She'd said it as a joke, he knew, but he turned away so that she wouldn't see how furious he was. He felt positively mad with anger. "We'll tell the press I picked it because it matched your eyes perfectly." He had picked it for that reason.

"Perfect," Marguerite said, slipping it onto her third finger. "Oh, I do love it, Willie. It's the prettiest ring I ever saw." She skipped toward him and flung her slight arms around his neck. "The thing is," she said hesitantly, "I was wondering . . ."

"Yes, darling?"

"If you loved me," Marguerite said, peeking up at him.

Willie's hazel eyes were unreadable. "No," he said. "But that's beside the point, isn't it?"

"Really, Willie," Marguerite said, drawing away. "You could have lied."

"That's one thing I won't do," Willie answered seriously. Except for this, he thought. I will never tell you I love you. "That's one thing you can't do, either. You can't lie to me. Do you promise, Marguerite?"

Why should she lie? Willie saw all and accepted all. She was marrying the best possible man in the world for her. "I promise, Willie. You're the only man I've never lied to," she said honestly. "And I intend to keep it that way."

"Let's go to bed," he said, his voice suddenly rough.

Marguerite smiled and turned her back so that Willie could begin with her tiny satin buttons. She looked at her engagement ring; it was so delightfully, preposterously *big*. "I think I'm going to be happy with you, Willie," she murmured. "I think we'll be happy together."

"I think we're going to give each other hell," Willie said, and with a sigh he buried his mouth in her creamy shoulder.

Olive had offered to move back into the Van Cormandt house permanently when the doctors told them Ned was ready to come home. Columbine knew that the gesture cost Olive dearly, for she cherished her independence. And she was touched, for she knew that Olive was aware of how much Columbine dreaded moving into the Van Cormandt house, and how heartbroken she was to leave Greenwich Village and Safe Passage House.

Ned moved into a room on the first floor, attended by a nurse. The sound of hammering while the workers rebuilt the library disturbed him, so the men stopped their work and the room was closed off. The house was so large that Olive and Columbine could go for days on the second floor without seeing each other unless they made a habit of having tea together a few times a week, which they did. Her pregnancy was a difficult one, and Columbine had been ordered rest by Dr. Dana. She wasn't allowed down to Safe Passage House more than once a week. Luckily, little Ivy Moffat took over like a whirlwind. Soon, Safe Passage House was a refuge for four women, six children, and one teenage girl.

Ned grew better slowly. Columbine came to enjoy the slow summer days, while she read aloud in the garden with Ned stretched out beside her in his chaise. He was often in pain, and she was often tired, so they made a quaint, companionable couple, so unlike themselves in the old days that they often laughed, remembering their hectic juggling of schedules, their shouting matches, their long, hilarious dinners. Neither of them mentioned their combustive sexual relations, however. Looking at Ned, Columbine had to wonder if he would ever have the strength to make love again. And most days, she wondered if she'd ever want to herself.

Autumn passed, and they now read in the cheerful, sunny morning room. Leaves drifted across the sere, small garden. Columbine grew large, and her ankles swelled. Dr. Dana ordered her to bed. One morning, she opened the paper to find that the newest star in New York's musical theater was young Daisy Corbeau, currently appearing in William Miles Paradise's *Wait for Sally.* And in the middle of December, on a night bitter with cold and brilliant with stars, Columbine went into labor. Twelve hours later, out of her mind with pain, exhausted, definitely resolved on never having sexual relations again in her life, and hating Elijah Reed with every ounce of her strength—such as it was—she gave birth to a girl.

Dr. Dana cleaned them both up and combed Columbine's matted hair. She helped her slip into a fresh nightgown, and she did not say a word about how Columbine had cursed Elijah Reed's body and soul at the end. She allowed in Ned and Olive, who arrived on tiptoe, all smiles. Olive insinuated a little finger into the girl's tiny palm and the small fingers closed around it.

"Lovely," Olive said. "Perfect."

Ned smiled. "Like you," he said to Columbine.

"You two are ridiculous," Columbine said, smiling down at her red, wrinkled baby. "She's hideous."

"Not at all," Olive said, shocked. "Look, she has blond hair. And the Van Cormandt chin."

Columbine turned away and fussed with the blanket. She had argued with Ned about telling Olive the truth. Olive would understand, Columbine felt sure. But Ned insisted that he wanted everyone to think the baby was his.

"And your mouth, Columbine," Ned said.

"I want to call her Hawthorn," Columbine said. She looked around at her room in the Van Cormandt mansion, saw the two people, blinking back tears, at her bedside, and looked back down at her daughter. For the first time since Elijah left, she felt at peace.

November, 1896
The Propaganda of the Deed

Twenty-One

COLUMBINE LOOKED OVER the edge of *Bleak House* at Ned. His head was thrown back, and his eyes were closed. She stopped reading aloud and closed the book.

"Go on," he said peevishly. "I'm not sleeping."

Columbine opened the book again and took up where she left off. While she read, she stole glances at Ned's face. As soon as she thought he was really asleep, she would stop. She was so tired today. Gradually, she saw his facial muscles relax. His mouth opened slightly. He began to snore lightly. Columbine closed the book.

Poor Ned. The doctors could not restore him to full health, and as the years passed he left his bed less and less. The internal injuries he'd suffered had marked him for life. He would never be completely free of pain. Constant pain had changed him; he was a different man than he had been. He was often querulous, and almost constantly depressed. The only person who could lift his spirits was Hawthorn, who looked at the fact that he remained in bed as an adventure along the lines of "The Land of Counterpane." She brought her toys and books into bed with him and played for hours, while Ned alternately played with her, read his newspaper, or napped.

The door opened quietly, and Olive stole in the room, checking Ned to see if he was asleep. When Columbine nodded, Olive beckoned, and Columbine followed her out, closing the door softly behind her. The years had marked Olive, too, marked them all. Olive's hair was beginning to gray; she was forty-seven, and as forceful as ever.

"Hawthorn will be home from the park soon," Olive said in a low voice. "I thought you'd like to spend some time with her. I can take over with Ned."

Columbine leaned against the wall. "He'll sleep for awhile, I think. He had a bad night."

"You look as though you could use a rest yourself," Olive said sympathetically.

"Yes, I'm very tired. Perhaps you could tell Hawthorn that I'll come up and see her for dinner in the nursery."

It was clear that this displeased Olive, but she merely nodded. "I'll tell Fiona to take your tea to your room today," she said.

"Thank you, Olive." Columbine started to turn away wearily, but Olive put her hand on her arm.

"Columbine, I must speak to you," she said. "I know you're tired. But will you come to my room for a moment?"

Columbine nodded, biting her lip. A request to come to Olive's room, except at teatime, always meant serious business. She followed her sister-in-law up the stairs and down the long hall to her bedroom and adjoining sitting room in the northeast corner of the house. The rooms were formerly occupied by Ned's first wife, Cora, but Olive had cleared away all the Louis XV furniture, with its curving lines and decorative frills, removed the ormolu and the marquetry tables and the taffeta hangings and put in the plain American furniture of her mother and father. A desk sat in the corner by the window, piled with the correspondence of a busy woman.

Columbine sat across from Olive in one of the comfortable velvet armchairs she'd installed. She felt rather like a niece who had been asked in for a "chat" to straighten her out about her propensity to overspend on her trousseau or to ignore her charitable responsibilities. Olive wore the identical expression of a disapproving concern not very well masked by an attempt at an air of disinterested friendliness.

Olive put her hands in her lap and turned to Columbine. "I'm worried about you."

Columbine smiled thinly. "Again?"

"Yes, again. You've been tired and spiritless. I know that Ned can be difficult, dear. But I hate to see you so affected."

"It's difficult not to be when he's so unhappy, Olive."

Olive nodded, her eyes troubled. "God knows, Columbine," she said with a far-off look, "if I could have seen the future, I would never have let you marry him."

The comment roused Columbine from her weariness. "Olive!"

"Let's be honest with one another," Olive said. "At last. You've been a good wife, Columbine, and I know you love Ned. But you lost your heart to someone else some time ago, that's perfectly obvious. You married Ned out of sisterly affection, concern, maybe guilt. And maybe," Olive said, a blush starting to stain her cheeks, "for a father for Hawthorn. No," she said quickly, raising her hand, "I'm not judging you, and I'm sure you both did it with the best of motives. It doesn't matter, anyway. Hawthorn is my niece no matter who her father is, that will never change."

Agitated, Columbine got up and went to the window. She pushed aside the curtains and looked out at the brilliant autumn leaves of the park. "Why are you saying this now, Olive?"

"Because I care for you very much, Columbine," Olive said. "You've truly become a sister to me. But part of me wonders how you can go on like this. You have been neglecting Hawthorn. Haven't you noticed how quiet she's been?"

Columbine didn't answer. Guilt swept over her, and she gripped the curtains convulsively. She loved her daughter, but she had so little to give her. And there were times that looking at her was torture.

Hawthorn's hair had remained blond like her own, but as she developed into a toddler and then a child, it had become obvious that she had Elijah's black eyes. And it wasn't just the eyes; there were other things. The way she'd frown, or a particular look on her face when she was happy and worried at the same time . . . it pained Columbine to look at her at times.

But that wasn't why she withdrew from her. She loved Hawthorn with all her heart, but the child took so much from her. She was questioning and intelligent and into everything. Her questions were unending. Sometimes it was just easier to leave her to Olive and close the door.

Columbine felt like a desert inside, wind blowing across a desiccated landscape. There was no joy springing forth anymore, no laughter. She had begun to feel pain in various parts of her body, little nervous tremors. She was turning into a neurasthenic upper-class woman, she knew, and she raged against it and despised herself for it and she remained trapped in her fears and her panics and her weariness. What kind of a mother did that make for Hawthorn?

"I know, Olive," she said finally. "She's been playing by herself awfully much lately. But I'm no good with her right now. I'm impatient and irritable. I feel it's better not to be around her."

"You need something," Olive said. "Can't you see that you need something other than this house? It's so obvious to me."

"Perhaps another trip," Columbine said haltingly. Two years ago, Olive had decided that Columbine should go to Europe alone. Ned protested, Hawthorn wailed, Columbine was terrified, but Olive insisted, and she got her way. Columbine had left for three months, months in which her weariness fell away and her depression lifted. She visited friends in London, she traveled to Vienna, she stayed for a month in Florence. The only place she did not go was Paris. She read new books and was electrified by Eleanora Duse and struggled through several lectures in Vienna by an amazing doctor called Freud. And then she returned to America, overjoyed to hold Hawthorn in her arms again, and within six months she felt the familiar dull pain stealing over her again.

"No," Olive said. "Not another trip. A nurse for Ned."

"Olive, you know perfectly well he's refused a nurse—"

"My brother is in pain, and God knows we can never know what it's like to lie in his bed, Columbine. But he has also become selfish and demanding. We won't use those words, you and I, but it's time we did. And I will no longer sacrifice you for Ned. You have to get out."

Columbine turned, shocked. She stared at Olive, who nodded grimly. "I know," she said softly. "You can't believe I'm saying these things. But I'm afraid that soon I won't recognize you, Columbine. The things I love about you are disappearing."

Tears gathered behind Columbine's eyes. "I know," she murmured. "I feel myself slipping away, too. I can't seem to help it, Olive."

"Yes, you can," Olive said briskly. She rose and came to her.

"You've had your dark night of the soul, and it's been long enough. You can't leave Ned, I quite see that. But you could could leave this house once in awhile. You could even take a lover."

Columbine gasped. "Olive, really—"

"You're only forty years old. You're still beautiful, even though you're determined to lose your looks. Columbine, you have to do something."

"A rest cure?" Columbine asked. It was the common solution for depressed patients.

Olive shook her head. "Certainly not. I've heard of these cures—Maud Hartley took one, and told me about it. Of course, she's a silly woman, so she thinks it worked. All that would happen is that some doctor would tell you to find consolation in your home and your daughter. Bunk. Columbine, you've been a political speaker, a writer. You had ambition and intellect and drive. And now your biggest concern is which volume of Dickens to read to Ned. And the only thing you look forward to is when you can start Trollope!"

Columbine had to smile at this picture of her days. "I have Hawthorn," she said. "And you. That's more than most women have."

A spasm of irritation crossed Olive's face. "Will you listen to yourself?" she demanded. "Home was never enough for you, you're not made that way. Why are you cramming yourself into such a narrow box? Columbine, resume your work, go back to Safe Passage House, more than twice a week. Every day if you must. You have to take an interest in things. You can't satisfy your nature sitting here taking care of Ned. And the man that Ned used to be, the man you thought you married, wouldn't have stood for it!"

Columbine didn't know what to say. She felt exhausted by Olive's energy. "I want to help him," she said. "He's hurting so. His life is over, he believes."

"I know." Olive saw that Columbine's lips were shaking. "Oh, dear, don't cry." She crossed to a small table and poured a glass of water, then handed it to Columbine. "Drink this. And don't cry, you know how I hate it."

Columbine obediently drank the water. "I'm sorry, Olive."

"Oh for heaven's sake, stop apologizing and do something. When was the last time you went out of the house? It's selfish of you not to be involved now, you know. The nation is in terrible shape, we're still in a depression. There's so much you could do."

"I suppose you're right."

"Safe Passage would be a good place to start. And I've gotten you into a study group, I think you'll enjoy it. It's called the Social Reform Club. Lillian Wald is in it, and Felix Adler—they're reading Dante now. They'd be delighted to welcome you."

"I couldn't—"

"Yes, you could."

Columbine crossed to the sofa and sat down. Olive's brisk good sense was tiring. It just wasn't that easy, she knew. She rarely went out anymore; she couldn't bear social life and Olive was right, her intellectual life had narrowed to newspapers and Dickens. Could she really return to the world, just like that?

A newspaper was lying on the table in front of the sofa, and she absently placed her glass on it. "I don't know, Olive," she said. "I don't have much energy these days."

"Just go through the motions," Olive said. "That's enough of a start."

Idly, Columbine's gaze rested on the table while Olive's words revolved in her head. The bottom of her glass had magnified the print of the paper. In large and wavering print she saw the name ELIJAH REED.

A tiny jolt sent a rippling wave of anxiety through her body. She moved the glass and picked up the paper. The item said that Elijah Reed, whose most recent novel, *Spencer's Man,* a most eloquent attack on Social Darwinism, had swept the country, was returning to New York City from Paris, where he had lived for the past six years, with time out to walk with Coxey's army of the unemployed to the nation's capital last year.

Elijah was back. Color flooded her cheeks, and her hand shook when it placed the paper back on the table. He would be living in the same city again. If she'd had any inclination to follow Olive's advice, it was squashed. She knew she did not have the strength to face Elijah Reed again.

"You see?" Olive cried, crossing back and taking her hands, "I was right! You look better already!"

• • •

"Tell me, Miss Daisy Corbeau," Edward Ferdinand Clinton said in his clipped British accent, "what is it like to be the most feted American musical star of your generation?"

"It is sometimes a trial, I must confess," Marguerite sighed.

"You have such a reputation for the feminine virtues," he said, "faithfulness to your husband, pureheartedness, modesty—"

Marguerite flipped over on the bed and pillowed her head on her naked arms. She raised one bare leg in the air. "All too true, Mr. Clinton. I'm afraid I'm an old-fashioned girl." She ran her fingers along Teddy Clinton's muscular leg, with its golden hair and smooth muscles.

"And they tell me that the chef of Delmonico's named a dish for you, some sort of blueberry pastry—"

"He called it Daisy's Cobbler. Monsieur Gilot is terribly sweet."

"And during the party that he presented it to you, I hear you pelted the streets below with the blueberries, isn't that so?" Teddy reached under a pillow to fondle a small breast.

"We were feeling so gay," Marguerite said with a pout. "I thought it terribly unkind of the papers to suggest we were making light of the city's hungry souls. I donated baskets and baskets of food the very next day."

He kissed the small of her back. "How wonderful you are, Miss Corbeau. A model of American womanhood," he said with a lascivious grin. "A pearl."

"And you, sir, are a positive swine," she said, sticking out her little red tongue.

He slapped her on her bare backside lightly. "Come on, Miss Corbeau—"

"That's Mrs. Paradise to you, sir."

"Mrs. Paradise, Miss Corbeau, Daisy, come over here. We have plenty of time for another go before we have to get to the theater."

"No, we don't," Marguerite said, avoiding his questing hand adroitly and rolling over to slip into a satin brocade dressing gown. "At least, I don't. I have an appointment, so you have to go, Teddy dear. I'll see you at the theater later."

"You minx, you drive me mad. All right," Teddy said with a sigh. "You've worn me out, anyway." He wandered off to the adjoining dressing room to get his clothes. Teddy liked to dress in front of a full-length mirror so he could admire himself.

He was an awful bore, really, Marguerite thought as she knotted her dressing gown and applied cologne to disguise the smell of sex. But he was so terribly good in bed. And she had gotten into the habit of seducing her co-stars. The show was winding down; Willie was looking for another show for her. She'd make sure she picked the male star this time. She was sure Willie had picked Teddy for his dullness more than his singing voice.

Since her debut as the young cousin from Kansas City, Sally Perkins, in *Wait for Sally*, Marguerite had been in play after play, handpicked by Willie solely for the interest of the female lead. She'd been a cowgirl, a tomboy, a serving girl at the French court, an explorer, and a dance hall girl. She was currently a cabin boy on a pirate ship. In every play, she showed her legs, sang sweetly, and fell in love, and though some were hits and some were flops, she remained a star through them all. Daisy Corbeau, America's Forget-Me-Not, married to the flamboyant William Miles Paradise, the couple all New York panted to read about. Their rows were legendary, as were their elaborate makings up, the diamonds they exchanged, the second and third honeymoons, the time Willie had bought out all of Delmonico's for Daisy's twenty-third birthday. And within the closed circle of the New York theatrical community, their adulteries were the stuff of legends.

"I'm going, sweet," Teddy said, coming back in the room and kissing her on the back of the neck. "My Daisy. Remember how I adore you."

She kissed him a swift goodbye; they both knew their minds were on other things now. One good thing about Teddy was that she knew he would forget her as easily as she'd forget him. He was too wrapped up in himself to make a scene when she broke it off. And there was a line of girls anxious to take her place, for Teddy was discreet, and no one knew for sure that he was her lover. Discretion was Teddy's only virtue, but it was one that suited Marguerite perfectly.

Marguerite sighed and began to run a brush through her unruly hair. She had been shocked, at first, at how easy it was to commit adultery. God knew Willie had found it so. She had begun to flirt with other men just to rile him, make him jealous, and it had flowered into an indiscretion so easily! Willie hadn't seemed to mind. He had gone off with a chorus girl from *The Merry Monarch.* That had been within six months of their marriage.

She heard the outer door open and close, and there was a rhythmic knock at her bedroom door. "Is that you, Toby?" she called.

He stuck his head around the door. Toby was still handsome, beginning to gray a bit at the temples, but as gay as ever. "It's me, petal."

"You know, I gave you that key for that one rainy afternoon so you could wait for me in comfort," Marguerite said. "What thanks do I get? You keep the key and use it every time you visit me. And you're always early! One of these days you're going to embarrass me."

"Nonsense, you are absolutely incapable of being embarrassed," Toby said, bending over and kissing the top of her head.

"Why are you early?" Marguerite asked crossly. "I thought you were having lunch with your latest conquest."

"He was dreadfully dull, no fun at all." It had only taken a few months in the theater for Marguerite to realize that Toby was that dreaded word, *homosexual,* like the notorious Oscar Wilde. Toby had been a little afraid of her reaction, but she had felt a mixture of fascination, relief, and pique that she no longer had to worry about breaking his heart.

"And how was your little escapade this afternoon?" Toby asked, waggling his eyebrows at her in the mirror.

Marguerite slapped down her hairbrush. "What escapade? I declare, Toby, you think I lead a much more exciting life than I do."

Toby laughed. "Petal, really. The bed is mussed, you're reeking of cologne—you always put on too much cologne after an escapade—and I just saw Teddy Clinton in the lobby. Do you expect me to be blind?"

She met his eyes in the mirror. "Yes, Toby, I'd appreciate it," she said dryly.

Toby's genial expression grew serious. "I wish I didn't see some of the things you do," he said.

Marguerite began to pin up her hair. "Don't start, Toby."

"You're absolutely miserable, and you expect me to say nothing."

"Yes," Marguerite said calmly, "because I'm not miserable."

"Yes you are, you don't know it, that's all. And how you could do this to Willie. He loves you, you know."

Marguerite sighed, exasperated. "Toby, do be quiet. Willie and I love each other, yes, but it's a different sort of thing."

"You're just trying to hurt him."

"Look, darling, I know you adore Willie, but he's quite content. As am I."

"How do you know he's content?" Toby bent over to sniff one of the roses Willie still sent to Marguerite every morning. He took it out and broke off the stem to slip it through his buttonhole. "One day he'll be gone, and you'll realize how stupid you were, playing with fire like this."

Marguerite ignored this. Toby had never been quite so blatant before, but she was in no mood to listen. "Toby, be a dear and order us some tea. I must eat a bit of something before I dress, and then come to the theater with me, will you?"

"Of course," Toby said. Reluctantly, he decided to drop the subject. "And where are you getting these British affectations from, pray tell? It must be from that fop, Teddy Clinton. 'Do be a dear,' indeed. I'll have you know that Edward Ferdinand Clinton, gentleman actor, was born right here in Brooklyn."

"Oh, Toby, really? That's marvelous. He told me he was from some little town in England named Clinton Hall."

And so the afternoon came to an end, as it usually did, with adultery, gossip, and tea. Marguerite hooted with laughter and teased Toby and put on her furs to sweep through the lobby tossing her head to the whispers and double takes. She sang and danced and received three standing ovations and an admirer sent an emerald necklace to her dressing room. But there was a shadow on Marguerite, a long shadow cast by Toby's question. Did he know something? Is that why he had asked her about Willie while he sniffed a rose and tried to look offhand? *How do you know he's content?*

When was the last time Willie had made love to her? Marguerite wondered as she removed her stage makeup. Had her transitory lust for Teddy distracted her from the fact that Willie was feeling neglected? Perhaps she should look into it, Marguerite decided.

Anyway, she thought, smiling at her pretty reflection in the glass, it only took her concentrated attention on him alone to make Willie come around. That would never change, she was certain.

"Mrs. Birch?"

Bell looked up. Lev Moiseev stood in front of her desk, holding a sheaf of papers. "I hate to disturb you," he said.

"Lev, I told you to call me Bell," she said. "And you're not disturbing me." She smiled warmly at him; she was fond of Lev. Only twenty-three, brilliant and capable, an engineer by training, he was the editor of the monthly cultural and literary journal, *Die Fraye Gezelshaft*, or The Free Society. Her health nearly broken from her years in jail and the factory work she'd taken on after getting out, Bell considered Lev a savior for giving her a job as translator on the journal the year before. She'd spent her time on Blackwell's Island perfecting her Russian and Yiddish, and with two years in a sweatshop, surrounded by Jewish workers, she was now fluent.

"Bell," he said, with an answering smile. "Would you mind looking at this? I needed to make some cuts, and it might have been too deep."

"Of course." Bell's position had expanded somewhat; occasionally, she did editorial work. They published the best of the Yiddish anarchist writers as well as Europeans such as Kropotkin and Sebastien Faure. She bent over the article Lev had asked her to look at and picked up her red pencil.

Lev broke into her concentration. "Bell, a group of us are going to Schwab's after work. There is talk that Kropotkin will come to America this next year. He's been invited to a conference in Canada. We must begin to plan. Will you join us?"

Bell hesitated. Lawrence would be furious if she was late again this week. Over the past year, Bell's involvement with the *Gezelshaft* had placed her among the premier anarchist and socialist intellects on the East Side. Even though anarchism had experienced a decline since a spate of violent activity, the core group still tried to keep the flame alive. She'd actually spoken at a few large meetings, and had written three articles which had been well received. She did this, however, in the face of Lawrence's growing opposition. Lately, he had been even more difficult than usual.

"I don't know, Lev," she finally said. "I—"

"Don't say no," he urged her. "Everyone is going, and we'll miss you."

"Well, perhaps just for a cup of coffee," Bell said, smiling at Lev's eagerness. If she got home early enough, Lawrence wouldn't know.

She was barely in the door when he spoke. He was hunched over the newspaper, his back to her. "You're late."

"Not so very," Bell said, taking off her coat and hat. "I had some extra work at the office."

"It couldn't wait until tomorrow, I suppose. Well, all right. I was fine here, I suppose."

"I'll just start dinner," Bell said. She crossed to the small kitchen and whipped an apron around her waist. Her salary from the journal was barely enough to keep them in food and coal. Lawrence's money had long ago run out, and he couldn't seem to hold a job. Bell sliced bread and spread a little precious butter on it. She took out the cabbage soup she'd made the day before and emptied it into the pot. With a few boiled potatoes, it would make a good enough meal, filling, at any rate.

While she was peeling the potatoes, Lawrence walked in the kitchen. "Dinner will be ready in a few minutes," Bell said.

Lawrence took a sip from the one glass of whiskey he allowed himself each evening. "Have you heard the latest about Schwab's?" he asked.

The knife slipped, and Bell nicked her finger. The potato fell to the floor and rolled underneath the table.

"Jesus, Bell, that was clumsy. We can't afford to waste food." Lawrence took another slug of whiskey and made no move to retrieve the potato.

She bent down and picked it up, then went to the sink to wash it off, as well as her bloody finger. "What about Schwab's?" she asked, with her back to him. Could Lawrence have found out how often she went there after work?

"Justus might as well change the name to Goldman's," Lawrence said bitterly. His pale blue eyes gleamed as he wiped his mouth. He hadn't shaved that day, and the blond stubble on his face looked rough. Once, Lawrence would not have been caught dead unshaven. He was not nearly the elegant man he'd been. "The little bitch has made up business cards with the address of the saloon on it. She's treating it as her private office."

Bell sighed. Lawrence's hatred of Emma Goldman had grown more fierce over the years. It was simply unfair, he claimed, that a woman anarchist should get all the press, when the men were doing all the work. He darkly accused her of being an informer in the case of her friend Alexander Berkman, who had tried unsuccessfully to assassinate Henry Clay Frick four years before and was currently serving a harsh sentence. And he would never forgive her for publicly horsewhipping his hero, Johann Most, when the anarchist leader refused to support Berkman's *attentat.*

"Mr. Schwab doesn't mind, I hear," she said, returning to the table. "He's fond of Emma."

Lawrence snorted. "How one can be fond of a viper, I don't know. A woman's place is by her man, making his home pleasant so he can think."

Bell put the potatoes on to boil. She hated when Lawrence talked this way. She had spent so much of her life resisting such ideas.

"Speaking of which, come make home more pleasant," Lawrence said. He took her hand and pulled her to him. Bell sat on his lap. She brushed the hair off his forehead and kissed his whiskey-scented mouth. As always, her pulse quickened at the taste and smell of him. It was out of her control, her lust, and she gave herself up to it again, every day, helplessly.

"Oh, I just remembered," she said, sliding an arm around his neck. "Lev says he'll look at your article. We have some space in the next issue."

"You call him Lev?" Lawrence asked, frowning.

Bell's heart skipped a beat. "We're very informal in the office," she said. "We're comrades, you know."

"Does he call you by your Christian name, then?"

His whole body was stiff, the earlier relaxation gone. Bell cursed herself for her slip. She got up and fussed with the soup. "Well, he called me Mrs. Birch for a year," she said. Seizing on that familiar wound, she turned. "Sometimes it's embarrassing for me, Lawrence. To call myself Mrs. Birch when they know very well I'm not married to you."

"Embarrassing?" Lawrence said, striking the table with his open hand. "For an anarchist? Ridiculous."

"No, it's not. I'm living in the world, Lawrence." Bell crossed to his side and knelt by his chair. "But it's not only that. I want to be your wife so much."

"You are my wife," he said. "In my eyes you are my wife. It is the individual that matters."

"I want to have your name. What if we should have a child? Lawrence—"

"You're trying to compromise my ideals as always! How like a woman." He seemed to rap out the charge mechanically.

"I'm only trying to be as much a part of you as I feel," Bell said softly. "In the eyes of the world, I mean."

"Bell, we've had this discussion before." He touched her hair softly. "You are my wife, my love." He leaned over and kissed her. His mouth opened, and he captured her tongue. Bell's insides melted, and she leaned into the kiss, feeling Lawrence's arms steal around her and grasp her to him.

"There, we are together," he murmured. "Turn off the soup, and let's go to bed."

Bell turned off the soup and the potatoes. He led her to the bed. Already, she was excited. He undressed her slowly, his hands lingering on her nipples. He left himself fully clothed, but he unbuttoned his fly. When she was naked, he pushed her down on the bed.

"Lawrence," she said dreamily.

"Don't speak. Lie down," he ordered. "No, on your stomach tonight."

She heard the slap of his belt as he opened it, and she gripped the pillow in the agony and delirium of waiting.

Twenty-Two

IT WAS OLIVE who forced Columbine to go to the Social Reform Gala. It was the event of the season for socialists, writers, settlement workers, and the society folks who supported them, an attempt to unite all the classes working for the same goal for one memorable evening. All of Columbine's old friends would be there—Ivy Moffat, now a force to be reckoned with in the taboo area of domestic violence, Florence Kelley and Lillian Wald from the Henry Street Settlement, Horatio Jones, Leonora O'Reilly, Josephine Shaw Lowell and Mrs. Russell Sage, who had worked so tirelessly in the suffrage movement. Even Elizabeth Cady Stanton, who left her apartment infrequently these days, was planning to attend. Olive couldn't understand Columbine's reluctance, especially since Elijah Reed was going to speak. Hadn't Columbine loved *Andersonville*, his novel about the Civil War?

There was nothing for it but to agree to go, even despite Ned's frown. He would not forbid Columbine to go, but he did not like it, and he made that plain.

Columbine dressed for the gala in her best gown, a shimmering green silk so deep it was almost black. Cream-colored lace edged the sleeves, and intricate black crystal beading embroidered the bodice. The dress was so pretty that she felt almost beautiful as Fiona helped her into it. When she looked into the mirror hopefully, her hands faltered as she fastened the small emerald earrings in her ears.

"Oh," she said, more an exhalation of breath than a word. Dull disappointment thudded through her. She hadn't cared about her appearance in a long time. Dressing like this, with her nerves in a flutter, had put her mind to the past, to six years before, when she was unmarried. She had somehow expected to meet the same face in the glass, a thirty-five-year-old woman fully in control of her power. But a forty-one-year-old matron looked back. Elijah would find her greatly changed. Columbine touched her hair, which seemed to have lost its brightness. She noted the fullness at her hips and the lines around her mouth. She looked at her hands, the hands of a mother and a nurse, capable, yes, but no longer slender and white. She shouldn't be ashamed of her hands; she was going to a gala where factory workers and settlement workers and nurses would be the guests. It was vain of her to bother about her hands. But she was bothered nonetheless.

"What is it, ma'am?" Fiona asked, adjusting the lace on a sleeve. "Don't you like the gown? I think it's lovely."

"Oh, Fiona." Columbine sighed. "The gown is lovely. But the woman in it looks so careworn."

What Columbine liked so much about Fiona was that, even in her capacity as a lady's maid, she was able to be deliberate and honest. Another maid would have fussed and flattered; not Fiona. She looked in the mirror with Columbine and gravely considered her appearance with narrowed green eyes.

"I don't agree, ma'am," she said finally. "Look at the sum, not the parts, if you know what I mean. You're a beautiful lady, Mrs. Van Cormandt. Now don't insult me by saying you're not."

Columbine had to smile. "Thank you, Fiona."

"Here, let me get your gloves."

That was one thing, at least a lady could wear gloves. No one would see the blister on her third finger from where Ned had spilled his tea, or the broken nail from playing with Hawthorn. Columbine buttoned up her long kid gloves and reached for her new fan of dark green silk. She took another look in the mirror. Maybe it wasn't so bad.

There was a knock at the door, and Olive swept in, dressed in her usual navy silk with the lace jabot. "The carriage is downstairs, Columbine. You look splendid. It's rather cold tonight, I'd wear your warmest wrap."

Columbine hid her smile as she slipped into her evening wrap, a heavy cloak trimmed with fur. Even when giving a compliment, Olive was completely matter-of-fact.

As they walked down the front stairs, Olive asked, "Do you want to say good night to Ned? I'll wait in the carriage."

"Yes, I should do that," Columbine agreed, though she would prefer not to. Ned had been so angry earlier this evening when she'd left him to dress. She suspected that he'd read in the paper that Elijah Reed was the featured speaker at the preceding dinner. They had not mentioned Elijah's name since their wedding day.

She entered his room hesitantly. He was sitting up in bed, a copy of the *McClure's* open on his lap. He barely took in her dress before he looked away.

"I've come to say good night, Ned."

"How kind of you," he said sarcastically, "to make my evening."

"Ned," Columbine said helplessly, "Olive insisted on my going to this."

He nodded shortly.

"I'll be home early."

"Don't bother," he said, turning away to lie on his side. "I'll be asleep."

Columbine stood for another moment, but Ned kept his back to her. Her silk skirts rustling, she turned away.

"Enjoy the dancing," he flung after her as she closed the door. Columbine leaned her forehead against it for an instant.

When she turned, she saw Fiona standing in the hall. The maid had heard everything, that was obvious. But Fiona didn't lower her eyes and scurry past Columbine. Some spark of empathy, some flashing accord, woman to woman, leaped from Fiona's eyes to hers. In that instant, Columbine remembered what she too often forgot—that Fiona's husband, too, had been injured in an awful blast, that he had remained an invalid for months before the attempt on Ned. James Devlin had died in prison within nine months of entering it. She wondered what Fiona's feelings were about her husband, though of course Columbine could not ask. Fiona had let her know years ago how painful it was for her to discuss James Devlin. It had taken the combined efforts of Columbine, Olive, and Ned to persuade Fiona that she was welcome to remain in the house, that they did not hold her in any way responsible for what her husband had done.

All of this went through Columbine's mind as she exchanged that short look with Fiona. She knew that Fiona had known guilt and suffering and how inextricably the two could be linked to make a particularly anguishing chain. She had heard the querulous voice, the jealous rage, the anguish of the bedridden, once vital man. She had known all of these things, her extraordinary green eyes told Columbine, and she understood.

He hoped she would be there, and yet he did not want to see her. Elijah straightened his tie for the thousandth time that evening, cleared his throat, and looked toward the door. He was supposed to be carrying on a conversation with Horatio Jones, but his responses were purely automatic. He was thinking of Columbine. Of course she must come, Columbine Nash belonged here tonight. Columbine Van Cormandt, he corrected himself hastily. He had never seen her, talked to her, as a married woman, and he did not think he particularly wanted to.

Not that he still thought about her in that way. The years had managed to reduce Columbine Nash to a burnished might-have-been studded with ifs. *If* he hadn't been the kind of man he was, *if* she'd hadn't been pregnant with Lawrence Birch's child, *if* he had had the courage at the end to beg her not to marry Van Cormandt, then, well, things would have been different, Elijah supposed. But he'd never spent time worrying about ifs and buts. He had devoted himself to his writing in a way he hadn't since he was twenty-three, writing *Look Away* in a fever. He had been heartsick and lonely and raging, and it had taken a while before those feelings dropped away, but they had. Paris seemed to intensify his feelings, but Elijah knew Paris, in all its melancholy, splendid beauty, was still a better place for him than New York. It had taken him six years to feel ready to return.

He looked over the head of Horatio Jones and there she was. Elijah's heart squeezed with pain, a pain so shockingly fresh he turned away for a moment to catch his breath. Columbine had been immediately surrounded by several women—he'd heard she did not go out much in society anymore—and she was flushed and laughing, kissing one woman after the other, squeezing their hands, and laughing again, somewhat taken aback at their pleasure at seeing her.

She looked exactly the same to him, not a whit older from across a room hung with rosy-globed chandeliers. Her blond hair was still that golden honey color, her skin still shone, and, if Horatio Jones would keep his damn mouth shut, Elijah might be able to hear that same, throaty laugh.

He waited for a break in Horatio's conversation and politely excused himself. Coughing again nervously, he headed across the room toward her, threading through the bright dresses and the perfume and the mustachioed men, seeing only Columbine.

Across the room, Columbine saw him. Her hands fell to her sides, and she stared, not caring, not knowing if anyone noticed. He was heading for her, and she didn't know what to do. She didn't think it would be like this. She hadn't thought about how it would be, but she hadn't thought it would be this awful.

He came up and nodded. "Hello." He wanted to say her name, but he couldn't quite get the words Mrs. Van Cormandt out. And it seemed, suddenly, just too intimate to call her Columbine.

"Hello," Columbine said.

He took her hand, but instead of shaking it, he merely held it for a moment and then let it go. He opened his mouth, but he didn't know what to say. If her eyes weren't telling him so much, he would have made small talk, or asked about Ned. But he knew that words would be inadequate, for her manner told him that she was just as affected at seeing him as he was by seeing her.

He could see now that she *had* changed, and he didn't care. She was still absolutely lovely. He saw that care and time had marked her, and that she was unhappy, and he wanted to pick her up and crush her against him. Unbidden, a thought of Columbine naked came to him, her skin damp, her hair wild down her back, looking up at him with that slow, drowsy smile she had after hours of love.

"Oh, Elijah," she said. The word came out slowly and softly, like a distant plash of oars on a still lake. *E-li-jah.* She might have added "my love," the tone was so intimate.

They were back in the bedroom of the West Tenth Street house, sure, at last, of what was between them. He was afraid to believe, longing to have, amazed at his luck. He was all of those things again, fresher and sharper than before. He had had six years of hunger in between.

"Columbine," he said. He reached for her hand again, and he brushed against her fingertips with his own. Even through her glove, she could feel the heat.

After Marguerite became a star, it was harder for her to meet her mother in secret. Once, at a restaurant on Second Avenue, she had been recognized. Marguerite scaled back her visits to one every few months and decided to risk coming to her mother's apartment, veiled and dressed in her oldest black coat. Jacob had moved up from the peddler cart and was keeping the books for a local butcher, and Sophie was able to arrange Marguerite's visits when he was out. Her mother was always so glad to see her that Marguerite usually spent the first half-hour trying to get over the guilt of not seeing her more often.

On a cold day in early December, Marguerite watched with relief as Willie went off to a luncheon with Maude Adams. Her suspicions had been allayed somewhat during the past weeks; Willie was as gay and offhand as ever. He was solicitious of her comfort, praised her new dresses, fetched her coffee in the mornings. The only thing that gave her pause was that they had not made love in awhile, she wasn't sure how long. Though the door between their adjoining suites remained unlocked, Willie had remained in his own bedroom. She would have to do something about that. Perhaps a new negligee from Paris, or a late supper in her room. She'd have to plan something, sometime.

Marguerite hired a hack on Broadway, relieved that she wasn't recognized. She got off on Canal Street and walked quickly through dark Ludlow Street to her mother's address. She was carrying a few presents, nothing that Jacob would notice, or, at least, what he would notice but not feel sufficiently enraged to throw away. Marguerite and Sophie had learned by trial and error what they could get away with to maintain the fiction that Marguerite was not contributing to the household in any way. A little bit of money, a cheese, some material for a winter coat. Once, she'd brought Sophie a new hat, and he'd thrown it out into the street.

She tiptoed past Mrs. Schneiderman's door, then ran up the last steps quickly. Two light knocks, and Sophie opened the door and held out her arms. Marguerite ran into them.

"I missed you, little one," her mother whispered. Tears were in her lashes as she held Marguerite at arm's length. "You get prettier every time I see you," she declared. "Come in, I made some cakes for us."

"Where's Papa?" Marguerite asked as she sat down at the kitchen table.

"Working. He won't be back until seven. And our new boarder is home at six." Sophie seemed happy as she bustled around the kitchen, warming the teapot, setting cakes out on a precious plate she'd brought from France.

"It seems as though he might keep this job," Marguerite observed idly.

"Take off your coat, love. I added extra coal, so you won't be cold. Yes, Mr. Cohen has turned out to be a gift from God. Even through these bad times, he hasn't let more than one of his clerks go, and him a bad worker anyway, and not married." Sophie set down the teapot in front of Marguerite. "And how is Mr. Paradise?" she asked.

"He's fine," Marguerite said shortly. "He's very busy." She rarely talked about Willie with Sophie; this exchange was made for politeness sake on both sides. Sophie hadn't disapproved of her marrying a Gentile, exactly. And she seemed to understand, or claimed to, why Marguerite wanted to keep her Jewishness a secret. Still, there was always a slight chill in the air when Willie's name was mentioned. It was hard for Sophie, Marguerite knew, for what was the good of having a successful daughter if one couldn't brag about her? So far, no one had connected Marguerite Blum with Daisy Corbeau. Marguerite had only lived on the East Side for a short time, and she'd been a rather nondescript, ungainly sort of child.

Sophie let out a breath and leaned across the table to examine her dress. "What a beautiful gown," she murmured in the respectful tone she reserved for clothes. "Such material. Is it from Paris?"

Marguerite nodded, pleased under her mother's scrutiny. It was getting harder and harder to come up with plain enough outfits for her trips down to the East Side. It was a delicate balance, finding a gown that would please Sophie without attracting too much notice on the street.

"I like the beading on the sleeve," Sophie said, nodding quickly as she scrutinized the garment. "I think I could copy it. Oh, you should have seen the fuss over the Levy girl's wedding. I was busy day and night making dresses. Everyone wanted to outdo the mother of the bride," Sophie said with a giggle. "That Mrs. Levy bragged so much about the groom I thought the neighborhood would hire one of those boys on Allen Street to hush her mouth."

Marguerite laughed and settled in for a good gossip. She nibbled at a seed cake. "Tell me about the dresses," she said. "What did you make, and for who?"

"Oh, for Mrs. Schneiderman I made a blouse, nothing fancy. They're having hard times, you know, with David out of work. But for Mrs. Fein—oh, Marguerite, you should have seen it. I copied that deep plum velvet dress you wore last time, do you remember? I used insets of green silk and some passementerie instead of the crystal. Of course, it wasn't as nice."

"I'll bet it was beautiful," Marguerite said. "What else?" she asked greedily. She loved to hear Sophie describe clothes in her sybaritic style; her mother was just warming up.

But the door opened, and Jacob Blum walked in. His eyes were on the floor, and he didn't see Marguerite at first. He set down his coat and hat on a chair.

With an anxious glance at Marguerite, Sophie rose. "Jacob? Why are you home?"

"Because Mr. Cohen has decided he no longer needs my services," Jacob said. "What is that—" He turned and saw Marguerite. "I should have known. It smells like a bordello in here."

Marguerite rose and began to gather her things. "I'll be going, Mama." She refused to engage with Jacob; she closed her mind against him as though it was a heavy oak door. She shut him out as she mechanically began to put her coat back on. In her mind, she was already walking down Ludlow Street toward Canal, hoping for a hack. Usually she would have to walk all the way to the Bowery. She was already taking in gulps of fresh, cold air while she walked.

Jacob sat down heavily at the kitchen table; he was too exhausted to yell. He put his face in his hands. "Don't I live with enough shame?" he asked in a low voice. "My life, my life. It's nothing. I have no homeland. No business. No family. What is a man without these things?"

Sophie went to her husband. She put a hand on his back briefly, softly. "You have a wife," she said.

"My house is full of whores," Jacob said, his face still hidden, and Sophie snatched her hand back and pressed it to her mouth.

Marguerite had paused by the kitchen door. She heard these things, though she did not want to hear them. But as she saw Sophie's humiliated face, black rage filled her heart. Jacob was turning on his wife now, without Marguerite there.

"You are an evil man," she said evenly to her father. "You are evil. You deserve nothing in your life, for you've made your women live a life of misery around you. Do you think God will forgive you?"

"Marguerite, hush," Sophie whispered, horrified.

"You're afraid of him, Mama," Marguerite said. "I am not. He's nothing but an old man. Dreaming of Odessa, not facing what he's become. I could forgive him his incompetence, Mama, but not his cruelty."

Jacob had not raised his face from his hands. "Go away," he said tiredly. His voice sounded unnatural. "Go away, both of you. Leave me."

Without a word, Sophie picked up her hat and coat. She followed Marguerite out the door and, putting a finger to her lips, led the way down the narrow stairway. She waited until they were out in the dark afternoon to speak.

"I'll walk you to the Bowery," she said as she buttoned her top button.

Marguerite nodded. She let the wind cool her hot cheeks. "Why don't you leave him?" she asked soberly. She didn't look at Sophie. "I could take care of you now. You wouldn't have to live on the East Side. I have plenty of money."

Sophie didn't speak for so long that Marguerite thought they would walk all the way to the Bowery and part in silence. She supposed that her mother was angry at such a suggestion. Leave her husband! Well, that was Sophie's problem right there, unable to conceive of a life without pain and misery.

When her mother finally spoke, it was in a meditative voice, and she said something that Marguerite had not expected at all. "There are things you don't know," Sophie said. "Things which might make it better for you or worse, I don't know. But may God punish me for what I'm about to say, I think I should speak."

A dart of fear nestled somewhere in Marguerite's ribs. "What is it, *Maman?*"

"It has to do with the Easter riots in 1871," Sophie said.

"The year I was born."

"Yes, yes, the year you were born, exactly. In December."

"What are you saying?" Marguerite practically snapped the question, irritated at Sophie's hesitation. "I've heard the story a million times. How you lived on pastries for two days. How Papa found you in the cellar."

"Jacob came home that day and found me in the cellar, yes. What I did not tell him was that the men upstairs had already found me. One of them had raped me. The others would have followed, but they were distracted. They were trying to push the piano off the balcony, and it proved difficult. That's when I ran downstairs. I suppose they would have found me eventually, but Jacob got there first. He didn't know what happened. Or what I mean to say is, he didn't want to know. He didn't ask what they did, and I didn't tell him. But I suppose he guessed. When you were born, nine months later, he talked so much about your inheriting his mother's black hair. He talked too much about it." Sophie ground to a halt.

Cold seemed to seep through her veins, freezing her responses. "Are you saying that Jacob isn't my father? Are you saying that some Russian drunkard—" Marguerite felt sick.

"I don't know, *ma petite*. Jacob *could* have been your father. We had made love the night before. That I remember clearly."

Her head down, Marguerite walked on, her skirt swishing above her boots. Why was Sophie telling her this? Why must she know? her heart cried. She didn't want to know!

"It wasn't until he saw you again that he began to change," Sophie went on. "When we arrived from France. I noticed it almost immediately. Perhaps he was wondering why you didn't look more Jewish, I don't know. Perhaps he was just defeated by his life, and the doubts began. But when you turned into a young woman, not a child, somehow that made him wonder and think. He confronted me, and I admitted the rape, finally. I could not hold out against him. He struck me, you see," Sophie said mildly. "And then he blamed me. He said I had encouraged it. Oh, you can imagine. Later he apologized, but the damage was done. I saw into his mind. I saw how completely he had changed. The world changed him, Marguerite. Everything he had pride in as a man had turned to dust. His brain, his abilities, his homeland, his Jewishness, his daughter, his wife."

"And so he turned against me," Marguerite said bitterly. "But aren't I innocent, Mama?"

"Of course you are. But," Sophie said, shrugging, "something turned in his mind, and he could not see that."

"Are you asking me to understand this, to forgive him?" Marguerite burst out bitterly.

"No. That's your decision. I'm giving you information, that's all."

"I don't know why," Marguerite said with a sob. "I don't want to know this, I can't know it—"

"But you have to see that it's not you. It was never you. It was me. It's still me, no matter how it appears. He can't do without me, and he hates me, but he can't say the things to me he says to you. Until tonight."

"But why does he hate you?" Marguerite asked, bewildered. "Why doesn't he hate that man?"

"Because of Roman Edelstadt," Sophie answered. There was only the barest hesitation in her voice.

"Mr. Edelstadt?" Marguerite asked, confused. Roman Edelstadt was the new boarder, a tall, quiet man with an enormous black mustache. He was a printer, Marguerite dimly remembered. He was trying to save money for his own place; he'd only boarded with the Blums for a few months. "Your boarder? What do you mean?" Marguerite asked. Then light dawned. "You mean—"

"Yes, that's what I mean," Sophie said. "We're together, Roman and I. And the only reason I'm telling you is that I don't want you to worry about your father anymore. Do you see why he said the things he did? Do you see that they have nothing to do with us? In the end, his suspicions were confirmed. I turned out to be a whore, after all."

They had reached the Bowery, and the bright lights hit Marguerite's eyes, dazzling her. She could not begin to understand what Sophie had told her, or what Sophie meant. The information sat in her stomach like a lump of lead. Her mother was sleeping with another man with a black mustache and big, ink-stained hands? Her real father was some faceless Russian Christian who hated Jews?

Sophie touched her arm timidly. "I love Roman, Marguerite," she said. "I never wanted Jacob to find out. But love is hard to hide."

Marguerite turned to Sophie. She hadn't noticed that her mother was still young, forty-three, and that during the past months she had filled out again, that her cheeks were pale pink, that her blue eyes were brighter. She hadn't noticed any of these things. Now, looking at Sophie, she did, and the sight enraged her. She didn't blame Jacob so much as Sophie, and she didn't know why. She hated her mother suddenly, hated her with all the irrational passion of a child. She thought of her mother lying with Roman Edelstadt and she felt sick.

"I have to go," she said. "I have to go."

"Wait, Marguerite. We should talk a bit. I'll walk with you." Sophie seemed desperate now, and she clutched at her daughter's sleeve.

"No, I have an appointment," Marguerite answered automatically. "It's very important. I must go." Raising her hand, she waved frantically at a hack, which clopped to a stop. Sophie still held her sleeve, and Marguerite brushed her off with a shudder.

"Don't touch me," she hissed fiercely, and she leaped into the hack. She could not bear to see Sophie's pleading eyes. She could not stand to see her mother. She didn't know if she could ever stand to see her again.

Never introspective, Marguerite burst into angry tears at her own inability to understand this reaction. She huddled in a corner of the cab, crying convulsively. Harsh sobs were wrenched from her, and she thanked God that the noisy street covered up the sound. She knew she had to gain some control of herself however. There was the lobby of the Fifth Avenue Hotel ahead, all resplendent light and glittering people. For the first time, Marguerite longed for a house. Privacy had never been something she craved, but she craved it now with all the desperation in her heart. If only she could pull up in front of a house on a quiet street, and unlock her very own door! If only Willie could be waiting for her in a quiet parlor, a glass of whiskey at his elbow and a fire in the hearth!

And then the longing for a home transformed into a longing for Willie. To pillow her head on his chest and feel his heartbeat, to feel his soothing hands on her hair, how she needed that! Willie would not care a fig if she was the product of rape, if she was Jewish or half-Jewish or Russian or French! He would keep on loving her, for he knew her through and through and loved her anyway. Just like Toby. Maybe that was why Toby understood Willie's love in a way that she did not. Maybe Marguerite could learn how to love, too. She was selfish and greedy and conceited, but selfish people could learn how to love, couldn't they?

These thoughts managed to dry her tears in a way that stern admonishments to herself had not. Through the confusion of her thoughts, Marguerite knew that she wanted Willie, needed him to help her sort it out.

Despite the urgency of her feeling, Marguerite didn't throw her caution aside. She had the driver pull up on a side street, instead of directly in front of the hotel. She thrust money at the driver and waited until he had pulled away before heading toward the corner. Willie should be back from his luncheon by now, however long it was. The gray afternoon had turned to dusk, and Marguerite drew her fur collar up against her face and hurried, hoping no one would stop her.

She was almost to the side entrance of the hotel when the door opened. She stepped back and melted into the shadows, for a person was leaving, a woman. She was well-wrapped against the winter cold, but as she moved forward Marguerite saw the sheen of her hair under an exquisite hat, bright red-gold hair, and slowly, she recognized Mollie Todd. But why would Mollie leave by the side entrance? You'd think since her career had been eclipsed in the early eighteen-nineties, she'd crave all the limelight she could get. Why wasn't she sweeping through the lobby, showing off that beautiful hat?

The door banged open, and another figure ran out. "Mollie!"

Marguerite's hand fluttered to her throat. It was Willie.

He ran lightly toward Mollie and pressed something in her hand, a wisp of lace and satin. Marguerite heard Mollie's low, throaty laugh.

"Now don't go thinking I left it on purpose, Willie," Mollie said, leaning toward him. "It's just that you make me forget things, darling."

And then Willie smiled, and put his hands around her neck, and drew Mollie toward him for a swift, warm kiss that seemed full of affection. When he drew away, she took him by the tie and pulled him back to her, and they kissed again, half-laughing. Mollie turned away and walked quickly down the street, with Willie watching her go, and with Marguerite still standing there, hope, urgency, need, everything draining from her slowly as she watched Willie staring at another woman and realized for the first time how very much she loved her husband.

Twenty-Three

If Ned noticed Columbine's better spirits, he did not mention it. Columbine did not make plans to see Elijah after that evening. It was enough that they had looked, and touched; they would see each other again. She resolutely set her mind no farther than that. With all her former notoriety as a scarlet woman, she did not think she could take a lover while Ned was an invalid. She could not find happiness that way. Perhaps seeing Elijah occasionally would be enough. But even that short meeting had given her energy. She became more involved in Safe Passage House, and she found that she enjoyed life again. She was better with Hawthorn, and she was more patient with an even more depressed Ned. Olive had been right, as usual.

With the end of December came heavy snows. Columbine was often unable to venture out of the house at all. She spent her time making up lost hours with Hawthorn, who was delighted to find her playful, high-spirited mother was back again. They had a festive birthday party for her with Olive and Ned, and then the Christmas preparations began. Columbine and Hawthorn plotted surprises and secrets, with Hawthorn carried away with the sweet knowledge of her own importance as she decided on the very best gifts for her father and her beloved Aunt Ollie.

The few weeks of tranquility ended abruptly with an invitation for a Christmas Eve open house at the Valentine-Hartleys. Columbine was going over the daily mail with Ned in the breakfast room while Olive was engrossed in the paper by the fire. She was about to put the invitation automatically in the "to be refused" pile when Ned stopped her.

"Wait a minute, Columbine. I think we should discuss this."

Columbine looked over her spectacles at him. "Discuss it? Ned, you know I don't call on the Hartleys."

"Exactly why this invitation is significant. They're making the first gesture at healing the breach. The Hartleys and the Van Cormandts have been close for generations. We have cousins in common. And Ambrose has changed since his heart attack."

"And Maud has not," Columbine said dryly. "She's still the silliest woman in New York, which is saying a great deal indeed."

Ned sighed and pushed away his teacup. His thin face looked weary, as though he'd already had the argument in his mind with her and had been exhausted by it. "Columbine, I want you to think about Hawthorn for a moment. Next year she goes to school. There will be parties and affairs to attend. And later, there will be suitors to choose from."

"Ned, she's six years old—"

"I'm thinking of her future, Columbine. She's a Van Cormandt. Sooner or later, she's going to realize what that implies. There are certain houses she'll be invited to, certain friends she'll make. And if she feels excluded from any of those houses, it will affect her. Do you see what I mean?"

"Why should she feel excluded from Maud Hartley's house? If she's worth her salt, Hawthorn will be flattered."

"Columbine, we're talking about a young girl," Ned said with asperity. "And Maud Hartley is a silly woman who happens to have a six-year-old daughter. Both of them could make things very difficult for Hawthorn. Do you want our daughter to be ostracized?"

"No, of course not. But I want her to recognize quality. She doesn't have to be welcome in every house in New York, Ned."

"Yes, she does!" Ned raised his voice, and Olive looked up from her paper.

"Ned, please don't," Columbine begged. She did not want to excite him; it tired him so these days.

"She's my daughter," Ned continued in the same angry voice. "She's the last in the line of a very old family. She has responsibilities to that name, and a social place. You can't ignore that, Columbine, even should you wish to. Ignoring it will only cause trouble for her later."

Columbine turned to Olive for support. "Olive, surely you agree with me. The Hartleys are such an awful example. We can pick and choose our friends."

Olive sighed. "I'm afraid, since you asked my opinion, that I agree with Ned, Columbine."

"Olive! I'm surprised," Columbine said, confused. "You can't abide Maud Hartley."

"But I see her," Olive pointed out. "I make it a point to go to her teas occasionally and her large parties. We're on the same board at the museum; we belong to the same charities. Columbine, I simply can't ignore society, unless I drop out of it completely, and that's something I don't want to do. There are Maud Hartleys, yes, but there are also Amelia Seldens," Olive said, naming a close friend who Columbine admired. "Society is a patchwork, not a monochrome."

Columbine frowned. Words Darcy had said to her years and years ago floated into her mind. As a Snow and a Grace, Darcy had been the social equal of the Van Cormandts. When she had been ostracized after leaving her husband for Tavish, she had sadly said, The Four Hundred isn't just a block of society on a ridiculous list. It's made up of individuals, Columbine. Individuals I've grown up with and loved. Individuals who can break my heart.

"There are certain things that Hawthorn will have to do," Olive continued calmly. "When she's older, she can choose her own life."

"But I never thought—"

"Well, you must think," Olive interrupted brusquely. "Think what it will be like when she goes to school, when she makes friends. Look where she lives, Columbine! We're not in Greenwich Village. We're on upper Fifth Avenue. This is your daughter's world."

Columbine stared at the invitation in her lap, biting her lip. But I don't want this to be Hawthorn's world, she thought in anguish. "I understand what you're both telling me," she said slowly. "And I will consider it. But I cannot go to this party. After that night, I swore I would never cross Ambrose Hartley's threshold again."

"I'm afraid I must insist, Columbine," Ned said.

At the steely tone in his voice, Columbine looked up sharply. "You're ordering me, Ned?" she asked. "What happened to your promises when I agreed to marry you?"

Olive stood, folding her paper. "If you'll excuse me," she said quietly, "I have some letters to write."

Ned waited until the door had closed behind his sister before he turned back to Columbine. "I must step in when I see you doing wrong," he said. "Hawthorn is my daughter. I am still the master of this house—"

"The master of the house! Ned, you've never used such language to me."

"I never needed to, Columbine. But I feel very strongly about this, and I must insist."

Columbine's face was stony, and her hands were quiet in her lap. "I do not take well to orders, Ned."

Relenting, Ned put his hand over hers. "Request, then. You need not stay long. But please go with Olive. Hawthorn is included in the invitation, you know. It would be good for her to meet other children. We are not enough for her, Columbine. Look at her party—just three of us old folks are not the best company for her."

Columbine sighed, knowing Ned was right in that. But she felt trapped, half-angry, frustrated, unwilling. She wasn't sure what was right, and she trusted Olive's good sense. And thinking of all she owed Ned, how could she refuse? She needed to think of Hawthorn as his daughter, not Elijah Reed's. "All right, Ned," she said. "I'll go."

As a supposed atheist, Bell found her reaction to Christmas puzzling. Yearning swept over her when she glimpsed a lighted tree behind a window, and she felt like bursting into tears when she saw people rush by her, their arms full of packages. It helped to work on the East Side, where there were few Christians, but around Tompkins Square lived some Christian German families, and their holiday cheer depressed her.

Politics had taken the place of religion in her life, but it had left a spiritual void. If Bell did not believe in God, for Lawrence had proven to her how such a belief contradicted her commitment, she nevertheless missed that belief. She found she still believed in the soul, and if she believed in the soul she believed in transcendence, but if she believed in transcendence she must believe in a higher force of some kind. It was all very puzzling. Next year, Bell decided, she would read philosophy. She felt a hunger for abstraction; she lived in a world of specificity, and she was discovering that it could, at times, be inadequate. Her mind was fed and her soul felt barren.

Bell was thinking these thoughts on Christmas Eve as she translated an extract from Zola into English and then Russian. It was difficult work, and though she tried to concentrate, her mind kept wandering. Outside her windows she could sense the quickening pulse of the city, as people finished up their work and looked forward to family and song and presents the next day. She would work on Christmas Day. Here at *Di Fraye Gezelshaft* it was like any other day, though Lev had delicately mentioned she could have the day off, if she wished. He confessed that though an atheist, he observed Yom Kippur in his own fashion. But what was the use of taking Christmas off when Lawrence would only disapprove, forbidding her to mention the holiday or buy him a little gift?

She heard low voices and laughter coming from Lev's tiny office, and she raised her head. Something about the laugh was familiar. Something from the past, something happy, warm with possibility. She couldn't place the feeling, and shrugging, Bell bent her head over her work again. Sentimentality was part of the season, she supposed.

But then Lev walked out of his office, and with him was Horatio Jones. "Look, Bell," Lev said, with a broad smile, "an uptown journalist wants to do an article on us."

Bell knew immediately that Horatio had known she worked here. His face did not show surprise, only a slight nervousness.

"Mrs. Birch, Mr. Jones." Lev made the introduction, and Horatio put out his hand.

"Mrs. Birch, it's good to see you again."

"Ah, you two know each other."

"Yes," Bell said. "In another life."

"In another life," Horatio echoed, smiling at her, and at the sight of his smile, Bell was suddenly very glad to see him.

Lev's quick dark eyes darted from Bell to Horatio. "Bell," he said, "I know you don't observe the season, but why don't you leave early today? There's nothing that won't wait until tomorrow."

"Thank you, Lev," Bell said gratefully. She didn't think she'd be able to concentrate on Zola anyway. Lev went back to his office, and she looked back at Horatio, smiling. "It's good to see you, Horatio," she said quietly. "You look well."

"You're as lovely as ever," Horatio lied, for Bell, though still beautiful, had lost something in the past years. Perhaps it was that serene, otherworldy look in her amber eyes. And she was much thinner, too. He could see her collarbones through her shirtwaist, and that swell of breast and hips that had been so alluring was gone. Her body seemed more angular. But she was still so womanly, with her long sweep of lashes and her abundant hair, her graceful hands.

"You're a terrible liar, Horatio," Bell said. There was a sardonic twist to her smile he'd never seen before.

That smile was painful to him. "Yes," he said softly, "I lied. You're even more beautiful to me."

Confused, Bell looked away, blushing.

"If you're leaving," Horatio said quickly, "would you let me buy you coffee, or tea? I know—a glass of sherry, to celebrate the season."

"I don't celebrate Christmas anymore," Bell said, taking her coat off the rack behind her.

"Well, I do," Horatio said, his brown eyes dancing. "So come on."

He took her to a small hotel on Broadway, near Astor Place. It was a respectable place, and Bell noted that there were other women there, drinking sherry with gentlemen friends or other women. She let Horatio press her into having one, and she was glad when she felt the warm, nutty taste slip down her throat. She hadn't had a glass of sherry since she'd lived with Columbine.

"This is lovely, Horatio," she said. "Thank you."

"Are you happy, Bell?" he asked suddenly. His gaze rested on her earnestly.

"Yes, of course," she answered composedly. "I enjoy my work.

And it's good to be out of jail," she added with a laugh. "Every day I wake up relieved to find I'm free again."

"It was a long sentence," Horatio said. "And the attempt on Frick didn't help your parole any, I'm sure."

"Yes," Bell said distantly, "I was due for parole, and the country went crazy about anarchists, so I didn't get out." She still couldn't speak of her disappointment without feeling that agony. She had lived for the day of her release, and it had been snatched away from her. She couldn't think of it now. She remembered turning her face to the wall, lying on her cot, not able to speak for days.

She looked around at the pleasant, warm room, as if for reassurance. "I'm here, however," she said. "It's behind me now."

"What about now?" Horatio asked. "Are you happy with him?"

The smile left her eyes. "Yes, of course I am. He's a brilliant man."

Horatio nodded; he did not point out that Lawrence Birch's brilliance had managed to escape every major figure in the anarchist movement. "Tell me," he said briskly in his reporter's voice, "is it discouraging to be an anarchist these days? After Berkman's *attentat*, the movement really slid into a decline in America. Especially since *Fraye Arbeter Shtime* closed," he said, naming the former foremost anarchist weekly.

"Only temporarily, we hope," Bell said. "But yes, it is somewhat discouraging. With the depression of '94, people's minds are on surviving, not ideology. But the seeds for renewal are planted, nonetheless. How can the people fail to see that the capitalist system is crushing them? That cooperation based on love is the only way economics makes sense for the many, and not the few?"

"You sound like a Nationalist, not an anarchist," Horatio observed. "Actually, you sound like Columbine."

"I take Edward Bellamy's ideas and push them a necessary step further. That's the anarchist ideal—cooperation, harmony, and peace. You're smiling, Horatio, and I find it extremely annoying."

"I can't help it—I find utopias pleasant dreams, not achievable realities. Besides, I'm a newspaperman. That's practically synonomous with cynic."

Horatio smiled so charmingly she had to laugh. "Well, we'll

never agree on politics," Bell said, "but I'm glad that we're still friends."

"As am I." Her hand was on the table, and he wanted to cover it with his own. Horatio forced his attention back to her face. "When did you marry?" he asked. "I didn't know about it. I suppose I should congratulate you."

"We married last year," Bell said quickly. She couldn't tell Horatio that she wasn't legally married to Lawrence. "And thank you."

An awkwardness passed between them. Horatio drained his tiny sherry glass, and Bell sipped at hers. "Another?" he asked, though hers was still half full.

"No, thank you. I should be going—"

"Of course. Can I find you a cab?"

"No, I'll just walk over to the El."

Glad to be moving, Bell gathered her coat and scarf. The cold air hit them as they left the hotel, and a few flakes of snow fluttered down against the white sky.

"Have you made any plans for Christmas?" Horatio asked, pulling on his gloves.

"No, no. I told you, I don't celebrate it any longer."

"Of course." They turned toward Cooper Square and began to walk. Two women walked by them, bags full of packages in their arms. The packages were wrapped and beribboned, and the women were murmuring excitedly. One of them said something, and the other laughed, a high, clear sound. "Do you remember Christmas at Columbine's?" Horatio asked in a meditative tone. "I don't think I've spent such a happy Christmas since. She always overdid the decorating, remember? That little parlor smelled like a pine forest. And all the food! I suppose it was her English Christmases. Oranges with cloves, apples, figs, gingerbread . . . and the three of you, Marguerite, you, Columbine—even in the lean years, giving such wonderful presents. Remember the year Columbine gave Marguerite that mauve cashmere shawl? She burst into tears."

"That was the last year we were together," Bell said.

"Was it? I suppose it was. How strange, I remember it as a happy time, and I was miserable, if I recall."

"Yes, I made you miserable," Bell said. "And it still pains me to think of it."

"Does it, Bell? But you were only honest with me."

"It pains me," Bell said with difficulty, "because had I taken what you offered, I think somehow I would be a happier person today."

He fumbled for her hand and pressed it quickly, then dropped it. "We can't choose who we love," he said. "I learned that."

"Yes," Bell said. "We can't choose who we love. We can only choose our friends."

"Perhaps we can be friends now," Horatio said.

"Perhaps we can," Bell said softly, knowing that it was impossible. Lawrence wouldn't hear of it.

They came up to the steps of the El, and they stopped. Bell turned to him. She looked young and pretty, with color in her cheeks from the wind, some wisps of brandy-colored hair escaping her black hat, snow falling around her. The expression in her eyes was very sad when she looked at Horatio. He knew that he had never known, would never know, what really drove her. And he still loved her just the same.

He opened his mouth to speak, then closed it. He took both of her hands in his. "Merry Christmas, Bell. And the happiest of New Years."

She gave the slow, gentle smile that he loved. "Merry Christmas, Horatio."

Columbine waited while the chattering guests filtered out of the Hartley's second-floor salon toward the tables set with candies and sweets set up in the gallery amid the Rembrandts and the Courbets. She stood by the French doors, looking out at quiet Fifth Avenue. The sky was white; it had been threatening snow, and only a few stray flakes had fallen. The moon was a round yellow circle, slowly rising over the branches of the trees in Central Park. Something about the night reminded her of the last time she had stood in this room, so miserable on New Year's Eve, in her fine gown and in the midst of all her confusion about Ned.

That night had begun everything, she knew now; she'd met Lawrence that night, she'd fought with Ned, and Elijah had come the next day. That night had precipitated the crack in her relations with Ned that had turned into a chasm. Funny how things could change, on just one night.

Things had not turned out as she'd expected. She had married Ned after all, and was now entwined in this aggravating role of New York society matron. She'd never expected that. Now Maud Hartley still simpered at her, but without the same superiority. Columbine was married, and somehow respectable in Maud's eyes, and she would be polite, for all she did not like Columbine. She almost missed Maud's acidity now, the tartness that had told her she did not belong.

Impulsively, Columbine opened the latch and walked out on the terrace for a moment. She remembered the horror of that night so many years ago, when the explosion had moved against their skin, the first explosion that had changed her life. Was this what the next century would bring, she wondered, such sudden, careless violence in the middle of plenty? If the world didn't change, perhaps.

Now, standing on the terrace, Columbine remembered that night clearly for the first time. She remembered having a cashmere shawl around her shoulders, she remembered how Ned had tenderly kissed her fingers under the cover of darkness. And she remembered smoke, and an acrid smell in her nostrils, the panic when the explosion had happened, the screams of the women. A woman had run across the street, shrieking, and Columbine realized with a shock that of course the woman had been Fiona, her maid, running full tilt toward her husband. And then, for the first time since she'd thought about that night, Columbine suddenly remembered leaning over the railing and watching a tall man walk rapidly down Fifth. With a slow, rolling sense of shock, Columbine realized that the man had been Lawrence Birch.

It was impossible. It was a piece that didn't fit. She must be remembering wrong. But Columbine closed her eyes and remembered the walk, the way the head was held on the neck, even the hat, and she was almost certain.

"Columbine?" Olive poked her head around the door. "What are you doing? It's freezing out here. Come inside, Hawthorn is looking for you. She got a prize in the fruitcake."

"Yes, Olive," Columbine answered mechanically. She turned

away, but she took one look back at the view of Fifth Avenue. The man she'd seen had been Lawrence Birch, she was sure of that now. But what she could do with such information, or what it meant, she had no idea.

Christmas Day was one of the few times Marguerite and Willie found themselves alone. Later, they would meet Toby at the Waldorf hotel, where they'd treat him to the most lavish Christmas dinner in the chef's power. There was always a slight edge of melancholy to Toby on Christmas Day, though Marguerite didn't know why.

Christmas morning was a time for Marguerite and Willie to be together, a family, sharing tender tokens of affection. It was a time that called for pure hearts and unstudied generosity, and so it was a time of awkwardness for them both. But what would the papers say if they knew Mr. and Mrs. Paradise could not bear to be alone together, even on Christmas Day?

Marguerite pulled out a house gown of patterned velvet in a deep shade of sapphire blue. The high collar of Valenciennes lace framed her pretty pointed chin, and worn over the dress as a sort of cape was a caftan of white satin which came over her shoulders in front on either side to the floor, like flowing scarves. In back, a train heightened the drama. Marguerite wove blue velvet roses through her hair, which she left loose. She left her ears and wrists bare in expectation of the new jewels which would soon adorn them. She was the picture of feminine grace, ready to graciously preside over the family Christmas. If only she was going out on stage instead of into the drawing room of a hotel suite she called a home, to meet a husband in the midst of a torrid affair, under a Christmas tree that had been bought and decorated by hotel staff.

Marguerite stared at her image, her hands arrested in the act of straightening a curl. I don't like my life, she thought. Toby is right, after all.

The knowledge cut her like a knife. She had told herself over and over that she was happy, for she had achieved everything she'd ever wanted, and it would be horrible of her not to be happy, almost as horrible as she really was inside.

Her success hadn't been without effort, of course, but it hadn't been very hard, either. She'd been in the theater long enough to have heard stories from other women of transgressions worse than what Edwin had done to her. She had simply been too naive, too blind to see the inevitable. And Edwin had been too weak. He was fat and married now, to Georgina Halstead. He had come backstage one night, sent roses to her for a week, and she had ignored him. Marguerite wondered briefly if Edwin were happy, then returned her attention to her own sudden, surprising pain.

If only she had Willie. If only she could go to him now, sink to her knees, and beg him to start their marriage over again. Toby, under pressure, had admitted that Willie's affair was common knowledge. That everyone was waiting to see what she'd do. That Mollie had said that she was damned if she'd give him up again for a woman who didn't love him. Marguerite had heard all these things as though Toby had stabbed her repeatedly with a knife. She moved about like a sleepwalker; for once in her life she could not form a plan to get what she wanted.

It was more than Willie, it was her lack of home, of child, of real friends other than Toby, of anything to anchor her life beyond the stage where she kicked her legs every night to roars of masculine approval. She missed Columbine, and sometimes she even missed Bell. If she had Willie, she could begin to plan those other things, a home, a child—maybe—a circle of friends who truly cared about her, not about Daisy Corbeau, but Marguerite. That night she had come home from Ludlow Street had changed her; she kept the picture of a home in her mind, a real building, with carpets and curtains and cushions.

And then she closed her eyes, an image rushing to the front of her consciousness. It was there always now, crowding out any other thoughts. It was how Willie had stood in the cold, hatless, coatless, and watched Mollie walk away. Mollie hadn't even realized her lover was still standing there. But he hadn't moved until the last flick of velvet cloak had vanished around the corner. Who did that but a man in love?

Then she heard, faintly, noise from the drawing room. Willie was tinkling at the piano. He was waiting for her. They would exchange Christmas gifts, gifts of guilt and propriety. Marguerite averted her gaze from the sight of her empty eyes and moved to her door. She went down the hall and pushed open the double doors to the drawing room. He was seated at the piano next to the tall, handsomely decorated tree, picking out "Silent Night" with a finger.

"A happy Christmas, darling," Marguerite said, crossing to him and kissing his cheek.

"Merry Christmas."

"Shall we have some eggnog, or some punch? They brought up both this morning."

"Some punch, I think."

Marguerite poured out two glasses of punch. She hadn't much use for Christmas. She had racked her brains for facts in the beginning, trying to remember what the Gentiles had done in France so she could invent family stories about past Christmases. But then she'd realized that her memories bored Willie, and she'd stopped. Now, the only good things about Christmas were the presents, and the opulent dinner with Toby afterwards.

"Come, sit by the fire," she said to Willie. "Let me give you your presents first."

He sat obligingly in the big brocade armchair while she piled presents around him. He opened them one at a time and thanked her dutifully for the cashmere dressing gown, the delicate gold dress watch, the softest linen handkerchiefs, the ruby stickpin and studs. Marguerite felt disappointed in his restrained reaction; finally, this year, she had taken time to pick the presents herself. Not since their first Christmas together had she spent so much time and effort.

"I thought the rubies especially fine," she said, hoping for a bigger reaction. "I can't wait to see you in your evening clothes."

"Everything is beautiful, Marguerite. Thank you." He leaned over and kissed her on the forehead. His lips were dry and cool. He reached into his inside pocket and took out a long, flat box. "Here, this is for you."

Smiling uncertainly, Marguerite opened the unwrapped box. It was a pearl choker, five perfectly matched strands, with a sapphire and diamond clasp. The pearls were breathtaking, it was exactly what she would choose herself, but Marguerite felt tears start behind her eyes. "Thank you, they're magnificent," she said in low voice, her face bent over the box. If only she could imagine Willie picking them out joyously, waiting hopefully to see her face. The way he'd been, half-shy, half-expectant, when he'd given her the sapphire engagement ring. Had he loved her once, then?

"I thought they suited you. Here, let me fasten them for you."

Marguerite turned obediently and let Willie fasten the pearls around her lace collar. Was this her only present, then? she wondered. Of course, they were fabulously expensive, she was sure, but couldn't Willie have picked up a few other small things, just to show he'd actually cared enough to shop instead of wandering into his favorite jeweler and pointing to something expensive in a case?

"Oh, yes, and you also have a standing order at Worth's for a new opera cloak and gown," Willie said. "You have only to choose what you want."

Marguerite nodded. Now she really wanted to burst into tears. She could order an opera cloak any time she wanted, and Willie knew it. But perhaps she was being ungrateful. She wanted this Christmas to be real, to be happy.

"Try on your new dressing gown, darling," she urged him. "I want to see it."

She helped him out of the silk brocade gown he wore, and Willie slipped into the cashmere one. "Perfect," Marguerite said approvingly. "You look very handsome."

"I feel quite elegant," Willie said. "Too bad I can't wear it to Christmas dinner. Can I get you more punch?"

"Yes, thank you." Marguerite folded over the dressing gown in her hands jerkily, wondering why everything felt so stilted, like a bad play. She felt something bulky in the dressing gown pocket, and she slid her hand inside. She fished out a slender book of poetry. *The Love Poems of John Donne* was embossed in the red leather cover. She didn't know Willie read poetry. Curious, Marguerite opened the book, and written on the flyleaf in an unfamiliar hand was: W, The words may be another's, my darling, but the sentiments are wholly mine. All my love, M.

Rage almost lifted her from the floor. Her scalp prickled and her hands shook. Willie turned and saw her face, saw the open book in her hands. He looked alarmed for a moment, then merely watchful.

She closed the book with a snap. "'All my love, M.' Well, I know it isn't me."

"No," he said evenly, "why would it be you?"

"Mollie Todd. Everybody knows about her, don't try to lie."

"I told you I'd never lie to you, Marguerite."

"Hah!" she spat. She shook the book at him. "And does this make you honest, Willie?" she taunted him. "Does this make you a good man, to be faithless but not to *lie* about it?"

Willie put down the two cups of punch. "Really, Marguerite, it's not as though your record is spotless."

But I didn't love any of them! she wanted to cry. Then why had she done it? Vanity—perhaps. Boredom—sometimes. Why had this all started, this contest between them? If Willie blamed it on her, she blamed it on him, and what did that get them?

Willie turned away tiredly. "So, is this little scene done now? Toby should be here soon."

"No, it's *not* done," she shouted, and he turned back, startled. "Not in the least. How dare you bring this into my home? Mollie Todd, that has-been!" She was trembling now. "How dare you humiliate me, how dare you drag my name through the mud, how dare you—" A great sob choked her, and she flung the book into the fire.

Willie leaped across the room, rudely pushed her out of the way, and thrust his hand into the fire while she screamed. He grasped the book where it lay in the embers and pulled it out, dropping it on the hearth, where it lay, singed but still intact.

"How dare *you*," he said, his face contorted with rage. He took a dangerous step toward her. "You silly, hard-hearted little bitch. You've been in every bed on Broadway. You've bedded every one of your leading men who would have you. What right do you have to say even one word of reproach?"

"It was different," Marguerite sobbed. "Different—"

"Why?" he demanded. "Why?"

"Because I didn't love them!" she screamed. She swiped angrily at her cheeks and faced him, defiant, half-afraid. There, it was out. Now he would know everything. That she wanted him, that she wanted his love.

Willie burst out laughing. He leaned against the piano and

laughed, a hard, cruel, mocking kind of laughter. Marguerite put her hands over her ears. She could not bear to hear it.

"Who are you to talk of love?" he asked contemptuously. "You've never loved anyone in your life."

"That's not true. I love Toby," Marguerite said, because she could not tell him that she loved him when he was laughing at her.

He laughed again. "Yes, you love Toby. He's your little pet, isn't he? You tell him your secrets and you buy him ties and you patronize him. Have you ever wondered how he lives, Marguerite? Who he sees, who he loves, what his passions are? Did you know he nursed his mother for two years and she died in his arms on Christmas Day two years ago? She was a great talent, fifty times better than you, and forgotten today—perhaps you might want to meditate on that. Did you know that Toby nursed a broken heart last year over that good-for-nothing Gregory Von Meter?"

"Why, he laughed about Gregory," Marguerite said nervously. "He said it was just a sad *contretemps*, whatever that is."

"He wouldn't tell you the truth," Willie said quietly. "You don't want to know the truth. You only want to talk about yourself, and when you don't talk about yourself you want to hear something lively, something gay. You have no curiosity about anything but your own concerns, and you have no tenderness."

"How dare you say such cruel things to me! Just because I won't sleep with you often enough," she flung at him contemptuously. She wanted to hurt him now.

One corner of his mouth lifted, and his hazel eyes were hard. "I wouldn't have you if you begged me on your knees, Marguerite. You don't know the first thing about what can be between a man and a woman. You've never become a woman. Some necessary thing hasn't happened. You're a still a child."

She tossed her head. "You didn't think so once."

"I'm not talking about sex," he said impatiently. "My God, can't you understand anything?"

"And Mollie Todd does, with her books of poetry and her inscriptions?"

He picked up the book with such tenderness she almost screamed at him again. "Yes, Mollie does. Perhaps it was best for her, not becoming a star. She had enough money to settle down in a little house. She took in her niece, a young girl, when her sister died. She is actually interested in things other than the theater, Marguerite. She talks well; she interests me. She knows about the theater, too, and not just what's a hot ticket on Broadway. She gave me Ibsen, she reads Shaw—you don't even know these people, do you?"

"Of course I do, damn you. And that Shaw play, *Arms and Men*, or whatever it was, barely ran two weeks last year, so who cares? Anyway, since when are you interested in bluestockings, Willie?"

Willie gave a thin smile. "Perhaps I'm growing older, I don't know."

"So I'm not smart enough for you, is that it?" Marguerite asked bitterly. "So that gives you the right to stray."

Now Willie only looked sad. She almost wished he would look angry again. "Marguerite, that's not what I mean. I wouldn't care if you never opened a book in your life if—" He stopped abruptly.

"If what?" she challenged him stoutly, but her voice shook. "If what, Willie? If I would let you do as you please? Well, I do let you do as you please, and look where it's got me. A box of pearls and humiliation."

He cocked his head and studied her as though she were a specimen. "I thought our arrangement was satisfactory for you, Marguerite. What about Teddy Clinton?"

"I don't love Teddy Clinton!" she shouted. "And you love Mollie Todd!"

Willie looked honestly puzzled. "What do you want, then?"

"I want you to love me again," she shot back. The words came out with no tenderness, only petulance and fury. She wanted to snatch them back. She put a hand to her mouth and bit on a knuckle.

Willie stood, staring, searching her face. The room seemed terribly still except for the sound of their breathing. "Did I ever say that I loved you?"

"I hoped that you did," she whispered. "I want it back, whatever it was."

"I'm sorry, Marguerite," Willie said finally. "I don't think I can oblige you. I wasn't terribly good at being a lapdog."

He spoke lightly, and she knew what her response should be.

She should tell him that she didn't appreciate him once, that she didn't know. That he was right, that she was selfish and vain, and that she needed him to teach her how to love, in the way he'd taught her how to eat a formal dinner, or how to dress, or how to sing. Lightly, teasingly, sternly, lovingly, generously. She should ask him to hang on, just a little bit more. She should ask him to dredge up a little more faith, if he could. And most of all, she should tell him that she loved him.

But what if she told him and he laughed in her face?

Hesitation marked her face, and Willie turned away in disgust. And as he turned, the door banged open, and Toby lounged in.

"Merry and happy, everyone. I must warn you that I'm prepared to drink several bottles of champagne, all by myself." He stopped, taking in Marguerite's white face, the way Willie was resolutely looking away. "Oh, dear," he said. "I knew this habit would get me into trouble. Perhaps I should go out and knock?"

Marguerite gathered herself up. She was an actress. She would be on stage today, after all. "Don't be silly, Toby," she said, turning toward him. Her voice sounded gay and slightly breathless. "It's nothing important. You've saved us from a quarrel on Christmas Day, so you're most blessedly welcome. Have some punch while I run and change. We'll have the merriest Christmas ever!"

Twenty-Four

THOUGH LAWRENCE WOULDN'T celebrate Christmas, Bell talked him into an inexpensive dinner at a small local restaurant to quietly celebrate the new year. Under the influence of wine and a succulent roast chicken, the indefinable sense of distance between them melted, and Bell, peeking into his ice-blue eyes, was relieved to see relaxation there for the first time in a long while.

On his third glass of wine, Lawrence even grew somewhat expansive. "This restaurant reminds me of another," he said, looking around at the cheerful fire, the small room, the checked curtains at the window. "It was in California. I went there with my mother. It was at a railroad stop."

"How old were you?" Bell asked a neutral question, hoping that Lawrence would keep talking. He never mentioned his past, and questions about it were forbidden.

But Lawrence's customary wariness of any attempt to pry into his past wasn't there; instead, he frowned, thinking. "I suppose about ten or eleven," he said.

Hardly daring to breathe, Bell asked, "What was your mother like?"

Lawrence took a bite of chicken. "I was a camp meeting child," he said offhandedly. "Do you know what that is?" When Bell shook her head, he continued, "At a revival meeting, the product of the moaning and the writhing can be sometimes more than, shall we say, a personal commitment to God. It's a rather more human connection, if you get my meaning, and voilà—a child is produced. That was me. My mother hooked up with this preacher, Herbert Thomas Bellows, something of a charlatan, as you might imagine. He advocated free sexuality, of course, at least for the men. When the Civil War started he took his followers into the Texas hills. He had several wives, including my mother. He believed that his children were the next tribe of Israel."

"And what did your mother think?"

"My mother thought he was God. She thought I wasn't good enough to be his son. She tried to mold me into his likeness with her fists."

Shock snapped her spine straight. "Lawrence—"

"Oh, yes, her Larry was a great disappointment. And then one day Bellows took off in the middle of the night with all of the church's money and one of his wives. Went back to California. My mother took me and followed him, but he didn't want her. Said he couldn't be sure I was his son. My mother," he said, his mouth twisting strangely, "blamed me for it."

"What happened? Did she—"

"Beat me? Yes, she did," he said blandly. "Many, many times. We lived in the same town in northern California as my father. On the other side of town. He ignored us, told the town my mother was crazy. They all loved him, so they believed him. Funny thing is, she started to turn crazy then, if she wasn't already. No one would talk to me. Not one person, isn't that funny? Because my mother said such vile things about that nice Reverend Bellows. I left when I was fourteen. Went to San Francisco. Burned down my father's house on the way." He said this flatly, spearing a potato with his fork. "It was my first experience with the Propaganda of the Deed," he said, chortling and almost choking on his potato. He took a long sip of wine.

"You never told me this," Bell said slowly. She was thinking of Lawrence as a little boy, beaten by his mother, rejected by his father, living as an outcast in a small town. His childhood had been a horror, as hers had been. Sorrow and tenderness washed over her. "How awful it must have been," she murmured.

"It wasn't bad," Lawrence said. "Shut up about it, Bell, will you?"

But she looked at him, clear-eyed. "It's why you understand me, isn't it. It's why we belong together."

"I suppose so. Eat your chicken, we can't afford to waste this meal."

Happily, Bell cut a piece of chicken and ate it. She felt close to Lawrence tonight, closer than she'd felt in years. For once she didn't worry if he regretted staying with her, or if he loved her at all. The sweet afterglow of a lover's confidence animated her, and she poured more wine for them and smiled at Lawrence lovingly.

He broke out into a soft smile. "How pretty you look tonight, Bell." He put his hand over hers, and she felt its warmth like a thrill deep inside her. She was overjoyed to find her love renewed. The thoughts of Horatio that had tormented her with doubts flew away as though they'd never existed. She had actually wondered if she'd made a mistake, those years ago!

The bell on the door of the restaurant tinkled, and Bell looked up and saw Lev enter with another man she knew, Morris Steimer. Damn, she thought, exasperated. She should have gone farther afield to eat tonight. Why had she stayed on the East Side?

Lev's dark face lit with pleasure when he saw her. He touched Morris's arm and they moved toward them.

"Good evening, Mrs. Birch," Lev said. At least Lev didn't use her first name.

"Good evening, Mr. Moiseev, Mr. Steimer." Bell wondered frantically if she must ask the two men to join them. "You know my husband, Lawrence Birch, do you not?"

Morris Steimer bowed. "I've not had the pleasure."

Already in a good mood, Lawrence's handsome face was full of welcome. He'd resented Bell's acquaintance with these distinguished men. Of course he'd reviled them behind their backs, but perhaps they weren't so bad after all. He shook hands with Steimer and Moiseev. "A pleasure," he said. "Would you care to join us?"

Lev looked quickly at Bell, then shook his head. "That's kind of you, but no. We have some things to discuss, and," he added playfully, "I have a rule never to interrupt a couple at dinner." He turned to Bell. "Actually, Mrs. Birch, we're discussing Kropotkin's visit to America. You've been so helpful with the plans. We wanted to ask you if you would sit on the dais with me, Edward Brady, a few others. Maybe say a few words? We remember your speech at the last meeting at Schwab's so well."

Bell didn't dare look at Lawrence. "I don't think so, but thank you," she said quickly. Her eyes begged Lev to go away.

He bowed. "Of course, this is not the time to discuss it. I'll see you at work on Monday. Good evening, Mr. Birch."

Lawrence nodded stiffly. The two men moved off to the back room of the restaurant. Bell stared at the tablecloth, her shaking hands in her lap.

He leaned over the table. "Give me your hand," he said.

She tore one hand out of the other and hesitantly put it in his, underneath the table. He squeezed it.

"So you are among the chosen, Bell, and I didn't know it," he said, squeezing her hand with increasing strength. "You give speeches at Schwab's and you will be among the honored few to sit on the dais while the Prince himself speaks."

"Lawrence, you're hurting me," she gasped. She thought he would break the bones in her hand if he went on. But the pressure only increased.

"And you didn't tell me. That is the betrayal, my darling wife, that you kept things from me. I cannot trust you, and I cannot love whom I cannot trust." His hand tightened even more on hers, and she bit her lip so that she wouldn't cry out. Her head was down, almost to her plate now, as the steady pressure went on. Tears started from her eyes and dripped onto her chicken.

"I have given you chance after chance, and you've disappointed me," he said. The pressure let up, just a bit, and his hold began to relax. Her hand was already throbbing. He dropped it abruptly and she brought it back to cradle it in her lap.

"You're a lying whore," he said. "You're probably the mistress of all of them, for why else would you get that far?" He stood.

"Lawrence, please don't go, please." She was crying in earnest now, not caring who saw. "Please."

"You look so ugly when you beg," he said, and turned and left the restaurant.

Fiona heard the signal as she was putting together the tea things for after dinner. A low whistle, repeated every two minutes or so.

Lawrence was outside, waiting. She checked the clock impatiently. She couldn't possibly get away now.

Luckily, everyone was busy either serving or cooking, for the Van Cormandts were still at dinner. Not bothering to fetch a shawl, Fiona eased out of the kitchen door and, shivering with the blast of cold, she ran to the stable. She skirted the corner and there he was, sitting on the ground in all this cold.

She crouched beside him and touched his shoulder. "What is it, love?"

"You have to get away."

"I can't, we've only started dinner—"

"You have to!" he said coldly, and she smelled wine on his breath. "Tell them something, anything. Just run. Now!"

The force of his words sent her back to the house at a run. She stopped outside the door to compose her face, then went back inside. The cook was bending over the roast. Fiona had long ago nestled her way into the woman's good books. Now, she would have to test how far her loyalty would go.

She staggered a bit and hit the table. Mrs. Plumb turned around. "What is it, Fiona?" she asked, turning back to the roast again.

Fiona came to her side. "I've had some very bad news," she said rapidly in a whisper. "My brother-in-law just called outside to tell me my sister is very ill. She's asking for me. Oh, Mrs. Plumb, she's all I have left in the world, you know."

"Maybe after dinner the master will let you go," Mrs. Plumb said.

"But I can't wait that long. My brother-in-law is leaving, and I'd be afraid to go downtown alone at this time of night. Mrs. Plumb, could you cover for me? Could you tell Mrs. Campbell that I took sick and went upstairs? I'd only be gone a few hours, I promise. You know how afraid Mrs. Campbell is of catching sick, she'll never come upstairs." The older woman hesitated, and Fiona widened her deep green eyes and put a sob in her throat. "I'd be ever so grateful to you. You know how I feel about family," she ended sorrowfully, for Mrs. Plumb had a large collection of sisters and brothers and nieces and nephews that she wrote to regularly.

"All right, dearie. I'll leave the door off the latch for you. But be quick, now. And wrap up warmly when you go."

"I will. Thank you." Fiona pressed the cook's meaty red hand for an instant, then ran from the kitchen.

In three minutes, she was out again by the stable, dressed in her warmest clothes. "Come," Lawrence said.

It was too cold to stay outside, so they struck out across the snowy park to the West Side, where they knew a small tavern. Lawrence ordered brandies, and they found a seat by a large, roaring fire. Fiona held her cold fingers to the blaze.

Lawrence sat back in his chair, cradling the brandy between his legs. He watched the play of firelight on Fiona's blazing hair, orange-gold on orange-gold. She turned, and the light caught that tiny triangle of gold in her left eye. Funny how Bell had faded, but Fiona had only grown more beautiful. She was a striking woman, Lawrence realized. Fiona was a good mimic; living in the Van Cormandt house had been a training ground for her. He could see how much more graceful she was in her movements now, more like a lady. Her posture and attitude defied her class now, and she had lost her angry defiance. Instead, she had copied something of Columbine's combination of elegance and easiness.

"What is it, Lawrence? Why are you gazing at me so?"

Her lilting voice washed over him, ran through his veins like the warm brandy he was drinking, and Lawrence suddenly felt better. The raging fury he had felt at Bell was still there, deep in his gut, but Fiona was here, and that was a balm of sorts.

"It's that woman, isn't it," Fiona guessed shrewdly. She would never mention Bell by name. She jerked her head back to the fire. "When are you going to do it, Lawrence?" she asked flatly. "When are you going to leave her? At first it was because you couldn't write bad news to her in jail. And then it was because she was too weak after she got out. And then it was because she was too fragile. And now it is because she brings in money for us. But I don't want her money anymore, Lawrence. I want you in a proper fashion, not sneaking around the city like two rats underground."

He didn't want to talk about this. Lawrence drained his brandy and signalled for another.

"I killed my husband for you," she said moodily, staring at her hands as she held them to the flames.

"Don't be melodramatic," he snapped.

"I'm going to hell, most likely," Fiona continued, not even hearing him. "I'm going to hell for you, Lawrence. You laugh at my religion, but you can't know how I'm tormented."

Lawrence took the second brandy off the tray and raised it to his lips. "You can always leave," he said.

She shot him a look of pure green ice. "You know I can't do that. I can't compound my sins."

"You know I don't want to hear about sins and penance and all that gibberish," Lawrence said tiredly. He reached out his hand and touched her back gently. "Fiona," he said softly, "I came to you tonight because I needed you." Her muscles tensed. "Come upstairs," he said. "They have rooms here."

She gave an almost imperceptible nod. He made the arrangements while she waited by the fire, and he led her upstairs to a small, sparsely furnished room. It was clean, though a bit cold. Fiona removed her hat but kept on her coat. Lawrence heaped more wood on the fireplace and the fire blazed more brightly. He hefted the thin mattress and laid it on the floor in front of the fireplace. Beckoning to Fiona, she came to him.

She knelt on the mattress and he knelt opposite her. Slowly, he unbuttoned her coat, smiling at her maid's uniform. He ran his hands over her breasts and her narrow waist, then ran them deliberately down her legs. Her head arched back and he saw her swallow. He placed his lips on her throat and kneaded her breasts through the wool of her dress. Fiona moaned and reached for him roughly. They kissed, their mouths wide open and moaning. They undressed quickly, breathing hard, watching each other. When they were naked, he pushed her down and covered her slight body with his own. Her red hair was a blaze against the white sheet, and her deep emerald eyes were wild. She looked feral, depraved, as she always looked during sex, the personification of the bad woman for him, of every perverse desire he'd ever had, and he loved her and hated her as he took her with a cry like an animal's cry.

Columbine smiled at her daughter. "But you already had Christmas, Hawthorn. And your birthday wasn't long ago. You can't ask for more presents, that would be greedy."

Hawthorn shook back her blond curls and fixed her black eyes on her mother challengingly. "But what if I'm a greedy little girl, Mama?"

Columbine quickly changed a smile into a deep frown. "Well, then, you'd be a bad little girl, wouldn't you? And you'd probably be sent to your room so you could think of how to be better."

Hawthorn nodded thoughtfully. "If I did that," she ventured, "could I have a pony?"

"Certainly not," Columbine replied. "If you came out of your room and asked for a pony, you didn't understand the lesson at all."

Hawthorn leaned against her knee. "But why can't I have what I want, Mama? Is there a *reason*?"

Hawthorn's enormous dark eyes were serious; she was a little girl who was tremendously fond of reasons. Quicksilver in her moods, creative in her play, she was nonetheless fiercely interested in the logic of things. And when she wanted something, she wanted it passionately.

Columbine helplessly looked over Hawthorn's head at Ned. His green eyes were laughing at her, and he shrugged.

Resting her head on top of Hawthorn's lightly for a moment, Columbine considered her reply. Why *couldn't* Hawthorn have what she wanted? If her mother couldn't, couldn't she at least give her daughter her heart's desire?

"Because it's not fair if just a few people have everything they want, when so many have so little," she answered automatically. "Remember when we went down to the East Side together? Remember how you said you didn't need as many dolls?"

Hawthorn nodded. "But I never said I'd give up a pony," she answered logically. "Besides, where would any little girls downtown keep a pony? Their houses are so close together." She ended on a triumphant note, and looked at Columbine expectantly.

Columbine gave up; sometimes, it was easier. She had a feeling that come spring Hawthorn would have her pony. Ned spoiled the girl. But then again, Columbine had had a pony when she was young, as well. Perhaps it would teach her daughter responsibility. "Didn't Aunt Olive want to read with you before tea, lovey?" she asked. "Why don't you go knock on her door? She's probably waiting for you."

Reminded of this precious engagement, Hawthorn ran from the room. Columbine turned to Ned with a smile. "She gets the better of me sometimes," she said.

Ned laughed. "She gets the better of all of us."

He looked almost well when he laughed; almost like the old Ned. The pinched look left his mouth, and his green eyes were sharp, the way they used to be, before painkillers had dulled them. Ned had been terribly low lately, and seemed to be in more pain than usual.

"It's good to share a laugh together, Neddie," she said in a sudden burst of affection.

Ned looked uncomfortable. "Yes, it is," he said shortly. "So much so that I . . . hesitate to bring up a sore subject."

"Oh, dear."

"The Bradley-Martin Fancy Dress Fete. I notice we got an invitation this morning."

"Oh, Ned. We're not going to argue about this, are we?"

"I dearly hope not. Are you planning to accept?"

Columbine sat up. "Accept? Surely you can't be serious. Ned, this is the most vulgar, *criminally* ostentatious affair I've ever heard of. Have you read the bulletins in the newspapers about the money they'll spend to transform the Waldorf into a replica of Versailles? The tapestries, the jewels, the flowers! The money they're spending on the orchids alone is staggering—five thousand orchids, Ned, think of it when so many are out of work! I can't go to such an affair. It would be against everything I stand for. Now, I went to that awful Christmas party at the Hartleys for you, I drank their punch and introduced Hawthorn to their horrid little girl, but this is too much."

"It will be the most important event of the season," Ned said soberly.

"But dear, it's not as though the Bradley-Martins are an old Knickerbocker family. If they were, they wouldn't be giving such a party."

"But nevertheless, everyone is going."

Columbine tried to control her temper. It was bad for Ned, but oh, this was infuriating! "Don't you value my reputation at all?" she asked him in a low, furious tone.

"That is precisely—"

"Not my reputation as Mrs. Ned Van Cormandt. My reputation as Columbine Nash. Ned, that's important to me. I won't be seen there. It would be morally repugnant for me to add my support. The whole thing makes me sick!"

"You must start going to these things, Columbine. You can't keep saying this about every large affair it's your duty to attend—"

"It's my duty to draw a line! It's my duty to hold to my convictions, not prostitute myself to gain my daughter points in a game of which I do not approve!"

"You've already done that," Ned said in a sudden flash of hot anger. "You married me. Wasn't that prostitution? Why are you balking now?"

She stared at him for a moment, shocked at his words. "Oh Ned, what's become of us?" Columbine asked sadly. She turned and walked from the room.

She went upstairs, but she could not stand the solitude of her room, stuffy and warm from the fire. She needed to walk. She gathered her things and rushed out, not caring that they would wonder why she did not appear for tea. She couldn't stand them now, not Ned, not Olive, with her quiet agreement to forcing Columbine to bend to the yoke she surely must have anticipated would be placed upon her. It wasn't fair of her to resist, she raged as she walked quickly down Fifth Avenue in the cold afternoon. Hawthorn was a Van Cormandt. She was the latest in a long line of proper ladies and gentlemen, not the illegitimate daughter of a rebellious, radical novelist.

She wasn't surprised when she found herself hailing a hack and traveling downtown. She wasn't surprised when she found herself at Elijah's door. But she was surprised at the sight of him when he opened the door. It was just that his face had lived in her dreams for so many weeks that it was odd to see it, fresh and clear on a dusky afternoon.

"Come in," he said.

"You're working."

"No, I've finished. Columbine, will you come in," he said with half-laughing impatience. "I'm freezing."

She walked into the parlor and stood in the middle of the room the same way she'd done that first time she'd come. "You've kept the same house. I'm glad."

"I'm glad you're here," he said quietly. His dark eyes were so like Hawthorn's they made her want to weep.

"I don't know why I'm here," she said, roaming about the room absently.

"I haven't called or come by because I did not think Ned would particularly want to see me. But I've thought of you every day."

"And I've thought of you every day," Columbine said, picking up a letter opener and putting it down again.

"I thought it was enough, just being able to think about you again," Elijah said. "But now I see you here, and I know that it's not."

Columbine stood at the window, looking out on quiet Eleventh Street. "I don't know what will happen with us."

"Nor do I," he said. "But I know what I want to happen."

She stopped and looked at him. "What?" she asked, with all the ingenuousness of a child.

His smile was slow and certain. "What do you think?"

Desire rushed through her. She stood, simply staring at him. "Oh, Elijah. Oh, my dear."

He took a step toward her and took her in his arms. His lips were very close to hers, and his eyes held the same passion.

"Don't," she said breathlessly. "Please, don't."

Another man would have kissed her. But Elijah let her move back in the circle of his arms. He kept his arms around her lightly, but even the suggestion of how they held her, could hold her, excited her.

"If you kiss me, I won't be able to stop," Columbine said. "I know that better than I know my own name. But I also know," she said painfully, "that I can't. I can't, not while I'm married to Ned. And I can't divorce him. So there we are," she finished, looking him in the eye. "I suppose that's what I came to tell you. That I still love you dreadfully. And that there's no hope."

"Where there's life, there's hope," Elijah said gently. "Columbine, you've placed me in an impossible position. I want to be your lover. But this time, I also want to be your friend. Perhaps we should start there."

They exchanged a rueful smile. "If we're going to start there," she said weakly, "would you please release me? I never claimed to be a saint, you know."

Marguerite woke at dawn. She lay alone in her bed and watched the light come up. She was wide awake, though usually it took her three cups of strong coffee to feel ready to leave her bed. In the first months of their marriage, when she'd woken in Willie's bed, he'd brought the coffee to her, padding out to the front room when the waiter knocked. He didn't want anyone to see her in the morning, he said. She was too beautiful, he said, too perfect. And he did not want her to dress for propriety's sake.

Marguerite closed her eyes, remembering the deep, languid morning love she and Willie had made. She pressed her legs together and turned over in bed, remembering. There had been such laughter and tenderness between them then. Color flooded her cheeks when she remembered Willie's words on Christmas Day: I wouldn't have you if you begged on your knees.

Abruptly, Marguerite threw back the covers and ran to the mirror. Her hair tumbled around her shoulders, and she brushed it just enough to look becoming, though it still looked tousled from sleep. Then she quickly slipped out of her satin nightgown.

Naked and barefooted, she ran across the carpet and hesitated only a moment at the connecting door to his suite of rooms. Hearing no sign of movement, she pushed it open cautiously.

He was still asleep. Good. She padded across the carpet as softly as she could. His face turned away from her, bare to the waist and probably naked under the covers, he slept on the far side of the bed. Holding her breath, she slid underneath the covers and moved carefully toward him.

She slipped one bare arm around his side and nestled her head against his bare back. He stirred, just a bit. She slid her hand along his front until she found him, satiny and soft, and she stroked him in a whisper-soft movement. She pressed her lips against his back and touched his skin with her tongue. He groaned, still half-asleep, and he shifted so that he was more exposed to her. Carefully, Marguerite slid around his body so that she was facing him.

She trailed her mouth down his chest. She licked and stroked as softly as a kitten.

"Marguerite," he said thickly. "What—"

She didn't answer, but continued her movements. She touched him with love and great tenderness, and he swelled in her mouth and hands and surrendered to her with a groan, holding her head between his hands and whispering "damn you" through clenched teeth, finally bringing her up against his body so he could see her, feel her completely.

They made love with the old passion. She had him, Marguerite thought, delirious with her desire, her legs wrapped around him. Her husband, her man, she had him, he still must love her, he must, he must. . . . And then it was over, and she was limp and bathed in sweat, and she was kissing his shoulder, not even aware that he was lying slack on top of her, not reciprocating her kisses, his face turned toward the wall.

Marguerite managed to convince herself that her marriage had been renewed. It wasn't necessary to talk about it, she told herself. How she hated people who had to talk about things endlessly! Willie hated that too. They were in complete communion now; they knew that the lovemaking that morning had signalled a new beginning.

Marguerite considered the proof of this when Willie had agreed so readily to going together to the Bradley-Martin ball at the Waldorf. Lately, they had gone to affairs separately, as was perfectly proper these days. But this was such an extravagant, splashy affair, sure to be great fun. Like everyone else, Marguerite gossiped about the preparations avidly, discussing what everyone would wear and how many jewels they would sport. The guests were all supposed to come as figures from the French court, but that did not stop Mrs. Bradley-Martin from confiding her intention to impersonate Mary Stuart. Her bow to the French theme was a ruby necklace once worn by Marie Antoinette.

Marguerite enjoyed the delicious question of her costume for several days. She toyed with the idea of going as a simple peasant girl, but she longed to wear her new pearl choker. Willie was no help. He answered all her musings with the statement that she would be lovely no matter what she decided. His replies seemed rather wooden, but Marguerite knew he was busy these days deciding on a new show.

When Toby asked her how things were with Willie these days, Marguerite could reply airily that all was well, and not be disturbed in the least by his worried nod.

Marguerite hummed her way to the theater one late January day. Her role in *The Lady Pirate* was becoming tedious, and she was looking forward to cajoling Willie into finding a new play for her. Her maid Celeste helped her into the satin dressing gown she wore while she put on her makeup, and she hummed the bars of the opening song as she reddened her lips and reached for her powder puff and Celeste laid out the ragged trousers which showed off her pretty calves.

There was a short knock at the door, and Teddy Clinton looked round. "You're here early," he said.

"Mmmm, there wasn't much traffic on Broadway. And I've been cutting it too close lately."

"I've finished with the paper, if you'd like it," Teddy said casually. He tossed it on the sofa. "See you on stage. Good audience tonight, I hope."

"See you later, Captain," Marguerite called gaily. She was glad that Teddy had stopped by. He had been petulant when she'd ended their affair, but obviously he'd gotten over it. She finished her makeup and went to the sofa, where she idly picked up the evening paper. She settled back against the cushions. Teddy, of course, had been reading the society pages, and her eye ran down the columns, searching for an amusing bit she could tell Willie later. Ah, here was the latest news about the Bradley-Martin ball.

Slowly, Marguerite rose to an erect position as she read that Miss Mollie Todd, once the toast of Broadway, had accepted the invitation of Mrs. Bradley-Martin and would appear at the ball dressed as Madame DuBarry, with a diamond and emerald necklace designed by M. Gustave Carteret, who just happened to be Willie's favorite jeweler at the moment.

Through a fog of bewilderment, she heard Teddy's voice directly outside her door. Teddy's teasing of the chorus girls was legendary.

"If you're not careful, I won't take you to the Bradley-Martin fete," Teddy said, as the girl laughed in a high-pitched squeal that got on Marguerite's nerves.

"Oh, and I'd wager you're not even invited," she said. "It's hard to get an invitation, especially for the likes of you." She laughed again as Teddy apparently made a face.

"It's not *that* hard to wrangle an invite, *if* you know the right people. Mollie Todd is going, and she's not even a star anymore. Maybe I'll get Willie Paradise to get me invited, too," Teddy said, and with another high-pitched giggle, the couple moved away from the door.

Celeste was smoothing out her gown for the second act. Their eyes met across the bright blue cloth. Celeste's face was scarlet; she was fiercely protective of Marguerite.

"Never you mind them," she said. "That Teddy Clinton doesn't know what he's talking about. He meant you to hear it, madam."

Marguerite didn't answer. She looked down at her hands, smudged with newsprint, and, looking up, she caught sight of her face in the mirror, grotesquely bright in her theatrical makeup. She knew that Teddy had stood outside her door deliberately, that he had spoken those words just to hurt her. But she also knew that what he said was true.

Twenty-Five

LAWRENCE HAD COME home late the night after the argument. Bell had been in bed, but sleeping had proved impossible. She'd smelled brandy on his breath, and something else, something unfamiliar that she might have thought was sex but was more likely perspiration and the smells of a barroom on his clothes. He undressed sloppily and came to bed. She didn't speak, afraid of his reaction, but she was relieved when he reached for her. But his touch was rough, and she stiffened. He flipped her on her stomach and lifted her flannel shift and took her when she was still dry and closed to him, roughly, angrily. Her mouth opened with the pain, and she bit the pillow. Dry sobs shook her body, sobs of shame without tears. He fell immediately asleep.

Bell awakened early that morning, and with only a shawl around her thin flannel shift, she washed herself, shivering at the cold water on her thighs, wincing when it stung. She sat in a kitchen chair with an untouched mug of tea and thought for the first time in a long while about Columbine's accusations of six years before. For the very first time, she faced the fact that they might be true. Lawrence's brutality the night before had given her a window into his mind. There was an engine which drove him which she knew nothing about. The thought frightened her, and she didn't want to face it.

But then Lawrence awakened, contrite, sick, his handsome face pale underneath its stubble. He shambled into the kitchen in his trousers, his suspenders trailing. He was so miserable, so like a child, and touched her hand so tenderly she was confused. Still angry, she made his breakfast in silence. He ate, drank an entire pot of tea, and then looked at her with those startling eyes, now cloudy with remorse.

"I've been thinking," he said. "I think we should get out of New York. We could go to Europe. Italy."

Too annoyed to speak, Bell sat quietly, hiding her impatience. She knew Lawrence was waiting for her usual immediate approving response, but she had to think.

At first the ridiculousness of it irritated her, but slowly, Bell began to consider it. Italy. It seemed so far away. That could be good, actually. But neither of them could speak Italian. She knew French and Russian and Yiddish—couldn't Lawrence pick a more convenient country? "Italy?" she asked.

"We could live cheaply there," he said, encouraged by the fact that she was talking to him. "It's warm. And the movement is strong there, Bell. It's growing, it's open to new influences. I wouldn't run into the same prejudice I do here." She made an impatient movement, and he saw that he'd taken the wrong tack. "But that's not important. We're important. We'd have sun and new hopes, not old influences. We'd marry, have a family."

"Marry?" she echoed.

"We'd have to, it will be easier for emigration purposes. Besides, Italy is a damned papist country. Bell, it would be a new start for us, can't you see that?"

"But how could we afford it?"

"We could borrow the money," he said.

"Borrow money?" she said, baffled. "But we don't know anyone with money."

"We know Columbine Van Cormandt," he answered.

Columbine asked the butler to repeat the name twice. Bell had rebuffed any attempt at meetings after she'd been released from prison. Columbine had been rather hurt at the time, but she supposed that as long as Bell continued to live with Lawrence Birch, relations between the two of them were impossible. But why had Bell shown up at her door?

"Show her in the morning room, please." Columbine picked the small room for its cheerfulness and warmth. It was snowing today, and a bitter wind was shaking the bare branches of the trees across the way in Central Park.

When she walked into the room, Bell turned. Columbine saw the changes in her face and her heart constricted with a fine pain. Bell looked tired and too thin. Deep shadows were under her eyes, throwing her pallor into relief. But her amber hair and her lovely eyes were the same, now with a sad beauty instead of their former sheen. She was nervous, and ironically aware of her nervousness; one arched brow quirked at Columbine in the old way. It was her old friend, her very dear friend, and Columbine felt moved at the sight of her.

"I'm so very glad to see you," Columbine said, and before Bell could draw back, she embraced her.

Something about the open friendliness, the familiarity of the hug made something break inside Bell. Tears welled in her throat and she leaned against Columbine's shoulder, feeling comfort there. A dry sob shook her body.

"What is it, dear?" Columbine murmured. "How can I help?"

Bell began to weep against Columbine's shoulder. She could not stop herself, and as she wept she realized how long it had been since she'd been able to cry. Was it since she'd met Lawrence? She didn't know.

Columbine patted her back like a child. Bell could feel that her old friend's body was rounder, and she suddenly remembered that Columbine was a mother, that she had borne Lawrence's child. Bell pushed away gently. "I'm so sorry," she said.

Columbine took her hand and led her to the small sofa in front of the fire. She gave her a clean linen handkerchief and waited until Bell had dried her face and blown her nose a few times.

"Now," Columbine said, "tell me how I can help you."

"I need money," Bell blurted out. "I'm so terribly sorry to come to you like this, but I don't know where else to go. I want to make a fresh start, Columbine. Everyone in New York knows me, knows my face—or maybe I just feel that they do. Everyone connects me to the bombing, even though I wasn't even tried."

"Yes, memories are imperfect. Once you've been in the paper, they can say anything they want about you, and they usually do," Columbine agreed. "I know that all too well. But what about Mr. Birch?" she asked hesitantly. She didn't even like to say his name.

Bell looked down. "We plan to go together. It was his idea, actually. But Columbine," she said earnestly, looking up, "I've thought and thought about it, and I think he's right. Not just for the reasons he says. But for me. New York is so oppressive for us now. But perhaps in Italy things would change between us. Patterns would be broken and re-formed, and pressures would ease. We'll marry and have a family, like a real couple at last."

Columbine stared down at the toes of her boots. She could not quite believe that Bell was coming to her for money to run away with the man who'd attacked her. But Bell had never believed that story. And she was in trouble.

"I don't think I understand," Columbine said finally. "Wouldn't living in a foreign country cause more pressures between you? You'd be thrown upon each other for everything then."

Bell leaned tiredly against the sofa back. "It's hard to explain, Columbine. I think I need to go to some strange place I've never been in order to find a new way to live. It's so hard to break out in the small cluttered rooms, among the same tired routines. I know it isn't . . . good, what we have. But it can change, anything can change."

"Bell, forgive me if I offend you. But if you want me to help you leave Lawrence, you know that there's always a place for you here," Columbine said, placing her hand over Bell's. "Or at Safe Passage House. Let me help you, Bell."

Bell shook her head slowly. Her voice was wooden. "I can't leave him. He's part of me. The best way you can help me is to do what I ask. I know I have no right to come to you, no right at all, except that once we loved each other."

"Then you have every right to come," Columbine said quietly. "But Bell, I'm worried about you. I don't know if this is the right thing." It was the most she could say. It felt like old times, to be sitting in front of a fire with Bell, discussing what should be done. Formerly, it had always been Columbine who was doing the confiding. But the same conversational rhythm was there, the same feeling, and though the circumstances were extraordinary, to say the least, Columbine drew a sense of comfort from the fact that Bell had come to her when in need. The friendship was a faint, flickering heartbeat, but it was there, alive between them.

Bell squeezed her hand. She hadn't expected to be so truthful with Columbine, but then, she hadn't expected so much open warmth from her old friend. "You must trust me when I tell you I don't know any other way," Bell murmured. "I can't leave him."

Suddenly, Columbine was afraid for Bell, and fear pushed her into irritation. "How do you know that?" she cried. "You speak as though you had no will, as though you were trapped. But nobody's trapped in anything, Bell." A shuttered look came over Bell's face, and Columbine stopped. Though she'd like to say more, she had a feeling Bell would bolt if she did.

The shuttered look passed, and Bell looked merely sad. "I don't feel trapped," she said slowly. "I don't know if you can understand this, Columbine. But I feel that the world is a world of strangers, and Lawrence is the only face that is familiar to me. That's how it's become. He *is* me. In all the world, I could never find a soul like his, so attuned to mine. He knows my baseness and my goodness, and he accepts all of it. I'd live for him and die for him, no matter what he does."

Columbine wanted to shake her. "But these are abstractions, Bell. These are desperate, romantic dreams. You aren't looking at him, you aren't seeing him, you're seeing something you're projecting *onto* him. He's treating you badly, I can see it. Look at you! I can see your misery, even if you cannot."

Bell stood and gathered her gloves. The intimacy that had sprung up between them again was gone now. Her face was stony. "Then you won't help me, after all?"

"Yes, I'll help you," Columbine said wearily. "I'll give you whatever you need, and you don't have to worry about paying it back."

"I'll pay it back."

"Whatever you want, but please be assured I don't expect you to."

"Thank you, Columbine," Bell said stiffly. "I'll be in touch when I make arrangements."

She held out her hand, and Columbine shook it. She would

have liked to embrace her again, but she knew that Bell would not welcome such a gesture.

Bell turned to go, then hesitated. "There's one more thing," she said. "It's awkward, but I must say it."

"You can say anything to me, Bell."

"It's about your child."

"Hawthorn?" Columbine was puzzled. "What about her?"

"I know that it seems ridiculous, seeing how things are. But I want you to know that if anything happened, we would take her. I just wanted you to know that. And I'd be a good mother to her, Columbine."

"But why would you take Hawthorn?" Columbine asked, baffled.

"Because she's Lawrence's daughter," Bell answered calmly.

Columbine stared at her. "Is that what you think? Is that what you've thought, all these years?" She reached out and grabbed the back of the sofa. "Oh, Bell."

"Columbine, you needn't dissemble. It's all right, really."

"Does Mr. Birch think this?"

Bell's mouth was a thin line. "We haven't discussed it."

Columbine straightened. "Bell," she said urgently, "Hawthorn is not Lawrence's child. I told you once that we never had an affair, and that's the truth. But even if you don't believe that, please believe that Hawthorn is not his. You've only to look at her to see it."

"I hear she's blond," Bell said tightly.

"So am I," Columbine said.

"You can't tell me she's Ned's!"

Columbine hesitated. She had promised Ned to keep their secret. But she knew Bell would never believe her if she didn't tell her the truth. "Elijah Reed is her father."

Bell looked into her eyes, and she saw that it was true. "Does he know?" she asked curiously.

Columbine shook her head. The pain in her face was so marked that Bell was taken aback. She saw that Columbine had a great, private pain that she held inside every day, never able to speak of it, never able to cry it aloud. Sympathy washed over Bell, and she reached out and pressed Columbine's hand.

"I'm sorry," she said.

She left silently, closing the door gently. Columbine felt that her last tie to the happy past went with her.

Marguerite was wearing a heavy veil, and already the snow had melted into ice which weighed down the veil and slapped her cheeks with frigid insouciance every time a blast of wind headed down Lexington Avenue. It was a ridiculous day to be out and about, and if she ruined her throat she would have only herself to blame. But she was in trouble, and she needed Toby, and he absolutely refused to go out. He was nursing a cold, and he'd somehow managed to get invited to the Bradley-Martin fete, which he would die rather than miss. So he was staying home with steaming towels and the excuse to drink as much brandy and hot water as he wanted.

She knocked on his door and heard a croaking voice tell her to come in. Toby was lying on the couch in the mohair dressing gown she'd given him for Christmas last year, a piece of flannel around his throat and a look in his brown eyes that was positively lugubrious.

"Really, Toby," Marguerite said, stripping off her soaking hat with relief, "if you didn't feel so sorry for yourself, you'd feel much better all round."

"Fine for you to say," Toby pronounced stuffily. "You're as healthy as a bloody horse."

Laughing, she shook out her skirts in front of the fire. "Delicate Daisy Corbeau as healthy as a horse? Don't tell the papers." She crossed to her things and took out a small paper parcel. "Look, I brought you lemons."

"Oh, you *are* an angel."

"I'll mix you a toddy, a nice strong one."

Toby glanced at her warily, his handkerchief halfway to his nose. "Why are you being so nice to me?" he asked suspiciously. "What do you want?"

"Just some gossip to cheer me up," she said in a bright tone that didn't fool Toby a bit. "Now don't move, I'm going to make your toddy."

"Are you sure you know how to boil water, petal?"

Marguerite laughed and went off to make the toddy. She poured in a generous amount of brandy, then added a bit more. When she gave it to him and he tasted it, Toby's eyes widened, and he gave her a look over the rim.

"Well, you have to be well for the ball," Marguerite said placidly, smoothing a blanket over his knees. She perched on the chair next to the sofa and looked at him expectantly.

Toby took a gulp of the toddy. "What are you wearing?"

"Well, I can't quite decide between Madame Pompadour and a peasant girl."

"Hmmmm. Why don't you go as both? Arrive as a peasant girl, then change your dress in a room upstairs, and come down as Pompadour. You'll be an absolute sensation."

Marguerite clapped her hands together, delighted. "What an idea, Toby! I knew you'd think of the perfect thing."

"But are you sure you want to come as Pompadour? Why not Marie Antoinette?"

Marguerite looked at him, her dark blue eyes shrewd. "I know why you're suggesting that, Toby, and I don't care."

"I don't know what you mean," he said loftily. "Oh, my head aches."

"You think I'm so ignorant I don't know that Madame DuBarry and Madame Pompadour were both mistresses of Louis XV. And you think I never read the papers and that I don't know that Mollie Todd is coming as DuBarry. But I know both of those things. And I know what people will say, and I don't care. I'm married to Willie. I've got him."

"Mmmm," Toby said, sipping his toddy.

"Haven't I?" she asked the question lightly, but her eyes stayed on his face.

"Of course you do, petal," he answered quickly. "Just as you say."

"Toby." She put a hand on his arm. "Please tell me. Is Willie really in love with her?"

"How should I know?" he asked crossly, fussing at the blanket.

"Because you know everything," she answered calmly.

He gave her a sharp look. "That's why you came here today, isn't it. It wasn't to bring me lemons. You never come within a mile of me when I have a cold. You've come to harass me, to pump me, when I'm on my deathbed."

"You're not on your deathbed, you have a cold. And Toby, I really want to know. Please tell me the truth."

The cross look left his face and surprise came over it. "You're serious, aren't you. Marguerite, this isn't like you."

Marguerite nodded. "I know. *I'm* not like me lately. Toby, I'm losing my life. I mean, I'm losing a life I didn't even know I wanted. Or rather, I'm losing the chance to make my life into something I want. Do you know what I mean?"

"No," he said. "But if you're telling me that you've come to your senses, I'm all for it. Do you love Willie?"

"He told me that I had no idea of what can be between a man and a woman. He said I wasn't a woman, that I was still a child. He said terrible things." Marguerite pressed her lips together. "And I thought, if I only, well, was nice to him—"

"You mean if you slept with him—"

Marguerite nodded, too upset to be embarrassed. "That he'd come back to me. But he didn't. So I need to know if he loves Mollie Todd. Because then I'll know what I'm fighting against, and I can fight harder."

Toby looked at her, and there was something in his gaze that made her uneasy. He looked almost as if he pitied her.

"Well?" she demanded. "Tell me."

Toby sighed. He wiped his nose. He put the toddy on the small table at his elbow. He did anything he could to delay speaking, for he did not wish to tell Marguerite the truth. The truth was too abstract for her, too slippery, too complicated, and that was the awful thing. Marguerite liked things simple; she could fight a simple truth, but she would struggle with a complicated one.

But maybe he was underestimating her. Maybe she really was changing.

"No, I don't think Willie's in love with her," he said slowly.

Marguerite leaned back against the chair and closed her eyes. "Thank God. Oh, Toby, thank you."

"Wait a minute," he said sharply. "I'm not finished. Marguerite, I think it would be easier if he was."

"Easier?" she asked blankly.

"He's still in love with you, I think," Toby went on, struggling to find the right words. "Not that it helps you. It's depleted him, this love. It's worn him out. And Mollie understands that. She gives him something you can't, Marguerite. Peace. And that's all he wants, I think."

Marguerite wanted to laugh. "Willie want peace? That's so silly, Toby. He likes drama and excitement and risk. If he still loves me, everything will be fine. I can win him back. Oh, I can give him peace and quiet, if he wants it, too," she said, shrugging. "I was thinking it would be fun to buy a house. I'd sit by the fire with him. I used to embroider, I can do that."

"Marguerite, it's not that kind of peace I mean. I mean—"

She stood up excitedly. "Oh, Toby, you don't know him. I know him. I'll buy all new gowns. I'll start at the Bradley-Martin ball—I'll wear such a gown! When he sees that everyone still stares at me, still wants me, he'll want me again!"

"No!" Toby shouted. "Listen to me. That's not the way, Marguerite. Why do you think that only jealousy excites love? Even if every man in the world wanted you, it wouldn't bring Willie back."

"That's an awful thing to say."

"Remember how you caught him the first time," Toby said impatiently. "Remember?"

"Yes, of course I remember," she said, matching his impatience with her own. "The play opened, and I was a hit. He bought me diamonds and roses, and we had champagne—"

"No," Toby was shaking his head, and he winced, for he had an awful headache that was getting worse. "That's not when you captured him. Didn't he ever tell you when he fell in love with you? Don't you remember?"

"I just told you. It was opening night, when I became a star. He—"

"No, it was the day you sang for him in the blue velvet gown. That day."

"That day . . ." Marguerite frowned. Why had Willie told Toby that, and not her? Why was he always confiding in Toby, and not her? But maybe Toby was making it up. He had a terribly romantic imagination, just like a woman's.

"That day you were yourself, Marguerite. Not Daisy."

She stared at him a long time. Then she said, her voice shaking, "You don't want me to get him back."

Toby reared back; he hadn't expected this. "What are you saying? What do you think I'm trying to do?"

"You love him. You love him better than me. You're jealous of me, and I never saw it." Hot fury bubbled in Marguerite, and she felt deliciously self-righteous. Toby wouldn't be telling her these stupid things unless he wanted her to lose. "Don't bother to deny it, I should have seen it. You were always hanging around us. You probably wormed his affection away from me!"

She had expected Toby to leap up from the couch, furious. But he only looked at her pityingly. "What are you so afraid of?" he asked, shaking his head.

"What are you talking about?" she demanded hotly. "Don't change the subject. We're talking about your treachery—"

"It can't just be Edwin," he said. "It must be something before. I know everything you've told me about your past is lies."

"It is not—"

"So what was it? What marked you? What makes you hurt the people who love you, the people that you love?"

"Nobody loves me!" Marguerite screamed. Her voice was the shriek of a wild creature; it seemed to come out from a deep place she hadn't known existed, someplace savage and frightening. Her mouth was open, and a deep sob rose up from that place inside.

Now Toby did struggle to rise. "Marguerite, it's all right, I didn't mean to upset you—"

"I hate you," she shouted with a face livid with rage. "I never, ever want to see you again, Toby Wells. I've shared everything with you—my money, my fame. And you never were a friend to me, never, never. You wanted my husband in your sick way, and you turned him against me out of spite." She gathered her things jerkily.

"Marguerite!" he cried. He pushed away the blanket and stood, weaving slightly from brandy, sickness, and confusion. "I've always loved you."

She stomped to the door, her arms full of coat and hat and scarf. "You're a liar," she said cruelly, and she slammed the door on his gaping face. Just like Edwin, she thought as she ran down the stairs, triumph in her heart, tears streaming down her face. Just like Edwin.

Once Bell had decided, she began to make arrangements. Within a few days she had investigated fares, given her notice to Lev, and received lists of people to look up in Italy, comrades in the movement, socialists, writers, kind people who would help them get settled. It really seemed as though it would work. They could do it. They *were* doing it.

Lawrence spent much of his time making more abstract plans. Every day he decided a different city would be better than another. He argued with Bell about how much money to ask from Columbine, for Bell had made the mistake of telling him the loan was open-ended.

Lawrence had made the suggestion that morning off the top of his head, and he was surprised to find events rushing out of his control. Bell was full of purpose, and he knew that she saw this move as her salvation. Lawrence both resented and admired this; he had always looked to Fiona for purpose, but he saw that Bell could be just as fierce. But he was irritated at her officiousness, so he gave up his plans and retreated behind his newspaper whenever she went over her endless lists in that new brisk voice he'd begun to hate.

"We really should be married here, before we go," Bell said, consulting her list. "At the end of this week, I should think."

Lawrence ignored her. "Listen to this," he said contemptuously. "These Bradley-Martins should be strung up. They're claiming they're doing the poor a favor by putting their money into circulation. Here's the latest—for the coachmen of the city, they're supplying four hundred carriages to bring their guests home. For the *coachmen*, they say. And now they're running lists of which decadent exploiter of the French peasants some fat American capitalist is going to portray, of how many diamond buttons will be on their coats and how much they will cost." He read from the paper in a disgusted voice. "'The beauteous Mollie Todd, who once graced the Broadway stage with that glorious presence that Titian would have begged on his knees to capture, will be appearing as Madame DuBarry in a gown of gold and a necklace of diamonds said to be a gift from an admirer of her great talent.' And people starving in the streets with this depression!" The paper crackled. "It's good we're leaving this place."

"Yes," Bell said. She hadn't told Lawrence, but Lev had asked her to participate in a protest line in front of the Waldorf that night. A coalition of anarchists and socialists would be there. Lev had asked her as a last gesture before she left, and she wanted to participate. But Lawrence, she knew, would not approve, mostly because he had not been invited to attend and would not want to go even if he had been.

But soon these kinds of petty problems would be over. Bell sighed and looked at her list again. She read over her tasks mechanically, and she remembered that there was one important task she had not committed to pen and paper. And since Lawrence seemed lost in the *World* she might as well take the opportunity now.

She rose and went for her coat. "I have to go out for a few minutes, Lawrence. Some errands. I'll bring back supper, all right?"

"All right." Lawrence didn't drop the newspaper, and his voice was abstracted as he concentrated on the paper.

Good, Bell thought as she tied a scarf around her neck. He didn't ask any questions.

Lawrence was oblivious to Bell as she slipped into her coat, laced her walking boots, and put on her hat. He was reading over the account of the Bradley-Martin ball, and he was thinking hard. Again and again he read the same paragraph, then returned to the detailed engraving of the beautiful Mollie Todd. And as he looked he whispered the words which had first set his heart and mind aflame with purpose, a purpose the women in his life had leached out of him with the endless, yawning cavern of their needs.

The Propaganda of the Deed.

It was so much the same situation of almost seven years before that they both must have thought of it, but if Elijah Reed did, he gave no indication. He was all politeness as he ushered Bell into his parlor like an honored guest, and he swept aside a pile of books to offer her the best place by the fire.

She sat, her gloved hands in her lap. "I'll get straight to the point, Mr. Reed. I'll be leaving for Europe for good next week. Before I go, there is something I must tell you. I'm afraid that I inadvertently gave you a false piece of information years ago, and I want to correct it."

Nervously, Elijah rummaged through his pockets for a nonexistent cigar, for he'd quit smoking in Paris. "Ah, yes, Mrs. Birch?"

"My husband did not father Columbine's child," Bell said with equanimity. "I know this for certain now."

Elijah felt embarrassed, even more embarrassed than he'd been the first time a lady of short acquaintance discussed such a thing with him. "And why did you feel the need to come and tell me this?"

"Because I think I might have . . . damaged your relations with Columbine in some way," Bell said slowly. "And I did not want that result, because I knew how much she loved you."

"Mrs. Birch, really—"

"I know this is dreadfully frank of me, and impolite. But I'm leaving, you see. I have to make things right. Please just let me finish." At Elijah's reluctant nod, Bell continued, "I think you should know that Hawthorn is your child, Mr. Reed."

Elijah stood up and sat down again. "Excuse me?"

"I'm sorry, I didn't mean to blurt it out like that. But I think you should know for certain. It would only take you a little while to start wondering, once I've left, who had fathered the child. And you would have to wonder if it were you, would you not? So I can't help it; I think you deserve to know." Bell stood. "That's all."

For perhaps the first time in his life, Elijah forgot his manners. He sat in the chair, stunned, while Bell waited for a moment, then seeing he could not speak, simply took her umbrella and went out, closing the door behind her. She sent up a fervent prayer, the first she'd prayed in a long, long time, that she'd done the right thing at last.

It had been Columbine and Olive's custom for years now to take tea together up in Olive's private sitting room. Ned usually napped at this time and Columbine later took a second cup with him. The two women cherished their time together, a time where they could speak quietly of books they were reading and dreams they'd had and observations about Hawthorn or Ned, or simply chat about nonsense or gossip.

Today, as they waited for Fiona to bring the tea, they were talking of Bell. Without mentioning the loan, Columbine told Olive of her sad feeling after Bell's departure. Bell had been so close to her for so long, and so wide a gulf separated them now.

Fiona gave a short knock and came in with the tray as Columbine finished sadly.

"So she has a—friend, then," Olive said, catching herself from saying "lover" just in time, for though they spoke freely in front of Fiona, there still were limits.

"Yes, I knew him quite well at one time. I don't trust him, and I don't believe he's good to her, but," Columbine said, sighing, "she is nonetheless fixed on him. She believes that living in Italy will start them on a whole new life. I do hope he marries her at last. She said that he would."

"This Mr. Birch, does he have a profession?"

Fiona knocked over the sugar as she placed it on the tea table between them. Her cheeks were scarlet. "Beg your pardon, missus . . ."

"It's all right, Fiona," Columbine said. "Just scrape it back in the bowl, no harm done. He's a writer, Olive, though he doesn't seem to get published. I don't know how they live. Bell supports them, I suppose. But she says it's Lawrence's idea to move to Italy, so I suppose he's also involved in this idea of a grand new start for them. They leave next week, on the eleventh."

Her hands shaking, Fiona scraped the sugar back in the bowl and replaced it on the table.

"Thank you, Fiona, I'll pour today," Olive said, and Fiona walked out like a sleepwalker, unnoticed by the two women. The door closed softly behind her.

Olive poured a cup for Columbine, and she leaned back with it in her chair. "I've been waiting for this all day," Columbine said, sipping at it. "It's been a horrendous week, hasn't it?"

"Yes, I've noticed the tension between you and Ned," Olive said. She usually was not so bold, and Columbine looked over her teacup at her questioningly. "I don't mean to intrude, Columbine. But

I presume you're still arguing about the Bradley-Martin ball."

"Yes," Columbine said. She took another sip of tea. "I don't understand him, Olive. He's become so hard. He's obsessed with Hawthorn's future. All the Christmas engagements I could normally refuse he was on me about. I had to go to this and that, and this again—oh, he's driving me mad. But on this issue I don't see how I can please him. I'm appalled by the waste, the indifference, the sheer amount of money it's taking to put on this fete. I don't care how many Astors and Rhinelanders and Van Cormandts are going."

"I know," Olive said. Her face was set and grave. Her teacup sat at her elbow, untouched. "But I think you should go anyway."

Slowly, Columbine put down her teacup. "Oh, Olive. Not you, too. I could see your point about the Hartleys. But this?"

"Columbine," Olive said clearly, her eyes never leaving her sister-in-law's face, "Ned is dying."

Columbine remembered a tumble from her horse when she was a girl, when the breath had left her body and she hadn't been able to speak. She stared at Olive. "What are you saying?"

"Dr. Temple didn't want to tell you. But I've always thought him a fool. He's silly when it comes to wives, he thinks they should remain in the dark or they'll be hysterical. Ned has cancer. That's why he's been so bad lately. Dr. Temple says it has nothing to do with his injuries from the bomb."

Columbine swallowed painfully. "Does Ned know?"

Olive nodded. "He knew without the doctor telling him. Dr. Temple confirmed his own suspicions."

"You've both known. . . ." Columbine turned away, pressing her face into the soft material of Olive's faded velvet armchair. "How long have you known?" she asked.

"Since before Christmas. Ned didn't want you to know, Columbine. He can't know that you know. He couldn't bear it, he said."

"How long—"

"Does he have? A matter of months."

"And this time you believe Dr. Temple."

Olive nodded, her green eyes pained. "Yes, there's no doubt this time. I feel it as well as know it."

Columbine nodded slowly. She wondered why she wasn't crying.

Now she thought of Ned's increased use of drugs, his obvious pain, the slight grayish tinge to his skin, and she was ashamed. She should have known it went beyond his normal discomfort. She should have known! She thought of every careless remark she'd made over the past month, every argument, every small irritation, and nausea swept over her. "Oh, Olive, I've been so terrible to him," she whispered.

Olive leaned forward urgently. "Now don't go feeling sorry for yourself. I didn't tell you so that you'd feel guilty. I told you because first of all, I think you've a right to know, no matter what Ned or the hallowed Dr. Temple thinks. And I also told you because you need to understand about Hawthorn. Ned needs to feel that Hawthorn will be a Van Cormandt, Columbine, that she will continue the family line. All of these engagements he's forcing on you are just a way for him to believe in that. He's afraid of Elijah Reed."

Columbine started at the sound of the name. "Why would he fear Elijah Reed?"

"Because he's Hawthorn's father. Ned told me. And even if he didn't, I saw you and Mr. Reed at that gala and it was perfectly plain to me that you were in love with him."

"I haven't—"

"I know you haven't. That's not the point. I'm thinking of Ned now." Olive reached out and grasped Columbine's hand. "You've done so much for him. Can you do this last thing? Can you make him secure in the knowledge that he will leave something behind? Go to the ball, Columbine. Go late and leave early, I don't care. Let him know that his position is important to you because it is Hawthorn's position. I'm begging you," she whispered, and there was a fine film of tears in her green eyes. Columbine hadn't seen Olive cry since Dr. Temple described Ned's injuries that first day in the hospital.

"Of course I shall go," Columbine said. "I'll do the best I can, Olive, and I'll keep the promise, too. Hawthorn will be raised a Van Cormandt."

Olive leaned forward and embraced her, and it was only then that Columbine began to weep.

Twenty-Six

OLIVE HAD ORDERED a costume for her, some sort of standard French royalty gown, all chiffon and velvet and a bodice encrusted with pearls. But the night of the Bradley-Martin ball Columbine looked at it laid out for her and knew she could not wear it. She took out her black silk instead.

Olive caught her. She knocked on the door and came in with a small glass of sherry and some biscuits and she found Columbine in her underclothes, holding the black silk with a guilty expression.

Composedly, Olive sat the tray down by Columbine's dressing table. "You're not going to a funeral yet," she said acerbicly.

"I can't wear that," Columbine said, pointing to the frothy gown. "I appreciate you ordering it for me, Olive, but I just cannot."

"Where is Fiona? Isn't she helping you dress?"

"No one can seem to locate her," Columbine said distractedly, looking from the black gown to her costume and back again. "Apparently Mrs. Plumb suspects a sweetheart. Don't tell Ned she's missing, I'm sure she'll return." Columbine did not mention that her gold gown was also missing.

"Of course I won't. Columbine, you can't be serious about the black silk. It's a fancy dress ball!"

"Mrs. Astor is wearing her black gown, I read it in the paper," Columbine said, feeling rather like Hawthorn.

Olive made a face. "Mrs. Astor doesn't dress up. You know she has not the slightest sense of fun, God help her, and she considers her personage too holy to desecrate. Besides, she already thinks of herself as royalty. Why bother dressing as a dead queen when she can impersonate herself?"

Columbine laughed. "Olive, you are too awful sometimes."

Olive grew serious. "Columbine, what will Ned think if he sees you in your black silk? You only wear it for formal dinners with the very oldest Van Cormandts, and well he knows it."

Columbine hesitated. "I just can't dress up," she said finally. Olive could see that her jaw was set in that stubborn way. "I can't walk into the Waldorf dressed as a queen with people starving in the streets. I'll just tell Ned the truth. I'm wearing it in honor of the starving poor, and to hell with the Bradley-Martins if they don't like it. He'll believe that I'm that wicked, I'm sure."

Olive's face lightened. "Yes, of course he will."

"Well, you needn't agree so readily," Columbine said grumpily, and two women had their best laugh in days.

Marguerite took two full hours to dress, even though her first costume was the simple one. Her dressmaker had worked like the devil to complete both in time, and Celeste was waiting at the Waldorf in an upstairs room with the real showpiece of the evening, which Marguerite would change into before the supper at midnight. That gown was a dazzling creation in the shade of deep blue Marguerite hoped someone, sometime, would name "Daisy's eyes" or something, and it had real diamonds sewn in the bodice, dozens of deep blue velvet roses, and seventy-five gilt tassels.

But for all the gown's magnificence, she preferred her peasant costume. She had cheated, of course. The simple, ankle-length gown was mousseline de soie of a fineness no peasant had ever touched, let alone worn. A deep rose satin belt was laced with a cunning strand of crystal beads. Just a drift of the palest peach chiffon covered her breasts over the low-cut satin bodice. Her slippers were peach satin, and they laced up her peach-stockinged ankles in a truly shocking fashion. She wore her hair loose and flowing, with only the hair ornament Willie had given her three years ago. It was sapphires cunningly fashioned into forget-me-nots, with sprays of diamonds as baby's breath, and it circled her hair like a wreath of flowers. She wanted to kiss the mirror when she was through.

But the exhilaration of the success of her costume wore off immediately, and she stared moodily at her reflection. She'd thought that her quarrel with Toby would help. She'd felt so self-righteous! But his words had filtered down as the days passed, and they had the uncomfortable ring of truth. She didn't understand her husband, she saw, and Toby was right—if she thought she could recapture him by wearing a pretty gown to a ball, she really was the child he thought her.

Willie knocked at her door and came in, looking handsome in his evening clothes and the ruby studs she'd given him for Christmas. Willie never dressed in a costume, no matter how much she cajoled him, and she'd given up years ago. Marguerite stood and twirled for him, the simple skirt whirling around her legs.

"Do you think it very shocking?" she asked.

"I would expect no less from you," he said. He couldn't help smiling at her costume. It was perfect, a mixture of demure simplicity and a daring disregard for conventions. There was the suggestion of her legs moving in the skirt that no lady would have found acceptable outside of her boudoir. And her ankles were showing quite plainly. Nobody but Marguerite could get away with such a gown without being labelled a hoyden. "It's an excellent choice," Willie said approvingly.

Marguerite beamed at his approval. "I thought and thought for days what would be best. And wait until you see the gown I'm wearing for supper and dancing."

"Did Toby help you?" he asked, fussing with a shirt cuff in a show of unconcern.

Marguerite's face darkened. "Only a bit," she said, turning to adjust the jeweled wreath on her shining hair.

"He told me you had a falling out," Willie said. "He's quite upset about it, Marguerite."

She shrugged. "I suppose he told you all about it."

"No, on the contrary, he wouldn't tell me a word. Just that you quarrelled." Willie saw that underneath Marguerite's blitheness that she was upset. Toby was really her only friend. He touched her shoulder gently. "He'll be there tonight. You two can make it up."

"He won't want to make it up," Marguerite mumbled.

"Of course he will. Why not? You're his best friend. He loves you, Marguerite."

"No, he doesn't. I don't deserve his love. I don't deserve anyone's love." Marguerite turned her deep blue eyes up at him. "If I don't deserve yours, what can I expect? You know me better than anyone."

Something moved inside Willie, and he was surprised to discover that it was his heart. It was impossible, for he thought that he'd managed to harden it against her. She was looking at him with such misery, but it wasn't the usual misery of a child who couldn't have what she wanted. There was sadness there, and resignation.

"I thought once that if everybody else loved me enough, wanted me enough, you'd stay with me. But that was foolish, wasn't it, Willie? It was the wish of a child," Marguerite said, looking at him in the mirror. "And it took me so long to be able to realize it. I guess now that I think you're going to leave me it doesn't matter anymore, it doesn't matter what I do, so I can say it. I love you," she said simply. Her heart was in her eyes, and for once she did not care. She felt as though she'd lost her best friend, and she had. Her husband was going to this ball to dance with his mistress, and as soon as she got to the ball she would become Daisy Corbeau, and no one would know she was miserable. Not even Willie. Not even Toby. Even with them, she had always acted her part too well.

Willie's hazel eyes met hers as he struggled to decipher her motives. He was used to motives with her. Why was she doing this when he'd had everything all figured out? In the simple gown, her hair down, she suddenly reminded him of when he'd fallen in love with her, standing on the stage in the shabby blue velvet gown, singing alone with such determination underneath the gaiety.

She saw the softening in his eyes. and hope flared in her heart. "Willie—"

"We'll be late for the ball," he said brusquely, and turned away.

The anarchists had decided to dress as Paris Communards, that most exhilarating urban insurrection of 1871 which had inspired both Bakunin and Marx. The choice of the Communards had been easy; it was a show of defiance against the American upper classes' exaltation of the decadent French kings. The anarchists and socialists had ended up arguing about tactics, however, so a unified front would not be presented. But still, many were going dressed ostentatiously in rags and little peaked caps.

Dressed as Louise Michel, the heroine of the Communards, Bell got ready in the empty rooms she shared with Lawrence. Everything was packed and already down at the docks, held there to be loaded onto the ship they were taking tomorrow. In the end, Lawrence had been understanding about her inclination to take part in the protest, and Bell saw it as a harbinger of better relations between them, a true marriage of minds as well as bodies. And Lawrence had been so romantic, packing a small bag for both of them. He had suggested they take just a little money from their precious store and stay in a hotel tonight. Bell would attend the protest, then take the streetcar downtown to meet him at the small but, Lawrence assured her, respectable hotel downtown. Picking up the small grip he'd packed, Bell looked around at the bare rooms. She didn't feel very much, not sadness, or nostalgia. Her life was ahead. She left the rooms on Tompkins Square without a backward glance, the grip slapping against her skirts.

The director of the New York Police Board, Theodore Roosevelt, had commissioned a large platoon of police to set up barricades outside the Waldorf and watch for any signs or gestures of disapproval from the crowd that had gathered to watch the grand carriages roll up and the guests, in their powdered wigs and jewel-encrusted costumes, alight from them. The street-level windows had been boarded up, in case of thrown incendiary devices, and detectives dressed in frock coats and jeweled-buckled shoes circulated among the crowd inside.

Guests entered in a bower of roses, with the falling petals soon making a carpet for elegant kid slippers. Overhead, the thousands of orchids were twined around chandeliers, and every pillar and mirror was festooned with more roses and orchids. Each guest and the historical personage they were portraying was announced to the Bradley-Martins, who sat on a dais on a pair of gold thrones. Three bands played continuous music, and the ball would begin with a complicated quadrille it had taken society folk weeks to rehearse.

Fiona knew all these things, and it did not help her nervousness. She sat in the fine carriage Lawrence had hired, nervously smoothing Columbine's gown over her knees. Her face felt set and tight with the white powder she'd used, and she kept checking the beauty spot on her cheek. She knew that as soon as she arrived she would be denounced as an impostor. Madame duBarry, indeed! She was a parlormaid, for heaven's sake. She had half a mind to jump out of the carriage.

Peeking out through the curtains, she saw that the carriage had crossed Thirty-Fourth Street and was pulling up in front of the hotel. There was a tremendous crowd outside the Waldorf. Fiona pressed a hand to her heart and ordered it to stop beating so fast. Just this one last thing she had to do, just this last thing. She could do it—Lawrence, that blackguard, had told her again and again she could do it. And she knew she could. She'd seen enough of fine ladies; she'd observed Columbine.

She flashed her invitation at the footman with powdered hair and knee breeches, then dropped her bouquet of flowers, as Lawrence had instructed. Then, as he bent to retrieve it, she dropped her glove. In the confusion of handing over the items, the next carriage drew up, and he gave her invitation a perfunctory glance and passed her on to the next footman. He missed the engraved name, Columbine Van Cormandt, and merely noted that she was, in fact, invited.

As she walked in, desperately trying to conceal her nervousness, she smelled roses and cologne and was momentarily dazzled by the light and luxury of her surroundings. Lawrence had told her to make every attempt to escape before being presented to the Bradley-Martins, but Fiona saw immediately and with horror that there was no way she could extricate herself without looking suspicious.

She whispered the name to the footman, and she swept up to the dais.

"Miss Mollie Todd," the footman announced in a ringing voice, "as Madame duBarry."

Everyone in New York had read of the beautiful Mollie Todd, even if they could not quite remember her brief stint on the stage, and heads swiveled to take in the elegant lady who was reputed to be the one woman who could steal Willie Paradise away from America's forget-me-not, Daisy Corbeau. And they looked and they whispered, for the papers had not exaggerated Mollie Todd's beauty. Her figure really was perfect, and her eyes glittered like emeralds. And who could miss that extravagant, blazing, red-gold hair?

Marguerite's back was to the dais when she heard Mollie Todd announced. She did not appear to have noticed, as she was engaged in charming a circle of men clustered around her. She waved her simple bouquet of wildflowers and wrinkled her nose and flashed her dimple, and not one of them had any idea that she was ready to stamp her foot and scream with rage.

As soon as she could extricate herself, she did. She turned just in time to see Mollie heading away across the ballroom. Rage filled Marguerite's heart, and she headed after her. She wouldn't lose Willie without telling that baggage just what she thought of her.

To her surprise, Mollie seemed to be heading away from the crowd, which tended to congregate near the dais while arrivals were announced. Probably too ashamed to show her face in such company, Marguerite sniffed, hurrying after her without seeming to hurry. She wanted to corner her quickly and return to the ball, since she'd hadn't yet fully enjoyed the sensation her gown had caused.

Mollie skirted an Indian with scalps dangling from his belt—apparently not everyone had taken the Versailles theme literally—and headed for a side door. Now Marguerite would not have stopped chasing her if someone had put a gun to her head. Undoubtedly, Mollie was headed for a secret rendezvous with Willie, who had disappeared immediately after they'd arrived.

She slipped through the door after Mollie just in time to see her run down the corridor and turn the corner. Marguerite sped after her, her feet noiseless in her soft kid slippers. She had no idea where she was now, for she was heading into the part of the huge hotel that would one day very soon connect with the Astoria next door. The Astoria had been built by John Jacob Astor, who had finally given in and razed his mother's home to make way for it, despite his irritation at his cousin, William Waldorf, who had built the towering Waldorf next door.

To Marguerite's surprise, Mollie disappeared behind a red velvet curtain that Marguerite had assumed was hung over the wall. She peeked behind it and discovered a long, dark corridor. It appeared unfinished, with none of the gilded opulence of the rest of the hotel. It was rather too late to turn back, but Marguerite wasn't thrilled with traversing such a dim, endless hall. But the thought of confronting both Willie and Mollie made her push the curtains aside and follow Mollie, now just a blur of satin in front of her.

She had guessed right; this corridor led into the unfinished Astoria. She was hurrying now, for Mollie was way ahead of her. A tiny beam of light showed as she opened a door. When Marguerite came to it, she reached out to gently turn the handle, but it was already moving, and she melted back against the wall. Mercifully, there was a curtained alcove there, and she quickly stepped behind the curtain, leaving only one eye peeking out.

But it wasn't Willie who opened the door again, and it wasn't Mollie Todd, either. It was an unfamiliar woman, with Mollie's titian hair, yes, but not her perfect face. But the real shock was the man. It was Lawrence Birch, looking rather silly in a brocade coat and knee breeches and white stockings, but it was Lawrence Birch nonetheless.

Something was not right. Not daring to breathe, Marguerite held herself still and listened. They were talking in low voices, and now that the door was closed she could hear them clearly.

"Why are you bringing this up now?" Lawrence was saying. "For God's sake, Fiona—"

"And when else can I? When you disappear off the face of the earth tomorrow, when you go to live in Italy?" The woman's voice was calm, but Marguerite knew a woman's fury when she heard it.

"I'm not going to Italy with her. Do you think I'm mad?" Lawrence grasped the woman called Fiona's arms. "I'm going with you. All you need is a passport. I have the money. Bell is meeting me tonight at a hotel downtown, only I'll never show up. She thinks we have tickets leaving from New York, but it's Boston. You and I will go to Boston tonight, after we're finished here. We'll sail from there."

"Show me the tickets."

"Fiona—"

"Show me the tickets."

There was something in her voice that brooked no argument. A pause. A fumble. Then Lawrence held something out. Marguerite wondered how Fiona could make anything out in this light. She squinted at the tickets while Lawrence waited. His back was to Marguerite, and she could see his hands working; he was nervous. But Fiona merely handed him back the tickets.

"All right," she said.

Marguerite could hear Lawrence's sigh. "All right," he echoed with satisfaction.

"If you left me, I would have tracked you down and killed you," she said flatly. "I've done enough sinning for you. When I took that oath that day three years ago, I was pledging to God that I would be your wife forever, and I meant it. We stood up before a priest, Lawrence!"

"I know. And I meant it, too. We're man and wife."

"All right, then. Let's go."

"You remember everything?"

"I remember."

They moved away, down the long corridor, and Marguerite reached out, finally able to steady herself. Her heart was beating furiously. She had gotten more than she bargained for. So Lawrence would leave Bell flat, would he. Her old hatred of Lawrence Birch returned in force, and her eyes narrowed. He was not the type to smuggle himself into a party just for the fun of it. Something was going on all right, but it was hardly her business. And she could not forget that Lawrence still had something on her. She comforted herself with the thought that at least now she had something on him. What would make her fun absolutely complete would be to use it.

Olive had gone off with a pack of the innumerable Van Cormandt cousins, and Columbine had been left talking to Converse Bowles, who had resisted Letitia Garth's clutches and was still a distinguished bachelor. He was charming, but Columbine wondered how soon she could leave. Then she saw Elijah Reed crossing the room toward her, and she forgot that she was bored and uncomfortable.

In a moment, Converse Bowles excused himself to head for the champagne, and they were alone. She sensed immediately that Elijah was different. There was some bit of awkwardness in his good evening, some odd stiltedness in the way he shook her hand.

"Is everything all right?" she asked him. "Are you all right?"

"Fine," he answered, not very convincingly. "You look very beautiful."

"I'm surprised to see you here."

"I read your name among the list of guests, so I came."

"Ned wanted me to come, and I—I couldn't refuse. He's concerned about Hawthorn. I have to do my duty as a Van Cormandt suddenly, you see."

For some reason, this remark seemed to trouble Elijah. He nodded and looked away. "Elijah," she said softly, "have I done something to upset you?"

"This isn't the place—"

"But if not here, where? We're never alone."

"Is she my daughter, Columbine?"

The lights whirled around her, the music rebounded in her head. His eyes were dark and troubled, like Hawthorn's eyes . . .

"She is," he said flatly.

"You're angry. Elijah, I couldn't tell you. You were going to Paris, dead set on it, and then Ned was injured—"

"Oh, God." He didn't speak for a few moments. "Don't you think I've thought of all that?" he asked in a tone that vibrated with anger. "Don't you think I've gone over it again and again? I didn't leave you any choice. I was a coward. I was everything I despise in everyone else, I left you, not wanting to know . . . "

She saw that he was angry at himself, not at her, and she touched his arm. "Please, Elijah. It would pain me to know that you blame yourself. We all do what we feel we must do. The trick is to be able to start over if we wish it. Can't we start over, Elijah?"

"I've never seen her," he said, and his voice broke.

"You shall," Columbine promised. "Someday soon, not yet, but I'll arrange a meeting." How awful this was, she thought despairingly, that her husband was dying, and she was able, standing here, to even think in the remotest way of her lover. But there it was. She loved Elijah. She wanted him to know his daughter. Ned couldn't know, it wouldn't help matters. She had promised Olive that Hawthorn would be raised a Van Cormandt, and she would. But Hawthorn would also know her father.

"I wish we could be alone," she whispered. "I wish we could be together."

"We are together," he answered.

Columbine smiled, and just then she saw the most remarkable thing. She saw her dress, her gold gown, through the crowd, heading away from them. Puzzled, she looked over Elijah's shoulder. She could not see the woman who wore it, but she thought the gown disappeared into one of the small rooms that held refreshments. Fiona, she thought.

"Will you excuse me, Elijah?"

He bowed. "Of course. May I take you in to supper later?"

"I would like that very much." She pressed his hand, and she moved away toward the refreshment room wonderingly. Why would Fiona steal a gown and come to this party? It didn't make sense.

She looked in the refreshment room, but Fiona wasn't there. Puzzled, Columbine came out and walked farther down the corridor. She didn't see anyone, but she kept going, past one turning, then the next, and she found Fiona standing with Lawrence Birch.

Their heads were together, and they were speaking together intimately. Columbine was so shocked she couldn't speak at first. Then Fiona looked up and saw her, and her face went white. She clutched Lawrence's arm.

He showed his surprise for only a moment. Then he smiled blandly. "Columbine! How lovely to see you again."

"Good evening, Mr. Birch," Columbine said coolly. "Fiona, what—"

"So you've found us out," Lawrence interrupted. "We are like naughty children, I confess. We just had to come to the party."

Columbine nodded, though she had trouble swallowing this. "I didn't know you were acquainted with Mr. Birch, Fiona."

"We've been acquainted for some time, ma'am," Fiona answered. She had regained the dignity that Columbine had always admired in her. "I'm sorry about the gown," she added. "I didn't think you'd miss it."

"I did," Columbine answered shortly. "I assume you took my invitation as well. I thought I'd misplaced it."

Fiona nodded carefully. "It was just a game," she said.

Columbine hesitated. "Fiona, I'm sorry, but I must say that it could be dangerous to play games with the likes of Mr. Birch."

Fiona smiled, her eyes glittering. "Thank you for the warning, Mrs. Van Cormandt," she said wickedly.

Lawrence gave her a triumphant look, and anger surged through Columbine. He would not do this again, stand there and demonstrate his power over a woman that she was fond of.

"How long have you known him, Fiona?" she asked quietly.

"Long enough to know him," she replied, shrugging. "Eight years last December."

"Eight years December," Columbine said. She took a wild, crazy guess, daring to because of the strange light in Lawrence's eyes. "Right before the party at the Hartley's, then. Did you know he was there that night?"

Fiona's defiant look slipped, just a bit. "He wasn't there that night. We didn't meet that night. We met before, and after, but—"

"Not that night," Columbine said. She shot a look at Lawrence; the triumphant gaze was gone. Fury was stealing over his face in a fascinating change. His cheekbones stood out prominently. The change in him reminded her of the night he'd attacked her. But Columbine wasn't afraid. She felt power surge through her, for she knew she was on the right track. She knew she was right.

"But I saw him there that night," she said deliberately. "I saw him running away after the blast. And I believe he caused it."

"You saw him . . . "

"I saw him, Fiona."

"I came to see you," Lawrence said to Fiona urgently. "Then I saw all the activity, and I left."

"I told you we were having the fireworks, that I couldn't get away," Fiona said. She was searching Lawrence's face, and suddenly the uncertainty left her eyes and her customary shrewdness returned. "That's why you asked me so much about them. You did it. You damaged them deliberately. And you knew—" Her hand flew to her mouth. "You knew that Jimmy was supposed to set them off."

"It wasn't supposed to go that way," Lawrence said. "I thought Hartley would be there."

"But you knew Jimmy would be," Fiona said through her fingers. "It's because of you he lost his arm."

"For God's sake, Fiona, what does it matter? We sent him to jail didn't we? Why are you having scruples now?"

Lawrence's words seemed to take whole minutes to sift through Columbine's consciousness. *We sent him to jail, didn't we?* Lawrence and Fiona, she thought. They were the ones. Not Bell. Lawrence. And Fiona had been his accomplice. She hadn't left the window open for Jimmy. She'd left it open for her lover. Had she known about the bomb? And if she had, what were the two of them doing here, tonight?

"Fiona," Lawrence said, "aren't we running away together? Don't spoil this night, don't . . ." Lawrence moved toward her. He reached out for her. Columbine prayed she'd move away. But Fiona did not. And then Lawrence took out a gun, and pointed it at Columbine.

Outside, the protest had fizzled. No one knew the anarchists had dressed like Communards, for they did not look very much different from the ragged crowd who was oohing and ahhing over the display of jewels and costumes and coiffures instead of rising as one solid mass to condemn it.

Bell clutched the grip and sighed. She should just leave. She thought longingly of the hotel downtown. Lawrence could be there already. She could be dining with him at this very moment. He had declared that they would order room service, no matter what the cost. But in her position, at the very front of the barricade, she would seem a defector if she left so early.

Suddenly she saw a slight figure run out from the Waldorf, wearing a voluminious black velvet cape trimmed in peach satin. She recognized Marguerite as the hood fell back to reveal a white face and darting blue eyes.

"Bell!" Marguerite shouted, and she ran across the street to press against the barricade. "I knew you'd be out here, I heard there was an anarchist protest," she said breathlessly.

Bell was taken aback; she hadn't seen Marguerite in seven years. Why this sudden friendliness?

"You must come inside," Marguerite urged. "I'm sure it would interest you."

"Why would I come inside?"

"Because it would interest you," Marguerite repeated. In a low voice, she said, "Lawrence is at the ball. I saw him."

"Lawrence? But that's impossible."

"Nothing is impossible in life, don't you know that, Bell?" Marguerite asked gaily. She seemed in high spirits despite the cold wind whipping down Fifth.

A policeman came by, slapping his nightstick against a white-gloved palm. "You'd better move along, miss. The crowd can be dangerous."

Marguerite shot him an impudent and highly flirtatious glance. "Don't you know who I am, Captain?"

"Why, you're Daisy Corbeau! Miss Corbeau, I didn't recognize you. All the more reason for you to move along, Miss Corbeau, ma'am."

"But Captain, I must take my friend with me." Marguerite held out her hand and pulled Bell's sleeve.

"She doesn't look like a guest, Miss Corbeau, if you don't mind my saying so, ma'am. And it's Sergeant Malley, ma'am."

"But she's *my* guest, Sergeant Malley, you see how we're dressed alike." Marguerite dimpled prettily at him.

The sergeant looked from Marguerite to Bell. True, both ladies were dressed in peasant garb. And he'd even seen an Indian tonight, so there was no telling what the swells were dressing as. And the lady behind the barricade *was* beautiful. She was another actress, most likely.

"Please, Sergeant Malley. Do you like the theater? I shall send you some tickets for you and your wife."

"That would be kind of you ma'am . . . . All right, go ahead. I suppose it's all right."

Taking Bell's hand, Marguerite tugged her forward, and Bell ducked underneath the barricade, hardly knowing why. "What are you doing?" she said underneath her breath to Marguerite as they ran toward the entrance.

Marguerite giggled. "I'm making something right, that's all. Something I did long ago." When they reached the awning, she looked at Bell a moment. Then she slipped out of her long cape and swirled it around Bell's shoulders. "There, that's better. Come along. We've got a bit of searching to do. But I think I know exactly where to find him."

Fiona had known that Lawrence had a gun, but she was nonetheless surprised when he took it out and pointed it at Columbine. "Let's go," he said.

"Lawrence, don't be silly," Columbine said. "This place is swarming with detectives."

"Just move," he said evenly.

With the gun hidden under a cape that was part of his costume, he led them away, down the hall toward the Astoria part of the hotel. This part of the hotel was quiet, deserted, and they moved quickly, almost running in response to Lawrence's hissed commands.

He took her down a dark corridor to an unfinished room in the Astoria side. Carpenters and wordcarvers had left some tools lying about, and there was scaffolding in a corner.

"What now?" Columbine asked.

"Now for the plan," Lawrence said. He went to the corner and rooted underneath a cloth, taking out a small package.

Columbine's heart began to pound. "No," she said.

"I'm afraid so," Fiona said. Her voice sounded wooden, and she went to stand next to Lawrence.

"It will take me a few minutes to arm it," Lawrence said. "And I wouldn't move, if I were you. I could make a mistake and blow us all to kingdom come."

He laid the gun down at his feet, but Columbine did not feel sufficiently brave to try for it. He threw off his powdered wig.

"Now," he said, "first, the detonator."

But the door opened, and Bell and Marguerite walked in. Marguerite was surprised to see Columbine, but the more the merrier. She had never been good at reading the atmosphere in a room she entered, since she always planned to change it.

"You see, Bell, I told you he was here. Look, Lawrence, I found Bell. And oh, Bell, I don't know if you know Fiona or not."

Bell stared from Lawrence to Fiona. She did not recognize Fiona as the maid she had met so briefly seven years before. "Lawrence?" she asked, confused. "What are you doing here?"

"Christ, Marguerite! You'll pay for this, you little Jew."

"He's here with his wife," Marguerite flung out. "They crashed the party."

"Wife?" Bell asked. "Wife?" she repeated stupidly.

"I'm Lawrence's wife," Fiona said.

"Legal wife?" Bell asked.

"Under God and the law," Fiona answered. She couldn't help feeling a tiny spurt of spite. At last she could claim it to Lawrence's doxy.

Lawrence screened them out. He bent over the bomb. There was nothing he could do now. His fate, as always, was in the hands of his women. How he would like to change that. He wanted to leave them both.

Bell's legs gave way, and she sat on the dusty floor. Everything fell away from her. She could not concentrate on anything but this information. She knew that as soon as she was able to feel, she would be torn apart by the pain. Believing in his reasons, she had waited for years. He had married someone else.

Lawrence picked up the bomb, and Columbine thought frantically. She had to get them out of here, all of them. Marguerite noticed the bomb for the first time.

"What's that?" she asked.

"It's a bomb," Fiona said matter-of-factly.

"Columbine?" Marguerite shot her a disbelieving look.

"I'm afraid so."

Bell looked up. "Lawrence, you have to stop."

He didn't answer her.

"Lawrence, it's no good. We're starting again, we're leaving for Italy."

"I think Fiona has something to say about that," Marguerite muttered.

"I'm leaving with him," Fiona said.

Bell looked over at Lawrence. She began to crawl toward him across the dusty floor. "Lawrence, tell me it isn't true. Tell me, please."

"We're leaving from Boston," Fiona went on. "He bought the tickets. He told you it was New York but it's Boston."

"But I booked the passage," Bell said. "Tell her, Lawrence."

"Stay away from me," he snapped. He'd begun to sweat, and he put down the bomb again and slipped off his brocade jacket. Fiona reached for it, and took the tickets from his pocket. She waved them at Bell.

"You see?"

In a moment, Bell was on her like a wildwoman, and she snatched the tickets from her hand. She looked at them frantically, and then, sobbing, she hugged them to her breast. "New York," she said. "New York."

Slowly, Fiona's face began to change. "New York. But Lawrence, you said it was Boston."

"You really should learn to read, Fiona," Lawrence said abstractedly. "I knew you were bluffing. I knew you couldn't read those tickets."

Bell moved toward Lawrence. "Darling . . . "

But she had blocked Fiona from his view, and Fiona whirled and scrabbled on the floor, rolling. And she came up with Lawrence's gun.

She trained it on him. "You're a dead man, you bastard," she said in a conversational tone. Bell gave a low scream.

"Don't be a fool, Fiona." Lawrence didn't take his eyes off her face. "I've armed the bomb. Do you understand?"

Marguerite moaned, and Columbine reached out to steady her. "Fiona," she said steadily, "this won't solve anything for you."

"What does it matter? He'll be dead."

"But do you want to die, too?"

"Certainly not," Fiona said calmly. "I'm getting away." She jerked the gun at Lawrence. "Pick up the bomb."

Hesitating a fraction, Lawrence picked it up.

"You two," Fiona said, indicating Bell and Lawrence. "You go first. Lawrence, you know where the door is. The rest of you, follow behind."

She kept them all under cover somehow, inching along the side as Lawrence, trying to shake off Bell's arm, moved out of the room. He pushed open a door and Columbine saw with surprise that they were on Fifth Avenue. There was still a small crowd at the entrance to the Waldorf, a half-block down.

"Keep going," Fiona said, and Lawrence and Bell moved forward.

"Fiona—" Columbine said.

"Shut up."

The police caught sight of them before they had advanced very far.

"He has a bomb," Fiona shouted clearly.

"No!" Lawrence shouted.

The police who were closest froze. One at the rear began to inch away slowly. Fiona noticed, but she didn't say anything.

One of the policeman recognized Marguerite. "Miss Corbeau, does he have a bomb?"

"I'm afraid so," Marguerite shouted back.

Fiona turned her body slightly, and Columbine realized that the police could not see the gun in her hand. Then she saw Fiona's object, and she was afraid. She wanted the police to shoot Lawrence. Fiona could get them all killed. And she doesn't care, most likely, Columbine realized. She hates Lawrence too much to give it a thought.

No one noticed a solitary figure, who had been leaning against the Waldorf, enjoying a cigar, when the strange group advanced. At the sound of Marguerite's voice he straightened, a foolish figure in a black velvet jacket, a white doublet, white stockings and black pumps. He threw away his cigar and began to inch along the wall.

Marguerite saw him. "Oh, my God," she said under her breath. It was Toby. She closed her eyes for an instant. *Please God, make him stop. He's not a courageous man, so what is he doing, anyway?*

Columbine grasped Marguerite's elbow and spoke in her ear. "When I tell you to run, run like mad, back the way we came," she said. "It's the only way."

Marguerite nodded, her blue eyes wide. If she ran, Toby would stop.

And then everything seemed to happen all at once, and yet so slowly. Sergeant Malley, suddenly an authoritative figure, called out to Lawrence to put the bomb down and walk away. He drew his pistol, and the other policemen did the same. Fiona backed away; Columbine squeezed Marguerite's arm, and she ran, but she ran in the wrong direction, toward the policemen and toward Toby, instead of back toward the Astoria. Not realizing Marguerite wasn't behind her, Columbine ran in the opposite direction. Lawrence bent to put down the bomb, but Bell stepped in front of him to shield him, and Sergeant Malley's arm went up. A loud explosion stunned them, but it was the gun, not the bomb, and Bell crumpled. Lawrence stood looking down at her stupidly, the bomb at his feet, and then another explosion happened, and the force of the bullet knocked him backward. He wasn't dead, and he reached for Bell, and that's when Fiona fired. Sergeant Malley fired again, and Toby, running for Marguerite, was caught in the crossfire, and was shot by one or the other, it didn't matter which.

The bomb did not go off. It had been a fake. Lawrence had planned to plant it merely to scare, to warn. He wouldn't risk going to jail again. But only he and Fiona had known that.

Dying, knowing she was dying, Bell crawled toward Lawrence. She saw at once that he was dead, and she lay her head on his shoulder and looked up at the wide black sky. She saw all her life, all the wrong and the pain and the mistakes, and she saw that she had loved a worthless man, and that she still, even now, took comfort from his body, and she knew that the long, hard road was finished, and she gave up with gladness and died.

Columbine went toward her slowly. She looked down at Bell, who looked as serene as she always had. Her amber hair was loose, and it spilled over Lawrence's shirt and was darkened with blood from his wound. Her lips seemed curved in a gentle smile, but Columbine knew that it was just the way Bell's lips curved, so delicate, so serene. Slowly, Columbine knelt by Bell's side. She adjusted the black cloak to cover her wound. And then she reached out and gently disengaged Bell from Lawrence so that she could lay alone.

The police were swarming toward the bomb, swarming toward Bell and Lawrence, leading Fiona away, and Marguerite screamed at them to help Toby, to get a doctor, for God's sake. She fell to the pavement on her knees before him. Toby looked up at her. She bent over him. She thought it was misting, but his face was wet from her tears.

From behind them, Willie had left the hotel, planning to meet Toby for a cigar as they had arranged. The police stopped him, and all he could see was Marguerite on the pavement. His chest felt tight, and he pushed the policeman aside roughly. "It's my wife," he said.

Marguerite cradled Toby's head. "You were very foolish," she said.

"I've played so many heroes, I got confused," Toby said, trying to smile.

"Toby. Don't die."

"I won't. I refuse to die while I'm wearing these silly pumps."

Marguerite laughed; he couldn't be dying if he could joke like that. "I didn't make it up with you, didn't tell you—"

"It's all right, petal. It's all right."

"You're always telling me its all right when it isn't," she said, tears dripping onto his lips.

"Then why should I stop now, petal?" he asked. He tried to squeeze her hand, and he discovered to his surprise that he could not. Marguerite was fading. "How extraordinary," he said, and then he felt himself slip back, back into a warm, black night, and he remembered to close his eyes, for he hated to think of them sightless, staring up at the starry sky. Such a tired device, he thought drowsily. I'm dreaming, I'm having my very last dream.

"Toby?" Marguerite wanted to shake him, but she was afraid he'd bleed even more. "Toby!"

A hand touched her shoulder with such tenderness she was finally able to look up. Through swimming eyes, she saw Willie.

"Come, my love," he said, and he raised her up, up, and clasped her in his arms.

April, 1898
In a Warm Room

Epilogue

MARGUERITE WOULD NOT tell Willie where they were going, no matter how he pressed her. She simply could not tell him, too afraid of his anger, his pity—she wasn't sure what, exactly. She would like to avoid taking him, but she had grown up in the past year, and she knew now that by turning away her eyes she could not make things disappear. And she had also learned in the past year a little bit of what it was to love. She had learned it was simple, after all. It was trust.

Willie finally gave up his laughing questions when she grew more quiet and subdued as the carriage rattled through the streets. He began to see that this was no gay surprise outing, but something important she could not tell him. He was anxious, but he was also glad, for it seemed, perhaps, that Marguerite might finally let him in on a secret about her. And perhaps he'd get a clue to the piece that he'd always felt was missing at the heart of their marriage, no matter how satisfying it had been in the past year.

As they went steadily east, her hand left his arm and dropped to her lap. He saw her fold her hands primly, and studiously avoid looking at him. As they clattered down Canal she seemed to shrink inside herself. Still, he said nothing.

Silently, he paid off the driver. Silently, he followed her down a dank and depressing street called Ludlow. He knew where he was, of course, though he'd never been there. He saw the men in black and the lights burning in the windows, for it was almost sundown.

She pushed open the door of a sorry-looking tenement and, not looking to see if he was even following, climbed the narrow stairs. He followed her up flight after flight, watching her neat little boots take the steps. And then they finally stopped and stood in front of a door. Marguerite knocked, and he noticed that her hand was trembling.

An older, very pretty woman opened the door. Her hair was a faded blond, but he saw her eyes, as blue as cornflowers, and he knew.

"This is my mother." Marguerite's contralto voice cracked. "Mrs. Edelstadt. Mama, this is William Paradise."

The woman shook his hand firmly, but he could see that she was nervous. "Please come in."

They walked directly into a small kitchen. The table was set for supper, but the candles were still unlit, and the room was dim. A large man with a black mustache sat at the table.

"This is my husband, Roman Edelstadt," Marguerite's mother said. "He's not Marguerite's father. Jacob died last year."

Willie shook hands with the large man, feeling his own hand completely engulfed. The man's smile was kind. "Welcome to our home," he said.

"Not for long, it won't be," Marguerite said nervously. She wanted Willie to know that she had finally persuaded her mother to let her buy a house for them.

"Yes, we'll be moving soon," Sophie said.

Willie had still not indicated, by a look or a word, what he was thinking. Marguerite thought of Lawrence Birch, the last awful night she'd seen him, how he hissed the words. *You little Jew.* She closed her eyes against the thought. Now she could not even look into Willie's face for a hint.

"Won't you sit down?" Sophie asked her son-in-law. She was a bit in awe of him, with his fine clothes. "It's the Sabbath. We're just about to light the candles."

Willie took his place at the table. The soft light surrounded them, and the sky outside was a deep blue, the color of Marguerite's eyes. He felt the smooth texture of the table, and the warmth of the kitchen, he smelled the smell of good things cooking, and he looked at the candles waiting to be lighted. He glanced at Marguerite's mother across the table, still lovely, smiling at her husband. At last, at last, he knew.

Sophie stood to light the candles. And finally, Willie spoke:

"Boruch atto adonoi elohenu melech ho'olom asher kidd'shonu b'mitzvosov v'tzivonu l'hadlik ner shel shaboos."

"Amen," Roman Edelstadt said.

The four of them looked at each other, and they all began to smile. And then Marguerite began to laugh. She laughed and laughed and could not stop, and the others laughed with her, not knowing why, but glad of the release of tension.

"What is it, *ma petite?*" her mother asked, amusement in her blue eyes.

"Who would have thought," Marguerite said, smiling fondly at Willie, "that I would have found a nice Jewish boy at last?"

Columbine poured the tea while Elijah frowned at the evening paper. The air was still cool in the evening, and they liked to sit in the rear study in Elijah's house on East Eleventh Street, which held the warmth of the late afternoon sun. There was a small fire in the grate, burning cheerfully and taking any chill from the breeze coming from the half-open window. The sky was darkening to cobalt outside, and the grass was a deep foresty green.

"The war fever is getting worse," Elijah said, "and more and more ridiculous. Speaker Reed is the only voice of rationality in the whole Congress. We're going to go to war with Spain, mark my words, Columbine, and for nothing but imperialism."

"Yes, I fear it may be so," Columbine said. "America is changing. There was a time in the sixties and seventies that I felt so encouraged—that we were beginning to face our problems, to do something for our workers and our women. And I'll fight with every last breath in my body for that. But for a nation, it's much easier to look without than within, isn't it." She handed him his cup.

"The last depression has marked us," Elijah brooded. "And I see this war fever as a bad sign. It doesn't bode well for the future. I don't know if America will ever really get a sense of class consciousness. We'll continue to exalt our individualism, and that's what might defeat us in the end. We're not a nation that understands community. We just want to elbow each other out of the way while we bluster about patriotism and grab for a piece of the pie."

"Elijah, I'm going to forbid you the paper before tea. Especially on a soft spring evening like this one. Can't we talk of pleasanter things, like our wedding?"

"I'm counting the days, love."

A shriek of laughter came through the window, and Columbine wandered over with her teacup. She looked out into the back yard and smiled. Hawthorn had somehow persuaded her aunt Olive to sit on the grass with her, and was earnestly telling her a story, her thin arms waving in the dusky light, her bright hair flying. Olive was listening gravely, chewing on a piece of grass.

Columbine leaned against the sill, lost in the pleasure of her daughter's happiness. It had taken Hawthorn awhile to come out from the shadow of Ned's death, but lately the old look of mischievous mirth was back in her eyes. She'd found comfort in Elijah's bear-like solidity, and she shouted with laughter at his sly jokes. Someday she would know that Elijah was her father, Columbine vowed.

Elijah had taken up the paper again. "It's that damn Hearst fanning the flames," he grumbled. "And the president is of no use at all. We're wasting time on a stupid war when we could be doing something here. What will the next century bring, I wonder. More foolishness, I suppose."

"Yes, darling," Columbine said, hearing Hawthorn's laughter as the cool spring air moved the curtains and she smelled the wet earth and the growing green shoots in the garden. "Tomorrow we'll start all over again. But tonight, come look at our daughter."